BETWEEN TESTAMENTS, MARRANO

Fernán Hernandes
A Trilogy of Novels inspired by life in 15th Century Spain

Book I

BETWEEN TESTAMENTS, MARRANO

PERRY JEFFE

BETWEEN TESTAMENTS, MARRANO is a work of fiction. Names, characters, places and incidents are the product of the author's imagination or are used fictitiously. Any resemblance to actual persons, living or dead, or events or locales is entirely coincidental.

All rights reserved under International and Pan-American Copyright Conventions. No part of this book may be reproduced or transmitted in any form or by any means, electronic or mechanical, including photocopying, recording, or by an information storage and retrieval system, without permission in writing from the copyright owner.

Copyright © 2001, 2007, 2014 by Perry Jeffe (P.E.Jeffe)

This edition is published in the United States, and printed in the United States of America on acid-free paper.

ISBN-13: 978-1512076318
ISBN-10: 1512076317

by Perry Jeffe for Ameon Media

THE FERNÁN HERNANDES TRILOGY

Book I
BETWEEN TESTAMENTS, MARRANO

Book II
A PASSAGE OF CLOUDS

Book III
THE OBSESSIONS OF ISABEL

The COVER ILLUSTRATION includes a retouched photo of the statue of Maimonides (Moshe ben Maimon) displayed in a patio of the former Jewish quarter in Cordoba, Spain.

For Barbara

Fictional Characters

Rafael Fernán Hernandes—son of Lorenzo/Celestina, aka Rafael Rivera
Naomi Melamed—a Jewish maiden
Abrahán Melamed—grandfather of Naomi
Lorenzo Hernandes—merchant, father of Fernán
Celestina Sarah Hernandes—wife of Lorenzo, mother of Fernán
Beatriz Hernandes—daughter of Lorenzo/Celestina
Cesario Hernandes—brother of Lorenzo
Blanca Hernandes—wife of Cesario
Antonio Hernandes—brother of Lorenzo
María Rahél Hernandes—wife of Antonio
Jerónimo—steward of the Hernandes household
Gaspar de Ribas—*converso* scribe
Diego Enríquez—godfather to Fernán
Rubén Halevi—farmer
Mosé—apprentice to Abrahán Melamed
Aharón—apprentice to Abrahán Melamed
Alfonso de Herrera—*converso* lawyer
Fernando Husillo—*converso* banker
Manuela—mistress of Pero Sarmiento
Paulo—servant in the Hernandes household

Historical Characters

Enrique de Trastámara—Prince of Asturias, heir to the throne of Castile
Juan II—King of Castile y León
Alvaro de Luna—Constable of Castile
Lope de Barrientos—Bishop of Cuenca, advisor to Enrique
Juan Pacheco—advisor to Enrique
Pedro Girón—brother of Juan Pacheco
Alfonso Carrillo de Acuña—Archbishop of Toledo
Pero Sarmiento—leader of the Toledan rebellion of 1449
Marcos García de Mora—lawyer, force behind the Toledan rebellion
Juan of Navarre—King of Navarre
Lope de Galvez—canon of the Cathedral of Toledo
Juan Alonso—canon of the Cathedral of Toledo
Fernando de Ávila—Captain of the Gate of Alcántara
Nicholas Leon Battista Alberti—Italian humanist, architect, theorist
Lorenzo Valla—Italian humanist, papal secretary, philosopher
García Álvarez de Toledo—Abbot of Santa María de Atocha

Glossary

alcalde—mayor
alcázar—fortress, castle
anusim—those Jews forced to convert to Christianity (Heb.)
ayuntamiento—town hall
barceloneses—citizens of Barcelona
bola—rope with weights attached at its ends
buena suerte—good luck
caballero—gentleman
Calatrava—major military and religious order
caporal—corporal
caravel—light sailing ship with two or three masts and triangular sails
cohuerço—meal after a funeral
cojones—testicles
comandante—commander
conde—count
converso—Jew or Muslim who has converted to Christianity, or a descendant of a converted person
convivencia—Christians, Jews, and Moors living together in peace
corregidor—governor
corrida de toros—bullfight
Cortes—Castilian parliament
dobla—19-carat gold coin worth 445 *maravedís*
ducat—375 *maravedís*
duque—duke
fracasso—fracas (Ital.)
hidalgo—noble
humanitas—devotion to studies promoting human culture
infante, infanta—child of a Spanish king other than the heir
judería—Jewish quarter
kettubah—wedding contract (Heb.)
L'Accadèmia della Traduzione—The Academy of Translation (Ital.)
La Fonda de los Reyes—The Inn of the Kings
La Scuòla della Spada—The School of the Sword (Ital.)
league—unit of distance equal to three statute miles
mano a mano—hand-to-hand, face-to-face
maravedi—standard monetary unit
marqués—marquis

marrano—pig, filthy person, abusive term applied to *conversos*, especially one thought to have relapsed to Judaism
matador—killer of bulls
mayordomo—steward, one who manages another's property or affairs
merced—favor, gift
meseta—plateau
mudéjar—part Islamic, part Gothic style of architecture and decoration during the 12th to 15th centuries
New Christian—*converso*
niño—boy child, infant
patrón—patron, sponsor
pensione—boarding house (Ital.)
picador—mounted bullfighter armed with pointed barbs
plaza mayor—central town square
Prince of Asturias—title of the heir to the Castilian throne
Puente de San Martín—Bridge of Saint Martin
río—river
salaam aleikem—Peace be with you (Arab.)
Santa Hermandad—rudimentary police force
Santiago—St. James
Sefarad—Hebrew name for Spain
Sentencia-Estatuto—Judgment and Statute
shivah—period of ritual mourning (Heb.)
shofar—trumpet made of the horn of a ram, blown during certain Jewish religious ceremonies and as a battle signal (Heb.)
Sierra de Guadarrama—range of mountains north of Madrid and east of Segovia
strappado—a form of torture
tax farmer—person who has paid a specific amount for the right to collect and retain taxes due from a specific governmental domain
teniente—lieutenant
Torah—the five books of Moses (Heb.)
torero—bullfighter
Trastámara—ancestral family of kings of Castile during the 14th and 15th centuries
umanisti—humanists (Ital.)

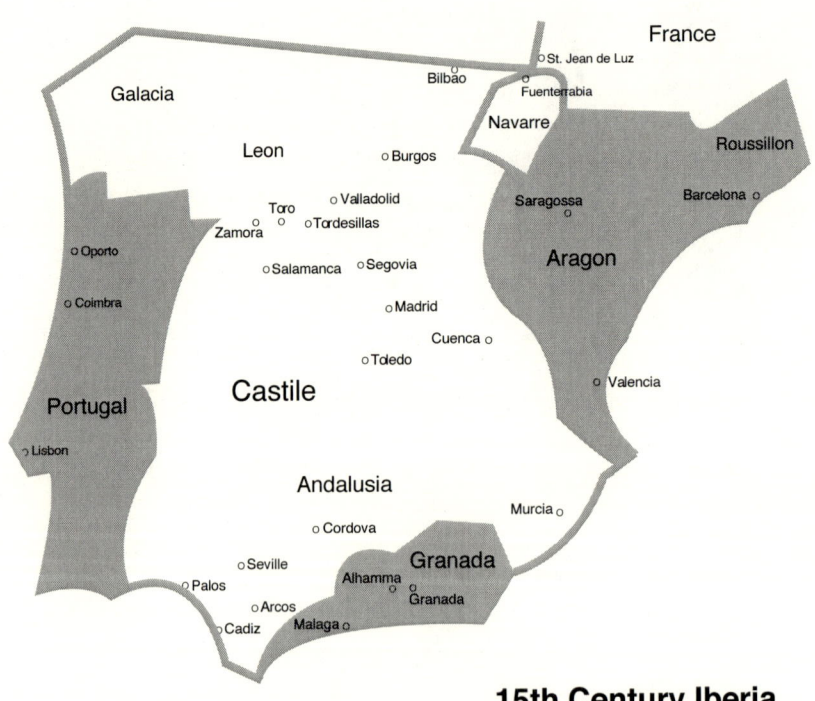

Between Testaments, Marrano

Part I

REBELLION

"…there were some men and women in the city of Toledo who were secretly celebrating Jewish rites, and who in great ignorance and peril to their souls, were not keeping either one law or the other; for they did not circumcise like the Jews… and although they kept the Sabbath and performed some of the fasts of the Jews, they did not keep all the Sabbaths or fast during all the fasts…in some households the husband kept certain Jewish ceremonies and the wife was a good Christian…and the members of the family concealed themselves from one another."

From a letter written by Fernando del Pulgar (1436-1490)
Secretary to Queen Isabel and chronicler of her reign
Quoted in *Fernando del Pulgar and the Conversos*
by Francisco Cantera Burgos
in *Spain in the Fifteenth Century* edited by Roger Highfield
Harper & Row, Publishers 1972

1

Late January of 1449, Toledo

Fernán raced through the twisting ways of a city newly buried beneath a layer of wet snow. He breathed deeply as he ran, inhaled the bitter draft and shuddered, but knew his body would warm as he ran and that the cold would lessen with each beat of his heart. How he loved Toledo in a new coat of white, the freedom of an unobstructed run past shuttered shops, the heady risk of narrow, deserted streets—deserted for the dark, for the snow, and for the spirits, demons, and cutthroats who tormented its nighttime courses.

Muffled cries startled the quiet night. Should he run against the wall or in the center of the cobbled street? Near the wall he would be less visible. In the street, a patrol would more likely see him. Though there should be no patrols until after the action Sarmiento had planned, and that might not be for a few days. No, it would matter little where he was—center or wall. Keep to the center.

Now that the storm had passed, light from a full moon fell on the whitened cobbles and, where unshadowed by bordering houses, glimmered within the fragile crystals. His run was clear. The snow-wet stones were uneven—he had best be careful. He drew his cape about him and thanked God his blessed boots were soft and quiet.

If he were stopped, what should he say? On an errand to the greengrocer for my mother, señor. Fool, at this hour the snores of the greengrocer keep his mistress awake—a babe knows that. Then, perhaps—Off to see my cousin, señor. Why so late, lad? My cousin is beautiful, señor, and she promised to wait. No. Then what? Best use the device Papá suggested. Delivering a message for my father, señor. What message might that be? My mother, señor, she is sick abed with a bad cough and fever. Sorry about that, lad, but why run toward the *judería*? The doctor is a Jew, señor. And you are a Jew? No, señor, a devout Catholic. *Marrano*, you mean—right, young swine?

Marrano be damned, he was as good a Catholic as they and, were his rapier in his hand, no man in Toledo, whatever his age or persuasion, would dare call him swine.

His boots splashed in the snow that had whistled out of the west bearing the biting cold. The Cathedral bells chimed their sacred song and a dog cadenced his bark to their rhythm. Eleven. Blessed God, so clear a night. The spire of the Cathedral rose like the finger of the Lord wherever one was in Toledo, beckoning, warning, directing him to consider the stars of heaven, the firmament of the Lord. He was wrong to act the blade solely because God had bestowed on him a talent for the sword. Danger lay within such arrogance.

Laughter smothered a sudden cry in a nearby house. Which house? Never mind, it was behind him and he had an urgent mission.

At home they will have retired, though Mamá will be alone in the great hall by the outsized fireplace, hands busy with needle and thread, worrying. Poor Mamá. Sons are a problem and he, running through the night alone and without a sword, must worry her indeed. But what a sight she had made with María, dancing after supper. And that sad old song Aunt María sang as the family sat at their long, oak trestle table, lethargic from the meal. While the servants cleared dishes and scrubbed the hands and faces of the little ones, Papá and his brothers sipped the rich dessert wine pressed from the dark grapes of the south, and the women chatted—all save María, dear, gay María.

"Dance with me, Sarah," María had said to his mother.

"Celestina, María. You know my name is Celestina, not Sarah."

"You will always be Sarah to me, sister, and I will always be Rahél." She spoke with a slight Hebrew accent, pronouncing her name with a soft guttural midpoint, not unlike the Arabic his tutor had taught him. "Come, dance and remember, dear Sarah."

"Too many years have passed, sweet one. Then I was too young to remember. Now I am too old."

Clouds above the Cathedral tower had darkened the moon and were swept away by bracing winds. The white road lay clear ahead.

He had spied on Mamá and Aunt María from the corners of his large brown eyes, as Fernán always scouted his elders—watching, listening for precious clues to secret lives. Papá sober as the women spoke.

María began a song Fernán remembered from childhood and had not heard since. Not since he had stared at his aunt, besotted with love from beneath the covers she tucked around his five-year-old body, won by a love for this dear woman with the thick russet hair and the faint aroma of honey—from baking, she told him laughing.

The Ladino words she taught him then now trembled on the quivering notes of her song and escaped her lips like frightened birds.

When God sent you, my love, to this world of pain,

She was only twelve years older than he, a mystery he still had to solve. Seventeen then, as he was now, she was married two years and so ancient to infant eyes.

As she sang the doleful melody, María had drifted around the table and touched each squirming child with her fingertips—as if those fingers had been dipped in holy water and she was the messenger of its blessing.

He neglected your heart, a heart for true love, my love.

The men muted their voices and sipped their wine, and the children covered their faces with their hands, peered between their fingers at one another, and giggled. Fernán had smiled at their antics. As she passed Fernán, María let her fingertips trail across his shoulders. Dear God, a shiver had run down his back, into his groin, and surrounded his private parts.

Be thou well, dear love, sorrow sours my heart.

He remembered the pleasure of her touch with shame. Her touch should not have aroused him. She was his aunt, married to his uncle. Must he confess this arousal to Fray Sebastiano? But how to explain?

For your love is a curse and your words a sharp sword, dear love.

And what penance would the Father impose for such an immoral response? A public penance? Dear God, pray never. His response was not immoral, but physical. He would control himself, recite a few Hail Marys, and surely that would do.

Find another to love, my love, find a passion more true.

María had smiled at the solemn words of her song when he was a child. Now, though, her words seemed to carry a burden—perhaps because she was childless. Though Fernán was hardly a child, he knew he was her favorite—more than her favorite. He loved her as he knew she loved him. Not as men and women love, God forbid. But he could not find the thoughts or words to describe the emotion he felt for her, and he opened his heart to her song and accepted the unbidden melancholy that passed to him.

For my heart is shattered, and your heart is a void, dear love.

María hesitated behind Celestina, then wrapped Mamá in her arms and placed her cheek gently against that of the older woman. Celestina first shied at the warmth and then acknowledged the intimacy. In mid-verse, María reached out and raised her sister from the seat. His mother shook her head, then smiled and, opening her hands to María, the two began a slow dance, sidestepping, holding their skirts above their ankles. With arms held high, they accented the rhythm of the song as they moved to and fro, fingers softly snapping, swaying to the forlorn melody.

Fernán had peered at his father, for Lorenzo Hernandes de Toledo was staring at the table, his jaw rigid. His right arm hung loose beside him and abruptly, he clenched his fist, raised it, and knocked twice on the table. The dancing stopped. The room was quiet.

"No more, María. It is not seemly. Especially dancing to that song."

"But Lorenzo...."

"Dear sister, you know that song belongs to another time, another people. You know that better than I. We are Christians, not Jews."

"I was a Jew, Lorenzo. We were all Jews not long ago."

"We were never Jews in this house and you are no longer a Jew, María," he said, his voice rising. "Do you want to be accused of heresy? Do you want us to be accused? We were born Catholic, María. We must behave like the good Catholics we are and so must you. We are servants of the King and must comport ourselves in such a way as to deserve his protection."

María turned to Celestina. Her chin quivered, her smooth forehead condensed into wrinkles, and her hand fluttered before her wet staring eyes as she turned and ran from the room. Fernán watched his uncle Antonio register dismay at the reprimand to his wife. Then Antonio excused himself, his expression reflecting the anguish of María. He mumbled something inaudible to Lorenzo and hurried after her.

Fernán examined his father whose features were flushed but impassive, and Celestina, who smiled a clouded smile Fernán knew well from past stormy times.

"Lorenzo," his mother pleaded.

"Not now, my dear."

Once more, Celestina smiled with compressed lips, then instructed the servants to put the children to bed and hurried down the stairs to the kitchen.

"Was that necessary, Lorenzo?" asked Cesario, his younger uncle.

"Are you simple, Cesario? You think we are not watched? You think our servants are innocents? You think they are iron that cannot be broken?"

Warm from his run, Fernán opened his cape. Did Papá think the servants spied? He could not accept that. Fernán had known most of their servants all his life—they were his friends. Papá was right in one respect though—anyone can be broken. His Moorish friend and tutor, Jerónimo the family steward, had told Fernán during one of their dueling sessions that no man was strong enough to withstand the *strappado* or the rack or the other machines of torture. And if Jerónimo said so, then it must be true because he was the strongest man in Castile. But what did he know of torture?

As he ran, a far-off voice broke the cold night as a pebble tossed into a pond shatters its surface, sending ripples to every corner. Fernán listened for galloping horses or running men, but heard only silence, and resumed his run.

His dagger slapped his thigh. He wished the weapon would lie still, though he was not afraid. If a patrol caught him, he would say his mother had a fever and then cough into their faces. They would surely back away and cross themselves, afraid of the pestilence plaguing the cities of Castile, happy to see the last of him. If that accomplished nothing, he would show them the note from Papá. The other note, the important note, was nestled deep in his boot. He took a breath and exhaled through his mouth, his running smooth, his heartbeat fast but steady.

Marranos, the commoners call us. Well, and he spat, they are swine.

Cesario had looked as if *he* might spit. Irritated by Lorenzo, by his attitude toward María, Cesario was about to leave the great hall when Lorenzo asked him to stay—asked, not ordered, his voice gentle.

Fernán understood his uncle Cesario—quick temper, sharp wit, generous heart—no artifice concealed his emotions. In that, he was Castilian to the core. Antonio was the hidden one. No way to know what he thought, except for the rare occasion when thoughts were bared on his face as they were tonight. María never knew. She had told Fernán that Antonio had a heart of soft Toledan steel—a conflict of terms, to be sure, but a wife should know.

The sounds of running. Had they caught up with him? Was there a shorter way? He had run as fast as he could, given the snow, the map of the city streets imaged in his brain. He was sure there was no other route, no way shorter than the one he had taken.

Then the clink of metal, boots on stone. Whoever they were, they were close. Fernán cut into a nearby alley, pressed himself against the cold brick wall, and drew his dagger. Minutes passed before five black shapes accented by the glint of steel jogged past. Fernán edged down from the street, keeping to the wall, pointing ahead with his dagger. The stench of garbage and human refuse oozed from each pore of the brick and stone wall of the narrow passage and made him queasy. He listened. The sounds of running had merged with the wind. This detour would cost him minutes. Would Jerónimo have slithered down this alley like a harried fox?

2

The Sarmiento house

Sarmiento counted the strokes of the Cathedral bells. "Blessed God. Eleven. Where is that damned idiot?" He drew close to the parlor window of the smallest of the three Mudejár-style houses that surrounded the cobbled courtyard below. A stately carriage, illumined by the warm light of sconces on the building walls, drove beneath the Moorish arch leading from the street into the courtyard.

The coachman reined in the horses and, as the carriage stopped, a footman dropped from his perch, brushed snow off the carriage steps, and helped a lady and gentleman out of the cab. Another servant emerged from the door of the house opposite Sarmiento, swept a path free of snow from the carriage to the building entrance and, capes spangled with snowflakes and precious stones, the laughing couple vanished into the bright interior. Sarmiento knew the pair—young, noble, rich, and stupid. The footman climbed atop the carriage step and the driver urged his team of horses around the courtyard and out through the archway.

Damn García! Damn him! Sarmiento gritted his teeth and squeezed his clasped hands together, whitening the knuckles. His mind on the audacious demand Luna had made to the Council earlier that day, Sarmiento was anxious to hear the news of the street García might bring, and now the man was an hour late.

Alvaro de Luna, Constable, grand military commander to King Juan, had presumption enough, soliciting a donation of money from Toledo as if it were a tribute city. Then, after a third written request and third Council refusal, to appear in person before the Council not seeking an outright gift but a loan. Sarmiento had voiced his extreme displeasure to the Council, his tolerance for the King and Luna, his bastard toady, ended. No gift, no loan. That opened a few eyes among the councilors, sleepy from a denied siesta. He was yet Governor of Toledo, a free city that owed tribute to no man—king, noble, or commoner—and certainly not to a king who offered and then retracted favors. Such a king deserved no gifts, no service, no allegiance. He would deny that weasel Luna everything, as Luna now sought to deny him his rightful positions of Governor and Chief Judge of Appeals.

Sarmiento threw himself into a chair facing the window, slung one leg over its arm, and began cleaning his nails with the point of a jewel-handled dagger.

"Why so nervous, Pero?" his mother asked. "You frighten me."

Had he money, he would have been out of this house long ago, and his wife and children, mother and father installed on the estate near Navarre far away, had it not been overrun and torched by the Aragonese. And why had their estate been savaged? Because he, Sarmiento, had supported the King in every foolish endeavor Juan had essayed, thereby incurring the wrath of the Princes of Aragón. Oh, but could he have the family off to Navarre and himself cavorting in the soft, ample bed of soft, ample, young Manuela—that sensuous hellion—then he would say to the Devil with Luna and the King. But he had too few *maravedís* and he damned the King and Luna and again damned García.

His mother paced to and fro, irritating every particle of his being as the woman always managed to do. Why was she not put to bed with the children? A low fire burned in the man-high fireplace. Nearby, his mute father sat static but for a right arm that trembled involuntarily—the residue of a second seizure suffered a month before. The sight of the father disturbed the son—disturbed, angered, and frightened. He remembered his father tall and vigorous and, when rich, bearing himself with the pride of a true Castilian noble. No longer wealthy and a half-step from the grave, the father trembled like the dead leaves on his burned estate.

It need not have burned! Sarmiento shouted soundlessly. Had his father not gambled, they would have had money enough to afford a fierce defense with which to repulse the invaders. Their estate would be alive and productive and they would be independent of the pitiful earning he drew as Commander of the Alcázar. When he had first reached manhood, he forbade his father to gamble and the broken man, the former nobleman, already reduced in stature and girth by the twin plagues of poverty and old age, had retreated to his chair by the fire where the fire dried his bones. Now he was as brittle as a cleft twig.

Sarmiento would not allow the King and Luna to remove him from his post as Chief Judge of Appeals, to remove him from command of the gates and other city forts, to reduce him to sole command of the Alcázar, a decrepit fortress. He would refuse to return the judgeship and gates and forts to Luna. Let events take their own damnable course.

A pale rectangle on the worn wall above the fireplace caught his eye. The antique painting that had protected the patch had been sold in September to an elderly French merchant who professed to admire its technique. Sarmiento knew better. His mother had graced the French bed for the better part of the summer and the purchase was generous payment for services rendered. He was astonished her juices still flowed. Or perhaps French vices were perverse. What difference, the painting had been old and mediocre and the cash welcome.

His eye fell on another patch—a large discoloration on the handsome Persian before the fire. The rug was ruined and he cursed his father and the seizure that had produced the vomit. And he cursed Hernandes, the *marrano* who had sold him the rug and must be laughing still at the outrageous price he had wrung out of Sarmiento. Then, after stealing his money, this *marrano*, full of himself, had the gall to boast of his son, not yet a man, whose swordsmanship, running, and knowledge of languages were peerless. His son, indeed. Peerless compared to what? What name had the brat? Yes, Fernán. Insipid. Then the *marrano* had the audacity to suggest that this Fernán could outpoint any man in Toledo with his rapier, when Hernandes knew very well that the rapier was the pride of the Sarmiento household and that he, Pero Sarmiento, was the most feared blade in Castile. Well, one day he would test the swordsmanship of this *marrano* son with bare points and teach the upstart true swordsmanship. And as payment for his unabashed hubris, Hernandes the *marrano* would be required to replace the rug—gratis.

Sarmiento had made the mistake of appearing for supper that evening unannounced, though not before his wife and children were in bed. His mother had been at odds with him since. The sorry meal sat uneasily in his stomach and he blamed her and her words for his discomfort. Disappointed in her only child, she had told him as much and, though he pretended indifference to her lecture, he was far from indifferent to her hectoring, and deeply offended and angered by her opinion. She would know better soon enough and faint dead away when she heard. But now her voice droned on and on and he would gladly have throttled her long since but that she was his mother.

"The King takes you for a fool, Pero. Sarmiento do this, Sarmiento do that." Her voice, mincing. "Tell him Pero Sarmiento does nothing that is not in his own interest."

He knew he should be silent but the rage within him retorted, "And what would that pronouncement accomplish, do you think?"

"Put the King on notice. You are a man of significance, a man of honor. The King and that whoreson, Alvaro de Luna.... Blessed Virgin! Alvaro of the moon, indeed. His whore-mother spread her legs under the moon for every son of a dog in Castile. Look at his teeth and know his lineage. His height—a child is taller than he. His head—bald as an apple. And that whore bastard treats you like a lickspittle. You, with your mother and father, your pure blood, your breeding, your brilliant teeth, your height, your thick black hair."

His mother paced behind his chair and spoke to the back of his head, another habit which tormented his soul. "Enough!" he said, more loudly than he intended. "My time will come."

"Time comes not of itself, my son. You seize time, command time, force time. Let time alone and you lose time. Find the right time, then strike. Our illustrious King Juan is weak. The man faces rebellion—his barons clutch at his gut, the Moors and Aragonese are boils on his fat behind, and fair Prince Enrique wants his crown before his stupid father is under the ground."

She seized his chair and shook it. Sarmiento groaned. "Pay me heed, Pero." He bit his thumb. "Learn from the Prince. You think that effeminate coward would dare defy Juan and Luna if the King were strong? This is the time to act. For the love of sweet Jesus, choose your weapon and thrust home. Fortify your position, then show King Juan and Luna your ass."

"With what should I fortify my position, dear Mother? I am no longer Chief Judge of Appeals, no longer governing head of Toledo—Luna has seen to that. Though I command the Alcázar, Luna has secured the gates and can take Toledo whenever his appetite demands. He can strip me of my command and my possessions, throw me in jail, torture me, banish me from Castile—whatever he cares to do."

His feet were spread before him, his arms draped over the sides of the chair.

"Are you as unconcerned as you look? Are you a son to your father?"

"You alone know whose son I am, dear Mother."

"Your father is your father, to be sure. But how can you bear to be treated like a servant by that whore bastard Luna, when all you need do is to raise an army, capture Toledo, and make the city your castle."

"Of course, how exceedingly stupid of me—raise an army and take the city. With what funds, Mother dear? What weapons? Do not...." He stared as she walked slowly to where her husband sat slumped in his chair, lowered herself onto a stool beside the old man, and peered into the fire. Sarmiento was apprehensive. A chill ran through him. A noxious stench filled the room.

Was it from the waning fire? He stirred the coals and the flame leaped upward, startling him. He sat back in his chair.

"You need no funds, Pero." Her voice appeared to come from a great depth. Or did his ears betray him? "An army is yours for the taking. Pay strict attention to what I say. The nobility of this city are cowards, they eat what Luna leaves. The clergy are women and *marranos* care only for gold. But though *marranos* seem ineffectual, the swine will serve you well.

"Consider this carefully. One group in this city has power—the people, Perito my son, the masses, those with nothing to lose. They are taxed again and again. They scrape their living from the streets and feed on hatred of the nobility and *marranos*. Nourish that hatred, Perito. The rabble are an army without pay, an army without a leader, an army of mongrels. They must be roused, they must be goaded as you would goad a bull."

Eyes unfocused, she stood behind him, hands clutching his shoulders. He stared at the sparks leaping erratically from the fire into the flue.

"How does one rouse a sleeping mongrel, Pero? With meat, dear son. So feed the mongrels swine, Pero. Feed them *marranos*. Their hatred for *marranos* is unbounded. But careful, my son. The dogs are ignorant. They must be kept on a short leash or they will devour your living, your property, and all the goods *marranos* have hoarded for you."

Sarmiento was stunned by her speech, a speech which seemed to grow out of the flames. García and he had agreed on their strategy weeks before and now, provoking his mother, ridiculing her words, expecting a vacuous return, here was their plan made whole in her mouth. Blessed Virgin, her vision was his. What did it mean? She sounded bewitched. He had felt a chill moments before his mother had spoken and then that stink had permeated the room. Was this vision pure? Were her words true or had the Devil possessed her as was the custom of the Beast? Who was that Frenchman? Sacred Jesus, was he being led into Hell by the unholy one? He thrust forward, freeing his body from her grasp.

"Mother?"

"Yes, Pero."

Her voice was her own, the hollow timbre gone.

"Are you well, Mother?"

"Quite well, but strangely tired. Perhaps the hour."

He heard footsteps in the courtyard and glanced out the window. In the brilliant moonlight, the formidable stone walls of the Alcázar, his command, loomed over the city. Marcos García and two priests walked through the arch, stepping carefully on the whitened cobblestones. García spoke to the priests. They nodded, shook hands with him, and shuffled back toward the street.

García peered up at the building where Sarmiento stood, his face lit by the sconces on the wall, his eyes in shadow.

"Marcos García is here. I will use this room." He would consider her words later, when the house was quiet, when he was alone.

"I will retire, son. And Pero," she rang a small silver bell, "promise nothing to that thief."

A servant in livery appeared and, with nose wrinkled and head averted, hoisted the old man into his arms as if he were a sack of soiled linen and followed his mistress out the door. Sarmiento locked the door behind them.

3

An alley near the Judería

Waiting at the entrance to the alley, Fernán listened for sounds of running men, but heard only wind and occasional street noises—a door closing, a horse neighing, a child crying. He inched down the alley between the buildings, his dagger leading, his boots crushing the virgin snow.

The remark Papá had made about the servants distressed him. Jerónimo was loyal, of that he was certain. More than once Jerónimo had reported disturbances among the servants to Lorenzo when Fernán was within earshot. And in years past, the hot eyes and deadly repute of Jerónimo had brushed abrasive toughs away from Fernán and his mother as they walked the streets—toughs who would have hurled abuse at them, called them *marranos*. No one dared abuse Fernán now. His reputation had been proved when, alone, he had been attacked by a gang in a poor section of the city. Five toughs, armed with swords of diverse size and vintage, had sought a quarrel, and Fernán had dashed their swords and cut more than a few arms and legs with dagger and rapier before they fled.

Earlier that evening, Fernán had been seated at the table with his father and Cesario when Jerónimo entered the great hall and stood by the door. Lorenzo had nodded and Jerónimo, in that precise voice that concealed a world, announced that don Gaspar de Ribas was waiting to see don Lorenzo. Jerónimo glanced at Fernán, the tinge of a smile on his lips, and Fernán winked. That may not have been proper, but they were friends, and the steward tutored Fernán in the martial arts of rapier, dagger, hand-to-hand, and in Arabic and much else.

"Has Ribas waited long?"

"Don Gaspar arrived a moment ago, don Lorenzo."

"Show him in, then leave us," his father said.

Jerónimo returned with a fussy little man who hurried to Lorenzo, shook his hand, and glanced around. The steward smiled to Fernán, left the room, and closed the door.

"You know my brother and my son, Ribas," Lorenzo said.

"Of course. A pleasure to see you both. I trust your wife and children are well," he said to Cesario and shook hands with him. Then he glanced at Fernán. "What about the boy?"

"Boy?" Lorenzo said, laughing. "Fernán? Fernán is a man of seventeen years, my friend. He is proficient in six languages, accomplished with long sword, rapier, dagger, and crossbow, and is an excellent horseman and swift runner—swifter than any man in Toledo."

Fernán waited against the wall in the alley listening for pursuers, and smiled at the boast Papá had made. Swifter than any man in Toledo was he? Then how had his pursuers caught up with him? And now he was proficient in seven languages not six—one for each day of the week. His father had not been informed that he had almost mastered Hebrew. Fernán kept that knowledge to himself, not knowing how don Lorenzo might react.

But Ribas had seemed subservient. How could the man be so humble before his equal? The exact opposite of Papá.

"I meant no offense referring to Fernán as a boy, don Lorenzo. I have known him since he was an infant and he has grown so remarkably. Forgive me, Fernán, it is that this business is so very delicate."

"And forgive me, don Gaspar," Lorenzo said. "I am a bit distressed. But sit down, old friend. You seem more troubled than normal. May I offer you something to eat or drink?"

"Not a thing, thank you, I have had supper. But I am troubled and for good reason." He then described the new tax that the Constable, Alvaro de Luna, had demanded Toledo pay for the defense of Castile. "One million *maravedís*, for the dear love of Christ. Tell me where in this blessed world will it come from? And of course Alonso Cota has been chosen to do the collecting." Ribas pushed himself to his feet and began pacing before Lorenzo. "Why do these people do this? The commoners hate us as it is. What if there are *conversos* like Cota who collect taxes—what of it? Cota is treasurer of the Council. The man must earn a living. Someone must do the work. You are a merchant, I am a scribe, so forth, so on. We earn our livings as best we can."

He sat again at the table. "And are we not as Catholic as they—better Catholics, most of us? What if our families were Jews? So? Ancient history. Were not Jesus Christ and His apostles Jews? Have not these Old Christians killed enough of us to make their point—convert or die? So we are not dead, we are Catholic, and they hate us for it."

"Ribas, please, what is it you fear?"

"I fear for our lives, my dear Hernandes—the lives of my wife, my children, my brothers and sisters, their families, all of us. I fear for our community, as you should, my friend."

"Why should we be afraid?"

"Why? Don Lorenzo, soon there will be another massacre—a slaughter as there was in 1391 and again in 1412."

"Nonsense. The King protects us. The victims of those massacres were Jews. We are Catholic."

"Except that Old Christians do not see us as we see ourselves, Hernandes. Not all Old Christians but most. They see us as Jews. And the rabble hate us—call us backsliders, heretics, *marranos*. They say we practice Judaism in secret." He jumped to his feet and raised his arms in supplication. "What a dreadful idea. Dreadful. Where would one begin? All those prayers to learn—and in Hebrew. Who knows Hebrew? Who can read that awful script backwards?"

"Come now, my dear Gaspar, Alvaro de Luna is our friend. The world is vastly different. This is not 1391."

"Is the world so different? Has it changed or is it in flux? Is the Constable a rock or do we stand on quicksand?"

"Gaspar."

"Ignore me at your peril, Lorenzo Hernandes. Remember when Alvaro de Luna—admittedly he is our friend—remember when he convinced King Juan to bestow the position of Chief Judge of Appeals on Pero Sarmiento. And then Alvaro reneged and restored Ayala to the judgeship."

"Yes, and I remember how Sarmiento fumed at the hurt, as well he might."

"Do not misunderstand me, my dear friend. Sarmiento sits neither at the right hand of God nor that of the King. Far from it. But how could Juan strip Ayala, bestow the judgeship on Sarmiento, and then spin around, twist the nose of Pero Sarmiento, and return the blessed judgeship to Ayala?"

Lorenzo shrugged. "The Ayala are the highest-ranking nobles in Toledo, Ribas, and Alvaro and the King need them, as you know. They need their wealth and their influence with the other high nobles. Sarmiento and his family are second-rate, if that, with little money and no influence. The man has nothing to offer except past loyalty that, unfortunately, is poor currency in our current politics. But come now, where are we going with this argument?"

Papá had begun to lose patience.

New sounds—feet on snow, walking slowly, cautiously, as he was. Fernán glanced behind him. The alley curved into darkness. Ah! The damned cobblestones were slippery under the snow. The sounds stopped. Fernán stepped gingerly down the sloping alley. Quiet. Not a breath.

Ribas had leaned toward Lorenzo and held his arm. Remarkable. Fernán had never touched his father so intimately nor had he seen any of the other friends of his father do so. Gaspar de Ribas was either desperate or had greater courage than was apparent.

"Sarmiento is dangerous, Hernandes. A cornered bull. The man has been used badly. Two years after this bewildering succession of twists and turns, control of the forts and gates are now denied him and he blames Alvaro de Luna, our friend, for this calamity. Arrogant, greedy bastard that Sarmiento is, he has only the hollow fortress of the Alcázar for his years of service. His horns have been blunted and he seethes."

"But what can the man do, Ribas? He has no force, no allies, nothing with which to threaten anyone. He is ineffectual." His father had looked at his friend quizzically. "Tell me, how do you come by this knowledge?"

"My situation has changed since our last meeting. I am now scribe to the Council, and this latest demand by Alvaro for this tax galls the Councilors. They will send a delegation to appeal to Alvaro de Luna tomorrow. But Alvaro is relentless and will turn them down." His hand shook and Lorenzo removed his arm. "Hear me, Hernandes. Those malicious eyes of Sarmiento burn. Who knows what he plans? I only know he has something in mind and that our position is dangerous. We are vulnerable."

"Do not fear, Ribas, Sarmiento is an empty shell. However, I will discuss this with the others."

"Good. Discuss it. But soon. The Council is distressed by the tax and word has sped through the city. The commoners…dear God, I hope you are right, that we have nothing to fear. I hope that is so. We will soon see."

Ribas stood before Lorenzo and took his hand. "I leave you now, my dear Hernandes. There are ruffians in the streets tonight. May be that they belong to Sarmiento. But would they be abroad as yet? Perhaps not. I would the night were overcast and dark as a cave. Though I dislike caves—you cannot see a blessed thing within them."

"Then bless Almighty God, Gaspar, for His moon lights your way."

The little man laughed weakly and left the room.

Lorenzo placed his fingertips on his eyes and massaged the bridge of his nose, a routine Fernán knew not to interrupt. Papá looked blankly ahead and then had turned to Cesario.

"We must rouse the *conversos*, Cesario. If Ribas is correct, we may be threatened momentarily, and we are few and vulnerable. Fernán," he said, "I will give you two notes. One to don Abrahán Melamed, the physician—you know the house in the *judería*. Put it in your boot. Show the other note in the event you are stopped. It will say that your mother is ill, God forbid, and that you need the assistance of a doctor. The note in your boot will put Melamed on guard and through him the rest of the *judería*."

"But why alert the Jews, Papá?"

"Because, my son, our position in Castile is unique and difficult. Even after the conversions, we remain a separate people and many of us, our house included, have family who are Jews. That is why we must alert them. For when we are threatened, Jews are threatened—their blood and ours are joined. But this is no time for explanations. Dress warmly, son, and hurry."

"I will go to Melamed, Lorenzo," Cesario said. "Fernán is too young."

"Thank you, Cesario, but Fernán runs swiftly and a youth is less likely to be suspect."

"Why is that?" Cesario asked. "Fernán is taller than I and looks older than his years."

"You speak in contradictions, dear brother. Too young or too old?" Cesario shrugged. "Never mind. You will warn our *converso* friends and Fernán will deliver our message to the Jews."

4

Some time later at the Sarmiento house

The hall doors opened, Sarmiento raised his head, and the servant announced García who entered, hand outstretched, words tumbling from his mouth. "Miserable night, don Pero. You must have thought I would never arrive. Thank God for the moon, for the streets are treacherous—wet, slippery, almost fell several times, but here I am."

The servant reentered, bearing a tray on which were two bowl-shaped glasses and a carafe of dark red wine. He placed glasses and carafe on a small table, decanted the wine, and retired. Sarmiento handed García a glass and raised his own. García inhaled the bouquet and drank.

"Excellent," he said.

"From our vineyards near Navarre, what remains of them. Damned Aragonese burned almost everything and stole what they could not burn."

"Nothing to be done?"

"Would you suggest I take up arms against the Princes of Aragón? I might as well slit my throat with this dagger. Perhaps appeal to King Juan? Well, as you know, the King and I have our differences. I doubt he would listen and, if he did, nothing would happen."

Sarmiento put down his glass and scrutinized García. The man was well turned out. Beard and hair carefully groomed. Shirt, doublet, cape, and hose in good taste though somewhat flamboyant. What Sarmiento could see of the shirt appeared to be silk and the doublet a fine cloth, carefully worked. The hose were tight around his stocky legs and the shoes were of the latest fashion. What fountainhead provided this stream of *maravedís*? The law paid, but not well enough to justify the quality of cloth the lawyer enjoyed, a quality that brought García almost to the level of nobility. And his aspect boasted good provisions—rosy cheeks, a solid paunch.

Stories proliferated, of course—questionable business interests, exchanges below the table, women. Sarmiento had observed the lawyer in court. The man was shrewd, always prowling for a chance, never quite finding it. But García possessed friends among the masses of people, the clergy, and the Old Christians of Toledo—an unlikely fraternity whose members shared the malice García harbored toward *marranos*. Valuable for this enterprise, if the lawyer could be trusted.

"What news, García?"

"Good news, bad news, but as you know, señor, bad news can be good." His laugh was a furtive gurgle interrupted by a cough and a frown. "Dear don Pero, I was distressed to learn how the King and Luna behaved toward you. I speak not of the loan but of their treatment of your person, señor. Removing the gates and the judgeship from your rule. Indeed, and after so many years of service to his majesty."

"Eighteen, García, eighteen long bitter years—advisor to the King, member of the Royal Council, Chief Butler. Worthless."

"I am desolate for you, don Pero, though not surprised."

"Why should you be? Juan is adept at removal—our royal master and his bastard puppy. Have I told you how the King removed Ayala? No? Then listen. These, señor, are our adversaries."

Sarmiento poured himself another glass of wine. García wet his lips.

"When King Juan was to come to Toledo," Sarmiento said, "Alvaro de Luna asked Ayala to prepare the royal rooms at the Alcázar for the arrival of the King. Then, when His Majesty arrived, he ordered Ayala to remove himself, that his presence would crowd that enormous edifice. Ayala left, of course—what choice had he—and the King turned over the Alcázar and the other trappings of governance to me—payment for loyalty. Ayala was out—payment for opposing His Majesty." Sarmiento sniffed. "Now, I am out—payment for nothing."

"Juan is a fox, don Pero, and Luna…well, one cannot trust the Devil, can one?"

"Never."

"Trust, don Pero, is blind. A wise man knows that trust emasculates him—locks his mind, dulls his senses, breaks down his natural defenses, and makes him vulnerable to attack."

Sarmiento toyed with the hilt of his dagger. "And you? Are you to be trusted, señor?"

García shifted in his seat and smiled. "As you would trust the stars that have caused our paths to align, don Pero."

"Remember. You said trust was blind?"

"Not when based on common motive."

"And your motive, señor?"

"To rid Castile of the bastard *marranos* and their Hebrew brethren."

"Your tongue is quick."

"You asked, señor."

Sarmiento sipped his wine.

"If you please, forgive me, don Pero, but what is *your* motive?"

Sarmiento stared at García. His eyes shifted to the bare patch above the mantle and to another on the far wall—the pale shadow of a picture that had fetched but a fair price—then skipped to the worn brocade on the arms and seats of the chairs and the ornate Persian rug he had purchased from Hernandes, that usurious *marrano* merchant, the rug now indelibly stained, its value destroyed.

He secured his dagger in its scabbard, wandered to the window, and sat on the sill. His voice sounded hollow. "Never forget, García," he said, "I am of a noble family, an old noble family. And I am first among the captains of the realm—the exact words of Prince Enrique."

The carriage had returned. Footman and driver waited in the snow for the young revelers to embark.

"But, García, what of good news and bad news. Let us assume, rightly, that my loss of the gates and deprivation of my lawful position in Castile are bad. Tell me, señor, what can be good about that news?"

"Your eyes have been opened, don Pero," he said, and waited. Sarmiento said nothing while peering through half-closed eyes at García, who stammered and then said, "When our eyes are open we see, señor. The outrageous repossession of your deserved properties by Luna was bad, but good in one way—it restored your sight which had been, forgive my saying so, blinded by devotion to the King. Now you see King Juan and Luna for the raptors they are and you are free to act."

Sarmiento took up his glass and drank the ruby liquid. He inhaled the exuberant spirit of the grape, but knew that the innocent fluid, distilled through his present state of mind, would be transmuted into a potion that would sour his brain and poison his sleep.

"Do you think me blind, García?"

"How could I possibly think that, don Pero? The King and Luna may assume your hands are tied, but they are mistaken, señor."

García studied his glass, sighed, drank the final drop of precious liquid, and lowered the glass slowly to the table.

"To the events at hand, don Pero," García said, and recounted the recent attacks and threats which, he said, weakened the King and presented an opportunity for Sarmiento. "And in addition to the dangers from Navarre and the Aragonese and the Moors in the south, now we have Pimentel, escaped from prison, safe at home in his castle at Benavente and declaring rebellion. The King is surrounded by troubles and the moment is yours to grasp."

"Pimentel escaped?"

"He is home and free."

"By the Sacred Virgin, captured at Zafraga and now free? Then God rules in Heaven. Hah! I swear Luna is the living Devil and should be buried alive." He peered at García. "What day is this, señor?"

"The twenty-fifth, don Pero."

"What month?"

"Why, January, señor."

"The day of the week?"

"Saturday. The *marrano* Sabbath."

"How very long this day has been. I would have preferred it were Monday not Saturday. Saturday is a void and Sunday as tedious. Though after Sunday there is Monday—momentous Monday." He frowned at García. "Why do you say *marrano* Sabbath, señor, when you know that Saturday is the Jewish Sabbath. *Marranos* are New Christians and observe the day of our Lord, Sunday."

"In name, don Pero, in name only. They make a good pretense."

"A good pretense. Perhaps." He loosened his dagger and slid it back and forth in its sheath. "I admire your wardrobe, García."

"Thank you, my lord."

"Are you entitled, señor?"

"Entitled?"

"Yes, García. You dress as a gentleman, with silks and other fine cloths. I would have thought homespun more your lot."

"I am a gentleman, señor."

"You were born a peasant, I am told."

"My father was an honored man, don Pero, a noble man. And I have the bachelor-at-law."

"And are very clever."

"Thank you, don Pero. As clever as I must be."

"And how clever must you be, señor?"

"As clever as will satisfy the moment."

"And will your cleverness satisfy the moment Monday? Are your people primed for momentous Monday?"

"At my signal, don Pero."

"They know the prize?"

"They have been briefed."

For the next hour Sarmiento and García reviewed their scheme. The lawyer impressed Sarmiento by reciting the entire sequence of events without notes—whose responsibility to secure which gate, when the gate would be secured, where to meet. By the end of the hour they had agreed on every point.

Sarmiento twisted toward the window and scanned the whitened courtyard. The carriage had gone. He turned back and, as he did so, the fire shivered. García was flushed, beads of sweat lined his forehead and glistened in the firelight.

"The fire too warm, García?"

"No, señor. The wine, perhaps. I drink so little." And he raised his empty glass.

"You do, indeed. Those men who were with you, García, who are they?"

"The men at the archway? Yes?" His left eye twitched. "Lope de Galvez and Juan Alonso, canons of the Cathedral."

"Priests?"

"Priests? Yes. Canons—priests."

"Do not trust priests, García. Their allegiance lies elsewhere."

"Their motives are mine, señor, absolutely—and yours. Closed vessels."

"Absolutely? If you slip do I fall? My name, García, must never be mentioned. We play with the lives of the mighty."

"You and I have never met, don Pero, and the priests are committed."

"Absolutely committed?"

"Depend on it."

"Must I? I suppose I must. But then, so must you."

García smoothed his mustache. "Rest easy, my lord. The priests are under my thumb."

"I will, I assure you, I will rest easy. But is your thumb large enough?"

"I own a very large thumb, don Pero."

"Is that so? Good. Very good. Remember, García, how in my judicial chambers you came to me with an ambitious scheme? I forget its purpose. And do you remember that I rejected your proposal and sent you away? You know, I was impressed with your cunning though I did evade your trap. You have a certain reputation as a hasty man. I am not hasty. I have waited eighteen years and were I forced to wait another eighteen, I would wait."

The fire damped again and Sarmiento glimpsed a moving shadow. Were his eyes overused or was it a messenger from Hell? Was this plan the work of the Devil? He drew his dagger and held it before him like a cross. García watched with wide eyes.

"Swear by this cross, García. Swear that if you or your minions mention my name, that if you or your priests whisper my name, you will be damned to Hell for eternity and burn in everlasting fire. Swear it, García!"

"Don Pero, I am loyal and committed."

"Then swear it. Kneel and kiss this cross."

Sarmiento held the dagger before the lawyer and García knelt. "I swear," he said, "in the name of our Lord, Jesus Christ, that your name will never be spoken. That if I or my people betray you, we will be damned to Hell forever." And he kissed the dagger.

"Good. You will administer the same oath to your canons," Sarmiento said, his voice now light. "We may continue. What were you about to say? Oh, yes, that Luna has provided us with an excellent pretext."

Shaken, García answered, "The Constable has played into our hands, don Pero. We required a torch to light the fire and Providence in the form of Luna has provided one."

"Who will light the torch?"

"Light the torch, don Pero?"

"Monday. For the love of God, García. Momentous Monday."

"An artisan has been selected, señor. Cota will collect taxes beginning Monday morning, assuming Luna rejects the delegation from the Council—and he will. A craftsman will resist the collection—a solid member of the common people with a loud voice and sincere reasons for hating *marranos*. He will be arrested and his outcry will spread throughout the city. That will hot the fire."

"And tomorrow?"

"Tomorrow, Sunday, our partisans will slander Luna, declaring that he received a bribe from Cota, the *marrano*, who profits from tax collection. They will spread the gossip at the Cathedral and other churches, and early Monday our good slanderers will circulate in the marketplace inciting the public. By midday the tinder will have been set, awaiting the flame."

"And by evening?"

"Toledo will be ours."

"Not ours, García. Mine."

5

Down the alley

The alley opened into a small square surrounded by shops and the stone walls of private homes. Streets in this quarter wandered like drunken guardsmen, but Fernán knew his way without eyes. A quick shadow at the narrow opening he had quit caught his eye as he felt a hard point pressed against his back.

"Drop the dagger. Turn about," a rough voice demanded.

He let the dagger fall into the snow and turned. A bulky man pushed Fernán against the wall of a darkened shop and held a sword to his throat. With the weapon under his chin, Fernán could not cough as he had planned, although the breath of the swordsman, heavy with cheap drink, clogged his lungs. In a choked voice, he recited the story about his ill mother. The man ignored his tale and demanded his name. Fernán told him.

"What family?"

"Chavez," Fernán lied.

Why was he not stiff with fear? Was it the practice with Jerónimo—the practice with dagger and sword—watching, planning, acting? Whatever the reason, Fernán waited, his mind cold.

Several figures emerged from the darkness. Three. This was not the pack of five that had followed him. Bad luck. This was an ill-kempt lot—hair and beards wild, clothes filthy and torn, weapons ill-made. One fondled a short-handled, double-edged ax. Another, a homemade pike crafted from a sickle tied to a bare bough—a lethal banner. The third swung a crude wooden club as if he were swatting elephants.

The ragged edge of the rusty sword pricked his throat. The polished swords of the pack that followed him had glinted in the moonlight. They might have treated him like a gentleman, though his allegiance differed from theirs. The scum Fernán saw about him now looked too miserable to care for niceties and were surely loyal to no one but the Devil. They were after his purse and clothes and, if he were lucky, a fat ransom for his life.

"Put your sword down or die."

Where the voice came from or who its owner might be puzzled Fernán, though the timbre was familiar. The ragged edge of the sword pressed against his larynx. He could not move his head.

"Jerónimo?" he whispered hoarsely.

"Shut your hole," the swordsman said.

"Good evening, Fernán. Steady, please. You with the sword, put it down. Now!"

The skirmish was over quickly. The bulk of the swordsman dropped away, swords flashed in the moonlight, men cried out, then running sounds and silence and Jerónimo stood before Fernán, smiling.

"You left the house too quickly, Fernán and, forgive me, but you run much too fast. Your father directed us to follow you but it was impossible. However, we knew where you were going and we took a shorter way."

"There is no shorter way."

"I know you are well-versed in most things, Fernán, and the gracious Lord knows that some day your knowledge will span this sphere we inhabit, as today many wise men conclude our world is formed but, as to the map of Toledo, your wisdom has a gap or two."

"What gap?"

"A gap in your memory of the streets of Toledo, young master, a gap through which we ran and which pared minutes from our trip."

"You ran past the alley…."

"And retraced our steps when we realized you had disappeared. Then, the good Lord blessed us and we heard voices."

Fernán stared at the crumpled figure of the swordsman. A dark stream ran from a knife in his throat over the cobblestones to the homemade pike that protruded from under a second corpse. Fernán picked up his dagger from the street, examined its edges, wiped it dry on his cape, and returned the weapon to its scabbard.

"Your knife in his throat?" he asked Jerónimo.

"Yes, Fernán."

"Thrown?"

"As a matter of fact. Prompt delivery was essential."

Fernán nodded his appreciation. "The others dead?" he asked.

"No, they knew they were dead when we appeared and so the dead men ran. I thought it prudent not to follow them to Hell."

"Who were they?"

"Thieves, cutthroats."

"Not Sarmiento people?"

"I think not, Fernán," Jerónimo said. "Sarmiento rabble would be better dressed and better armed."

Fernán saw four servants from the Hernandes house standing against a building across the square, talking quietly. He called out his thanks. They doffed their hats and one asked if the young master was well. Fernán replied that with the help of God and their sharp swords he was well indeed.

"Forgive me, Fernán," Jerónimo said, "but your throat is scratched and there is blood on your cape."

"His damned sword was jagged. Only a scratch."

"Then with your permission, we will accompany you the rest of the way."

Jerónimo and the four servants escorted Fernán to the Melamed house—two ahead and two behind, swords drawn. The walk downhill was slippery on the crisp snow, but they were soon at the house in the *judería*.

Unlike most houses in the Jewish quarter, the Melamed house was not cheek by jowl with its neighbors. The entrance was through a walled garden that separated the house from its neighbor to the right. On the left, a narrow street led to the river. The brick-and-stone dwelling was about fifteen feet wide and thirty deep with balconied and shuttered windows on each of its three stories.

Fernán hesitated a moment, then knocked on a door recessed into the garden wall. After a second knock, a light appeared in a third-floor window and, several minutes later, a barred panel in the door slid back and a sleepy face appeared. Fernán told the bearded man that he had an urgent message for don Abrahán. The panel closed.

They waited a quarter hour in the cold before Fernán heard footsteps crunching snow. The panel opened briefly, a pair of tired, wise eyes examined him, and then the door opened. Fernán told the four servants to wait and he and Jerónimo walked into a small courtyard that contained a few olive and fruit trees and some shrubs dressed for winter, the branches blanched with snow.

"I am Melamed," the physician said to Fernán. "You have a message?"

A multi-colored, long-sleeved caftan clothed the spare frame of the man who faced Fernán. His head was covered by an embroidered turban that rested on a brilliant fringe of curly white hair fused into a full beard and mustache. Two large young men with jet beards and similar clothing framed the doctor.

"A message from my father, don Lorenzo Hernandes, señor."

"Don Lorenzo is your father?"

"Yes, don Abrahán."

"Then we will go inside. Summon your men. This strange weather can cause harm to the lungs and there is hot drink in the kitchen."

The study was warmed by a small fire. Books and scrolls piled on every surface obscured the floor. A trestle table stretched wall to wall.

"Come close to the fire, young man," he said. "Ah, yes, I did detect something more than a shadow beneath your chin. What have you done to your throat?"

Fernán explained the fracas with the hoodlums that caused the dirty bruise while Melamed cleaned the wound.

"You have good luck, apparently, in that your servants were close behind you. Now we will dress the wound, Rafael, and it should heal properly."

"You know my name?"

"Don Lorenzo has but one son to my knowledge—Rafael Fernán Hernandes," he said, while completing the dressing.

"True, my name is Rafael Fernán, don Abrahán, but I prefer Fernán."

"Then I shall call you Fernán. Now what is the message from your father?"

Fernán removed his boot and retrieved the note. Don Abrahán sat on a bench before the table, head bowed, hands clasped before him, and read the letter. He looked up at Fernán.

"You are familiar with this letter?"

"I am, don Abrahán. My father asked me to read it before I left our house."

"Good. And are you concerned?"

"No, señor. God watches over us."

The eyes of the physician, which had been studying the letter, rose like twin moons. A snowy eyebrow and one corner of white mustache were elevated in what Fernán interpreted as an expression of amused interest.

"And to which God do you refer?" Melamed asked.

"There is but one God, señor."

"Ah, yes, of course. One God, many peoples. And you think God watches over us and takes care of us—all of us equally—Catholic, Jew, Muslim, and so forth."

"If we are good."

"Good. An intriguing word—good. And if we are bad?"

"Then we are alone in the world."

"Alone in the world? Isolated? Unprotected?"

"Yes, señor."

"And the stray lamb, Fernán? She who is alone not because she has trespassed but, one might say, because of the will of God?"

"The lamb is not alone, señor. She may be lost, but can be found and saved."

"Found and saved," don Abrahán said, and his eyes filmed over and, as quickly, the watery film dissipated. "Stay tonight in this house, Fernán. You said the sword blade was jagged and rusty. I treated your wound with an ointment before I wrapped it. I will want to see its appearance in the morning. You may dismiss your servants. They will inform your father that you are here and safe."

"Is there a reply to the message, don Abrahán?"

"No. A reply is not necessary."

Fernán excused himself and entered the kitchen, where he found Jerónimo and the servants drinking heated wine with Aharón and Mosé, the assistants to don Abrahán. Fernán could not decide what to call them. They did not appear to be servants and yet they protected the doctor.

"Are you well then, Fernán?" Jerónimo asked.

Fernán repeated what the doctor had said and Jerónimo asked if he was sure he wanted to stay. Why Fernán wanted to stay the night, he did not know, but don Abrahán attracted him and he wanted to talk further with the doctor.

"I will stay the night, Jerónimo. You and the others return to our house and inform my father that the message was delivered and that there was no reply. I am well and will see him tomorrow. And, if you please, tell my father nothing of what happened. I will tell him myself." He took his tutor by the hand. "Good night and thank you, my friend."

6

Sunday morning

At first light, Fernán turned toward the window. The square panes partitioned the cloud-filled sky as his mind was sectioned by a motley of images—running in the night, the beady eyes of the swordsman, the ragged sword against his throat. He winced. His neck pained him, but the bed was comfortable and he had slept well.

He washed his hands and face in a plain ceramic basin on the wooden dresser. The water was warm—someone had filled the basin earlier that morning while he slept. Perhaps Naomi. The doctor had said Naomi would make up the bed. Fernán had been too tired, though, to ask who Naomi was or to continue their conversation.

As he remembered, the kitchen was two flights down. He would wait there for the doctor. Fernán dressed, found the stairs, and descended. Don Abrahán sat at a table in the center of the small kitchen munching on a piece of dark bread and a healthy slice of light yellow cheese.

"Good morning, Fernán," he said. "Please join us."

Fernán saw no one except the doctor. "Thank you, señor."

"You slept well?"

"Except when my throat bothered me. Yes, señor."

"We will look at the throat after you break your fast, then you can be on your way. Ah, Naomi," he said, smiling at the space above Fernán, "this is Rafael Fernán Hernandes. You will call him Fernán."

Fernán turned in his seat. A young woman stood several paces behind him holding a pot and ladle. He first saw eyes rimmed with thick lashes outlining the pure white orbs in which her irises floated—a deeper brown than his, almost black. Her skin was smooth and pale, but with a pink tinge. And her features were of such harmonious proportion that they seemed designed—yet not static but mobile, varying with her mood. Younger than he, fifteen or so, she wore a simple white dress which revealed enough of her figure to charm him. A patterned scarf covered most of her chestnut-colored hair. Fernán could think only with his eyes and he struggled to his feet and nodded stiffly. She was not tall, the top of her head was below his chin.

Naomi looked up at Fernán as he stood, her smile restrained and brief. "Good morning, Fernán," she said, her voice not low, not high. Unlocking herself from his eyes, she said, "Grandpapá, the cupboard is quite empty. I will have to shop today." She put the pot on the table. "Will Fernán have soup?"

"Ask Fernán, my dear, not me."

"Thank you," Fernán managed, "it looks delicious."

He searched her face and was again transfixed, then shook his head to clear his sight and glanced around the room for another stool.

"Thank you, Fernán," she said, "but I have eaten. Sit, if you please."

He wondered that she knew his thoughts, but he sat and she ladled soup into his bowl and left the room.

"Here is bread and cheese," don Abrahán said. "Naomi baked the bread and the cheese is from a nearby farm. Both are excellent, though the bread is a day old, since yesterday was the Sabbath."

"Naomi is your granddaughter, señor?"

"Yes. Her parents are gone, God rest their souls."

"I am sorry, señor."

"Thank you, Fernán. An old loss."

The doctor turned to the window, his face void.

Fernán hesitated, then tore off a piece of bread and spooned the thick soup into his mouth—wholesome plain fare. The girl was young to have lost both parents. He said nothing to the doctor and ate the bread and soup, waiting for Naomi to return. When he realized that she might not, he suffered a curious sense of loss, an experience with overtones difficult to judge. And although he could not recreate the exact form of her face, his eyes had been filled with her and he knew that she was beautiful. But she was a Jew.

"Don Abrahán," he said between mouthfuls, "will there be trouble for your people?"

The doctor raised his eyebrows and moved his head to one side. "My people, Fernán? You and I are of the same people, my boy. Take away clothing and a few drops of holy water and we are the same." He stroked the beard on his cheek. "You know who you are?"

"I know my great-grandparents were Jews and that they converted to Catholicism. My mother was converted when she was quite young."

"Your great-grandparents, when did they convert?"

"During the massacres of 1391, my father said."

"And why did they take such drastic action?"

"To save their children and themselves."

"What do you know of Jews, Fernán?"

"Very little, señor. My father has been Catholic all his life and, therefore, so have I. Our family is Catholic. I know little of Judaism."

"Understandable. Your family chose another way."

Don Abrahán cut a slice of cheese.

"You asked if there will be trouble for my people, Fernán." He sighed. "I do not think so. Not this time. This time we sojourners will be untroubled. We are so few now, so insignificant—the haters have so few of us to hate. Our time will come again, but not now."

The doctor ate the cheese and looked straight at Fernán. Other than the whites, which had traces of pink and red shot through them, his eyes were twins to those of his granddaughter—the almond shape, the frame of lashes unusual for a man, the near-black irises. His eyes, however, conveyed a sense of melancholy whereas hers brimmed with intelligence and life.

"Now is your time, Fernán, I am sad to say. Now is the time for the *anusim*, whom you call *conversos* and they call *marranos*. Trouble lies at your doorstep, my boy, you who wear the garments of the oppressor. An oppressor who will turn on his changelings in this land of olives and grapes and once again transform this ancient soil of *Sefarad*—this sweet, beautiful land in which we Jews have tarried since the time of Hadrian—into clay stained with blood."

7

The study of don Abrahán

The morning sun shone through two large windows, and Naomi waited in the sunlight, her face aglow.

"Does your throat pain you, Fernán?" Melamed asked.

"No, señor, my throat does not hurt."

"You said that it bothered you this morning."

"Did I? Yes, don Abrahán, I suppose I did."

"Let me see. Naomi, bring that white jar, if you please."

Half of him, attentive to the words of don Abrahán, satisfied convention while the other half lay suspended on a different plane. Though he never glanced her way, he perceived the beginning of an attachment made almost painful by the obligatory gulf between them, and he concluded that the hurtful sensation he now experienced was not unique to him but had, as its reflection, an equal intensity within her.

The doctor unwound the dressing he had applied the previous night and pronounced the cure satisfactory. "However, young Fernán, you will be required to apply this ointment twice a day—when you arise and when you retire. It is not necessary to cover the wound after today since the lacerations in your throat were shallow and have closed. But remember to use the ointment for the next few days. Then come to see me."

Naomi handed her grandfather the jar, then raised her bright eyes to Fernán and smiled. He rolled his eyes and she laughed. The doctor turned.

"What have we here?" Melamed asked. "Pranks behind my back?"

"Señor, forgive me. I was being foolish."

"Folly is the privilege of youth, Fernán. Nothing to forgive."

Fernán looked around, but once again Naomi was gone. Had he embarrassed her?

Melamed applied the ointment and bound it with a clean cloth. Then he sat at the table, wrote in a journal for a few minutes, and said, "Do not remove the dressing until tonight."

"Yes, señor. If I may ask, don Abrahán, how did you become a doctor?"

"Study and practice."

"And where did you study, señor?"

"In Italy, a school of medicine at the university in Padua. After years of study and practice you learn a technique or two that may help your patients, and so they call you a doctor."

"Might I become a doctor?"

"If it were something you wanted to be. Do you?"

Fernán had asked the question blindly, impulsively. With no immediate response at hand, he said, "My father has planned for me to become a merchant, to continue in his trade, though I am not sure of my aptitude for buying and selling. Other occupations interest me more. Study interests me. I would prefer to study in a university, though I have no idea what course to pursue. And Castile is in such turmoil."

"You are growing, my boy—your mind is expanding. Give it time. As for Castile—Castile is changing as well and is about as confused as you seem to be, though it has had many more years to adjust. Castile and you shall have to wait and see." Melamed turned to Fernán. "Your father told you nothing more about me?"

"No, señor. My father said nothing but that I was to bring the message."

"Curious. You know who you are but not who I am. So then, if your father did not tell you he must have intended I should."

Melamed sat on the edge of the table, hands folded before him. He sighed deeply and nodded a few times as if readying himself for prayer.

"My grandmother bore eight children, Fernán," he said. "All gone now, of course—may they rest in peace. My father and your great-grandfather were two of those children. I was the only son of my father, a Jew of Toledo, and one of the very few who remained in this city. Our family name is Melamed as was yours before your great-grandfather converted during the massacres and took the name Hernandes." Don Abrahán smiled warmly. "You and I are cousins, Fernán—distant cousins, but cousins. Blood of our common ancestors inhabits your veins and those of your father, myself, and Naomi."

Fernán nodded but said nothing. The affinity he felt for this house, for don Abrahán, and for Naomi was at least partly explained. His contact with

Jews had been occasional, and meeting a Jewish cousin who was a doctor and a female cousin whose beauty possessed him, would take time to digest.

"So, now you know who you are and who we are."

"Thank you, don Abrahán, for that knowledge."

"Not at all. You should know. Now where are you bound for?"

"Home. There is just enough time for me to attend Mass."

"Of course," Melamed said. "Be careful in the city."

8

A street in the Juderia

He retraced his path from the preceding night, avoiding the alley of offensive odors and brutal memories, and plunged into the puzzle he had created, or God in his wisdom had created, though he could not presume God would express interest in the details of his personal affairs. For he had walked into the Melamed house the night before and found himself at home in this Jewish atmosphere, yet never having visited a Jewish home. Was it similar to his? Not to his mind. His home was a replica of the homes of his friends—Old Christian or New. There was a Castilian formality to them, a Catholicism of crucifix and prayer and decoration that was, of course, absent from the Melamed household, although he was certain that other forms were present of which he was unaware. The familiarity of their home—of its configuration, scent, food—was indefinable. At the same time, an exoticism within the house spoke to something hidden within him. Though alien, he was certain he could find his way around the kitchen, that nothing within the house would surprise him.

So deeply was he engrossed in his speculation that he almost passed the key to his puzzle without noticing that she was a few steps ahead of him, her arm through a market basket, head erect, a shawl draped around her shoulders. He shut off thought, lengthened his stride, and ten steps later was beside her.

"I missed you," he said.

As he spoke he wondered if she would understand what he meant—that he had failed to see her leave, not that her absence distressed him. Or was that what he meant? But he came abreast of her so suddenly that he doubted she had heard what he said because his voice startled her.

"Oh, Fernán!" she said. "I could not imagine who would speak to me in the street."

"I am sorry, Naomi." They walked together in silence for several minutes. There were few people on the street that morning, Jew or Gentile. Naomi nodded to one Jewish matron who glanced at Fernán and hurried by.

Fernán halted abruptly and Naomi turned to him.

"Do you think it strange that we met this morning?" he asked. "I do. And stranger still that you and I are cousins."

His arms hung like immovable weights, while his eyes reabsorbed her image, dwelling on new details he had failed to notice—the delicate tracing of her eyebrows, the pink shell of her ear, the slight pout of her lips. Her simple shawl covered her head and shoulders, framing the face his mind had captured, seemingly forever.

"Friends of mine have cousins among the *anusim*," she said.

"What does that mean—*anusim*?"

"Forced ones—Hebrew for those converted against their will."

"I have not come across that word in my studies."

She peered at him as they resumed walking. "You study Hebrew?"

"Yes. I like languages."

"You know many?"

"Six well. Hebrew well enough to read but not to speak."

"That is quite a lot."

"Not really. There are many similarities between them. Spanish and Italian are very alike, and Latin is the core of both. Hebrew is quite different, though it has echoes in Arabic. And Ladino is Hebrew Spanish."

"You speak Ladino? How wonderful. Have you traveled?"

"No. Toledo and the few villages around us are all I know."

"I would have thought that, knowing so many languages, you would want to travel."

"I will one day," he said.

"I too will travel some day," she said, and she raised her eyes to the clouded sky. "Toledo is so small and the world so large."

"Do you speak other languages?"

"Only Spanish, Hebrew, and Ladino."

"Then I can teach you Latin, Italian, and Arabic."

"Would you?"

"Indeed. I want to."

Her cheeks were flushed. He credited the air that retained some night chill. Much of the snow had disappeared with the morning sun, though patches of white remained against the walls of the narrow street where the sun had yet to penetrate.

"I have known for a long time that your family and ours were cousins," she said.

"How could you know?"

"My grandpapá and your father speak to one another—they have spoken many times."

"When? I never knew."

"There may be a few other things you do not know," she said.

The corners of her mouth were turned up, suppressing a smile and creating a dimple below her cheeks. His eyes were fastened on hers and on her smile now fully opened to him as he stared nakedly at her. She laughed, and he saw that her teeth were clear, white, even miracles.

"Have you never seen a Jewish girl before?"

"Never so close."

"And what do you see that is so different from the girls you know?"

"I know no girls."

"But you must. So nice-looking a young man...." Then, perhaps realizing what she had said, she asked, "How old are you, Fernán?"

"Seventeen."

"And no wife, no fiancée," again the smile, "no lover?"

"Of course not. Certainly not. Other things concern me."

"What, for example?" she asked, hurrying to keep up with his pace which had suddenly quickened.

"The situation in Toledo, for one, which seems to worsen."

"Worsen for whom?"

"For us, for *converso*s. Old Christians despise us."

He had been about to say that Old Christians consider them Jews, as don Gaspar had exclaimed the night before, but thought he might offend Naomi. She, though, plunged straight ahead, voicing his thought.

"But you are no longer Jews, you are as Catholic as they are."

"That seems not to matter—they act as if we were never baptised."

He slowed his walk to allow her to keep up with him, and told her that her grandfather had discussed the relationship between their families with him this morning. He apologized for prying.

"But you were not prying, Fernán. It would be unnatural for you not to be interested, although there is not that much to know."

He asked how long she had lived with her grandfather.

"Ten, eleven years," she said. She had forgotten almost everything about her parents. Her grandfather reminded her of her father, the little she did remember. "Grandpapá says I look like my mother."

"What happened to them?"

"They were lost at sea. My father was a merchant like your father. He traveled throughout the Mediterranean and Mamá went with him. They were very close, Grandpapá says. One year they failed to return—weather or pirates had killed them, we think. Their ship was never found. My grandmother died quite young and Grandpapá became father and mother to me."

What was reflected on her face? Old sorrow? Wonder at what life might have been had they lived? He wanted to hold her, to say he would make her life splendid, to tell her about his family and how they would love her. Flustered, though, he asked her age.

"Almost sixteen," she said.

The way she spoke, her assuredness made her seem more his age. "Who are Mosé and Aharón?" he asked.

"Brothers, as you may have guessed—apprentices to Grandpapá. In this case, however, Aharón is the silent one and Mosé wordy."

"I once thought I might become a doctor."

"Did you?" Naomi smiled. Then she motioned toward an alley that descended toward the river. "Forgive me, Fernán, but I go this way—to the Jewish market. Would you feel uncomfortable there, do you think, out of place?"

"No, I would not be troubled, Naomi, but I cannot now. My family will wonder what has become of me."

She nodded as if in accord with some unspoken promise and he wanted to touch her, perhaps to verify her reality, but was bound by chains. He said a painful goodbye and she wished him a good day and he watched as she turned and waved and walked down the alley toward the Jewish market.

9

The Cathedral Plaza

Idlers and those hurrying past the crowd of over two hundred artisans, shopkeepers, and laborers who had gathered in the plaza stopped to listen to the shrill tenor of a thin, angular priest who stood before the doors of the church exhorting his flock to oppose the new tax. A haze had appeared from the north, and the light, which had been brilliant in the chill morning air, was now dull as a tarnished blade.

Fernán had heard the priest speak before and disliked his manner. Pero Lope de Galvez, canon of the Cathedral, was an effective speaker, he thought, but a hateful man, priest or not.

"What law forces you to support the wars of this king?" Galvez questioned, his voice silk. "If King Juan cannot finance and fight the wars he starts, he cannot be much of a king, can he? Can he?"

"Not much!" the crowd shouted.

"No, my sons and daughters, he cannot. Not that we like him the less for it." Jeers and catcalls. "But does Juan support you, provide for you? Help you when you are sick or needy?"

"No," the crowd cried. "No help there. Not in this world."

"No, not in this world. But he does tax your wages, does he not? Oh, he taxes you. Yes, he sucks your lifeblood. Takes the earnings from your labor and puts the money in his coffers."

"He does, God knows."

"So why give more of your life and money to Luna to support an old man who has yet to stand on his own feet? Why buttress King Juan when you know the man will let you fall? Never a hand up for you, dear people."

The crowd barked, "We know!" and wailed, "Damned if I pay the tax! Rot in hell before I do! Luna the bastard gets his cut from Cota the *marrano*!"

Their words alarmed Fernán and he hung back at the corner of Town Hall across from the Cathedral.

"Dear sons and daughters," Galvez shouted over the crowd, his voice now shrill, "reject the war tax of Alvaro de Luna! Stand up against the tax collector and, if the *marrano*, Cota, hails a guardsman to force you, if he tries to deny you the earnings of your sweat, defy the guardsman and the *marrano*, the anti-Christ. Defeat the tax. Refuse to pay for war."

Voices in the crowd. "Cota takes half the tax. Half the tax in the pocket of a *marrano*? Damn him! Down with Cota! Down with the *marrano*!" An earthy female. "Cota bribes Alvaro, the blood-sucker." A basso. "So who is the *marrano*, Luna or Cota?" The mob guffawed. A woman. "Who can tell? Both smell like pig to me." Squeals, grunts, screams from the mob, and then a shout. "Tomorrow is when Luna gets his bribe." The basso. "Shit tomorrow. What he gets from me is pig shit."

Voice coarsened, Galvez shouted above the shrieks, bellows, and snickers, "Go home, good people! Go home now. Tell your neighbors of the war tax, the Luna tax, the *marrano* tax. Tell them what you know."

"We will, Father!"

"Tell them to refuse the Luna tax. Tell them to refuse the King his war tax. Pero Sarmiento proclaimed Toledo a no-tribute city. Toledo owes nothing to King Juan or his bastard lackey."

"To hell with Luna!"

"And Monday—listen now—Monday, when Cota tries to collect his tax, what do you tell him?"

"No tax!" they roared.

"What do you tell the *marrano*?"

"No tax!" they screamed.

"Bless you, my children," Galvez said, blessed them with the sign of the cross, and retreated into the Cathedral followed by several acolytes.

"Bless you, Father!" they shouted.

The crowd grew more boisterous as Fernán watched—repeating the words the priest had proclaimed, shouting to one another. Street vendors hawked food and drink and the potent spirits took hold. The raucous crowd became nasty. Young hoodlums ran into the mob, ducked between legs, grabbed skirts, snatched purses, and took cuffs on the ear or kicks on the rump when near a broad arm or leg. Those Fernán knew from the shops, artisans who worked for his father, tradesmen who sold his mother goods, others several hundred strong, all became roaring, shouting drunk.

"What does the priest know about us? His food is on the table."

"Shut your mouth. The priest knows what he knows."
"Why against the King? Juan is a good man."
"Good to himself, you mean."

A fight began, then another and the brawl spread. In no time the scene was a melee. Men fought, screamed curses, hands clubbing, feet kicking as they rolled in the dirt, arms and legs tangled. Women were roughed, and drunk, fell where pitched, receiving kicks from toppled bodies and blows from tossed cobbles.

"Fascinating to watch the animals play. What do you think, young man?"

The speaker was one of several onlookers peering around the corner of the building where Fernán had positioned himself. Stocky, a head shorter than Fernán, the man was well-dressed and wore a fine sword. Fernán did not know him, but he nodded and said, "Quite a spectacle."

"Marcos García de Mora," the man said, introducing himself, "and you?"

His bearing reminded Fernán of the swordsman of the night before, although the difference in their stations could not have been more apparent.

"Rafael Chavez de Castro, señor, a visitor to this city," Fernán lied.

"Well then, you have received quite an introduction to our fair town."

Dizzy with drink, the greengrocer who served the Hernandes house spied Fernán near the building and roared, "A *marrano*—get the little bastard!"

Fernán drew his dagger.

"Best run, young man, they look to be in a rough mood," García said.

"Thank you, señor, but I am well-trained."

"Your life," García said, and hurried off.

Fernán was alone. Stones landed near him. The noise of the crowd rose.

"Look at the length of weapon the beggar sports!" a tradesman howled.

"About the size of a baby weenie," a blowzy woman cried. Another. "My baby has a weapon twice the length. Never get near me with that pricker, *marrano*." Another. "Your wee one, *marrano*, does he wear a cap or did they cut the poor thing off entire?"

The mob surged toward Fernán. He backed away. Two boys darted out of the crowd then veered off. More stones were thrown and Fernán took a blow on the shoulder. A young man rushed him, screaming, a knife in his fist, and Fernán waited, sidestepped, and struck the youth with the pommel of his dagger, sending him sprawling.

A voice in the crowd shouted, "My boy, you hit my boy, you bastard!"

The crowd streamed forward and Fernán ran. His legs carried him past Town Hall, through narrow alleys and courtyards where the locals watched with startled faces as the youth streaked by, until Fernán realized that he no longer heard the screams of the frenzied crowd, slowed his pace, and jogged home.

"The family is at Mass, Fernán," his father said, "but I waited. What is that cloth around your neck?"

"I fell last night and scraped my neck, Papá. Don Abrahán treated me and wrapped it with cloth."

"You seem winded."

"I ran home."

"Why run?" Lorenzo asked.

"I wanted not to be late for Mass, Papá. Also I listened to a harangue by Pero Lope de Galvez outside the Cathedral. He opposes the new tax and drove the crowd into a frenzy against Alvaro de Luna, the King, and *conversos*— Alonso Cota in particular. Our greengrocer was in the crowd. He saw me, tried to run me down, and the mob followed. But as you see, I ran too fast."

"Thank God your mother is at Mass, Fernán. She would have died of fright."

"No cause for alarm, Papá. The plebes were drunk and God was with me."

10

The following morning

"The day before yesterday, Fernán," Jerónimo said, "that magnificent bay, Montaña, threw a shoe. And this morning at the blacksmith shop, while waiting for the bay to be shod, who should appear at the shop of the armorer next to the smithy but Alonso Cota, the tax collector, insisting that the armorer pay the new tax."

"The tax Alvaro de Luna demands?" Fernán asked.

"The same. Close your left side."

They were practicing with rapier and dagger in a small armory set aside for sport and weapons storage near the stables.

"I opened my left side to divert your eye from my sword."

"Perhaps," Jerónimo said, "but you would be dead from the fake, young master, before you could use your weapon."

"Never."

"No?"

Jerónimo engaged Fernán with his dagger and swung his sword flat against the open side.

"Dead."

"Agreed. Dead. Fair or unfair."

"Death is unfair, Fernán, but you should have anticipated my stroke. Shall we stop?"

"A wicked stroke, wickedly delivered."

"To be learned, a lesson must hurt. And I struck with the flat of the blade. Imagine the consequence had it been the edge."

Jerónimo stripped off his shirt and dabbed at his upper body with a wet cloth. Then he donned a fresh shirt, poured ale into a mug, and drank.

"Fernán, my friend," he said, "when I say *hurt*, I truly mean startle, surprise—to gain your attention. Pain surprises us, awakens us from slumber. However, I would never cause you real pain except to save your life."

"I know that, Jerónimo. Your sword woke me, that was all. But you were saying."

His pensive face—sharp aquiline nose, deep-set dark eyes, and prominent cheekbones—now shone with his usual humor. "I was saying, Fernán, that the blacksmith and I thought it odd that Cota himself would do early rounds instead of passing the chore to one of his hirelings, so we wandered over to the armory and listened. We were startled to hear the armorer refuse to pay the tax."

"Refuse?"

"Just that."

"Were guardsmen with Cota?"

"They were indeed, decked out in their fancy garb. Two nasty specimens, looking like a pair of those squashed-faced dogs the nobility favor. We were impressed with their colorful appearance until they turned to face us—like following a shapely woman expecting a beauty and finding a hag."

Fernán smiled and Jerónimo said that the blacksmith and he could not control their hilarity. They were reduced to giggling convent girls at the contrast of fancy costumes and ugly faces and almost came to blows with the guardsmen who must have felt as ridiculous as they looked.

Removing his shirt, Fernán dipped a cloth into a bucket of water and washed his torso. His side bore a red imprint where Jerónimo had struck him.

"What did señor Cota do when the armorer refused to pay?" he asked.

"Nothing. The armorer, though—Rodríguez, you know his work—called señor Cota all manner of vicious things and spit in his face. Of course, the guardsmen dragged him off to prison, all the while Rodríguez screaming obscene epithets about their lineage into their faces. Shouting to the heavens about not paying the Luna tax and damning the King for his war and Luna for being bribed by Cota."

"The same harangue the canon gave the crowd outside the Cathedral yesterday. Were there others with Rodríguez at his shop?"

"A large number for the time and place. For the sun was not yet up and the shop is far from the center of town, as you know."

"How many?"

"Fifty or more—townspeople, commoners."

"And what did they do?"

"Shouted at the guardsmen to release Rodríguez. A few bold women tore at the fine clothes the guardsmen wore and were smacked down for their audacity. Then the guardsmen threatened the crowd with their pikes. That turned the crowd as lunatic as Rodríguez and they took up his cry, shouting, 'Death to *marranos*! Death to Luna, their bastard friend!' And the words became a chant that followed the guardsmen and Rodríguez to prison."

"The crowd followed them to prison?"

"Just so, gathering people along the way and urging others to join. Those hanging out their windows and on their balconies added to the torrent of rough talk, screaming at the guardsmen to free Rodríguez. A circus, to be sure."

"And you followed?"

"This was an event to be witnessed and so, yes, I did follow," Jerónimo said. "The blacksmith turned back though he was as amazed as I. But his shop was open and horses need shoes. I followed the rabble to the prison and, by then, many hundreds were gathered, screaming and shouting their chant of death to *marranos* and Luna. Not a pretty thing to witness. I stayed but a moment, though, remembering that by then Montaña must be shod, and so I returned to the blacksmith shop, collected the bay, and rode back here."

At that moment, bells rang.

"What bells make that punishing sound, Jerónimo?"

"The Cathedral bells, young master, but for no virtuous reason."

Fernán had heard cathedral bells all his life but not at this hour on a Monday. And these were cathedral bells disfigured. Not bells to mark the steady beat of time, nor bells whose hymn called multitudes to prayer. These were the discordant bells of carnage and fire—bells of war.

"We must attend whatever assembly is being called," Fernán said.

The house was empty of Hernandes men. Lorenzo and Cesario were calling on the wealthy, reporting on commissions and deliveries, and Antonio had left for a few days to bargain with local artisans for merchandise. For the first time, Fernán experienced the full burden of manhood.

"Jerónimo, assemble the male servants and distribute weapons to senior members of the staff. I will speak to them after I see my mother. Then you and I will go to the Cathedral."

"What shall I tell the servants, Fernán? They will be concerned."

"Tell them we may be attacked and that they will be expected to guard the women and children and the house. Now hurry."

He found his mother in the parlor playing chess with María while his eight-year-old sister, Beatriz, watched.

"Mamá, there may be trouble today. You heard the bells?"

"A dreadful sound, Fernán dear. Who could have played them so poorly?"

"You are quite rude today, Fernán," María said. "No hello, no kiss for Auntie?"

"Forgive me, Aunt María, the times are difficult and I must hurry."

"Why must you hurry?" his mother asked.

"Because these bells foretell trouble, Mamá. Listen, if you please. I am the only man of our house present and I must take precautions as Papá instructed."

He told them that the staff would be armed and responsible for their safety until he or his father or his uncles returned. The women and children were to find something warm to wear and, if there was an attack, they were to hide in the storage room with the door bolted. If the house was set on fire they were to retreat through the rear door toward the river, make their way to the gate of Cambrón, and wait outside the city walls. The servants would accompany and protect them. They must not panic and must not delay by gathering their valuables.

"You understand, Mamá? These are the instructions Papá gave me."

"You are a good son. We will do as your father instructed. Let us pray there is no need for extreme measures. Where will you be?"

"At the Cathedral, learning why the bells rang. Jerónimo will accompany me. We will be armed and on horse."

He kissed his mother, aunt, and sister and joined the men servants and Jerónimo in the armory. Fernán repeated the instructions he had given his mother and emphasized that, in the event of an attack, they were to guard the women and children with their lives.

"An attack is not expected, but we must prepare for one. Paulo," he said to a tall, rugged young man, "you will be in charge until Jerónimo returns. Place two men away from the house toward the Cathedral to warn of an attack. If the house is fired, retreat through Cambrón, set up defensive positions, and wait. Above all else, protect the women and the little ones."

"You may depend on me, don Fernán," Paulo said. "My life is devoted to defending the family."

They hurried to the stable. Jerónimo took Fernán by the arm. "Why choose Paulo?" explaining that Paulo had caused some problems of late—the women servants had complained of his advances and he had laughed off Jerónimo and his warnings.

"Like many handsome men, he thinks all women love him."

"But will he protect the women and children, Jerónimo?"

"Let us hope it does not come to that, young master."

11

In the Cathedral

A pall had been cast over the sky, the air damp and cold. Fernán had neglected to take a cloak and gloves, and his hands were numb on the reins, the chill penetrating as Jerónimo and he rode through the streets. Once their horses and weapons were stabled near Town Hall, they ran across the plaza to the Cathedral.

The nave was crowded, all pews full. Those unable to find a seat stood beside the pews, in the transept, and behind the nave. On Sundays and holidays the first pews would have been occupied by nobility. This day, however, no noble or councilor or other leader of the city was attending. Seats the highborn and affluent normally occupied, those seats where Fernán and his family and other well-to-do *converso* families sat, were filled with the masses—laborers, artisans, and shopkeepers who leaned forward on the benches, bodies tense, hands grasping the tops of the pews before them, listening to the speaker with rapt attention.

Fernán sent Jerónimo toward the transept to absorb the mood of the community, count the number of those in attendance, and note the faces he knew. From a distance it was difficult to distinguish the features of the speaker who stood high above the audience, his body hidden behind the lectern.

"Pardon, señor, but who is preaching?" Fernán asked the man next to him. "I am a stranger in the city."

"Well, you had best learn his name, friend, for tonight it will be on every tongue in Toledo. That is Marcos García de Mora, bless his soul. He speaks for the common man—his words are golden."

The man with the fine sword. His memory jogged, Fernán now recognized the large square head, black hair cut straight below the ears, sharp straight nose, and sensuous mouth of the man who had spoken to him the day before near the Cathedral Plaza.

García resumed speaking. His voice, a shade above normal volume, carried distinctly through the length of the hall.

"I am saddened," García said, "that King Juan and his Constable, Alvaro de Luna, having emptied the royal treasury, now demand money from the humble to continue their wars and pleasures. That they seek to empty the meager purses of the common people so as to defend fair Castile against the ravages of Juan of Navarre and the Moors is, indeed, sad, but to demand that we finance their extravagance is obscene."

García sighed and lowered his head. After a moment, he raised his eyes, looked out over the assemblage, and moved his head from side to side, gathering the silent people to him before he spoke, his voice strong, the tone bitter.

"Are the wars and extravagances of the King and his court a matter for our concern? Must we pauper ourselves to support the court and its splendor? Must we impoverish our families and deprive our children of food and clothing to fill the bellies of courtiers and bureaucrats who toady to the King—most of whom call themselves New Christians, or *conversos*?" His voice incredulous, pleading, rose to a wail. "And who are they, these *conversos*? Why, they are but Jews in Christian clothing!"

A collective sigh, a unified voice of despair, of fear that their toil had been useless, their few *maravedís* stolen, their children denied a meager meal, worn clothing torn, lives reduced to servitude—this sigh rolled through the Cathedral like a desert wind, scorching hope out of each heart and consuming faith.

García lowered his voice again. "You all know Alvaro de Luna the Constable, advisor to the King. A talented, greedy man who has ruled Castile for forty-five years, usurped sovereign authority, filled his own pockets to overflowing, and furthered the careers and stuffed the purses of Jews and their New Christian brethren, the *conversos*. And these *conversos* have thanked Alvaro de Luna with generous gifts.

"Now, dear neighbors, Luna wants more and the *marranos*, the New Christians, are quick to help him fill his purse. And why not? His purse is their purse. Collect the money, he commands the *marrano*, Alonso Cota. Take your usual usurious slice of pie, señor—I will take the rest. Who will know?"

A man in the first pew rose and shouted in a clear voice, "We will know!" Another joined, "We will know!" and others stood and shouted until García leaned forward in the pulpit so that only his face showed above the lectern. The mayhem diminished and García spoke again, his voice low but with the intensity of fire.

"Yes, dear neighbors, you and I will know. We who pay our taxes to Luna, the friend of *marranos*, we will know. We whose sweat and torment earn the *maravedís* that are now grasped by the claws of Cota and Luna, we will know. We will know!"

The desert wind grew from a growl of "We will know," to a rumble of far-off thunder, to a cry of pain in which *marrano* was repeated and repeated as if it were being ground into the earth.

"And if we refuse, if we refuse to pay," the voice of García transcended the cries of the crowd, "as brave Rodríguez the armorer yesterday refused to pay, what then will happen? Why, we will be imprisoned and tortured and killed and our goods confiscated by the Crown—as happened to our hero, Rodríguez. Is that not so? And so we ask our dear Lord—what can we do to prevent this disaster, sweet Jesus, we who are but your poor servants and have no weapons with which to defend ourselves? What can your poor people do?"

"Tell us, don Marcos, tell us, what we can do?"

"I will tell you, I will reveal to you what our dear Lord has revealed to me!"

The crowd hushed and García walked slowly down the stairs from the pulpit to where the archbishop would have stood delivering his blessing were he not with the King in Benavente. Fernán saw that García was clothed as a member of the group he addressed, in black overshirt and mouse-gray hose.

When Jerónimo returned, Fernán whispered, "Note the monk with a cowl standing near the right wall of the nave." Jerónimo nodded. "That is Pero Sarmiento, Commander of the Alcázar, former Governor of Toledo. He glanced this way and I saw his face beneath the hood. I met the man when Papá sold a carpet to him two years ago. Look, he turns his head."

"I mark him, Fernán, and he marks me. He is the Devil."

The hall was still except for García on the stairs and a man coughing. Sarmiento pulled his hood down and hurried from the Cathedral.

García stood at the center of the nave, hands clasped before his body, eyes closed as if in prayer, As one being, the people sighed. García opened his eyes and stretched out his arms in supplication.

"What I say now, I say with great reluctance, dear Lord. No man should raise his hand against another. Your only son, our Savior, Jesus Christ, taught us to offer the other cheek, to love our enemy."

He paused, arms extended, his voice addressing the heavens. "What, though, dear Lord, if that enemy betrays our sweet Jesus? What if that enemy be Satan? What then? How can we tolerate abuse of our sacred beliefs? How can we tolerate a threat to Jesus Christ himself?"

García stepped back, his eyes wide, his arms at his side.

"But I go too far," he said in awe.

"No, don Marcos, tell us, tell us!"

"Then, my dear friends, I will tell you." He brought the palms of his hands together in an attitude of prayer and was silent for several minutes. A man coughed into the heavy silence. García lowered his arms and spoke.

"You know me. I am of you, born poor and unprivileged but of good Castilian stock. I am pure of blood, as you are. And like you I have been exploited by the nobles, but most of all by *marranos*. They have stolen our birthright, gathered our livelihood to themselves, and risen to the highest levels of power by their greed and lust. Why do these *marranos* who call themselves *conversos* submit to baptism, knowing that they cannot accept the teachings of Jesus Christ, knowing that their blood is polluted? Why?" He looked from side to side, his hands pleading for a response.

"Tell us, dear don Marcos. We wait for your words."

"I will tell you. Listen to these true words." His body leaned forward so that each person before him felt that he spoke to him alone. "Jews," he said, "are forbidden many things—as is right, the children of Satan should be denied everything. But *conversos, marranos*, can amass wealth, usurp our government, marry our pure, young Christian girls, and behave as if they themselves were pure of blood. But dear souls, friends in Christ, *marranos* are not Castilian, they are of foreign, alien stock. They betray us to our enemies, they flee our battlefields causing us defeat, they pollute our city with their presence."

Unintelligible cries arose from the crowd. García raised his arms and there was quiet. "What can we do against these enemies, these *marranos*, my dear friends?"

"Oh, guide us, Marcos de Mora. Guide us, good soul."

"I will guide you. I will tell you what we must do, my dear people." And he opened his hands again in supplication and his voice, smooth and tempered, rose as he spoke. "We will drive out these *marranos* as we drove out the Moors. We will arm ourselves and drive them from this sacred city of Toledo as surely as God drove Satan from Heaven, as surely as Jesus drove the moneylenders from the Temple! Then, dear friends, then our ancient city of Toledo will be as pure as Heaven. Our homes will be cleansed, our children will be safe, our goods secure. Our city will be ours once again!"

The people looked from one to the other and then one by one they stood and began to shout. What had seemed impossible to them now was simple. Drive out the *marranos*. Return the city to the people, to Castilians, to the pure of blood. And they laughed into the faces of their neighbors, and thumped each other on the back and thundered their approval as at a bullfight, delighting in the words of García as they might in the performance of the bravest *torero*.

García raised his voice above the clamor, "Now, my friends, now we must act! Act to save our city! Rid ourselves of *marranos* by ridding ourselves of Cota and his tax! Close the city from those who would attack us so that we may purify Toledo from within!"

Standing at their seats, standing in the aisles, the people began to comprehend. Their heads nodded and they said "Yes," and spoke one after the other, "Yes," and then a chorus of voices asked, "What must we do, señor? What must we do, blessed don Marcos? Tell us what we must do!"

García smiled. "Be seated, my neighbors! Sit and I will explain."

Fernán took Jerónimo by the arm. "The entertainment is over. We have work to do."

And they left the Cathedral.

12

Sounding the alarm

He was relieved, once he straddled his mare with his sword at his side. García had chilled him more than the frigid weather, though Fernán was familiar with the myths spread throughout Castile and Aragón about Jews and *conversos*. Most frightening was the sincerity or appearance of sincerity García exhibited—the hatred at the core of his speech that formed the foundation of his lies.

"Jerónimo, if you please, return to our house. If my father or uncles are not yet home, oversee its defenses while I ride to the Cota house and warn them to leave the city. We must gather our friends. I do not know what we shall do, there are so many against us. But my father will know."

"We are in the hands of God, Fernán. You will return home once you have warned Cota?"

"As soon as I warn Cota and Melamed. Father would want the Jews put on guard."

"Then take my cloak. I will soon be inside and warm."

The Cota family lived in the *converso* quarter, not far from the Hernandes home. Fernán tied Margarita to one of a series of iron rings set into the stone wall of the main house and scanned the facade. Like many large homes fronting on the street, access to the interior lay behind an arched entrance.

The house, to his eye, was constructed for defense—with limited access, visual or physical. The entry was headed by slabs of granite that converged on a pair of iron gates leading into the courtyard. Windows at the four levels punctured the front wall of the building, each level of window designed in a different style—plain, gothic, Moorish, arched—the lower windows taller than those immediately above. The wall appeared to be a stack of horizontal panels that stretched from one end of the building to the other, except where interrupted by red brick borders surrounding the windows and gateway, terminating in a notched design of granite blocks and filled with random patterns of cement that enclosed rough-cut gray stone. The cement and stone repelled the eye as successfully as it might an enemy, producing an effect at once dynamic and forbidding.

Fernán had been there on many occasions, the last being a meeting of the *converso* council where he accompanied his father. Today, the house appeared vacant—the gate fastened, windows shuttered tight—as if the family had departed for their country home. But it was winter, an unlikely time to leave the city, and don Alonso was in town to collect the tax.

The street, wider than most in Toledo, seemed deserted. Fernán called out, "don Alonso, I am Fernán Hernandes. I have a message." He repeated this several times before a voice, emanating from what seemed like the sky, whispered hoarsely, "Fernán, go to the alley beside the building. There is a side entrance down the alley."

The alley, which appeared to be part of the building, was closed off by an iron gate. Fernán tried the gate latch, found it open, and stepped through. The side entrance, about twenty feet from the gate, was open as well.

"Come in, Fernán."

Fernán recognized don Alonso and entered the house. As he did so, a servant slipped by him and scurried toward the gate. Fernán stood in a hall with several doors on either side and realized he had entered through the service entrance. Before him stood Cota, dressed for travel. They shook hands and don Alonso asked Fernán to follow him. A door in the hall led to a sitting room where Cota motioned him to a chair.

"My servant will stable your horse, Fernán," he said, and looked at Fernán quizzically. "While always pleasant to see you, my young friend, I am anxious to know what message brings you here."

Fernán related the substance of the meeting in the Cathedral. "I urge you to leave the city at once, don Alonso. García has roused the rabble against you and they will undoubtedly seek you here and commit some mischief."

"And your family?"

"Our problem is not as immediate as yours, señor, but we are taking precautions." Fernán rose. "I am sorry to be abrupt, but I have another call to make before I return home. I beg you, don Alonso, do not hesitate. García and the others were most alarming. Gather your family and leave. The *Puente de San Martín* would be your best exit from the city."

"You are right, Fernán, we will depart immediately. I am deeply indebted to you and your father. Simón will show you to the door near the stable. If God wills it, we shall meet again."

Simón, the servant who had darted up the alley to latch the gate, had returned and asked Fernán to follow him. After proceeding through a series of halls and doors, they exited the house onto a large U-shaped area formed by buildings on three sides. The center of the space was devoted to a modest formal garden encircled by a graveled drive. Fernán caught a whiff of stable and saw his horse being led to him, neighing and prancing. At the same time, a large coach-and-five was driven to the central entrance. Simón directed Fernán out of the property and he mounted and rode off.

He chose a circular route within the city walls, avoiding the more direct interior city streets and confrontation with the mob he imagined had by now erupted from the Cathedral. His course led him past the Gate and the Bridge of San Martín. He prayed that Cota would expedite his departure—García seemed determined to make an example of the tax collector. And if Marcos García was serious about Cota, then he was serious about sealing the city, San Martín, and the other bridges and gates—Visagra, Cambrón, Alcántara. All would be closed.

Closed gates represented a considerable obstacle to an invading army. But if shut, how could his threatened family leave, and Naomi and don Abrahán whom he now regarded as family?

He rode past what had been the synagogue Kneset Haguedola, but was now the church of Santa María la Blanca, down a side street toward the river, and tied Margarita outside the wall of the Melamed house. A bell, unnoticed the other night, hung to the right of the door. Two days and so much had changed. He pulled the bell-cord, the bell sang its happy song, a few minutes passed, and then Mosé slid back the panel and peered at Fernán.

"Ah, Fernán. *Buenos días, amigo!*" and he opened the door.

"Is don Abrahán at home, Mosé?"

"Indeed he is and will be delighted to see you. Come in out of this sudden cold."

Mosé then asked after the health of Jerónimo and what pleasant event returned Fernán so soon to their neighborhood and was the afternoon not bleak and the studies he and Aharón were attempting so difficult and was Fernán tutored and…. They were at the study, the doctor seated at his long table, a profusion of papers scattered left and right, his head bent close to his writing.

Mosé coughed and said, "Don Abrahán, Fernán is here."

Melamed looked up from his work, gathering his thoughts from other worlds. "Fernán?"

"Don Abrahán," Fernán said. "I have important news."

"Yes, of course," he said, his eyes now focused. "Come in, dear cousin, come and sit. You look cold. Warm yourself by the fire. Would you care for something to eat or drink?"

"Ale, if it is convenient, señor."

"Of course it is convenient. Nothing else? No? Mosé?"

Mosé left to fetch the ale, and Melamed smiled. "And your throat, how is it?"

"Healing, don Abrahán, but terrible things are about to happen."

"Not to your throat?"

"No, señor, to Toledo."

"Oh, well then, before we speak of Toledo, let me examine your wound." He shuffled away from the table, sat in a chair opposite Fernán, and removed the cloth covering his throat. "Good. You have the jar of ointment I gave you?"

Fernán said he did and Melamed said, "Then continue to use it for the next few days. You will not need the cloth, it has served its purpose. Now, tell me terrible things about Toledo."

Mosé returned with a mug of ale. Fernán thanked him and Mosé backed out of the room as he would in the presence of a king. Fernán laughed, then remembered why he was there, and told Melamed what had happened outside the Cathedral the day before, and in the Cathedral and the Cota house earlier that day.

"You have had a busy few days, Fernán," Melamed said.

"Yes, señor, busy and disturbing. I have no idea what may happen next, but if the mob takes the city and García rules...."

"Then we must prepare for the worst. However, Fernán," and he inched closer to his cousin, "we must not allow fear to possess us. We are afraid because we are ignorant of the future. Therefore, to control fear we must weigh the future, balance bad with good, and take their measure." He walked behind his chair, inclined his head, and pointed his forefinger toward the ceiling as if he were lecturing a congregation. "Let us say that Marcos García prevails and the gates and city are closed. What would proceed from that?"

"We would be isolated, at the mercy of García and the commoners."

"True. So then we must ask how long the city would be closed—how long the traditional rulers of Toledo, the councilors and nobles, would allow it to remain closed. Whether the King who must protect us—or not be our King—would allow García to rule Toledo, and so on. Do you see?" And he spread his open hands. "The future is not imponderable. We have the facility to exercise our imagination and to anticipate what might happen. Then we may judge which result is more likely than the other and, from this exercise, take hope and silence fear. For at the edge of the future, Fernán, at the very edge, lies hope."

Fernán had listened attentively but was not reassured. The exercise Melamed had outlined seemed unrealistic—for while imagining the future and balancing bad and good, the actual future could overtake them. The plan Fernán would hope to initiate was not speculative but active—the stockpiling of weapons and provisions and preparation for conflict. That would mean gathering *conversos*, appointing leaders, and establishing a defensive posture. He had learned that from Jerónimo, who was a master strategist. Now, with Melamed warned and the immediate future planned, Fernán prepared to leave, knowing he would be needed at home.

He had hoped to see Naomi, but she was not about and he asked the doctor where she might be. Normally pensive, don Abrahán became solemn.

"My dear Fernán," he said, as if heading a letter, "I have no idea where Naomi is at the moment. The girl has duties and she does them and that carries her to odd places at odd times. However, let me deliver my own message of caution."

Melamed sat in his chair, relaxed, as much as the hard back of the chair would allow, and interlaced his fingers across his abdomen.

"Naomi," he said, "is very young, Fernán. She is a Jew and you are Catholic. Therefore, do not expect a favorable result to come from your attraction to her."

"I am more than attracted to Naomi, don Abrahán, though I have nothing but the most honorable feelings for her."

"Of course you do, my boy. I would expect nothing less from you, but...."

"I love her."

"Oh, Fernán," Melamed said, "you are a good and a brave young man. I know who you are perhaps better than you know yourself, and I have become very fond of you—now that we have finally met. However, how can you say that you love Naomi? Forgive an old man, Fernán, but what does a boy know of love? He sees a lovely girl and he wants her. Wonderful and natural. But love? Love, as the poets often say, is a flower that is sown in our hearts and, like all living things, must grow and blossom, and that requires a spring and summer in which to mature. Love is not a passion of the moment, Fernán. Wait, you will see."

His brow wrinkled, head tilted to one side, an expression informed the face of the doctor that Fernán identified with his father—neither a sad nor happy twist of the eyes and mouth that bore traces of both emotions.

"Find another girl, Fernán. With your handsome face and worthy background, I should think girls would trip over themselves to capture you." He wagged his head. "Naomi is not for you."

On his way out of the house, a dispirited Fernán passed the kitchen where he saw Mosé consuming a huge dinner. The apprentice motioned from Fernán to his plate, his mouth too full for words. Fernán, his heart heavy, smiled wanly and shook his head—he wanted to be gone. And so he left the Melamed house, opened the courtyard gate, turned toward where he had left his mare, and received a kiss on the cheek from Naomi who was waiting outside the wall.

"Naomi!" he cried, and reached out to hold her. She smiled impishly, backed away, and ran through the courtyard gate, leaving behind a befuddled Fernán who touched his cheek where she had kissed him and then put his fingers to his lips.

Seeing her, his heart betrayed him and he was suffused with a joyous abandon. Though he acknowledged her youth and that she was a Jew, that no longer mattered—his life had been turned over as a field is plowed in spring and made ready for seed. And although he did not truly know her, except for the few words they had exchanged, he knew her for the soul revealed in her eyes, for a face which had seared itself into his consciousness, and for other precious details that were now intrinsic to his being. For these things and for others that he sensed would complete his life, he knew that one day this young woman would be his bride.

13

The Gate of San Martín and the Cota house

Dazed, absent thought, Fernán retraced his ride from the *judería* toward the Cota house. Hungry now, not having eaten since morning, he was anticipating supper. While he might have eaten at the Melamed house, he had refused, disheartened by the remarks the doctor had asserted with such conviction. After seeing Naomi, however, after her kiss, his spirits had soared and he felt hunger of several varieties.

Cousins, they were cousins, but distant cousins, and distant cousins do marry. The barrier was not cousins, but the Church. He could not marry a Jew. The marriage would be sacrilegious and he would be declared heretic or, if Naomi were to consent to baptism, her grandfather would die of grief. María had converted to Catholicism to marry Antonio and told Fernán that her family had forsaken her. She was dead to them—a wound that would never heal. Dear God, he prayed, help us find a way.

Margarita sensed the slack reins and idle heels and chose her own pace to the plaza of San Juan de los Reyes near the Gate of San Martín, where she pulled up short. Fernán was surprised that the mare had stopped and asked in a soft voice what troubled her. She neighed and shook her head and he reached forward to soothe her, stroked her mane, and spurred her lightly. But she was stopped hard. He trusted her senses and looked around him but could find no reason for her obdurate behavior until he saw several commoners carrying pikes and swords running toward the Gate of San Martín. His mare shied and Fernán tightened the reins and calmed her.

"Where are you running?" he shouted.

"The bridge," a pikeman replied. "San Martín is to be taken and the city shut as tight as the pocket of a Jew. And who might you be?"

Fernán said nothing, pulled Margarita around, and rode back to the nearby terrace, a site that would afford him an unobstructed view of the gate and bridge some hundreds of feet distant. Aligned along the edge of the terrace were monks and a scattering of townspeople, some of whom Fernán knew. Dismounting, he led his horse to the edge and looked out over the river below. The sun, completing its round, peered from beneath the low-hanging cloud cover, coloring the dense fringe of clouds pink and magenta. On the far side of the river, golden *palacios* spotted among the steep wooded hills observed Toledo with indifference.

From the terrace, Fernán saw the pikeman he had hailed, running past the intersection with Cambrón and down toward the Gate of San Martín. At this distance he could distinguish a small knot of men gathered before the gate and the faces of defenders in the tower. The glitter of swords below and helmets above sparkled in the late sun like early fireflies. Had Cota and his family escaped?

The gate had been dropped—a defensive measure—the captain of the bridge offering resistance. Several men on horseback, one in a guardsman uniform, rode to and fro behind the armed men assaulting the gate, most of them dressed as commoners. Suddenly, a flash followed by a dull report—a gun, perhaps an arquebus, clumsy, occasionally effective, but frightening. Arrows rose in clusters from the attackers below, some penetrating the open tower windows. If all else failed, the rebels would fire the guardhouse, he thought, or blast the door with gunpowder and attempt an assault on the stairs.

The air was still and cold, a sharp breeze blew from the north and, with the lowering sun, the clouds hardened into a thick blue-gray soup. Those on the terrace were silenced by the action below, from where Fernán could hear the voice of the rebel commander shouting orders.

Unexpectedly, activity ceased. The attackers had gathered around a horseman in plain clothes who raised what appeared to be a sheet of white paper that fluttered in the breeze. His voice was clear but the words garbled. The effect of his gesture, though, was immediate, for the men began yelping and cheering. Soon Fernán saw a group of guardsmen emerge from the gate. The skirmish was over—San Martín had been taken.

He led his horse away from the terrace, mounted, and continued toward home. The warmth of the Melamed fire and the euphoria of the kiss had faded. Fernán turned over the effect of closed gates on the city. For one thing, merchandise for his father would be stopped and confiscated. Merchandise be damned, he thought, their lives would be confiscated.

Again Margarita halted at the intersection with Cambrón. Fernán rose in his stirrups and looked about him for other men with weapons. There were none—the street was deserted. Then he smelled an acrid odor. "Dear God," he said, "the Cota house," and urged the animal on, forcing her at a trot up the darkening street where neither of them wanted to go.

The house was burning—exterior walls and chimneys scorched and charred though standing, the handsome interior gone. Horse and rider skirted the building, as far from the fire as could be managed, the horse brave but skittish. Fernán tied her to a tree and raced back to the blazing ruin, drawing his sword as he ran.

No glass remained in the windows. The front gate had been demolished and lay bent and broken. He approached as near to the house as the heat would allow, peered though the bare windows from front to rear, but saw little except burnt and burning timber. The floors had cascaded into the cellar and the ironwork was scorched and peeling. Furniture had tumbled into flaming heaps and ash covered every surface. Beyond the far wall, a glorious oak that had formed a sizable part of the landscape had caught fire and was now a blackened skeleton.

Cota was alive, Fernán thought, and he and his family would be safe wherever they landed. The tax collector would find haven in Aragón, across the Pyrenees, or in another country, but would never return to Toledo, not to the memory of this destruction.

The vigorous wall Fernán had admired and respected earlier that day—the wall of panels and patterns of cement and brick, diverse windows, and elegant stone—was a scorched shell. On its surface, the words, DEATH TO MARRANOS, had been painted in large white letters below the crude caricature of a giant skull. Some letters retained their original white. Others, scorched by fire, varied in hue from orange to deep brown. The wall had been reduced from its former symbolic arrogance to a humble, blackened cipher.

Tears ran freely down his cheeks. Fernán wondered at them, knowing the tears were not for the wall or the house or Cota. Perhaps the tears were for lost hope. For though he strained his imagination, he could not visualize the edge of the future, that edge where don Abrahán had declared hope lay.

14

The following morning, the conference room of the Alcázar of Toledo

"You allowed that rabble to sack and burn that magnificent structure!" Sarmiento snapped. "What had you in mind? And what has become of the pictures and furnishings? Gone? Burned? Anything saved, for the love of God? What?"

His face reddened to his scalp, Sarmiento stalked around the table, sword in hand, and swiped at without striking the drapery and other sundry objects in the room, his rapier whining in despair.

The canons Galvez and Alonso and the captains drawn from the plebeians and the regiment of the Alcázar cowered in their seats while striving to appear brave. García, though, seemed unmoved.

"Don Pero," he said in soothing tones, "the men followed your exact orders. You instructed me to restrain the people and the guard from sacking *marrano* households other than the Cota house and, señor, that is precisely what they did."

"But burn? Did I say burn the Cota house? Sweet Jesus knows I did not. I said *sack*. Do you know the word, García? Plunder, loot, pillage, put in a bag, a sack, from the Latin *saccus*, from the Greek *sakkos*, from antiquity long before. And you, a scholar of all people, should know the word and its meaning. Not burn! Never burn. What good comes from burning? Goods burned become smoke, without substance, without value. Ah, dear God," he wailed, "hopeless, hopeless," and, sighing deeply Sarmiento collapsed into a chair at the head of the table and then bolted upright. "Was anything salvaged?"

"Not to my knowledge, don Pero. The men were rabid with hatred for *marranos*—Cota in particular. They did not have time to think."

"They cannot think," Sarmiento said and slumped into his chair. "Do not expect them to think." He sprang to his feet and paced from wall to window and back again. "But you, García, you I expect to think and to act rationally—to listen to my words and understand their absolute meaning. Without that, we fail, and we cannot fail."

He gritted his teeth, scanned the table and, finding vacant faces and tops of heads, realized he had taken a wrong turn. He must soothe these men, assure them he was pleased with their performance, bring them to his side.

"What I say, señores, is true for all of us, myself included," he said, his voice now tempered. "What we are attempting…no, not attempting…what we will accomplish is the total revision of the monarchy, the elimination of Alvaro de Luna, and the recognition of the rights of the city of Toledo and of the people of Castile. Even more important, the heart of our mission will be the elimination of *marranos* from Toledo and all Castile."

Heads nodded vigorously while García smiled. Sarmiento wondered whether the smile was one of pleasure or derision. Damn García, the man was difficult.

"For this mission," Sarmiento said, "we need all our faculties, all our collective wisdom and experience, all our strength. We cannot tolerate missteps, explicable or not. We must root out all weakness, all indecision, all hesitation. We must be strong, decisive, ruthless."

He halted at the head of the table and stared at each face in turn. García looked vacuous. What was wrong with the man—had he no blood, no sensation in his body? Sarmiento depended on him—the lawyer was his link to the riffraff. But how can the man control his face like that? Impossible to read.

The priests looked down and avoided his eyes. Ineffectual playthings. The captains, however, met his gaze. He must learn their names. Some, Sarmiento knew by sight from the Alcázar, but not their names. They were his strength, these men who controlled the gates and access to the city. With the captains he owned Toledo. Whatever else they might be, though, García and the captains were commoners and depending on commoners was troubling.

He removed himself from the table and sat on a chair against the wall. Why so restless, Pero? Because of the day, because of the day.

"García," he said, "review the day for us, if you please."

"Certainly, don Pero, with pleasure."

García exhibited confidence. Was the confidence real? The tongue-lashing forgiven? The inspirational sermon and its emphasis on *marranos*, though brief, seemed to have elevated his spirits. Well and good. Be happy, García—for now.

"After the speeches at the Cathedral," García said, reading from notes, "men of the common people, those who could be trusted, were assigned as captains and the captains to gates." García raised his eyes. "The list is here, don Pero," he said and returned to his notes. "The captains were provided with horses and weapons obtained from the Alcázar and the weapons were assigned to their platoons. The few guns we could acquire were allocated to San Martín, Visagra, and Alcántara."

The recitation annoyed Sarmiento, though he had requested its reading. He had no patience with lists, and meandered to the window, sat on the sill, and played with his sword.

"The gates fell quickly, except the Tower of San Martín, which surrendered after a brief but vigorous assault. Captain Higuera, describe the attack on San Martín, if you please."

An ungainly giant struggled to his feet. Dressed in a shirt of dubious origin, a doublet that strove with little success to close across his girth, long hose showing heavy wear at the knees, and a cape that was undoubtedly borrowed from a short man, Higuera leaned on the table—an ape with hairy knuckles. A bastard sword and dagger hung at his hip.

"Don Pero, don Marcos, and others of lesser rank here assembled," he said in a phlegmy voice. "I, Francisco Higuera, captain of the Bridge and Gate of San Martín, will tell you as best I can how the Bridge and Gate of San Martín were taken. As all of you assembled here know, we captains were chosen by don Marcos García some three or four weeks hence…."

Hence? What is the fool saying? Sarmiento peered through the window in desperation. A miraculous material, glass, though faulted with slight imperfections. Through it he could see the darkening sky preparing for night with almost as much clarity as with his bare eyes. And this momentous day, though like the glass marred by minor ripples, was now ending. A miraculous day, a day whose close found him elevated well above the imperious nobles who had dismissed him as second rank. He had gained power without revealing his complicity and tonight would accept the mantle of Governor.

Tomorrow morning, Luna will be served a surprise for breakfast that will stick in his throat and throttle him and, in the future, King Juan will think twice about rejecting Sarmiento of Toledo. Let him call on Sarmiento when his bastard puppy Luna fails and, perhaps, Sarmiento will save his crown. Oh, how Luna will hurry his privy council to frantic meetings. Dear me, what shall we do? The King and his army are at Benavente surrounding brave Pimentel. Poor dears. I fart for them.

Higuera groaned on with his detailed description of the engagement—an engagement in which García commanded the troops astride a black stallion, and Higuera, chosen for his enormity, was held in reserve for the expected assault on the tower—in which action he was expected to die. However, the captain of the Gate chose to surrender instead of fight and Higuera, reprieved, was placed in charge of prisoners, all of whom immediately reversed allegiance and joined the rebels.

A red-faced Higuera resumed his seat amid applause from the captains and García.

"The gates," García said, "are now under the control of the captains."

"Thank you, don Marcos," Sarmiento said, reviving himself. "One more piece of business before we adjourn, at which time you will return to your posts until the ceremony this evening."

Sarmiento removed his sword and dagger and lay them on the table. "Unlike you, señores, I go unarmed this evening. Our meeting, which will be attended by nobles, councilors, and commoners, must be seen as the first encounter between us. We have never met—do you understand? Your orders have come from García, whose genius organized this rebellion. Now you have come to bargain with me, a nobleman, Commandant of the Alcázar and Chief Judge of Appeals, for my approval."

The latter title brought García awake. Sarmiento nodded. A smile leaked past his lips.

"You will ask me to approve your conduct in this engagement. You will convince me that the tax placed on the city by Alvaro de Luna forced you to take these steps. You will say that by taxing Toledo, immediate and vigorous action was required—for who of us knows what further restrictions of our rights might have been enacted by Luna. You will urge me to join you in effecting the removal of Alvaro de Luna from his positions in Castile, and convince me of the necessity to protect our sacred Toledo from further violation of its rights. You will urge me to join you in repelling any attack by Alvaro de Luna and in convincing His Highness that your only thoughts were for the good of Castile and Toledo." Now a somewhat bitter potion. "However, all matters regarding *marranos* will be left for the future. That is critical. *Marranos* have friends among the nobility and we must be prudent. Be patient, señores, their time will come, and soon."

Nothing stirred. No one moved. They sleep with their eyes open.

"I will," Sarmiento said, "after some deliberation and debate, applaud your actions. You will then turn over to me the keys to the gates and swear you will yield to my authority in all matters. I shall declare myself head of the administration, commander of its military, and rightful Chief Judge of

Appeals. Then we shall have a small ritual, wherein my role will be consecrated by the Church and blessed by the former administration. Is that clear?"

Murmurs of approval from the seated captains and canons while Sarmiento, Governor of Toledo, paraded to the foot of the table and posed, chin high, hands clasped behind him.

"I shall meet with you again this evening. Don Marcos will brief you on details. Thank you, señores, for a job well done. García, I will see you in fifteen minutes."

The captains saluted in various manners and degrees, each observing the other and adding stolen bits to his own performance. Sarmiento nodded, dismissed the meeting with a back-of-the-hand gesture, and left the room.

"Where in the name of God did you find such a pack of dolts, García?"

"For the work that was needed, don Pero, these men were the best that the common people and the Alcázar could offer."

"How dreadful."

"Not actually, since they accomplished the tasks set before them with little comment and no argument."

The room where they sat, a room in which Sarmiento received lower-rank visitors to the Alcázar, was sparsely furnished, since the cost of furnishings would have come out of his pay as commandant and he could think of a dozen better uses for the money.

"But that—what is his name? Lligerez?"

"Higuera, don Pero."

"Higuera. Where did that specimen originate?"

"Under the finest rock in Castile." Sarmiento looked annoyed. "You see, Higuera is helper to a mason and spent his days bearing all manner of fine rock."

"Very clever, García. Lose him. Take him to a wood or the edge of a cliff and dispose of him. San Martín is too important to trust to a Higuera."

"As you wish, don Pero."

"The others seem acceptable—if you vouch for their loyalty and deeds. However, remember that it is one feat to storm a post guarded by idiots and quite another to confront a King—and we will confront the King."

"Understood. The captains will be as well drilled as their men."

The two sat on facing chairs across a straight-legged table at which Sarmiento composed his letters. Marcos García had carried their weapons into the correspondence room with him and the matching sword and dagger lay on the table between them. Sarmiento drew his sword, a handsome rapier with an ornate though functional hilt.

"I much admired the weapon you wore to my house the other night, García. I see you have it on. What do you think of this tool?" and he handed the sword to García.

"This is not a tool, señor, it is an instrument. One might play melodies on this steel." García sighted along the blade and tested its balance. "The lady is well-balanced. She is engaging, though light, and cuts a fine figure. She must give you much pleasure." He returned the sword to Sarmiento who smiled and sat on the edge of the table.

"Indeed, she does please me, García. Though, to be truthful, this sword and dagger now cause me bitter tears."

"Why should that be, don Pero?"

"I have learned that their creator is dead, needlessly. You knew him, Rodríguez the armorer, a poet in steel, taken by the guards and killed."

"I knew him, don Pero, and also mourn him. His death was unexpected—the game with Cota went too far."

"At whose insistence, García? Yours?"

García eased out of the chair and walked to the window, forcing Sarmiento to turn. The glass was dark as night and Sarmiento viewed an imperfect García in the mirrored reflection.

"Rodríguez was told that the role he proposed to play was hazardous," García said. "That he should protest the tax until he entered the prison gate and then repent and pay, saying he had drunk too much ale that morning. He was instructed to apologize and beg forgiveness and he agreed to the terms.

"However, Rodríguez hated *marranos* even more than I, don Pero. Odd how each of us is driven by various humors—love, money, fear, hatred. Rodríguez was driven by passion and sincerity—in truth, the armorer was a poet. However, once his choler had risen he could not be restrained by reason, but required that his bile be put to rest by physical means. Working steel all day must have imbued him with some of its qualities. So, in his anger, he wrested a pike from one of the guardsmen and was quickly run through by the sword of another. A high price to pay for rebellion, but good work is never bought cheap."

"You should have foreseen his actions."

"Don Pero," García said, turning from the window with a smile, "could I foresee the actions of men, I would rule the world. As it happens, I am a man like you and suffer the failings of mankind."

"I am not pleased with your failings, García. First Rodríguez, then Cota, then Higuera."

"If you wish to replace me, Chief Justice," García smiled and shrugged, "you might choose Captain Higuera. He would be most willing."

"Do not jest. I am in earnest."

"I am also in earnest. What I do, I do out of sincerity and passion—as did Rodríguez. Strong drives as you know, don Pero. I hate *marranos*, you hate Luna." García circled away from Sarmiento and drew his sword. "Why not play a round, señor. Test our steel. Our swords are equal, both fashioned by Rodríguez. Perhaps the armorer is watching from Heaven."

"Or Hell. No, I will not engage you, García."

"Because you would lose the masses if I were killed?"

"You will not die. Though if you did I would disavow our relationship. The rabble are committed. They smell blood. The men will follow me."

"Then you have nothing to lose, except this servant, and that is little enough. Play a round, don Pero. No daggers, no cuts, points only."

Sarmiento sighed. "I take no pleasure in this, García. One round."

They faced off in the center of the room, saluted one another and engaged. Sarmiento knew he was much the superior swordsman and reacted mechanically to the preliminary thrusts of his opponent, analyzing García while waiting for an opening to score. He planned a light touch, not enough to pierce flesh but sufficient to halt this folly. After several passes, he became familiar with the style and limitations of his opponent. The man was quick, aggressive, and schooled, but not half a Sarmiento. A few passes, García overextended, and the riposte scratched García just above his heart.

"Oh," García said, "a touch."

"That is the round. We will stop. Rodríguez will not have noticed from his post in Hell."

"Agreed. A bad idea made worse by losing. You and I appear to be bound together—like prisoners." García sheathed his sword. "Until later."

"Remember, García, the King will attack."

"How can I forget, Excellency? We will be prepared."

Sarmiento watched García leave. Swordplay cleared his mind. The focus, the logic of thrust, slash, parry, riposte. Play, though, was for the young. He was Governor of Toledo, and his dependence on García and the mongrels to maintain that title, despite his occasional denial of their importance, galled and disgusted him. Bound like prisoners? Conceded—but for the moment. Soon he would find a noble reservoir of support. For the rabble were detestable and lawyer García aspired to heights beyond his station.

Part II

TURMOIL

"Let man remember all the days of his life
that he is being led to death.
Stealthily he journeys on, day after day;
he thinks he is at rest, like a man who is motionless on board ship,
while the ship is flying on the wings of the wind."

The Journey—Moses ibn Ezra (1060-1139)
The Penguin Book of Hebrew Verse (1981)
Edited and Translated by T. Carmi

15

Early February, 1449, the Hernandes house

Fernán entered the great hall of the Hernandes house and stood beside the doorway. Jerónimo waited outside. Nine days had passed since the Cota fire and the Sarmiento rebellion, as it was being called, though he thought it more a García rebellion, having heard the lawyer speak so demonically in the Cathedral. During those nine days his father and Juan de la Cibdad had placed the borough on alert, organized night watches and, when Fernán was not studying or practicing swordplay with Jerónimo, he served as messenger for both men. Several times he had scaled the city walls to deliver messages to *conversos* outside, returning with vegetables and other fresh foods in short supply within the city.

He had met Naomi only once, since patrols were everywhere—some in makeshift uniforms, others declaring their allegiance with bright red scarves or headbands. The night they finally met was quiet and cold, and the half-moon hung in the sky like an adornment within a bed of faint stars. He had waited several nights on end with no success and, believing this night both safe and providential, stationed himself outside the Melamed house, his cloak drawn about him. Rewarded when Naomi opened the courtyard gate and hurried off in the direction of the Jewish market, he glanced up and down the street and followed discreetly, not wanting to alarm her. Although she wore dark clothing, she was made visible by her outline against the charcoal houses and the dim shadow that trailed her figure.

The market was closed, its stalls shuttered and latched, but when Naomi knocked quietly at one of the larger enclosures, a door opened a slit, a ray of candlelight leaked onto the street, and she was welcomed inside.

Fernán concealed himself between two shuttered stalls on the far side of the narrow street and waited. Some minutes later the door opened again and Naomi, carrying a sack, stepped into the street and walked toward home in the shadow of the wall.

"Naomi," he whispered. "It is I, Fernán."

She inhaled sharply. "Fernán. Come quickly. Keep to the shadows."

He took her sack and they walked through the back alleys to the Melamed house. Naomi unlatched the courtyard door and led Fernán to a bench.

"I have waited for days to see you," he said.

"Waited for me?"

"Of course. Though don Abrahán does not care for me."

"Grandpapá is fond of you, Fernán."

"And you? You kissed my cheek. Are you as fond of me as I am of you?"

She turned her face away and then looked into his eyes. "I am fond of you, Fernán, though Grandpapá is right—I am a Jew."

Fernán took her hand and brought it to his lips. "Naomi, I have no words to describe how I feel. There must be a way."

"To describe how you feel?"

He laughed. "No, sweet, to be with you. Why do you frown?"

"I worry about Grandpapá."

"God will take care of him."

"I have no trust in God. He betrayed my mother and father."

"Then why are you a Jew?"

She folded her arms beneath her breasts. "Because my mother was a Jew. Being a Jew is my heritage, my home." Naomi took the sack from Fernán and walked to the courtyard door. "You must go now, Fernán."

He looked down at her. The top of her head was at the level of his chin and he kissed a wisp of hair that had escaped her scarf. Then he raised her face to his and kissed her lips.

"Please," she said, "go now."

He stepped through the courtyard door and heard the latch click. Fernán sensed Naomi waiting on the other side and he stared at the door as if the power of sight would cause it to open. "We will find a way, Naomi. We will." After a while he heard the door to the house open and close and he stared at the courtyard door with burning eyes for several minutes before he turned and trudged up the street toward home.

That was two nights ago. Now he must tell his father that the guests had arrived, usher the servants out, and latch the door to the hall. After the door was latched, Jerónimo outside and he inside would ensure that no stranger entered or overheard what was said within.

Cold meats and cheeses, bowls of fruit, dishes of sweet pastries, and several varieties of wine and ale had been laid out on the dining table. Fernán was amazed at the quantity of provisions the women had assembled despite the locked gates of Toledo.

A horseshoe array of stools fronted the fireplace, some already occupied. Those seated had placed their wineglasses and dishes of delicacies on one of a series of trestle tables that formed a parallel horseshoe in front of the stools. Three men stood at the open end of the horseshoe warming their chilled hands and feet before the heat of the steady fire, as if their only distress was the frigid night air that made for an unusually brisk walk from their homes. The ambiance of the room conveyed no sense of panic. The mood was unexceptional—a meeting of the *converso* family council held punctually once every two months.

Before he assumed his post at the great hall door, Fernán positioned himself and Jerónimo at the entrance to the Hernandes house, where they welcomed and accounted for the guests. Both wore swords as a symbol of strength and respect as well as evidence of determination. Twenty-one heads of the prominent families had arrived, no larger a group than usual, and each had recited the words, "Equality and justice," as he entered the house.

Fernán had known these men since he was a child. He had studied languages, history, and the catechism with their children, played games and fought mock battles with their sons, attended parties, celebrations, and weddings at their homes, and paid his respects at funerals for their young and old. Their families were his community. His godfather was in attendance, as were his honorary uncles and those who had comforted him during difficult childhood times. He was secure in their company. He knew that when he reached his majority he would take his place with them as their equal, and wished that time was now.

In normal times, his father would have looked to these families for a bride for his son. But Fernán dismissed that thought as meaningless. He would marry Naomi. Of that he was certain, despite the problems marrying a Jew raised within the Church, problems that dismayed him. But with the business of the evening ahead, he replaced thoughts of Naomi with the sober images of the Cota house and the Gate of San Martín. Now endangered,a shiver of apprehension for all their families trembled within him.

His father was seated, engrossed in conversation with two men who leaned toward him, wineglasses in their hands. Fernán hurried over and told his father that the tally was complete. Lorenzo stood and announced, "Everyone who was to come is here. Take your seats, if you please, señores. We have much to discuss."

The servants hurried from the room and Fernán latched the door from within and stood before it. The men took their seats. The murmur of voices drifted into silence as Lorenzo began the meeting.

"For nine days now Pero Sarmiento has ruled Toledo. When Gaspar de Ribas first warned me of Sarmiento, I discounted his fears. I thought I knew Sarmiento, having done business with him, and that a man without money, a man whose family had no influence among nobles and councilors, a man who had been rejected by Alvaro de Luna and whose control of the gates and judgeship had been taken from him, such a man would be no threat." He shook his head. "I was wrong. I apologize to you, Gaspar, and to all of you, my friends."

Many stood to protest that an apology was unnecessary. Fernán almost shouted his objection but remained quiet though he churned within. He had never heard his father apologize. Gaspar de Ribas rose and Lorenzo said, "If you please," and raised his hands.

Bernardo de Cáceres, a young man who had inherited a prosperous family estate, mounted his stool. "Don Lorenzo," he said, "I see no reason for you to apologize."

"Absolutely," the assembled men chorused.

Ribas and the others resumed their seats. The room was still. The figure of the gangly Cáceres stretched like a pole above his stool. "None of us could have anticipated the Sarmiento rebellion," he said. Giggles trickled from three young men seated near Cáceres. He nodded to his claque, his mouth curved in a smirk. "The Sarmiento rebellion was well hidden behind the bulk of García."

The claque burst into laughter. Fernán flushed and his hand went to his sword. The Cáceres remark had been unacceptable in the context of the times and outrageous in one so young.

"We thank you for that most valuable information, don Bernardo," Lorenzo said. "Now descend from your childish perch, if you wish to join us."

"*Olé*, Lorenzo!" someone called. Fernán smiled. "Señores," Lorenzo continued, "misjudgment of Sarmiento is behind us. Sarmiento has shown himself to be an opportunist. He has used hatred of New Christians to avenge himself against Alvaro, raised the townspeople into an army, and dared Alvaro to attack. We, therefore, must answer the questions raised by this impertinence. What will happen to our city? What will happen to New Christians? What must we do to protect our families?"

Cáceres had stepped off his stool but remained standing, a hand on his hip. "You ask many questions, don Lorenzo," he said. "How can we answer them? How can we decide what to do when we are all equally ignorant?"

"Your wit, don Bernardo, however poor and ill-timed it may be, is perhaps appreciated by some, Lorenzo said, "but that appreciation is restricted to the street and several of the more tawdry ale houses." And he turned his back on Cáceres. "Now let us begin discussion, for we face a serious threat and must choose a leader. That is the first order of business."

Why had Cáceres baited his father and acted the fool? Fernán wondered. What was his game?

"Señores!" The voice of Juan de la Cibdad was deep and commanding. "Our council is not of the mold where officers are chosen because they can afford a stable of braying donkeys." Laughter relieved the tension. "Truly, we have no use for someone who struts about making inane remarks without regard to propriety, assuming the role of ass."

"*Olé*, don Juan! *Olé, amigo!*" several voices called out.

"No, señores. We reject those who pretend to stand high and mighty. We need a man of true stature, a man whose voice is clear, whose mind is sharp, and who is loved. Don Lorenzo is that man."

"Don Juan," Cáceres said from his seat, "Don Lorenzo may be able—he has declared as much on several occasions—but why place our future in the hands of a man who…. Oh, forgive me, I believe I may have stepped out of bounds again."

"Cáceres," Cibdad declared, "we are gathered here for good reasons. Our families are in mortal danger. We are cut off from the world, we cannot leave Toledo without permission from Sarmiento, and soon the King will attack. If you are to be one of us, if your small brain allows you to perceive danger, then stay—but watch your mouth. If you want no part of this, then leave—but watch your back, señor. And if you desire satisfaction, I will be most happy to oblige. Decide, but decide quickly."

Fernán stifled a shout, and then realized that the community would need every man, even a Cáceres.

Cáceres blanched. Everyone in the room, other than his circle of cronies, stared at him. A taut smile flickered on his lips and then disappeared.

"It is my turn to apologize" he said. "I play the fool when wise man is the proper role. Don Lorenzo, don Juan, señores, my heart is with our cause, my mouth will follow my heart."

"Don Bernardo," Lorenzo said and looked squarely at Cáceres, "we may not agree on all matters and we need not, so long as we differ only in how best to serve our community." He turned back to the assembly. "But enough wasted words. Don Juan has raised my name. I raise his. He is used to commanding men and I for one would be most comfortable under his command."

"And soon be sick of my orders, my friend."

Calls of "No, no, Cibdad. Lead us."

"Friends, if we fight I will lead. But if we talk then I will listen. Don Lorenzo can talk and listen and fight, if necessary. He should be our leader."

Several men expressed other views and the unceasing debate discouraged Fernán. The enemy would move against them while they argued. He believed they should make preparations for battle, not jockey for power and dispute fine points of governance.

The most revered among them, Diego Enríquez, his godfather, then spoke. A white-haired man of over seventy years, bent, often confined to bed, he had survived the massacres of 1391. As a boy, he had witnessed his father hacked to death and his mother thrown from a parapet of the Alcázar before he and the remnant of his family were converted.

"Señores," Enríquez said, "time passes quickly. I suggest that we allow the master of the house we now occupy to moderate our discussion as we have done in the past. Matters of substance should be settled by a majority. We remain equals, but since we are in the Hernandes house, Lorenzo should retain the chair and we should move on."

"An excellent suggestion, don Diego," Cibdad said. "Are we agreed, señores?"

The ayes overwhelmed the few nays and Fernán blessed Cibdad.

Lorenzo led the discussion back to the questions—"What will happen to Toledo? What will happen to us New Christians? What must we do?"

After some discussion, they concluded that the future of Toledo must rest in the hands of the councilors, the nobles, and the King.

"When we say King," Cáceres said, "remember we mean don Alvaro."

"Agreed," Fernando Husillo said. "Alvaro is our friend, but if he is displaced our future will darken."

"We must also ask if councilors and nobles will accept the governorship of Sarmiento," Alfonso de Herrera said. "Will councilors and nobles tolerate rebellion against the King?"

"Or will they fight Sarmiento?" Cibdad asked. "And if they do, will they fight beside us? Or do they hate us as do the commoners?"

"Why should we care if the nobles hate us so long as they fight?" Cáceres called out.

"Because," Cibdad said, "we must count our friends and enemies. We must know whom to trust and whom to hate, who will help and who will not, and who will close his door but nevertheless not inform against us."

"And who may be persuaded by words or gold," Enríquez added.

The discussion lasted an hour. Fernán distinguished three factions. The largest, led by Cibdad and Lorenzo, favored soliciting help from the nobles and councilors and aligning with the King. The center, led by Husillo, advocated neutrality and patience. The smallest faction, led by Cáceres, argued for accommodation with Sarmiento.

"We are seen as opponents of the rebellion and enemies of the new regime," Cáceres said. "I agree with Husillo, that we should be neutral. But I differ with him in one respect—our neutrality should be active. We should accept the new role Sarmiento has assumed, understand that commoners have grievances that must be addressed, and cooperate with the new administration."

Herrera leaned on the table before him. "How can we cooperate with those who hate us?"

"If we demonstrate our friendship, the rebels will welcome us."

"Are you mad, Cáceres? Where have you lived your life? The townspeople detest us."

"Perhaps, Herrera, the commoners hate us because some of us, I will not name names, are proud and arrogant. Some of us look down on the townspeople and take advantage of them."

"You say this? You? You sound like Sarmiento and that filth, García."

"I spell out their accusations, Herrera, I do not approve them."

"Señores," Lorenzo said, "be calm. Nothing can be gained by accusing each other of bad will. We are here to reason together."

"Don Lorenzo, señores," Cibdad said, "as you know I am a soldier. I ask you not to underestimate Sarmiento. I have seen him in battle—he is formidable."

"And I, señores," Herrera said, "am a lawyer and have argued against García. I have won and lost, and when I have won I have seen his eyes—they were heavy with rage. He is clever and obsessed."

Fernán had stood by his post without moving or speaking and now speech boiled over. "Señores," he said, "I know I should not speak and am aware that I am not the equal of any man here. I surely do not presume to instruct. However, I was present in the Cathedral when García spoke and probably am alone in that regard. I pray I be allowed to relate the tenor of his speech and how it was accepted by the people."

"Does anyone object to hearing these remarks?" Lorenzo asked. "No? Proceed then, Fernán."

The men turned so that they could see Fernán. Several whispered to their neighbors and a few smiled.

Fernán related how he and Jerónimo had gone to the Cathedral and listened to García. He spoke clearly and took pains to articulate his speech so that all might understand. He told them that he was amazed by the quality of the oratory—that García had held the people captive and manipulated their minds.

"He is a craftsman with words, señores. He caught the people as flies are caught by a web. They were powerless before him. So that when he had raised their humor to a fever, with a twist of a word or an accent or an emphasis, he roused them to that action which resulted in the burning of the Cota house and the seizure of the gates. He is not an ordinary man. His hatred is on fire. He is not to be discounted, señores. I beg you. García is a danger to us all."

"Fernán," Herrera asked, "did you hear Sarmiento as well?"

"No, señor. Sarmiento did not speak. However I saw him disguised in a Dominican cowl standing against the Cathedral wall. Both Jerónimo and I marked him and Jerónimo pronounced him a devil."

16

The Sarmiento house

"Delicious," Sarmiento said, sucking piglet juice from his fingers. "The cook is to be praised. Is he new, Mother?"

His wife, Clara, glanced at her mother-in-law. The older woman gazed ahead without blinking, her face a mask. Clara blushed and replied, "Yes, Pero. Your mother engaged him three days ago. He had been with the Ayala family."

"Good choice, Mother. A well-seasoned suckler. The Ayala have taste as well as riches." He motioned to a servant and the man poured more wine. The bottle of red had not turned as had so many others of their vineyard relics. The stock would need rejuvenating, perhaps with an Italian or French grape.

"What will you do with the Ayala, Pero?" his mother asked, as if waking from a dream. "Arrest or banishment."

"Neither, for the moment. They are too well-connected. The rabble are good for nothing and the Ayala influence may be required sooner than I expected." He laughed. "Our good councilors are wondering who will be next." He washed down a slice of pig with the wine. "No need to deplete their ranks further, though. Enough that they fear me—and they do."

He snatched an apple from a basket of fruit. Where was the King? Could he still be sieging Penamente? The man had a truly royal anger.

"And Arias de Silva?"

"Silva, Mother? Silva loves *marranos*, unhappily, and he is much too strong. If he becomes troublesome, I will test his mettle."

Ten days. Ten days since Toledo had bent to his will. A rush like the cry of an eagle rose within him and, had he been alone, would have poured out in a peal of triumph and pride. For now he could buy the best cook, the Ayala cook, eat the best food, better than a baron, order rich new clothes for his family and himself, dress the part of Governor of this ancient city, and be more powerful than any governor in the long history of Toledo. The city was his.

Were the Toledan councilors and nobles preparing a counter-revolution, sending messages to the King or Luna? Those who truly rivaled him had been jailed or exiled and were wandering the countryside. But he was above them all now and they knew better than to cross him. Sarmiento severed the apple into eighths with swift cuts of a small ornamental dagger, skewered a section on the point of his dagger, and thrust it into his mouth. None of them, councilor or noble, had supported the rebellion. They would regret their detachment. He would curb them—prosecute them for treason if necessary. Noble or cleric, he would stomach no challenge. They would bend the knee.

"The children are sleeping, Pero," his wife said.

Had he asked after the children? He could not remember.

"The children are sleeping?" he asked.

"Yes, Pero. They miss you. I had them wait, but they were so fatigued I could not put them off any longer. Poor dears were desperate for rest."

"Could not be helped, Clara. Work must take precedent."

He quaffed more wine, stuffed roast pig in his mouth, and once more relived bedding Manuela that morning. By God, the woman was a maenad, a true wanton. What she would do. He shivered from the memory. Since the rebellion his appetite and potency had grown and she had responded vigorously to his need. His genitals stirred. Perhaps Clara would suffice during siesta. Perhaps not.

"You never see them, you know. They never see their father."

"Who never sees them?"

"You. Your children, Pero. Your children never see you."

"Their father is Governor of Toledo, Clara. Do they know that?"

He would see his children when consolidation was complete. Make up for his absence and neglect when he could trust the garrisons at the gate and the regiment in the Alcázar, when he had routed out the weak and traitorous, when he could face King Juan with an impregnable city and muster support from a source other than rabble. Then he would smother his children with kisses and Manuela with his body. Now he must work. The mob was unsatisfactory—no substance, no grounding. Their victory might have been a freak. He must have noble assistance, dependable and consistent. How else could he defeat Luna? And then, with Luna gone, might the King abdicate in favor of Prince Enrique? Or would Juan of Navarre overthrow the lot? Either would present him with an opportunity now that he had achieved national renown. He would step into the void created by the demise of Luna.

How he wished he could voice these thoughts to a friend—a friend he trusted to share secrets. His isolation irked him. García was no good—the man was a peasant with designs of his own. He could confide in no one except his blessed mother, and his mother was his mother. How many men considered their mothers confidants? None. Clara was certainly no confidant. Hardly a wife. Good for an occasional joust, but passive, limp. Manuela, though, God protect that beautiful devil. Sly, self-serving, but responsive to each need, each mood. He felt his member stir. God, how she roused him. To hell with Clara, he would visit Manuela after dinner.

"What will you do with the *marranos*?" his mother asked.

"*Marranos*? You said *marranos*? Why, I shall prosecute them as traitors."

"How will you justify that?"

"Justify? Need I justify everything? I suppose I must, to be safe. Well, I might argue that we are at war with Alvaro de Luna, the dear friend of *marranos*, and that *marranos* conspire with their friend to defeat us. Therefore, they are traitors to the rebellion and the city and must be prosecuted. Simple."

"You believe that, Pero?" Clara asked.

"To satisfy the mob, so long as I need the mob, I will think anything and do anything. You see, my dear, *marranos* are the focus of mob hatred. García and his little band of rebels and priests have fomented the delightful notion that the commoners, the people, rebelled to rid themselves of the economic yoke of *marranos*."

"And is that true?"

"For the love of God, Clara, truth has no part in this. What wonderful pig. However, if you insist on truth," he said, wiping the plate with a chunk of bread. "Many people owe money to *marranos*. However, commoners owe a great deal to everyone." He laughed, shoved the chunk of bread into his mouth, emptied the wine, and beckoned the servant.

"But why do *marranos* differ from us, Pero dear? We are all Christians."

"Oh, dear God, Clara, they were Jews. Jews! You and I are descended from Castilians. Our blood is pure, theirs is polluted." He sighed, pushed his plate away, and wiped his mouth on his sleeve. "*Marranos* are available prey, my girl—identifiable, distinct, valuable. A few owe me.... That Hernandes fellow, for example. What is today? Wednesday? Thursday? He was to bring a new rug. Where the devil could he be?" He grimaced in exasperation. "*Marranos* mean nothing to me, Clara. That is, except for one proposition that Mother outlined just prior to the rebellion."

"What was that, Pero?" his mother asked.

"You forget, Mother? I will remind you. Generally, *marranos* are reasonably bright and industrious, as are the Jews from whence the beggars sprang. Therefore, many have accumulated considerable wealth of assorted kinds—gold, houses, art, all that. So, once we prove that they are traitors—and that is simplicity itself—we will confiscate their blessed assets and, thereby, become immensely rich. Remember now, Mother?"

17

The Alcázar of Toledo

Saturday night Sarmiento wallowed in Manuela, finding it impossible to satisfy her hunger or his own. Whether true or assumed, her passion stirred him as no other woman ever had, and he felt his own passion lighting her fire—or so he thought. At daybreak, after an intense, brief coupling, he dressed, mounted his horse, and rode the animal to the Alcázar, his sleepy personal guard trailing a horse-length back. He marveled at the strength of his carnal appetite and attempted to adjust his seat and relieve his private parts of the jiggling rhythm of the stallion, whose motion stimulated his flesh. He was anxious to subdue this boyish preoccupation, but his member ignored his entreaties and saluted the day with rigid attention.

He avoided the Cathedral, wanting no contact with the sycophantic canons, Galvez and Alonso, who would sidle up to him with simpering flattery and introduce minor matters that should have been disposed of by García a month before. The two priests turned his stomach. He could not dismiss them entirely, though, since Galvez had been appointed Vicar of the Cathedral and head of the church judiciary while Alfonso Carrillo, resident Archbishop, was tarrying with the King and his court at Benavente.

As he rode through the city, the sky played host to dawn, the sun appeared from behind the hills, and the day modulated from deep blue to azure, frigid to cool. At the Alcázar, Sarmiento dismounted and handed the reins to one of the guards, a sullen monster, entered the spacious interior court of the Alcázar, and climbed the broad steps to his rooms, dismissing salutes from the sentries.

García was waiting. Sarmiento instructed his orderly to lay out a change of clothes, then washed leisurely, taking care to scrub his genitals. In general, he was pleased with García. He had known the lawyer to be perceptive but, since the rebellion, he had observed just how perceptive García could be—sometimes annoyingly so.

They breakfasted handsomely while reviewing the week. The King topped the list, followed by the nobles and *marranos*.

"It appears that Juan is still besieging Benavente, don Pero," García said. "He hopes, vainly, to capture Pimentel inside his castle. His army has not begun a move toward Toledo."

"Bless Pimentel! May he torment Juan from Hell to Hell!"

"Luna is furious. Sending message after message urging Juan to lift his siege of Benavente and attack Toledo. But you cannot very well command a King whom to love and whom to hate, and Juan hates Pimentel."

"You know that to be so, García?"

"We have spies with the King, don Pero. We are not without resources."

"Of course, of course. Very impressive."

And where were his other spies? With Manuela? In his soup?

Nobles were a delicate issue. He needed his fellow nobles, though they and the councilors no longer controlled Toledo. For though he was supreme and could, for the most part, do as he blessedly pleased, there were annoying limits to his power. Those limits, he had found, were defined by the will of the commoners on whom he relied for military strength—at present. And the plebeians had their own surprising and confounding ideas, damn them. He needed to be free of commoners. He needed nobles. Yet the nobles had done nothing during the rebellion. Perhaps divided between abhorrence of *conversos* and aversion to commoners, they had studied the affair from their palacios and town houses, said little, and did nothing. Those councilors not noble had been dismissed—some banished, some jailed, others tolerated.

"Do you know Silva?" García asked.

"Arias de Silva—a traitor, friend to the King."

"So he is, don Pero, and should be watched. His family is second only to the Ayala, and yet he befriends *marranos*."

"Then watch him, García. By all means, watch him."

"I do, señor."

Sarmiento smiled. García was subjecting him to a display of power. Good. Better to know than to guess.

"I doubt you have visited our new salon of horrors, García. Would you care to join me? There might be something there for you—as inspiration. You might even wish to accompany me to my chambers. We have Diego Enríquez in chains."

"The banker? Enríquez is quite old."

"Quite."

The torture chamber was a floor above the bowels of the Alcázar where political prisoners were incarcerated. Sarmiento detested the place. The stench of sweat and excrement rising from the cells was overpowering. He presumed García would respond with similar aversion and anticipated the reaction of the lawyer with pleasure.

"What do you know of torture, don Marcos?"

"Very little," he said, his voice muffled within a scented handkerchief.

Three male prisoners were in the chamber when they entered, naked except for loincloths which covered their hips and genitals. One appeared to be dead, supine on a long table, head fallen to one side, eyes closed. Another sat before two Dominicans, one of whom interrogated the prisoner while the other recorded the testimony. There were no sounds other than the feathery questions of the Dominican inquisitor that were lost in the corners of the room.

A third prisoner stood on a platform twelve feet above the stone floor, hands tied together behind his back. A rope led from the bound hands through an iron ring set into the ceiling and back to a cleat fastened to the platform, where it was tied off. As Sarmiento and García watched, the executioner, a huge man, grasped the upper arms of the prisoner and dropped him off the platform. He fell ten feet before his arms were jerked up behind his back by the taut rope, the stress of his full weight and sudden fall borne by his shoulders. The prisoner screamed, then uttered a piteous cry as he hung from the rope, arms distorted by their abnormal reverse extension.

"Are his arms pulled from their sockets?" García asked.

"They do not appear to be," Sarmiento said, "not this time."

"Will they drop him again?"

"Oh, yes. Depending on his condition, what they need to know, how the executioner appraises the moment."

"What do they call this torture?"

"*Strappado*—an Italian word. The Italians have a bent for that sort of thing."

"Does anyone escape intact?"

"Some may, I suppose. I observed one who suffered six falls without dislocation. He was in excellent condition, though, as you might assume. This prisoner, however, is stocky. A heavy man is worse off."

The rope was eased off the cleat and the prisoner lowered to the floor. Water was poured over him by another masked executioner, to no effect. The prisoner lay prostrate on the floor, apparently unconscious. Another douse elicited a groan.

Sarmiento called to the head executioner and asked him how many drops the prisoner had endured.

"Three, Your Excellency, including this last. The prisoner did well considering he bears substantial weight."

"Has he confessed?"

"The usual lie—not spying for Luna. Another drop should do it."

"How long will you wait to drop him again?" García asked.

"Ten, fifteen minutes, señor. He should be coming around in a minute or two. We will douse him again—that should bring him up. A simple plan, Your Honors. Four drops should do it."

"Do you not give him time to confess?" García asked.

"No, señor, not worth the effort. He knows nothing, but will confess all the same—to stop the pain."

"I disagree, Executioner," Sarmiento said. "This prisoner is well-informed. I want to know when he has confessed. In particular I want names of friends and family who may have conspired with Luna against the rebels, and traitorous words spoken by the councilors. Be diligent."

"Indeed I will, Your Honor," the executioner said, and returned to his profession.

"We must be ruthless, García. Torture them until they confess to conspiring with Luna—whether or not they have done so. Having secured a confession, we judge them guilty of treason, execute them, and then confiscate their possessions. An efficient system. The administration needs funds and *marranos* are a ready store of cash. Our people need to be set an example and blood inspires obedience above all else. Besides, the commoners hate *marranos* as much as you do. They enjoy watching the rich and powerful cut to pieces."

"Who is this prisoner?"

"The one dropped? Gaspar de Ribas, scribe to the Council. Knows everything the Council said or did. A fount of knowledge."

As they rode past Zocodover Square, Sarmiento noticed a crowd and remembered that several executions had been scheduled for the afternoon.

"This should prove amusing," he said, and they walked the horses closer to the crowd, where they sat their mounts and watched the proceedings.

The crowd howled as a man in a loincloth was forced onto the platform and tied to a rough wooden table discolored by human effluents from previous executions. The executioner stood back as the prisoner was secured and then selected an ax. He wore a stained black leather apron and a black mask that covered his eyes and head. His legs, twin blocks of ropy muscle shaded by dirt and blood, protruded from beneath a black overshirt.

"An inspiring vision of Death," Sarmiento said. "The ultimate butcher and his tools—ax, curved knife, hatchet—each tool specific to an action. First he severs limbs from torso."

The blow was delivered. With each stroke the howling grew, and high above the screech of the crowd rose an agony of a scream beyond the range of the human voice. Each cut of steel fed the appetite of the mob and their roars increased in volume and pitch with the swell of their murderous hunger. "Now he draws the bowels!" one fat-bellied villager cried. And as the executioner drew the living duct from within the near-dead body, the swarm squealed as if their own guts had been sucked from their bellies. "The ax for the head." Another shriek as the ax came down with a savage thwack. "Quarter, quarter, quarter!" the mob chanted and their cries rose to an orgiastic scream as the torso was split throat to groin like the carcass of a pig and the scarlet halves separated.

García turned his horse away. "Gruesome affair. I hope they derive pleasure from this sport. I admit I do not."

"A weak stomach, García? I would never have guessed."

"My stomach weak? Not likely. But I would rather run a beggar through than watch his bowels drawn and his body hacked to pieces."

"Then perhaps we should discontinue killing?" Sarmiento asked and turned his mount about. His mouth twitched uncontrollably and he bit his lips to conceal the fault.

"No, we should continue. We need funds to pay wages and buy arms and we need the commoners to guard the gates and fight the King. Blood keeps them happy."

"Then we shall do what is required, whatever that may be. Yes, García?"

García was quiet as they continued to the judicial chamber in Town Hall.

Diego Enríquez stood in chains between two guardsmen, his hair and beard trim and white, his large gray eyes aglow beneath white eyebrows. Herrera sat on a chair against the wall, but leapt to his feet when Sarmiento entered. García remained near the door as if he might bolt.

"Well, Herrera," Sarmiento said and sat behind a large table set upon a platform. "What have you to say for your client?"

"Your Excellency, Diego Enríquez has been accused of treason for conspiring with Alvaro de Luna. Don Pero, señor Enríquez is innocent of the charges which have been brought against him."

"He has been judged guilty by the court, Herrera. Do you say the court pronounced incorrectly?"

"I do, don Pero. The charges are false and always were false."

"But, Herrera, that is exactly why your client must be put to the test. No one can possibly lie under torture, and in this way his innocence will be proved."

"Excellency, I plead leniency for this man. Don Diego Enríquez is old. Torture will kill him. He is a good man and a loyal citizen and could not have conspired with Alvaro de Luna. How could he have left Toledo to contact Luna—the gates have been closed and guarded since the rebellion?"

"Oh, Herrera, there are many ways to circumvent a closed and guarded gate, as you well know." Sarmiento inclined his head. "Don Alfonso, Enríquez is a *converso*, as you are. Is it not a matter of record that you *conversos* favor Alvaro de Luna?"

"With all due respect, Excellency, that is conjecture. Your Excellency, this man has a wife, several children, and many grandchildren. He has been accused of treason and convicted—that we know. But we do not know his accusers, those who have attacked him. We cannot question them. Under this system of law, where one can be accused of heinous crimes without knowing his accusers and without being able to face them, none of us would be found innocent. Guilt and innocence, good and evil become one."

"Herrera, you oppose the times. The times determine what is good and what evil, who is innocent and who guilty. What appears good to one era may become anathema to the next. Move with the times, señor, and be careful I do not mistrust your motive."

Enríquez began to speak. A guard ordered him to be silent.

"Let him speak," Sarmiento said. "Nothing will come of his speech."

"Excellency," Enríquez said, "these may be my last words, but even amongst savages a man who will soon die is given the right to speak. I thank you for granting me that privilege. As you have said, Your Excellency, my words can cause no harm.

"Of what law I have broken, I am ignorant, Excellency. If I have spoken against injustice and that is now a crime then, indeed, I am guilty. If the court needs money, the court may have mine. I give it to the court freely. Money has little true worth in our lives and no value in the grave. Your Excellency, I would save this life God gave me for a few years more, or as long as God has willed I may enjoy it. Not for money nor for my welfare but for the sake of a woman who has been my good wife for over forty years, and who will surely die of grief if I am tortured and killed. But if God has willed that I must see His face, then know that the woman is innocent of wrongdoing and it is for her that I make this, my final request. Grant me, Excellency, a few days to prepare my wife and family for this death."

"Your request is denied, señor."

Enríquez bowed his head beneath the sharp response and Herrera cried out, "Make his torture slight, Your Excellency. Don Diego will confess at the sight of the instrument. He will confess now. Nothing can be gained, Your Excellency, by subjecting him to the pain you know his body cannot endure."

"Pain is good for the soul, Herrera," Sarmiento said. "Pain washes away the sins of corruption and leaves us pure, as pure as fire. Pray God, Enríquez will confess his treason and reveal his conspirators, then he will require no greater purification than is necessary. We know his conspirators, of course, but for the sake of justice we need corroboration. Enríquez can supply the added proof."

"Torture *me* then," Herrera pleaded, "not Diego Enríquez. This man is the soul of good will, the soul of our community, Excellency. Our people will be distraught. They will never be reconciled."

Sarmiento eased himself out of the chair and faced Herrera. "Have you learned nothing, Herrera? Then listen. You and your people are of no importance except as an example, a symbol. You will soon understand. Do not tempt me further." Sarmiento waved the prisoner away.

Enríquez looked up at one of his guards, a tall young man. "Your father, Bartolomé, he is well?"

"Yes, señor. I am truly sorry, don Diego."

"If I am to be with God, so be it. These are mysteries of which we men know nothing."

"Take him out!" Sarmiento ordered.

The guards marched Enríquez out of the room. Herrera followed, his eyes a well of tears. García watched as they left.

"You look pale, García. Are you ill?"

"The old man looks not unlike my father, don Pero. He was pitiful."

"You continue to surprise me, Marcos. I thought you despised *marranos*."

"I do—a *marrano* wronged my family." García stared into the air and then spoke in a voice Sarmiento scarcely recognized. "When he was a young man, my father incurred a foolish debt to a *marrano* landowner. He borrowed a sum of money to acquire land he coveted for its fertile soil. The land he owned was promised as security. As so often happens in Castile, the weather changed and our land withered—no crops grew and there was nothing with which to pay interest on the debt. The *marrano* refused to wait, he had debts of his own to repay, he said, and he took our land. My father had not a *maravedí* in his pocket and he cursed the *marrano* and drew his knife. The *marrano* defended himself and my father was killed.

"I was ten at the time. I was there when he died. Since then I have hated *marranos*. Yet, the resemblance of this man Enríquez to my father has moved me, though my father was much younger. It will pass."

18

A week later, the Hernandes house

Supper that evening was solemn. Even vivacious María was subdued. The little ones sensing a disturbance, a rumble of far-off thunder, a shiver in the earth, ate their food and, holding hands, followed the servants to bed like small pets. The women retired soon after and the four men sat and stared at their wine glasses or their hands or the wall.

"Did he die quickly, Lorenzo?" Cesario asked.

Lorenzo shrugged and shook his head. "A man his age could not survive one drop of the *strappado*."

"Herrera said Sarmiento was obdurate," Antonio said, "determined to set an example."

"Example of what?" Cesario said. He pushed away from the table and strode around the room. "Diego did nothing. Is that the example Sarmiento wanted to set? Do nothing and die?"

"That may well be the message Sarmiento delivered," Lorenzo said. "No matter what you do, no matter how saintly you may be, or because you may be a saint, if you are a New Christian you will be tortured and die horribly—like Ribas, poor soul." Lorenzo clenched his teeth and brought both hands down hard on the table so that the tableware jumped. "I should have killed this Sarmiento when I had the chance—cut his throat like you would kill a mad dog."

From across the room Cesario shouted, "I will not die like a beast in a slaughterhouse!" Agitated, he paced back and forth and struck one hand with the other. "If I die, it will be in a fight with a knife or sword or by my own hand. What is done with my body when I am dead is of no importance. My body will have served its purpose. My soul will be free."

Fernán listened and absorbed the words with each drop of the red wine he was now allowed. He had eaten little of his supper. The smiling face of don Diego was before him, speaking to him, comforting him. Almost fifty years separated their ages but, in the absence of his grandfather, who had died when Fernán was six, Enríquez, his godfather, had become his friend—a precious link to former times. Though don Diego had several children of his own, they were now men with families of their own who lived in Segovia, Ávila, and Burgos, and he sought out Fernán and conversed with him as he had with his own children when they were young.

They would walk together and Enríquez would talk of old Toledo when Jews, Muslims, and Christians lived and worked in mutual harmony, a *convivencia*. And they would stroll through the Jewish quarter and his godfather would point out the two synagogues remaining from the ten or more that had been active during the time when Jews were a significant part of the Toledan population—the synagogues Kneset Haguedola, now called Santa María la Blanca, and the Synagogue of Samuel Levi, called El Tránsito, a masterpiece of *mudéjar* art that was built less than one hundred years before their time. He would describe to the boy the work of the School of Translators of Toledo, within which Jews, Muslims, and Christians worked side by side during the time of King Alfonso X translating classic Greek, Hebrew, and Moorish works into Latin and Spanish.

When Fernán would question why there were now two synagogues when there had been ten, Don Diego would answer that there were more Jews in those times. The boy would ask why. "Many Jews converted to Christianity, Fernán," Don Diego would answer. And why was that? "Because they wanted to be Christian or because they were forced to convert." Was my father forced? "No, your great-grandfather was." Why were they forced? "I cannot answer that, Fernán. Ask Fray Sebastiáno to explain." But Fernán had never asked his confessor and when he questioned himself, he realized that he was afraid to ask.

As if by accident, while walking through the city, they would happen upon a shop that sold marzipan, their favorite confection. "Oh," Enríquez would say, "look where we have come, Fernán. I did not realize we had walked so far. My, my, my—see the various forms of marzipan in that shop. Shall we look more closely?" Soon they would be in the store and then back on the street again, laughing like schoolboys, with marzipan in one form or another in their hands.

Fernán was stunned when Lorenzo told him Ribas had been taken and killed. But when he learned about don Diego, his blood froze. Madness had seized Toledo. There was no safety, no hope. The senseless acts of Sarmiento and his crowd were deliberate. There was a plan to kill *conversos* one after the other—no excuse would be heard, no protestation of innocence heeded, no plea attended. Yet something within Fernán rebelled against the thought. Could this methodical butchery continue unabated? Was there no law? He must speak to don Abrahán.

His father had been speaking. "We will not sit here and wait for the door to be broken in and all of us arrested."

"Did the nobles offer opposition to Sarmiento when you spoke to them?" Antonio asked.

"A few offered sympathy from their balconied *palacios*, but only one offered help—Arias de Silva, second in order among the councilors. Don Arias assured me that his arms and his company of men were at our disposal, and for that I said we would be grateful all our lives. He is loyal to the King and his precepts, including protection of New Christians and, when the King attacks, as he will, Silva will be in the van."

"God bless him," Antonio said.

"Ayala, on the other hand, was the patrician—so very cordial, so very polite. He smiled that simpering smile and washed his hands of us. That we are of the same religion and have served the city and the nobility for so many years is a matter of indifference to Ayala. He plays the game of politics and we are not markers on his golden board, a site he has reserved for the head of Alvaro."

"Forget Ayala. Arias de Silva is the man I will follow," Cesario said. "Did Silva suggest anything?"

"Yes, brother. He approved setting patrols, but said that patrols were not sufficient and that we must establish armed companies and seal the borders of our borough to prevent the plebeians from seizing us."

"I am for that, Lorenzo," Antonio said, and raised his glass.

"And I," Cesario added, and drank with his brother. "What does Cibdad say?"

"He approves and has begun to form a company."

"Then we must do the same," Antonio said. "For don Diego and Ribas and ourselves."

"Papá," Fernán said, "I must be part of your company. I am of age and as fit as any soldier in the ranks of the King."

Lorenzo turned to his son and smiled. "This engagement will not be swordplay, Fernán. Sarmiento has armed his company with weapons from the Alcázar. You will be our mouth and ears from one company to the next. We have men of fighting age, but no one as fleet as you."

19

That evening, the Melamed house

Dressed in black, Fernán strapped on sword and dagger and left the house. The prospect of a fight stirred him. Lorenzo had attempted to instill a mature perspective in his son, saying that in battle there were no winners, that war was a futile exercise, that in the end talk terminated conflict. Fernán listened, but sober words whistled past his ears—his spirit was high.

The street was as clear as the night sky. The three-quarter moon had risen and long black shadows blanketed Toledo. Fernán kept to the dark. He dared not ride Margarita, as she would attract the enemy or villains lying in wait for passersby.

Why was the moon full and then gradually diminished until it disappeared? There were times when he saw part of the moon he should not see, but saw it dark, as in shadow. And why did the cycle take four weeks? Jerónimo had said the moon was a sphere which circled the earth once every twenty-eight days and that the moon we see is the part lit by the sun. Take a ball, he said, light it with a single candle, then walk around the ball and you will see the phases of the moon, from new to full and back again.

What strange ideas Jerónimo entertained—no doubt brought by the Moors from across the sea. He said that the moon and its phases drew the tides of the ocean and the periods of women. Fernán had nodded his head as if in agreement, though he knew nothing of the tides of the ocean, never having seen a larger body of water than Río Tajo that wrapped around Toledo. He knew almost nothing about women, save that he was fond of them, those he was close to—his mother and sister, María, and now, above all, Naomi.

Of course he knew women were not made like men. A visit to a stable or barn told him that a mare and a stallion were dissimilar and that a cow and bull differed in their hindquarters and horns. He had witnessed stallions mounting mares and dogs copulating in the street, and though men and women were not animals, in that God had bestowed reason on man, humans were fashioned in a similar way to beasts. Women had parts he did not and parts he had they lacked. But of what did the parts of women consist? He saw the bulges of breasts and hips, but had no experience to teach him, as some of his acquaintances boasted they had, those who told him weird tales about women they had experienced. He was not even sure what they meant by experience. Women were a mystery and he detested mysteries. This was not the sort of thing he could ask Jerónimo or Cesario, and certainly not Lorenzo. But he must find out. Seventeen was too old not to know. He was a man.

The passage to the Melamed house went without incident, although Fernán witnessed the arrest of one man. He had watched from the safety of a dark alley as a patrol apprehended the fellow and dragged him away. All the while the man protested and cursed his brother-in-law who had insisted he visit that night to discuss family business, else he would be in bed and safe.

Fernán and Melamed sat before a quiet fire in the study.

"I felt I must talk to someone who is not involved," Fernán said.

"And who might that uninvolved person be?"

"Yourself, don Abrahán. You said it was not your turn to be troubled."

"However, I did not say that we were not involved, my boy. We have always been involved and always will be. These troubles stem from our very involvement. But they are a short prelude to the immense troubles to come—and they will come, Fernán, again and again, like waves riding in to shore. Do you know the ocean or the sea?"

Fernán was surprised by the question. "No, don Abrahán, I do not. But I expect to some day."

"Without doubt, Fernán, you will know the waves of the sea."

When he was young, Fernán had often lain in bed, fingers in his ears, listening for the sound of waves his friends had said he would hear. The sound he did hear had been a low roar. Was that how the ocean sounded? He had asked his father and Lorenzo put him off, saying that Fernán would judge for himself one day.

"The waves of the ocean," Melamed said, "are more spectacular than those of the sea. This trouble we are passing through is like a sea wave—controlled, deliberate. The ocean, however, is a chaos independent of any presence, other than God. This trouble foretells a chaos yet to come."

Normally, Fernán listened to don Abrahán and his prophesies and metaphors with great interest, but not tonight. "The chaos is with us, don Abrahán. My godfather is dead and others have been tortured and killed."

"Fernán, I know it is terrible to lose friends and to bear witness to the apparent disintegration of your world. Believe this, though—your world will not disintegrate although it may seem to do so. Change, yes, your world will certainly change. But take heart, dear cousin, the world is old and has seen many catastrophes—yet, we live."

The small room was filled with the voice of the doctor and the memory of Naomi—her smile in the light of the sun. But he dared not ask about her, although he realized that as much as he valued the words and company of don Abrahán, his visit to the doctor was an excuse to see Naomi, and after their borough was closed, it would be difficult to visit. How long might that isolation continue?

Their talk went on for some time, don Abrahán raising one subject after the other as if reluctant to release Fernán. The doctor told him that torture and execution of *conversos* at this stage was political, a contest between Sarmiento and Alvaro. That was why those who had been tried were accused of collusion with Alvaro and convicted of treason. In the future, he said, persecution would take on a religious cast.

"Religious hatred," he said, "passes to a child with the milk of its mother, and is a boil on the ass of mankind." Fernán started at the word and then laughed. "No laughing matter, young man. Heresy needs only accusation, not proof. Who can prove what is in my mind or yours? And accusation is so small a matter—a few words. Heresy has the further benefit of prosecution by the Church, a defense of the words of God—as the Church interprets His words—whether they are, in fact, His words or the words some man or woman has written to be placed in the Holy Mouth. Prosecution for heresy is malignant, deadly—as pernicious and virulent as the Black Death."

Fernán left don Abrahán, his head awhirl with thoughts of the change evolving in the world. He was not afraid but he was confused. He had no experience of battle, had never seen his borough closed and fortified, had never lost his godfather to torture, or witnessed his father and uncles in such an agitated state. And heresy was a new force. Although he knew the meaning of the word, he could not imagine heresy applied to those he loved. For if convicted of heresy, Fray Sebastiáno had said, you are burned at the stake and will roast in Hell forever. God save us.

His mind preoccupied with heresy and his eyes on the ground, he failed to see Naomi seated on the bench under the olive tree in the speckled moonlight, and walked directly to the gate.

"Fernán," she called softly.

He turned to her, his thoughts still with don Abrahán, and stood for a moment transfixed.

"What is wrong, Fernán?" she asked.

He walked to the bench, sat beside her, and took her hand. "I have been talking with your grandfather. I am sorry, but I am very confused." He kissed her hand and placed her palm against his cheek.

"What did Grandpapá say to confuse you so?" She touched his other cheek, drew his face close to hers, and kissed and held him. He enfolded her in his arms and repeated the substance of his conversation with don Abrahán.

"Fernán, you must not worry. Grandpapá has told me that the King will not allow Sarmiento to govern. He will attack the rebels and Toledo will be as it was."

"I honor and have great respect for your grandfather, but I am afraid Toledo will never be the same. The people have repressed their hatred for New Christians and now that hatred has burst forth. Shopkeepers my family has bought greens and meat and other goods from for as long as I can remember, I have heard cursing us, Naomi, calling us *marranos*, threatening us with death. How can we live together in the same city, how can we buy from them, knowing that they hate us and want us dead?"

"Oh, Fernán, now you are again like Jews."

He held her away from him and looked into her face. "If I were a Jew as you are, dear Naomi, I would be happy. I would know who I am. But I am not like you and can never be like you."

20

Saturday morning

The *conversos* closed their borough and divided the troops into two companies—Lorenzo commanded the right and Juan de la Cibdad the left. Arias de Silva would form a third company and guard the center. Silva and his company were professionals, whereas the other two were composed of men with little or no experience of battle, some of them servants.

The task was demanding. Wooden beams, barrels, and carts were pulled together to barricade the streets. Houses fronting the city were fortified—windows and doors barred and shut, lookouts assigned to the roofs, and women positioned with cauldrons of boiling water to repel attempts to fire the houses with torches or scale their walls. Some houses had common sidewalls, others had courtyards, alleys, or streets between, but even walled yards were difficult to defend. At each such break in their line of defense, the captains assigned men bearing long bows and crossbows. When the enemy charged, the bowmen would launch arrows and then fall back while pikemen and swordsmen advanced.

The difficulties were immense. How to rotate the small army they had assembled so that men could rest and be fed. How to prepare for the inevitable casualties. How to protect women and children if their line was overrun. Confidence was scarce, but Fernán heard few complaints.

Before the companies were organized and in place, before barricades were fully erected, Sarmiento threw his force against the *conversos*. As the first attack advanced, Fernán studied the approaching pikemen. Their attack was cautious—he felt their indecision. Though the *conversos* were as green as the rebels, the rebels were not defending their homes, and the attack of pikes and swords, a probe to test their defense, was beaten back with minor loss to the defenders.

Ordered to hold himself ready to run messages, Fernán cried out as he watched the blows and counter-blows of the engaged troops, and his body twitched and his arm ached to swing his sword. Then, called upon to run a message, he sprinted behind the lines from captain to captain, repeating the message to himself, shouting so as to be heard above the clamor of battle.

"From Hernandes. Holding here. Casualties light. Your status?"

The enemy launched an attack in force at dawn Sunday against Lorenzo on the right. Bowmen in houses opposite hurled an avalanche of arrows, followed by a sortie to the center by pikemen and swordsmen with breastplates and helmets. Lorenzo stood his ground while his bowmen shot arrow after arrow at the attackers. The rebels retreated under the deluge. *Converso* forces cheered and pursued but were restrained from a counterattack.

"From Cibdad. No counterattack. Conserve troops."

Later that morning, a mass of clouds blew in from the west, blackening the sky. A light mist grew into a steady, chilling rain and the ground between the two forces became sodden. Attempting to stay dry, the men crowded under makeshift shelters or in the lee of houses, taking turns guarding and resting. With one eye to the front, they ate what food there was, quenched their thirst, and waited for the next charge.

The rain continued through Monday when a half-hearted attack against Cibdad bogged down in the wet. The rebels were unable to do more than slog through the mud, presenting easy targets for bowmen.

And Fernán dashed from captain to captain. "From Silva. Maintain watch. Several hit by snipers."

Dawn Tuesday, attacking sappers blew the doors off five front-line houses but were repulsed by scalding water spilled from upstairs windows and by arrows shot from within the buildings. Fernán winced at the pitiful screams of the burned and wounded. In response, the maddened enemy assaulted the windows of front-line houses with arquebus and bow, while crossbow snipers picked off several defenders.

By noon, the sun had dissipated the early mist and the ground had firmed, but there was no general attack.

"From Cibdad. Reinforce upstairs windows. Repair, barricade doors."

Wednesday, an expected attack never materialized. Snipers with arquebus and crossbow traded shots and arrows across the lines, but pikes and swords were missing. That night, the captains—Lorenzo, Cibdad, and Silva—sat in the great hall of the Hernandes house, commandeered as headquarters, discussing the course of battle. They argued over food and water, how to husband their remaining troops, whether to attack the enemy or to let the enemy waste his resources attacking them. Fernán attended in the event there were orders to run, half-listening, his face rough with stubble, his mind weary with talk. The sounds of battle reverberated in his ears, although the night was quiet since night was reserved for patrols.

Cibdad had said the enemy would attack only during the day, and was proved right. The rebels probed at night and the defenders checked the enemy, harried its men, and recovered the bodies of the wounded and dead they could not retrieve during the day. But night or day, Fernán could not rid himself of the shouts of men dashing with pikes or swords, the whoosh of arrows launched toward the defenders, or the thwack of enemy arrows plunging into flesh and the explosive cries of shock and pain that followed. These sounds lived whole in his head, peopled his days, and haunted his nights.

Most of the night, the captains counted heads, arrows, and casks of gunpowder, calculating how long their defense could be maintained and what options were open if they did collapse. Silva and Cibdad dominated the argument—when to retreat and how and where and with whom, or whether to consolidate and regroup into a single salient. They avoided talk of surrender, if surrender were possible. More likely, Cibdad said, there would be a massacre. And that opinion settled the issue—no surrender.

All week long, Fernán had raced from captain to captain, memorizing messages, barking them out, forgetting what was said as the week progressed and as one skirmish blended into the next.

Early Thursday, the rebels struck the center with a light force and the Silva company countered and forced a rebel retreat. With Silva extended and exposed, a larger force of rebels attacked Lorenzo. Reduced in bowmen, Lorenzo fell back, exposing his left flank. Silva ran to defend, opening a hole in the center. The original rebel force again attacked the center, but Cibdad led his men from the left, leaving a skeleton force to cover his flank. The attackers were beaten off and the line held, though Cibdad was struck by gunshot.

Fernán had been taking a message from Cibdad when a ball hit the captain and knocked him to the ground. A diffusing red well appeared in his chest and a shout went up from the rebels. The defenders drew back, confused, not knowing who was in charge. Bernardo de Cáceres raised his sword and shouted, "To me, to me!" and men rallied around him. "For Cibdad!" he shouted and the men took up the cry, "For Cibdad!" and charged the rebels.

"Run, Fernán." The voice was a croaking parody of the Cibdad voice he knew. "Run. Tell them I am down and bad."

"My arm is strong. I can help here."

"Your arm cannot fight guns and arrows. The captains must be told I am down. Run!"

"We will carry you to safety."

"I am dead, Fernán. The wound is a river. I am faint and cold. I command you to run."

Fernán looked into the near-dead eyes. "Go, son." Cibdad closed his eyes. Fernán turned. A wall of men were fighting several feet away. He had no time. "Come to Cibdad!" he shouted. Several men joined him. "Defend this man with your lives!" he cried, then ran to alert his father.

As he ran he looked back and saw the defenders under fierce attack. Unable to hold the line or drag Cibdad to safety, they retreated. The rebels advanced, swords flashing, and Fernán lost sight of Cibdad and Cáceres. His eyes teared as he ran and he shook his head to clear his vision. Sarmiento will kill Cibdad. Torture him for secrets and kill him in some hellish way. Cibdad would tell them nothing.

"Cibdad down!" he shouted as he neared Lorenzo, fighting tears, breathing great breaths, teeth bared in a grimace of anguish and rage.

"Taken by the enemy! Cibdad down and captured!"

Lorenzo looked up from the wet earth where his brother Cesario lay, his arm and leg bloody. And Fernán, moved beyond reason by the sight of his wounded uncle, seized the long sword beside Cesario, raised the great weapon high, and cried, "To me, to me!" and raced toward the fight.

"Fernán!" his father called, but the son heard nothing, his mind frozen. "To me, to me!" he shouted, his voice frenzied, his eyes wide, his face a savage mask. Tears of rage ran down his cheeks and Jerónimo saw the face of his young master and cried out, "To Fernán!" and ran after him with sword and dagger. The men joined the rush and a great roar of voices rose as they followed Fernán, their swords leveled at the enemy.

Fernán dodged maces and pikes, rose high, blocked axes, and flung puny swords aside as he swung the great sword. Both hands locked to the hilt, the mass of the sword alive, he whirled the weapon, decapitated a pike, and sliced through a buckler and the breast behind it. The razor edge lopped off arms and legs and faceless heads, slicing the flesh of rebels as he tore through the pack and felt the hesitant crunch of the sword as steel severed bone. Back and around, he was a swirl of death, splitting the enemy into two bloody knots while Jerónimo and the men with him punished the rebels and strewed the ground with wounded and dead. The rebels, surrounded by horror, fled in disarray to their lines.

Wild-eyed, Fernán reared to throw his sword after those retreating, but Jerónimo held his arm and spoke quietly, dissuading him. Fernán stared at the hand that held his arm and then at the Moor.

"I have been mad, Jerónimo," he said, and then examined himself. "Merciful God, see my arms, see my body. I am scarlet, Jerónimo—awash in blood. How many have I killed?"

"More than five, Fernán, and many grievously wounded."

"Five or more? What will almighty God think of me killing His creatures as if they were beasts? Five? Only five dead? Why not five hundred? Why not five thousand? Come back!" he shouted to the rebels, "Come back and be killed! Oh, dear God, what have I done?"

"Defended your home. God will forgive you, friend. You fought in a righteous cause. A man must defend his loved ones."

"Must he kill? Is there no way but to kill?"

"When you are attacked, no other way."

"Might I not have reasoned with them, Jerónimo? My voice is as strong as my arm. You have taught me to reason and persuade. I should have argued, not killed."

"Remorse is noble, Fernán, but your actions were just. Their minds were stopped."

"You think?" Fernán sat on the ground and held his head, his eyes filled with tears. "I can think of nothing, Jerónimo. My mind will not work."

"You are a lion, young master, but even lions must rest."

21

On the street that night

The sky was overcast, the night dark, redolent of fresh rain. Fernán wore a black hooded cape and waited at the alley entrance until he was sure he heard no enemy patrols. Before he stepped into the street, he discussed the route with Jerónimo. His friend had asked why he must see the doctor tonight after the enfeebling fight they had barely survived, and Fernán told him about Naomi—that he loved her and would marry her.

"She is a Jew, Fernán."

"That does not matter."

"Will she convert?"

"No. Conversion would kill her grandfather. She is at home in her religion."

"You are mad from the battle, my young friend. You, a Catholic, want a Jew who will not convert? Is there some key to the story you have omitted? Or do you torment me?"

"Antonio married María."

"And your aunt converted to Catholicism, as you well know. You are teasing this Moor." Jerónimo shook his head and smiled. "Of course, now I know. You have a wench in the city and your blood has become so hot from the fight that you are mad. So now you must cool your manly juices to restore your sanity."

"That is not so. I am ignorant of women. In that respect, my education has been deplorable. I know one thing only—Naomi will be my wife, our match was ordained by Heaven, and without her I will be dead."

"Ah," Jerónimo said, "more serious than I imagined. Then there is nothing to be done, young man. You must follow the way of the Lord and trust in His beneficence—that He will countenance your path to happiness. May God watch over you. We will talk of women and love when we return."

"When I return."

"And I. We go together."

"I go alone. My nurse died years ago, God bless her soul, and I have need of no other."

"I am no nurse, dear Fernán, but a friend with a sharp sword to ward off the evil spirits that haunt the night. I will not interfere with you courting the lovely Naomi—though you are mad. But if you deny me your company, I will weep and be inconsolable for I will never see you again. Either you will be taken by the rebels and killed or you will survive, but either way your good father will have my head for not protecting you."

Fernán sighed and accepted the inevitable.

When he had walked a hundred paces down the street, he stepped into a shadowed archway. The street was empty and he turned and watched Jerónimo detach himself from the alley and follow, moving in and out of doorways and alleys. The steward was a wraith. Had Fernán not known Jerónimo was there, he would have been invisible. He heard Jerónimo whisper, "*Buena suerte*," and the steward was off to the bend in the road where he stopped and waited for Fernán. And so they continued, one bypassing the other.

Fernán tried to concentrate on where he placed his feet, but his thoughts were on Cesario and Cibdad. He had heard the sounds of battle and his father shout and then his sword cut as if governed by a force other than his arms, and everywhere blood.

Cesario would live, though he was out of the fight. A third of their soldiers were dead or wounded. Though they had beaten the enemy back and rebel casualties were twice theirs, they could take no consolation in numbers, for the enemy was ten times their size.

Cibdad and Cáceres were gone, presumed dead, and Lorenzo and Silva had divided the Cibdad company between them. They must fight on, for surrender would lead to massacre. They had no allies, no friends. The King had not moved against Sarmiento, but instead wasted his resources laying siege to Pimentel. De Luna was impotent and Sarmiento, king of Toledo.

Could they retreat? Could they move so many men, women and children? And where would they go? If they did retreat, they would leave behind everything for which three generations of their people had labored since they became Christian. His head was heavy with grief and foreboding—his people were trapped within the walls of a city surrounded on three sides by a river and attacked by overwhelming force. They would die, but they would inflict remarkable damage on the enemy before they disappeared into the dark and joined Christ in his Kingdom. But in that Kingdom would Fernán find those men without heads and arms, the men he had killed? God alone knew and He was silent.

His senses opened to the clink of steel, the tramp of feet. He stepped into a door recess and drew his rapier and dagger. How light his rapier felt compared to the long sword—that deadly poleax of weapons. Limbs and heads had littered the ground after the engagement, something a rapier could not do. One slice of that long sword and the fight was done, limb severed, blood spurting. Damn the bloody blade! The rapier felt sweet in his hand—manageable, intelligent.

A six-man rebel patrol dragged past the intersection with the next street, lugging their pikes. No threat there. Then the last was gone and Fernán sheathed his rapier and dagger, waited a moment, and sidled up the street to join Jerónimo.

22

At the Melamed house

Mosé opened the barred panel in the courtyard door. "Is that you, Fernán? And Jerónimo beside you? Good evening to you both. But from where have you come? I was told there was fighting between the rebels and New Christians and we were concerned for your safety. Of course, I would not approach your part of the city and I cannot imagine what it might be like to fight a battle—I certainly do not engage in such conduct and I hope I am never called upon to do so but…God forbid, are you here because you are hurt? And here am I, talking through a door and you may be injured and in need of aid."

"No, Mosé, we are both well," Fernán said.

"And I still talk through a door. If you please, come in and welcome." Mosé opened the door and led them through the courtyard.

As he passed the bench where Naomi had kissed him, Fernán grasped that he was no longer the young man of that evening, the youth who had lamented with such conviction that he, a Christian, and she, a Jew, were not and could never be alike. Where were those thoughts now? The killing had changed him. He had aged, was closer to the Angel of Death.

"We are all here," Mosé said, "and not yet in bed, except for Aharón, who is not in bed, surely, but off somewhere in Castile buying or selling goods to pay for our apprenticeship. Here is don Abrahán."

They entered the study where Fernán had seen Naomi aglow in the morning sunlight and where his throat had been salved, his heart lost, and the path of his life made clear. A low fire illuminated the room and Naomi sat in the firelight mending a shirt. She lay down the garment and looked into his face.

"Fernán," she said, "you are so thin. Are you well?"

He smiled at her—a wan smile. "Yes, Naomi," he said, savoring her name. "My body is well, but my soul is ill."

"Why is that, Fernán?" the doctor asked.

"I fought and killed many men."

"Fernán defended his home," Jerónimo said. "He was splendid."

"How can one be splendid and kill men?" Naomi asked, her eyes fixed on Fernán.

"Señorita, permit me," Jerónimo said. "You are young—a wonderful season, but a season that will pass as spring passes into the fullness of summer. When you are within the next season of your life and have a home and children, you will treasure a man who can defend his family as my young master Fernán defended his today. Fernán is as true a man as I have ever known. That is why he killed—as a lion will kill to defend his pride—out of necessity."

Though the light was dim, Fernán could see the color rise in her cheeks.

"I see," she said. "But how will Fernán cure his soul?"

"Time will cure his soul, Naomi dear," don Abrahán said. "Fernán stands at the border of manhood and will pay the price of admission to that state many times. He has paid a heavy price today and the burden weighs on him. That is natural, though regrettable. As he grows into manhood, his soul will strengthen and the burdens he must bear will weigh less heavily upon him. That is when he will make peace with life."

Melamed rose from his chair and placed his hand on the shoulder of his young cousin. "I am saddened to tell you more unpleasant news, Fernán." Melamed sighed. "The dead body of Juan de la Cibdad was dragged through the streets to Zocodover Square, hanged head down, and mutilated by the commoners."

"Dear God, I was with him when he was shot, don Abrahán. But how can such a man have no honor in death?" Fernán lowered his head and closed his eyes. "Oh, Señor, Señor, where are You that You permit this outrage? Must we be butchered like animals? Do You not see? Do You not hear?" He turned to Melamed. "Bernardo de Cáceres. Have you news of him, don Abrahán?"

"No, Fernán. No news."

"May I get you something to eat or drink?" Mosé asked.

Fernán looked up sharply and Mosé saw his tortured face and stepped back. The only sound in the room was that of the crackling fire. Melamed asked Fernán how the battle was progressing. Naomi put her arms around her grandfather and, in a reduced voice, Fernán recounted the events of the week. Melamed asked what the *conversos* would do.

Fernán shook his head. "Sarmiento and García are committed to our deaths."

"But where is the King?" Naomi asked.

"We do not know, Naomi," Fernán said.

"Perhaps this action was rash," Melamed said.

"Rash, don Abrahán? They arrested us, tortured us, killed us, cut us to pieces—my godfather, Gaspar de Ribas, others. What choice did we have but to resist?"

Melamed advised caution and Fernán said, "Caution may now be a luxury, señor. You see how they treat our dead. We must go now, don Abrahán." They shook hands. "Thank you for your good counsel. Goodbye, Naomi."

She held his hand. "Goodbye, dear Fernán. When I see you again, may there be a light in your eyes."

How could he say that she was the light in his eyes? That must wait for a better time. He bowed his head briefly and he and Jerónimo followed Mosé into the courtyard.

23

A meeting of the Converso Council, the Hernandes house

Two days later, all was quiet. The unsettling month of March opened to a taste of spring. Fernán sat on the ground with the other exhausted *conversos*, their backs against a wall, the long sword by his side, watching swallows flit about following paths their precursors had followed. In this year-in, year-out pattern, he found reassurance.

The rebels had vanished, melted away without warning. No shots were fired, no arrows sang their deadly tune. Children played on the street in the afternoon sunshine and families exchanged sympathies at the gravesides of fallen kin. Peace was distant, but Fernán prayed that fighting had blunted the rebel taste for blood. He was grateful for the respite but wary, as were the others who remained vigilant, ate quickly, and slept in battle dress.

Fernán had retained the long sword, though he was troubled when he held the weapon. Naomi had asked if one could be splendid and kill men and, though Jerónimo had defended his actions, Fernán was uncomfortable with his deadly talent. He could fight and kill, his mind cold and reactive, but killing was abhorrent to him and he was ill with its memory.

The day dragged. The pace of the past week lengthened the hours of this idle day. Fernán lay about waiting for the first flight of an arrow, his nerves taut, and relived the dark walk to the *judería* and the sight of Naomi. Almighty God, how he lived to see that dear face, kiss those sweet lips. But he dared think no further, for the furtive run to Zocodover Square flooded his mind and the image of its grisly contents distorted his dreams.

Evening, and the smells of cooking drifted up from kitchens where the women, tension relieved for a moment, unwound in song and chatter. And then supper—quiet, suspended.

Night fell and the council met in the Hernandes great hall. No meats or cheeses, bowls of fruit, dishes of pastries, or bottles of wine—food and drink were scarce among the *conversos*. Talk was quiet, faces somber. All came armed.

Fernán now sat with the other men, his prowess granting him the status age did not, while Jerónimo stood by the door, armed and alert. The air was charged when Fernán described the outrage done to Cibdad.

"Juan de la Cibdad was dead of gunshot," he said, "God bless his immortal soul. Despite that, they tied his dead feet together, lashed the rope to a saddle, and a rebel on horseback dragged the body slowly through the streets to Zocodover Square. All the while, the commoners threw stones at his corpse and lashed at the body with rope and branches and whatever implements they could find.

"Señores, these are the words of Mosé, apprentice to don Abrahán Melamed, who witnessed these events and recounted them to us. I repeat them as best I can."

"How could a Jewish apprentice have seen this?" Herrera asked.

"He wore a plain cloak and was disguised."

Fernán drank some wine. "When the body was delivered to the square, its clothing hung in shreds and it was covered with blood and dirt and the excrement people had thrown. A wooden platform and frame had been constructed and the body was hung by its feet, head down, its arms flailing about. The people pelted the poor body with stones and struck it with poles and clubs and shouted and cursed Cibdad, calling him swine and spawn of the devil. Then, their wits stretched beyond sanity, they took knives and swords to the mutilated corpse.

"Señores, here gentle Mosé stopped, for he was overcome with horror and ran from the square. But the shouts and screams of the crowd carried almost as far as the *judería* where he lives and where he told this to us."

Fernán stopped and cleared his throat. He was near nausea but drew a deep breath and curbed the impulse to retch.

"The hour was late when Jerónimo and I arrived at the square. The plaza was empty of people. Señores, I tell you what follows because it is my obligation. I would spare you these details but you should know the depth of derangement to which the people have descended—how far their hatred has borne them."

He coughed and waited a moment, quieting mind and body, distancing himself as best he could from the images he had seen.

"What hung from the rope could not be recognized as human. The rest of the body was scattered about the square. Dogs were at the remains."

Fernán excused himself and left the room. When he returned the men were deep in debate. He sat near his father and Lorenzo touched his arm. Fernán looked into the eyes of his father—they were wet with restrained tears. His father tried to smile. Fernán said quietly, "We will have our revenge, Papá."

Lorenzo was about to reply when they heard someone at the door. The men drew their swords. Jerónimo looked to Lorenzo, who said, "Open the door." Jerónimo opened the door and stepped aside and Bernardo de Cáceres stood at the doorway, his clothing torn and dirty, his right arm bound with a bloody cloth, his left arm raised to knock again. He started to speak, but Lorenzo went to him and said, "Sit with me, Bernardo. Jerónimo, if you please, fetch wine and bread."

Cáceres was short of breath and Lorenzo helped him sit.

"Do not speak, Bernardo, until you have eaten," Lorenzo said.

"I will eat after I speak." Cáceres closed his eyes. "I bear a message."

"Where have you come from, Cáceres?" Herrera asked.

"From the rebels. My right arm was cut in the battle and I could not hold my sword. I prepared to die, but one rebel told the others to take me to García and they led me from the battle. They tied a knot around my arm to stanch the bleeding and bound my eyes and hands and led me…somewhere. I waited in a small room. I could not see and I lay on the floor and slept, expecting to be taken from there and tortured. I was afraid I would tell them what they asked. I am not a brave man."

Jerónimo brought a jug of wine and a mug, a plate with bread and meat, and a knife. Cáceres took the mug and drank deeply, then closed his eyes a moment.

"How long I slept before they came for me I do not know, but I prayed to God to give me strength. They brought me to Sarmiento and unbound my eyes. I had met the man several times with my father and, after my father died, I saw him alone. He remembered me and asked about my arm."

"How is your arm?" Lorenzo asked.

"The bleeding has stopped, the pain is bearable. I have no feeling below the cut."

"Our doctor will examine the wound."

"Thank you." He looked up, his eyes weary. "Sarmiento said he wanted me to carry a message to the New Christians. He said New Christians, not *conversos* or *marranos*. For the first time I thought I might live and I said…I said that I would carry the message. He made me repeat his words until I had them by rote. This is his message."

'New Christians, lay down your arms. If you do so we will not attack. However, if you refuse, we will attack without mercy—confiscate your possessions, burn your buildings, and destroy your community. As for those who have been agents of Alvaro de Luna and opposed the rebellion, we ask you to lay down your arms and we will end the matter and release those who have been detained. We have removed all soldiers of the rebellion from the vicinity of your borough and have ceased offensive operations as a gesture of good will. Your response to this generous proposal must be delivered to the Alcázar by noon Sunday or we shall resume hostilities. There will be no further concessions.'

Cáceres looked at the faces around him. "That is his message."

"Sarmiento imitates a king," Herrera said.

"The King of Toledo," Silva said.

"But who trusts him? Was he sincere, Cáceres?"

"He appeared so."

"Those were his exact words?" Lorenzo asked.

"He forced me to memorize them."

The men wandered away and formed small groups, where they continued to argue the merit of the proposal and the consequence of refusal.

"Let us be seated, señores, and consider this matter," Lorenzo said.

Cáceres began to eat the food Jerónimo had brought. Fernán watched. His hunger seemed genuine—though Sarmiento was shrewd and would have starved a false messenger. Jerónimo had reminded Fernán of the words of Cáceres and his bent toward accommodation. Fernán needed no reminder. He remembered how Cáceres had spoken to Lorenzo and he continued to scrutinize the messenger. Cáceres glanced up at Fernán, his mouth working, his face without expression.

The men had taken seats and Silva said, "Señores, let us apply reason to these words. I argue for compromise. My company has been much reduced by this battle and I see little profit in fighting when we are made a proposal such as the one Cáceres has brought. I urge you to conserve your resources. What do we achieve by fighting tomorrow? We lose good men. Whereas, if we postpone the fight and accept the proposal, we will live until the King attacks and restores order to Toledo. The nobles want this tyrant out and out he will go. Sarmiento must surrender to the King eventually and, when he does, he will be punished and life will return to normal. I advise compromise, patience, and acceptance of the proposal."

"You believe his promise, don Arias?" Herrera asked.

"I have the opinion of Cáceres that Sarmiento appeared to be sincere, and I know what refusal will bring. But, señores, I do not share your dilemma—I can leave at any time with my men and my freedom. Therefore my judgment should carry little weight."

"Why should Sarmiento make this offer?" Husillo said. "How does it benefit him?"

"Does the nobility pressure Sarmiento to withdraw?" Herrera asked.

"I am not aware of pressure," Silva said. "That does not mean pressure is absent."

"Perhaps Sarmiento feels indirect pressure," Herrera said. "If he kills us, how can he make peace with King Juan—if that is his objective. He is outside the law now and further unlawful acts will compound his guilt. Though he is noble and, in that sense, beyond the law."

"Does killing *conversos* matter to the King or the nobility?" Fernán asked. "They are the law. But is Sarmiento his own man? Does he not answer to the commoners? They maintain him, and their actions will never be prosecuted. They could dismember a thousand Cibdads and never be held accountable. Don Bernardo, what does Sarmiento intend?"

Cáceres started. His presence had been ignored. "What do you ask?"

"What does Sarmiento intend?"

"He intends to withdraw if we lay down our arms."

"That is all he intends?"

"Who can say?"

"And you trust him?"

"Do I have a choice?"

"We all have a choice," Husillo said. "We must choose life or death—to lay down our arms or fight. I choose life."

"The life you choose may be your death," Herrera said. "Arias de Silva has said we should accept the proposal, that in doing so we will be alive when the King reconquers Toledo and rights the wrongs committed by the rebels. However, who is to say that Sarmiento will hold to his word or that the King will appear and punish the rebels. I say continue the fight and pray the King comes soon and behaves like a King. If we must die, we will die fighting, not torn to bits by commoners and dogs."

Fernán drew his father aside. "I do not trust Cáceres, Papá."

"Nor I, Fernán."

"Why then treat him with such gentility?"

"I am a gentleman."

"Of course, Papá, forgive me. What will happen now?"

"Silva will win the argument—if a tragic outcome can be called a victory. We will lay down our arms, there will be the semblance of peace, and persecution will resume. Sarmiento is the Devil and one does not make peace with the Devil—he enjoys tormenting poor souls. We will hide our weapons and pretend to love peace while we safeguard our homes and pray for deliverance. This peace will be short-lived."

24

The following day, the Alcázar of Toledo

Sarmiento sat at his writing table in the Alcázar twirling a quill between thumb and forefinger while he reviewed the week, composed his thoughts, and reduced its events to ink on paper. He followed the practice religiously, week by week—compiling daily notes and organizing them into logical categories and compact prose on Sundays. When so moved, he would play with words and poetize a verse in a manner foreign to prose or spoken language. These airings of hidden emotion he kept in yearly folios—as a history of his achievements, as amusement for a mind that required intellectual play of an order he rarely encountered in social intercourse, and as a source for some future when inspiration might be fallow.

His last entry included an evaluation of the attack against the *marranos* and the logic of the message he had sent to the so-called New Christians through Cáceres. One of his agents had reported the previous night that the wounded Cáceres said a final decision by the *marranos* had been postponed until morning, but that capitulation seemed assured. Now he must wait, though he was confident of surrender. They must capitulate, having suffered so many casualties. Nothing could be gained by further resistance.

García and he had broken their fast early that morning with bread and thick slices of ham. Sarmiento had washed down his food with a fermented concoction of honey and water encountered during a journey through England several years before and which, subsequently, he introduced to his cookery. The beverage generated only mild intoxication and was suitable to slake thirst at any hour.

García, however, drank red wine every day at all hours, and Sarmiento marveled at the volume García swilled without revealing a hint of inebriation. In fact, he thought García improved with drink—his vocabulary expanded, his responses sharpened, his wit grew more devastating. Manuela had laughed when he told her about the contrary effect of tippling on García. She taunted Sarmiento with, "My dear Pero is jealous of poor Marcos," and questioned whether the sexual prowess of the lawyer also benefited from drink.

"Convey your fermented García to me," she said, "and I will test his performance with and without wine and report to you—Excellency."

Sarmiento had been amused by the thought of rotund García bedding sleek Manuela, the impertinent, glorious bitch, but then he began to seethe at her insolence. She was too young to presume so much—her familiarity, her teasing was a trifle like taunting. She must know her place. His outrage, though, was interrupted by an orderly who announced that messengers from the New Christians had arrived.

"More than one?"

"Lorenzo Hernandes de Toledo, Excellency, accompanied by his son, Fernán, and his steward."

"Hernandes. This should be diverting. A wager, García," Sarmiento said, "a hundred *maravedís* the *marranos* have capitulated."

García lowered his wine glass and smiled. "You are too optimistic, don Pero. I would undoubtedly lose and I require *maravedís*—they comfort me."

"My comfort derives from gold as well, but indirectly," Sarmiento said. "However, García, logic dictates that if the *marranos* agreed to our proposal they would reply, and not the opposite. We shall see." And he told the orderly to send in Hernandes and the others.

How long had it been? Three, four years, since he had seen Hernandes, since the man had sold him that miserable rug for his home and the carpet for Manuela at such an exorbitant price, and then included a few odd pieces of rubbish at no charge to obscure the insult. But Hernandes had not yet replaced the stained piece. These Jews—always some trick, some dissemblance.

Hernandes strode into the room accompanied by a tall youth with strong features and a confident air that Sarmiento found annoying. A Moor followed, a swarthy man of medium height with sharp features and black eyes pointed as daggers. They stood before the governor and bowed their heads briefly.

"So, Hernandes, a messenger now. A basketful of talents, señor."

"A minor talent, Your Excellency."

"And who is that with you?"

"My son, Fernán, and my steward, Jerónimo."

"Your boy has grown considerably since we last met. What is your age, young Hernandes?"

"Seventeen, Excellency."

"You appear older."

"So I am told, señor."

García sauntered over to the visitors and peered up at Fernán.

"I know this youth, don Pero," he said.

"Do you, indeed? Under what circumstance, García?"

"I happened along as young Hernandes was observing Galvez harangue a crowd outside the Cathedral shortly before the rebellion." He stepped back and looked Fernán up and down. "And did the people chastise you, young man?"

"No, señor. When defense fails, I run, and God has made me swift."

"A practical philosophy, though not always effective," Sarmiento said. "Is this the youth, Hernandes, of whom you boasted so brazenly when we first met?"

"Not boast, Excellency. My remarks were modest and accurate."

"So you say."

A soldier entered the room and whispered to the lawyer. García turned and asked, "Are you sure, Ruano?"

"There is no doubt, don Marcos."

García glared at Fernán. "Don Pero," he said, "Captain Felipe Ruano, assigned to the *marrano* borough, has informed me that we are in the presence of a master swordsman."

"What are you saying, García? I have no time for games."

"During the skirmish Friday, young Hernandes killed eight of our troops with his long sword and maimed an equal number."

Sarmiento walked around his table and confronted Lorenzo.

"Is this true, Hernandes?"

"The number may not be exact, but that is apparently what happened."

"Why apparently?"

"Fernán recalls the fight but not the details."

"Then convince me why he should not be arrested?"

"My son, my steward, and I are messengers, Excellency, unarmed and outmanned. Such an action would be unworthy of a nobleman."

"These are difficult times, Hernandes. Customs that apply to noblemen in times of peace may be discarded in times of war."

"Then do with us as you wish. However, if we fail to return to our people, the battle will resume, and your name will be blackened. I cannot imagine the King taking such an action lightly."

Sarmiento smiled. "King Juan is at Benavente, attacking my good friend Pimentel and, if I know the resources of count Alfonso Pimentel, Juan will be busy in Benavente for a long, long time. Do not depend on the King, Hernandes."

Sarmiento sat on the edge of the table, folded his hands across his stomach, and stared at the floor for a full minute. Then he said, "What your son did was done in the fury of battle and may be understood in that light." He sat absolutely still for a few more minutes before saying, very quietly, "Care to try me, young Hernandes?"

"Your Excellency mocks me," Fernán said. "I am young and inexperienced. The episode Friday was the result of uncontrolled passion—I was seized by rage. Would our purpose here be served by a match between us? I think not, Excellency. I think this visit should remain on a diplomatic level, untainted by emotion."

"My, my, Hernandes, who tutors this young man? I should hire him for my own. But he is correct." Sarmiento walked around the table. "So then, Hernandes, what have you brought me?"

"Our council has accepted your proposal, Excellency. We will lay down our arms. In turn, we expect your administration to abandon the arrests and persecution of our people."

"Persecution?" Sarmiento said. "When have we persecuted your people? You presume, Hernandes. Those who have been arrested and tried were agents of Alvaro de Luna. They admitted to treason. We have never persecuted New Christians, our brothers in faith."

"As you wish."

"Not as I wish but as it is." Sarmiento drew his sword. How sweet it would be to run this popinjay through and send back the corpse with his conceited bastard. However. He handed the sword to Fernán and said, "Tell me, young Hernandes, what does a master swordsman think of this weapon."

"Master of nothing, your Excellency. However, I see that this sword is a Rodríguez and beautiful, as are all swords made by that craftsman." Fernán balanced the weapon and then extended and swung the sword from side to side, watching the blade flex and feeling its heft. "Sad to say, there is a fault in the balance, and the blade responds with insufficient dash. Jerónimo?"

Handed the sword, Jerónimo performed similar moves and then nodded to Fernán. "I agree, young master. A beautiful weapon with severe faults."

"You are both wrong," García said. "I tested the sword."

"No, García, the boy is right. Rodríguez made beautiful but imperfect weapons." Sarmiento returned to his table and said, "Don Lorenzo, many thanks for your message. Our attack is halted. Go in peace."

He watched as Ruano escorted the *marranos* to the door. "One moment," he said, and the four turned at the doorway. "There is a matter of the deaths."

"But, Your Excellency, you dismissed us and forgave the deaths," Lorenzo said and stepped back into the room.

"I dismissed you, not your son, and I forgave nothing. I said that the deaths of our men at the hands of young Hernandes might be understandable, but said nothing about forgiveness. Death demands a price—the widows must be compensated, the law obeyed."

"What price?" Lorenzo asked.

"How much are dead men worth, Hernandes? Let us ignore the wounded. I suggest we apportion the cost—a cash penalty, some merchandise, a banishment. That seems reasonable."

Lorenzo attempted to walk toward Sarmiento but was blocked by Ruano. "To pay a penalty, Your Excellency, may be reasonable. We will pay the penalty and bring you merchandise to select from, but banishment is not reasonable."

"Hernandes, how can you fail to understand? Eight of my people are dead and eight others suffered grievous wounds, all at the hand of your son. Many others died or were wounded during the battle, but his actions were the most grave. The people must be served and I am their servant. If left to their own devices, the people would demand death for the offender. And here I place my life in jeopardy by offering you an alternative and, as thanks, have your ingratitude. I offer you a modest payment and that the offender should leave Toledo as retribution and you question my charity? How can you insult me by refusing such a reasonable offer? What offer could be more modest?"

"But, Your Excellency, Fernán is my only son and young."

"Old enough to kill, old enough to be exiled."

"Then we must break off negotiations. Your conditions are unacceptable."

"Do you realize what that means, Hernandes? We will fall on your community with all our resources—which are considerable, as you know. We will destroy your homes. Your people will be decimated, the entire New Christian community of Toledo will be demolished. Nothing will remain. Is this what you want?"

Fernán spoke quietly to his father and Lorenzo shook his head.

Sarmiento threw up his hands. "Well then, have it your way. In light of our past acquaintance, you may choose an older substitute. A small price to pay for the survival of your community. But do not insult me, Hernandes. I will not be so lenient again. You have a brother. I recall you have two. Choose one and be content it is not your son."

Lorenzo bowed his head. Fernán spoke to him, and again Lorenzo shook his head. "No," he said to Fernán, "I will not allow it."

Sarmiento yawned. "Enough of this chatter—this endless contention exhausts me. So like you to haggle, Hernandes. Raise the money, collect the merchandise, choose a brother—but let me know your decision by first light tomorrow, no later. And you must replace that rug you sold me for so exorbitant a price. The material does not reject simple stains. Now go quickly before I think again."

Lorenzo was about to speak when Ruano pushed him out the door.

Fernán stared at the captain and Ruano drew his sword and slammed the door behind the four of them.

Sarmiento sprang to his feet, laughing, "I told you it would be diverting."

"We should arrest that young snip."

"No, don Marcos, that would be wrong, absolutely not. Who knows what those *marranos* might do in their anger. Young Hernandes has become a hero to them—they might go berserk, and then our troops, to right the wrong, might destroy the entire enclave. There are many fine buildings the *marranos* have constructed filled with silver, gold, and other merchandise of great value. I covet those buildings and currency—for our cause. Be patient, friend. Their guard is down, their taste for battle soured. They will provide a brotherly exile and we will police their borough and take them singly, judiciously."

"How, judiciously?"

Sarmiento sat on the windowsill and tapped on the glass. "These lovely days stretch before us like beckoning virgins, García, do you not think so? Nevertheless, one lovely day, very soon, the King will awaken from his dream of hate and realize that he has a kingdom to manage and that we defy him, and his royal anger will shift to Toledo. When that occurs we may need the law as a buckler—a shield, not a weapon. Therefore, if we arrest these *marranos*, try them, and eliminate them, it must be for cause."

"You confuse me, don Pero. As a lawyer, I am paid to confuse others and am not easily bewildered. But for what cause can we arrest them that we have not used? We have accused them of connivance with Luna. Why not continue to do so?"

Sarmiento stared out the window. He never tired of observing clouds reconfigure themselves against the blue Toledan sky. Today, the sky was magnificent with cloud puffs scattered throughout the heavens. His mind, though, was empty. He had no cause for arrest other than conspiracy, and conspiracy was a weak argument—difficult to prove and difficult to promote among a people who sympathized with conspirators. Was not conspiracy the precursor of rebellion, and were not the commoners rebels? No, there must be another stick with which to beat this dog. Oh, Manuela, I have grown sick of this game. Take me to your arms, Uelita, envelop me in your warmth, let me enter your portals and release this pain.

Manuela. Yes, what was it Manuela had said last night as they lay entwined in bed, her clever fingers busy between his thighs? No, those were not her words but those of Clara at dinner. When? A month ago? Clara? How in the blessed name of God could he confuse mistress for wife? But what had Clara said? Something about a difference. Yes, yes. How do *marranos* differ from us, she had asked, we are all Christians? Or words much like that. And he had answered that *marranos* were the progeny of Jews and that was a chasm they could never cross. We are descended from Castilians, our blood is pure, while their bloodline is the polluted effluent of Jews.

"Precisely, our blood is pure," Sarmiento said and turned to García. "They were Jews, García. *Marranos* were Jews. If we prove they are now Jews, that they never truly accepted Jesus, what then?"

"Then they would be heretics, don Pero. The Church would find them guilty of heresy, relax them to us, and thus avoid blood on its pure white hands. We would burn them or throttle them or both. And with Archbishop Carrillo in Benavente with the King, Galvez is now Vicar and controls the judicial offices of the Church in Toledo. Therefore, conviction of those apprehended would be assured. Excellent thought. Most impressive. How do we start?"

"Start? Well, you are a fine orator, don Marcos. You will address the populace in the Cathedral. Expand on the theme of Jews and Christians who betray our Lord through pretense and such drivel, and the tune will play on the fear and hatred of the people. We require their compliance and support. Then…but let us discuss this later at some length. My thoughts race ahead of me and I sleep poorly and need rest."

"What a trap we will spring, don Pero. What a trap for those swine. We will take those *marranos* by the throat and strangle them."

"Yes, of course, García." Sarmiento returned to the window and the white clouds that transformed themselves endlessly in a sky blue as the eyes of his mistress—product of a Visigoth in the bed of her great-grandmother, no doubt. Now that the plan had been designed, he had lost interest. His mind flew elsewhere. Details remained, but they were trivia that García could manage. There were more important matters for his attention.

A pity young Hernandes refused to play at swords. How he would have loved to tickle the ribs of that boy with his imperfect weapon. The hothead had been right, though—a blade should be flexible and the balance perfect. Ah well, he would refine the weapon and then play—soon. And he smiled at the sky.

25

The Cathedral of Toledo

García sat through the bulk of the Mass reviewing what he would say. He knew that words would come as always, unbidden, responding to an inner call, responding to the faces of the people, his people. Among those faces in the nave was Sarmiento, seated in the first pew, a seat befitting his position. He sighed. This partnership with Sarmiento had become such a contest. At times he thought the man mad, at other times, a genius. García understood that was the way with brilliant men—their minds overwhelm them, occasionally drown them, inducing impotence in the face of conflicting themes.

His temperament was not the same as that of Sarmiento. His mind was clear, analytical, like that of his father. Choice came to him through careful study. He would weigh benefits, balance negatives, and make deliberate choices. That was his strength. He was imperfect, aware of his sins, his faults—fond of many of them. His strengths, though, made his faults possible, in fact, desirable. He would be nothing without his faults—a bundle of dull strengths without joy.

This morning, his sermon, if it could be called that, would twist these little people into a fierce knot, a cudgel with which to strike *marranos*. Don Pero had called it a tune. García thought anthem more appropriate. He would compose the anthem note by note, measure by measure, so that it resounded like a clarion. And as he had called them to battle *marranos* before, so he would call them to judge *marranos* now. But not yet. Save passion for the pulpit.

The Mass had ended and Lope de Galvez, Vicar of the Cathedral, his dear friend, nodded to him. García was a bit faint. Many nobles and councilors, now ineffectual but potentially alarming and indisputably the hereditary rulers of the city, were seated in their customary pews. The rebellion had taxed his traditional loyalty to the King, the secular Vicar of God in Castile, and to those chosen by God to rule Toledo. Had it not been for *marranos*, García would be a true and loyal subject of the King. But one cannot swear allegiance to a King who permits swine to rule his kingdom.

Patience. Step by step we will pull them down. Another step today. Would he do well? Could he persuade the people that *marranos* constitute a menace that must be destroyed while protecting his own innocence, his neutrality? Prayer had always escaped him. Instead, he relied on a muse that hovered within him—his guardian angel, his pagan spirit—he knew not what to call it, except that he knew these otherworldly creatures abounded despite the disbelief of the Church. He would be foolish to deny them, as his priestly friends encouraged him to do. García knew better. He knew they delivered his strength and led the words from his mouth, and he blessed their power, whatever the source.

He rose from the wooden bench on which he had listened to Mass, the surface of the bench polished by the innumerable rumps it had accommodated, and stood for a moment gathering his strength and will. After a moment, he walked to the stairs leading up to the pulpit and stopped to gaze at the ceiling high above the altar—the windowed, groined structure fashioned like a giant starfish he had once seen on the Aragón shore, supported by scaffolding which hid much of the layer upon layer of ecclesiastic gold ornament that embellished the depiction of the saints and their works, beginning at the ground and stretching to twenty or so feet below the crest. In his mind, he saw the remainder supporting further saints and, at the top, the golden figure of the crucified Jesus, His arms outstretched.

García breathed softly. "Find me worthy, dear Lord," he said. He mounted the spiral steps, counting the number until he arrived at the pulpit. Thirteen. Unlucky? Not likely within this house. He grasped the edges of the lectern and turned his grave face to the people.

Their faces were blurred. His eyes had weakened in recent years—near and large objects were all he could see clearly. A mortal impediment for a swordsman. He had scarcely seen the point of the sword when he dueled Sarmiento. But the Governor never knew and never would. Sarmiento was seated, waiting. He recognized the commanding figure even though the face was indistinct. They had discussed what García would say, how he would proceed with the attack.

"A religious attack is pure," don Pero had said. "It requires no proof such as is demanded when one must prove treason and collusion, such as the proof we forced out of those we punished. The people understand heresy without proof. The idea appeals to their love of Christ and abiding hatred of the Jew. They are won to our side before the first word is spoken."

García needed no explanation. The rationale was built into his heritage. And so he began.

"Dear friends and neighbors. We have met in this glorious Cathedral before. When last we met it was to protest the tax imposed by Alvaro de Luna, a tax that was to be collected by Alonso Cota the *marrano*, now fled."

Were the whispers throughout the audience the effect of unease or joy? Never mind, the people will respond.

"When last we met, we gathered our forces and defeated that unfair tax. We defied Alvaro de Luna and captured Toledo. We arrested many *marranos* who had collaborated with Luna and punished them severely, as you well know. And when the *marranos* barricaded their quarter, all of us, under the leadership of our brave Governor, don Pero Sarmiento, attacked the *marrano* quarter, won a magnificent victory, and received a surrender from their forces, payment of a penalty, and banishment of their leader. Sadly, some of you lost loved ones during that encounter and for those lost we offer our prayers for everlasting life at the side of our Lord, Jesus Christ. Amen."

A murmur of amens flowed through the nave.

"Now my dear friends, I have told you I was born Castilian and am pure of blood as you are. Like you I have been exploited by *marranos* and wondered why I was so badly used. Why are these so-called brethren of mine antagonistic? You may remember that when we last spoke I reminded you that *marranos* were the descendants of Jews—surely not a new thought. But I did not tell you that which was hidden from me then and what you must know now."

"What must we know, don Marcos?" A clear voice from the floor.

"What you must know is this." And he looked from left to right of a great blur. "Although I said that these *marranos* were Jews, that their grandparents and great-grandparents were Jews, what I did not say, what I have since learned, is that the *marranos* who live in our city *today* are Jews."

A great intake of breath and undertone of whispering. Some in the front pews, the nobles and councilors, spoke out in their normal voices. "Nonsense. The fellow is mad. Why should we stay and listen to this?" And others behind them cautioned, "Be quiet. You know nothing. We must hear. He is better informed than you."

García waited until there was silence. "What I have told you some know already, is that not so? But many in this sacred hall do not know and need to be informed. And that is my holy duty—to reveal the truth. For now, today, these so-called *conversos*, these so-called New Christians, these *marranos*, practice the accursed laws of Moses."

The nave erupted with opposing voices. "No, it cannot be. Yes, it is true. It cannot be so. No? Well, I know it, I have seen them myself. I have seen it."

"Dear neighbors," García intoned over the crowd, "I have learned that these *marranos* express their abhorrence of our holy days by observing the holy days of the Jews. Now, today, they eat no pork, nor milk with meat, and practice the other dietary laws of the Jews. Now, today, they are Jews and practice the old religion that was denounced by Jesus Christ and his Apostles and by all the saints."

Several men in the front pews stood and called out, "You spread vicious lies, García. Your soul will burn in hell for falsifying within these walls. Yours is the voice of the Devil." And they walked out of the church accompanied by their families amid shouts from the rear of the nave. Those shouting shook their fists and were barely restrained by the holiness of the place from striking blows against those leaving.

"Peace, my friends, peace!" García cried. The Cathedral quieted. "Let them go. They are friends of heretics."

"Heretics!" they shouted. "Heretics!"

García was pleased with the reaction. "These people who call themselves *conversos,* who claim conversion to Catholicism, who have submitted to baptism and submitted their children to baptism, sin against the Church. These *marranos* who masquerade as Christians while knowing that they do not accept Jesus Christ, that they cannot accept Jesus Christ in their hearts, know that they profane the sacrament because they know their blood is foul. These *marranos* are the brood of Satan."

Shouts of "Yes, yes!"

"They are not Christians like you and me, they do not worship our God, our Lord Jesus Christ. They do not accept the sacred doctrine of the Trinity nor do they accept the Holy Testament. And why? Why is that? Why do they reject all that is holy to you and to me and to our Church? Because they cling with obstinate tenacity to the teachings of Moses and cannot accept the truth of Christ and his mission on earth. And, dear friends," he hesitated and then spoke with revulsion in his voice, "they seek the downfall of our Holy Church."

"Never, never!" The people rose to their feet as one and screamed into the air, and the sound reverberated off the walls of the Cathedral. "We will defend our Holy Church to the death! Bless our Church! Bless Jesus! Keep us from the Devil and his evil brood! Save us from the Devil!"

García knew he must bring them down from this climactic outburst to a more rational state. And so he held up his arms and used the full power of his voice.

"Dear friends! We must reason together. We must take action to protect our Church—but only through reason. If you please, let me proceed."

The people submitted to his call, abandoned their wild pleadings, and resumed their seats, waiting to hear what García would say.

"Thank you, gentle folk. Thank you." He waited until the nave was again quiet. "Though we know these *marranos* are evil, were that all we knew, we could forgive them their ignorance and hatred, for Jesus Christ directs us to forgive our enemies and bring them to the truth and so we should. Were these *marranos* Jews in name as well as in practice, we would pity their ignorance and teach them the truth. But in fact they are Christians in name and hidden Jews in practice, and that is a grave deceit and we call that deceit heresy. Yes, heresy. For these Jews in Christian garments are heretics and must be punished for their transgression. They and their children and their grandchildren were baptised in the Holy Church and partake of the Eucharist, and their transgression from the laws of the Church, from the dogma of the Roman Catholic Church, must be punished. For there is one law and that law is the canon of the Roman Catholic Church by which all who are baptized are bound and must obey, and transgression from that law must be punished."

"Punish them, punish them!" The chant rose and filled the Cathedral, and García let it swell and diminish in its own time.

When there was quiet, García spoke. "My friends, there are some among the *marranos* who are sincere in their devotion to our Church. These souls we must treasure. We must take care to find only those who have committed grievous acts against the Church—heretical acts. But you ask, how shall I know them, these hypocrites? And I will tell you—by their acts shall you know them.

"Look about you. Do you see a *marrano* who lights candles on Friday nights? A *marrano* in her best clothes on the Sabbath of the Jews? Do you see a *converso* who does not observe Sunday as the holy day of the Lord? Do you see a *marrano* who walks with Jews. Do you know a New Christian who will not eat pork? These *marrano*s are Jews, no matter that they wear the garments of Christians. And as good Christians you must go to your priest and report them, for they are secret Jews, heretics, and traitors to Toledo, to Castile, and to Christianity. We must find them and pluck them from the fabric of the Holy Church."

He continued for another quarter hour detailing who was heretic and what they should do, and the people responded and blessed him and he blessed them and they left the church. García was dizzy with fatigue. This short talk to a friendly audience had sapped his strength. He had given much longer speeches to hostile crowds. But had he accomplished his task? He thought he had. He needed wine, but there was none except the sacramental wine and it was watered and he would have none of that. The church was silent and he sat on the wooden bench on the altar and gathered his thoughts. Galvez had gone and Sarmiento as well. He had hoped don Pero would have come to the dais and honored him with words of praise.

"Well done, don Marcos." He would stand in the iridescent light of the altar, smiling, his grand head haloed by golden saints.

"I am drained, don Pero."

"You gave us everything today, don Marcos García de Mora. Your energy, your soul, your very being were your holy gifts to those fortunate ones in church this morning. Your everlasting soul is pure and blessed by God, brave man, and your energy will be replenished. Come, dear friend, let us enjoy a good dinner together and plan our future."

However, once García had completed his talk and thanked the audience and the good people of Toledo for their attendance, he waited in the pulpit raised high above the multitude and watched as the Cathedral emptied. Sarmiento remained seated until the nave was bare. Finally, the governor stood, glanced up at the pulpit for a moment, and walked out of the Cathedral without a sign or a word to García.

26

The Hernandes house, two weeks later

The house was still and dark, the moon new, and Fernán lay awake. He had fallen asleep instantly, as was his habit, but awakened some time later and lay in bed peering into the dark, not knowing why sleep had escaped him. Then it was clear. Antonio had left the house, banished from Toledo, and the fault was his. Had he not taken up the long sword and killed and maimed rebels, Antonio would be asleep in a room above him with María. Had he protested more forcefully that he, Fernán, should accept the banishment.... Dear God, forgive me.

"Antonio," he had said, "I must accept this exile. It is my due and a sentence I can bear." But he knew neither Antonio nor Lorenzo would permit him to be banished—they would die first.

"Nephew," Antonio said, "I will go because I have no children and Cesario must recover from his wounds. Do not be disturbed. I am familiar with strange places and customs. Do I not travel frequently to foreign countries in pursuit of business for the family? I will continue that pursuit, Fernán, and we will be rich." Antonio held him and looked into his eyes. "Soon King Juan will reclaim Toledo and he will take this Sarmiento and hang him in Zocodover Square. Then I will return." And he laughed in a bluff way Fernán knew was unlike his uncle, a facade that concealed his honest sentiment.

Over two weeks had passed since Antonio had ridden away and Fernán now mourned as if his uncle were dead—worse, as if Fernán had killed him. Tonight Antonio should be in Toledo and Fernán in some foreign city or roaming a strange countryside—not an altogether bleak prospect. If the courage to convince his father had been his, this wound in his gut would not burn, this guilt that woke him in the dark, his heart pounding.

Fernán slipped out of bed, took the candlestick from the table beside his bed, walked the few steps to the smoldering fire, and selected a hot coal with a pair of tongs. He blew on the coal, lit the candle, and watched a shower of sparks from the dying embers retreat up the chimney. Naked and chill, he replaced the candlestick, crept into bed, and let his thoughts drift.

He could not understand why Antonio had not taken María with him. The morning Antonio left, the family had gathered in communal sorrow in the street outside the house.

"The way is fierce and dangerous and no place for a woman," Antonio said.

"Then how can you go, husband?" María said, her eyes swollen with tears.

"I am not a woman, María, as you well know," and he kissed her.

Fernán had never seen his aunt and uncle express affection openly, and his heart broke for them.

"The climate in Toledo will change," Antonio said. "When it does I will return."

"And will I be here?"

"Where else in this blessed world would you be, María?"

"Nowhere, except with you. But we live in strange times and who can know what will happen. Oh, go quickly, husband, I cannot bear this endless leaving."

Antonio mounted his big dappled horse and rode off, his servant following on a mule bundled with goods, provisions, and clothing. After horse and mule and riders disappeared beyond the curve in the road, María turned to Fernán who stood beside her and held him so hard he lost his breath. Her rhythmic sobs crushed her breasts and belly against him and his guilt stifled the reassuring words he should have spoken. Blanca, the wife of Cesario, took María in her arms and led her weeping sister-in-law into the house.

His mother took Fernán aside. "Be wary, son," she said.

"What of, Mamá?"

"María. She is tender now. Her soul is raw, exposed, her heart bruised." His mother looked into his eyes with great sadness and said, "She loves you, Fernán."

"I love her."

"Of course. I know. You have loved her since you were a baby, but as a baby and a young boy loves. María, though, is a woman who needs the strength of a man. I see how she looks after you when you leave—not as an aunt looks at her nephew, but as a woman who hungers for a man."

"I have done nothing to encourage her, Mamá. Have I done something wrong?" he asked.

"You have done nothing wrong, Fernán dear. I tell you this so that you may be aware. Women are complex—wanting to please, wanting to be protected, to be loved. I do not want you or María hurt. Nor do I want a scandal. María is like another child to me and, all at once, you are a man. Be cautious, son."

Her words confused him. She had never spoken to him about such things. And so he became cautious as his mother advised and, when María approached, he managed to be polite but somewhat distant. Her eyes were quizzical, amused by his changed attitude.

"Are you cross with me, Fernán?" she asked.

"Certainly not, María. How could I be? I have no cause to be."

"You are much different than you were." She smiled. "Are you in love?"

"What? Why would you think that?"

"Because you are a young man and young men fall in love."

"No, María, I am not in love. Other young men may fall in love, but my mind is distracted by important events." And he made an excuse and removed himself.

His love for Naomi was sacred and not for gossip. But he had not seen Naomi for almost a month. March had passed and spring had come and he was sick with longing. Jerónimo carried notes to Naomi, since Fernán could not continue to make excuses for visits to their house, and Jerónimo was party to his secret and adept at subterfuge. Then, last Thursday, while Melamed visited relatives in a small town north of Orgaz, Jerónimo arranged for Fernán to meet Naomi in the Melamed courtyard. Patrols still roamed the streets, but their vigilance had been tempered by the long siege that was not a true siege, and patrols rarely stopped anyone.

The moon was shy of full and he waited impatiently for Naomi to open the courtyard door. When he heard the latch, he burst through.

"Oh, Fernán," she said, laughing, "you are sudden."

He kissed her and she took his hand and said, "Come sit with me on our bench."

"Don Abrahán is here?" he asked.

"No, he left this morning and will be gone for several days."

"May we go inside?"

"I think it best if we sat here," she said. "The wind has eased and the night is mild."

He smiled. "Do you trust me?"

"I do, Fernán. We may go in if you would like."

"No, we will sit here. The weather has turned warm."

He kissed her brow and cheek and lips and, holding her, became conscious of the delicate substance of her body.

"I feel the bones in your back," he said.

"And I can feel your muscles. You must be strong."

"What do you know of muscles?"

"I assist Grandpapá in his work sometimes. I know the body and how it is made and what each part does—as much as Grandpapá knows." Her expression was serious. "I am not a foolish girl. I could be a doctor if it were allowed. Grandpapá said so."

She smiled and he laughed and looked at her with wonder.

"This separation is so cruel," he said.

"What can we do?"

"Is your grandfather still opposed to our friendship?"

"Were ours a friendship, dear Fernán, Grandpapá would be content. But you know that you and I are more than friends and so does he."

"Some day, Naomi, we will marry. I promise you."

"Why promise what you cannot fulfill, Fernán?" There were tears in her eyes. "You know we can never marry."

He kissed her lips and neck, then knelt and held her and kissed her dress at the swell of her breast. She sighed and he placed his head in her lap. She fondled his hair and he could feel the softness of her thighs against his cheek. "I will allow you almost everything, Fernán, because I love you," she said. "But we must take care that our love is more than passion."

Fernán returned home, after several hours of kisses and caresses and joint explorations through layers of clothing, floating on a swell of unfulfilled desire—tormented physically but transformed. Nothing was the same—the world was filtered through the prism of his love with colors and qualities richer than any he had known. Could he have flown, he would have found it natural. She is magic, he thought. In his room, he undressed, touched his swollen organ and, released from torment, lay on his bed in a state of reverie, blessing Naomi.

Two days later he returned to the Melamed house. A strong wind blew, carrying with it the last chill of winter. They sat in the garden and Naomi told him that don Abrahán had returned from Orgaz. Something in her demeanor disturbed him and he tried to kiss her but she demurred and he asked if she was well.

"Very well, thank you," she said. Then she walked to the gate and opened it and he followed. Her arms were crossed beneath her breasts. She looked at the ground. "I must tell you, Fernán...." She glanced at him and sighed. "Something has happened over which I have no control. I am not content saying this. I have been free all my life. I have done my chores and respected my Grandpapá and loved him—but my life was my own. Now my life is not my own and I am ruled and no longer free to see you."

"Why? What has happened?"

"Grandpapá has arranged for me to marry."

"How can he have done that?" He tried to hold her but she disengaged from him. "Who is he?"

She shook her head. "What does it matter?"

"He is a Jew and I am a Catholic. Is that the reason?"

"Fernán, if you wish to please me, do not torment yourself. The affair is settled, the contract signed. Nothing can change." She turned away from him. "Nothing can happen between us."

He held her arms and forced her to face him. "I must speak to don Abrahán."

"No, Fernán. Grandpapá is fond of you, but he will not see you. And if he did…." She shrugged and lowered her head.

"Look at me, Naomi. You knew this before."

Her gaze was steady. "What did I know?"

"That don Abrahán would arrange this marriage. You knew when last I saw you—when you let me hold you, when we kissed and I touched you. You knew then."

"I knew nothing, Fernán. How can you think that? Grandpapá spoke of the possibility of marriage, but it was in the future—far off in the future." She raised her hand but then lowered it. "I could not have let you touch me if I was betrothed."

"When will you be married?"

"Later. In the spring." She faced him. "Fernán, nothing can change what has happened, not even our love. I would kiss you gladly. I would hold you and let you love me and revel in our pleasure of one another, but I cannot—not now. Do you see? It is not allowed. We must not be with one another."

She stared at him. "I must go, Fernán. Now I will not have Grandpapá or you. I am alone. I have no one. Do you understand? Goodbye, Fernán." And she walked toward the house.

He followed her for several steps, and she turned to him. "Fernán, dear, sweet friend, do not make me cry. Do not make this hurt more than it does." A pulse beat in his temple, and he stood rigid, then turned and walked through the open gate.

The wind blew in hard gusts down the street. His cloak was blown open but he felt nothing—neither wind nor cold—and he waited opposite the gate. The gate had blown open and swung back and forth with each gust of wind. He expected Naomi to return and close it. But the opening remained dark and he heard the door to the house close. He waited, hoping she would return, hoping to see her again, hoping that what she had said was a fantasy the wind would whisk away. He waited for a long time but she did not return and, at last, he walked down the street where they had walked together, toward home.

That was then. He covered himself with a blanket. He was a fool. For while he kissed her breast, don Abrahán was signing the marriage contract. And the doctor had told him that all that separated him from Naomi was a few drops of holy water. A few drops of water to which Fernán felt bound more by custom than belief. Why should custom separate them when they loved each other?

He tried to sleep, but realizing the futility of seeking what was denied him, opened his eyes and watched the candlelight flicker on the walls of his small room.

27

Some time later

In the cold depth of night, a floorboard creaked and a beam compressed with a sharp report. The creak came from the room above. Perhaps María, restless as he. Fernán had heard the sound before.

An unusual house. Reconstructed by his father and uncles after his grandfather died, the original building had been modified to provide accommodation for the three families. Each occupied one of three adjoining two-story structures atop two floors of common spaces. The central structure was home to Lorenzo, Celestina, and Beatriz, his young sister. Cesario and his wife, Blanca, and their four children occupied the right wing, and Antonio and María the left. The great hall, studies, and parlors comprised the upper common rooms, and on the ground floor were quarters for servants, pantry, buttery, and storage. Kitchen, bakehouse, armory, and stables for horses and carriages occupied smaller quarters behind the main building.

When he was thirteen, Fernán, the eldest of the children, had decided to sleep apart from the family and convinced his father after much argument to allow him to do so. His bedchamber was a small study off the great hall, a quarter the size of the bedchamber for Cesario and his wife, in which Lorenzo, Cesario, and he had met with Jerónimo after the steward returned from the sermon by García at the Cathedral. The meeting in his quarters was an accommodation to Cesario, who was slowly recovering from his wounds. They drew up chairs to the large bed.

"Did Sarmiento see you?" Fernán asked Jerónimo.

"No, Fernán. He was seated in the first pew and, had he seen me, would have thought me a brother, for I stole his disguise and dressed as a monk."

"Jerónimo," Lorenzo said, "wherever did you learn these deceptive skills?"

"You cannot have forgotten, don Lorenzo, that I was a slave and that a slave is an animal in the eyes of his master and must hide his humanity. Slaves must deceive or die. But, señor, permit me to tell you what was said." And he repeated the substance of the sermon.

Fernán sat up in bed. Did he hear steps in the great hall? The noise stopped and he lay back.

"Many Old Christians reproached García for his accusations, and stood and denounced him," Jerónimo had said. "Many from the best families. The commoners, though, shouted the Old Christians down and cursed them as they left the Cathedral."

"And what have you heard since?"

"Bad tidings, don Lorenzo. People say that *conversos* will be investigated for heresy and that Sarmiento has appointed a tribunal of judges for that purpose."

"What else would one expect from Sarmiento?" Cesario asked. "If it is true, and I trust it is, the judges might as well be Sarmiento, García, and Galvez. We will all be accused of heresy and, whether guilty or not, convicted and burned."

Again, steps in the great hall and then a quiet knock. Fernán seized the dagger from the table beside his bed.

"Fernán?" a voice whispered. The door opened. "I saw light beneath your door," María said. "I thought you might be awake."

"As you see, María, I am awake. Sleep forgot she was my friend."

"Why should that be, Fernán? Young men sleep like posts."

"Perhaps my life is moving too quickly. Now we *conversos* are accused of heresy and a tribunal appointed, and other happenings too distressing and numerous to recount, not the least of which is Antonio exiled. I should be the one exiled, not your husband."

"Antonio and I discussed his decision, Fernán. He will do well for *Hernandes y Familia* in the East. He has traveled extensively and you have not. His decision was correct. Accept it and do not let it keep you from sleep."

She was barefoot and her nightdress hung loosely about her body. The pale cloth was thin and there were shadows at her breasts and between her legs.

"And why are you awake, María?"

"For the same reason as you. I sleep and wake and sleep and wake and God knows that is poor rest." She sat on the edge of his bed. "May I stay with you and talk, Fernán, since you are awake? That is, if you will put your dagger aside."

"I had no idea who might be wandering about," he said, while replacing the dagger in its scabbard, "though I would have made a ludicrous figure fighting an intruder—naked but for a dagger, like an ancient Greek."

"Indeed, you would have cowed me, señor. I would have submitted in an instant," she said, smiling. "You wear no night clothes?"

"Never. They twist around and make me restless. Then I turn and they twist even more."

María laughed. "What a curious young man you are, Fernán."

She sat on his bed and he became aware of her scent. "Is this wise, María? What if you are seen?"

"And who will see me? The house sleeps and we are merely talking."

"If a servant saw you leave this chamber and said something to someone who said something to another someone, as he might, there would be a scandal."

"Poor dear Fernán, you have become a worrier." She yawned. "I am so tired, yet I cannot sleep and the night is cold. May I lie near you?" He stared at her, his mouth open. "Go ahead, silly, move over. You forget that when I was first married and came to this house you were a babe and I bathed you and cleaned your mess when your mother was indisposed. I know your body as well as she. Your nakedness frightens me not at all."

"I am no longer a babe and you frighten me, María."

"No, Fernán, you frighten yourself and for no reason. Would you turn this pitiful woman aside when I cry for help? I am alone, dear heart. I need your warmth."

Reluctant and apprehensive, he slid across the bed and turned his back. She raised the cover and lay beside him. "Oh, the bed is so very warm where you were. Can your body be that warm?" And she touched his hip.

"Ah," he cried, "your hand is cold."

"Then I will warm my hands between my thighs and you will not be chilled. There. They are warm now."

She moved closer and he could feel her soft breasts against his back and, through her linen, the roundness of her warm thighs against his buttocks.

"You are not prudent, María. You should not behave this way."

"Why?" she said, "What have we done but keep warm and talk." She slid one arm under and the other over his body and held him against her. "Now I am truly warm."

"And I am truly frightened."

"Why frightened, dear Fernán? This is your Auntie María, not a stranger." Her arms closed around his middle and lay against his belly, and her thighs pressed against the backs of his thighs. "That is better. Now tell me about the girls you know."

"I know no girls."

"Oh, but you do. I have a spy in the other camp, a friend with eyes and ears. Though my father disowned me and considers me dead for converting to marry Antonio—his loss, poor man, and mine—there are some who pity me and will nod or say hello, though I hide my face from them. Most ignore me. Except one, my oldest friend who loves me, and she has warned me of the Melamed girl."

He turned toward her.

"Your secret is sealed in my heart, dear Fernán. I love you, sweet boy. I would die rather than hurt you. Be calm. Tell me your story of love and let me live through your words."

Her touch and the warmth of her body had roused him, but now he was relaxed and he lay on his back and told her about Naomi and their love, her refusal to convert, and the approaching marriage.

"Naomi is dead to me, María, as you are to your family. She was so cold when I last saw her, so different than she had been." He looked at her. "But why would your friend warn you about Naomi? Does she think Naomi would harm me somehow?"

"No, Fernán. I used the wrong word—I meant that she informed me."

"I wish Naomi had informed me earlier about the marriage. I might have done something. She must have known. Don Abrahán would not have surprised her with so final a contract. And why would she not let me speak to the doctor? Yet she said she loved me. She had no right to trifle with me so, to make me love her. I have suffered pain I did not know the world allowed. I no longer trust her or any woman. I thought in my madness that if I prayed, God in his bounty would return her to me. But she does not trust God and, besides, I want her no more—not now. I never knew her and I hate what.... And my prayers are Catholic and cannot govern Jews. I no longer desire to see her. I only pray that our family will be reunited and happy."

"Take heart, dearest Fernán," María said, "so many beautiful girls live in Toledo. You will find someone. Naomi is young and a young woman has no control over her life. She meant no harm. You will find another girl to comfort your youth."

And she kissed his face and stroked his hair and he was aroused again and embarrassed by his tumidity.

"When you were small, Fernán," she said, "you would sometimes come into my bed and your little friend would raise his head and I would kiss him," and she laughed.

"María."

"Be still, Fernán. God made us to enjoy our lives, and to enjoy life one must be free of fear and open to pleasure. And those were such innocent days.

Oh, Fernán, you are my angel and I love you for the comfort you have always brought me."

Then she lay her head on his chest and breathed, "I am afraid of Lorenzo."

"Afraid of Papá? Why? He loves you."

"I have no child. And with Antonio banished, Lorenzo may send me away." She put her finger to his mouth. "No, Fernán, let me say what I fear. We are not of the same flesh—you and I, your father and I. There is no blood warmth for me in his heart. He thinks of me as a Jew and therefore a threat, especially now. I sing a harmless Ladino song and he rebukes me. He is afraid and fear breeds distrust and distrust, hatred."

"He cannot hate you, María."

"Not yet, perhaps. But let this persecution continue and witches will pop out of the fire. We will all seek shelter and those without shelter will burn." She raised herself and half-lay above him, her full breasts almost visible through the neck of her dress. "I want a child, Fernán. I need a child. With a child my life would have value and meaning. Why am I here in this world? Am I a plaything? Am I here to bake bread and attract the eyes of men—to satisfy desire with no end in mind but sexual pleasure? No, Fernán, I am here to be a wife and a mother and though I am a wife, my husband wills me to remain barren."

She lay back and took his hand and laid it on her stomach. He withdrew his hand and she replaced it and held it there. "We love each other, you and I, and what I say to you I would say to no other person in this world." She put her other hand on top of his. "Antonio wants no children. He believes children he would father would be mules in this world—not Jew, not Catholic, without being—as he feels about himself. When we lie together he spills his seed where your hand and mine now lie. No argument of mine, no pleading, no tears can convince him to do otherwise."

María turned to Fernán, lay on his chest, and whispered quickly in his ear. "Sweet Fernán, lend me your seed that God may create life within me. As God gave Hagar to Abraham when Sarah was barren, let Him give you to me that He may bring forth new life within me. God will look down on us and approve our act as He blessed Abraham and Sarah in their old age with the child Isaac. And I will bless you for your beloved self, for the solace you bring me, for the refuge you afford me."

Fernán turned from her. "María, think what you have said. You are a married woman. You are my aunt. We would be committing a sin, as we now most probably are, and be damned to everlasting fire by God and the Church."

"Oh, Fernán, do you truly believe that?"

"You do not?"

"Of course not. Who are priests to instruct us in the thoughts of God? We speak to God through our hearts, not through some middleman who takes his profit from our penance. You and I are not blood relatives. God loves us and loves our lives and protects us from improper relations through His laws. But all laws allow exceptions, Fernán, and God would allow this exception."

"And if you were to have a child, who would Antonio believe was the father?"

"Himself. Oh, Fernán, I am so ashamed to beg love, to steal life from you." She whispered, "Antonio lay with me the night before he left and, as I sensed he was about to discharge his seed, I closed him inside me and held his body tight with all my strength and I felt him release within me. He was very angry and had good reason to be since I disobeyed him. But I told him that I was not fertile and calmed him and he was appeased.

"I did not lie, my sweet. My time was unseasonable and I knew I had not conceived. Then Antonio was gone and I was desperate with fear and I thought of you and I waited. I would seduce you, I thought. But I cannot, dear soul, I love you too much. I cannot trick you, Fernán, I can only beg you, as you love me, to grant me your gift of life so that I may live through my child."

"I am a young man, María, and you have posed me a problem fit for a Solomon. Would Jewish law allow such behavior?"

"No more than Catholic law. But the ancients were much wiser than we about the generation of life. Life was more precious to them. This is a matter, love, where law must be ignored, where we must search our hearts for the sanction of God. I examined my heart before I came to you and found no obstacle."

She sat cross-legged on the bed before him.

"Consider this, sweet Fernán. Do you know women? Let me teach you so that you may please your love and not fumble or be coarse like some ignorant youth. And as we proceed, nothing will prevent you from saying, 'Stop, María,' and we will stop. Regard what I will say and do as I instruct you. Love is both science and art with pleasure as its reward so that, as you might study a new language with Jerónimo, I will instruct you in another idiom."

He began to protest but she closed his mouth and continued. "How else will you learn of women, my sweet, except from some whore who will take your money and leave you with the pox and no knowledge? And then you may become weak and never be able to father a child."

Fernán was deeply troubled. María had been the focus of his fantasies for as long as he could remember, and to have her revealed to him in a way he thought morally questionable, if not totally wrong, was a misery worse than ignorance. As for Naomi, she had gone from him and he had no faith that prayer would prompt her return. Why should he not pity María? Why should she be denied that which God and nature had intended her to have and for which she was so well endowed? He would steal nothing, kill no one. The impulse was positive, affirmative, life-giving. The work of his sword would be balanced. Life beat strongly within him and gradually he became amenable to persuasion. He sighed.

"What has your heart told you, Fernán?"

"My heart remains troubled though my reason is persuaded. But if my heart disagrees with my actions as we progress, I will say, 'Stop.'"

"Bless you, dear, sweet Fernán. Can you see me in the candlelight?"

He said that he could, and she said that she would first explain the parts of a woman and then show him how a man should please her.

"First, close your eyes and I will lead your hand to my secret places."

He closed his eyes and she disrobed and lay beside him and took his hand and, as he touched her womanly parts, she described what each was. Fernán lay there, his mind exploding with strange delights.

When she had completed the round, she said, "Now when I tell you to open your eyes, you will touch me again but see what you touch, and I will explain what you must do to give me pleasure. For if you please me, you will enjoy the greatest pleasure yourself and that will lead us closer to our intent. Now open your eyes and look at me."

Fernán opened his eyes. He had never beheld a nude woman. She had removed the bedcover and the candlelight played on the soft curves of her silken skin and she lay back and spread her legs and took his hand and repeated her schooling, this time demonstrating where he should touch and where kiss and how he should move and when. After they had completed the round again, she told him to lie on his back.

"María," he said, "no more."

"Oh, dear heart, how can you deny me now, Fernán? Have pity on a poor woman who will otherwise be cast into the fire."

"I am miserable, María."

"Do not be, dear Fernán. You do nothing wrong. If God smiles on me then a new life will be born and, indeed, God will smile and I will be saved and you will have been my savior."

And she bestrode his body and led him into her and he could not contain himself. Afterward, he wondered if his motive had been pity, or that his pity was trivial and lust his motive. And he could not answer the question.

28

The Sarmiento house

While his father sat statue-like before the dormant fireplace, Sarmiento explained that the Commission of Inquiry he had appointed on the eighteenth of March had completed its investigation within a week, and had concluded that *conversos* were, for the most part, secret Jews who practiced Jewish rituals and customs. He withheld the fact that the Commission, composed of hand-picked anti-*conversos*, had been given orders to find what they had found. That was of no consequence to his father.

He stared at the old man, light from the window illuminating one side of the old face, and saw lines newly etched on the creased and sunken cheek and brow that had once been full and smooth. The man had withered, was aware of nothing, had no knowledge of the biased judges selected for the religious tribunal that was now ruling on actions against Judaizers. Yet Sarmiento continued his recitation. The tribunal, the ecclesiastical court, had been authorized by Pero Lope de Galvez, the Vicar of the Cathedral Church. Taking advantage of the absence of Archbishop Carrillo, Galvez had dismissed the Archdeacon and issued death sentences to those unrepentant heretics found guilty by the tribunal, despite having been prohibited from doing so by Carrillo.

"You see, Father, Galvez has flouted the ban Carrillo imposed because Carrillo is the lackey of the King. To obey the Archbishop and oppose the will of the people would have been treason, not that Galvez would have considered scorning the people. And several weeks ago—you may remember my telling you this—García announced in church that Christians must report the heretical actions of *marranos* to their local parish priests. We have had an enthusiastic response to that appeal so far—many accusers have come forth—and I am pleased to tell you that this will be a very successful operation."

Sarmiento leaned forward and spoke in a hoarse whisper. "I also think, Father, you will be pleased to know that the administration—that is, your son—has confiscated possessions of the heretics and that these confiscations, added to those goods we have retained to date, fatten our coffers considerably. We are in excellent financial condition, Father, excellent. We have begun refurbishing the estate and restoring the vineyards. And this house has undergone an overdue renovation, as you may have noticed."

The elder Sarmiento neither moved nor uttered a sound and the son rose impulsively, stood behind his father, and stared down at the pink head covered with scarce strands of thin white hair. His fingers trailed over the chair frame. The chair was new as were the other chairs in the room, the rugs, and several tapestries on the wall—one covering the formerly bare space above the mantel.

He leaned on the back of the chair and his voice rose. "Quite a number of *marranos* have been processed so far. The number is past fifty and there must be a hundred or more still to appear before the tribunal. Men and women arrested, accused, sentenced to death, burned in the square, goods confiscated—and more to come. A goodly number of women, Father, a surprising number. Several burned." He sat on his chair, his torso projecting forward, his foot tapping automatically. "As I said, Father, neither the Pope nor the Archbishop authorized the proceedings—only the Vicar. He assured me that the trials were proper and he is correct. A bit bothersome, this matter of the Pope and Archbishop, but justified—part of our responsibilities to God and Church."

His voice broke. "Why, Father, when I need you to hear me are you deaf and dumb? I find this very disappointing. Very disappointing. Not your fault, I know, but it is maddening. Whom do you expect me to talk to?"

Sarmiento stood beside the window, stared at the empty courtyard, and allowed his voice to clear his mind, knowing that the words went unheard, yet compelled to speak, to hear his voice, to know he was there. "You must realize that unless we have noble support we cannot hold out for long with only the rabble for backing. Those low people will bolt at the first shot. They have behaved well so far, but cannot be trusted for long. Not one can be trusted. Not one."

He spoke now to the cobblestones in the courtyard in a lowered voice. "The King is on his way, Father. He has broken off his siege of Pimentel and is encamped at Fuensalida. We have spies in their camp, they have spies in ours. I have written to Navarre. Slimy bastard. But what choice did I have? Navarre has assured us of his support. Oh, yes, I know his patronage is not worth one *maravedí*. Another who cannot be trusted, damn him."

He turned to his father, hovered over him, and spoke quietly into his face, ignoring the fetid odor exuding from the old man. His own breath caused hairs on the white eyebrows below him to quiver. "I watched the burning from my horse, Father. Lord God, the stench was horrifying. And the screams of the women—far worse than the men. My mount became agitated. The prisoners appeared to be in a bad state to begin with, most of them. Well, they are Jews after all—what can one expect? Thought I would vomit. Pig smells good burning—not Jews, I can tell you that. Something in them stinks when they burn. Sins, maybe. Sins burning, do you think? Do you hear me?" The door opened. He seized his father by the shoulders, shook him, and shouted, "Answer me, for the love of God!"

"Why do you shout at your father?" his mother asked. "Why shake him as if you were emptying a sack?"

Sarmiento straightened and glared at his mother. "I am not shouting. I am not shaking him."

"For the love of God, leave the poor man alone, Pero. There is little enough left of him. He has done all he can in this world. Let him die in peace."

Sarmiento contemplated the ceiling. "Why am I here? I never want to be here, so why am I here? Why talk to this relic? I must have lost my mind. And why do I talk to you, Mother—dear? Some day you will be alone and then you will talk to the walls as I do."

"Leave your father in peace. He is dead, Pero, except that his body has not yet discovered the difference between life and death. It will, soon enough."

Sarmiento returned to the window. "Too much wine too early. I have become García. My head is a morass."

"You act like a child, Pero. A man your age does not shout at the dead. It is bad form. Did I hear you name Navarre?"

"You were at the door, Mother. You heard every word."

"I could not make out all the words."

"You are a package of goods," he said, and sat on the window sill. The street beyond the arch was alive with activity—carts, horses, people striding by in the sunshine, full of energy, about their business. "Navarre has assured me of his support."

"Navarre? You amaze me. Are you aware that you amaze me? Why, for the sweet love of Jesus, do you fool with Navarre when Navarre laughs at you? He helps the Aragonese burn our estates and you beg for help? Really, Pero." She sat in the chair he had vacated. "Must you always be with the low crowd—the commoners, the outcasts? That toad García, for example. What is he? One of those effeminate things who toys with children?"

"Your son is Governor, señora. Have some respect for the Governor and his associates."

"Respect? You earn respect when you travel in the best circles, not act the toady to vermin like Navarre, who is no friend to Castile nor to us. Why not lick princely boots? Some day Enrique will be your king."

"I lick the boots of no man, Mother—king, prince, duke, councilor, no one."

"Really?"

"Just so."

A young man walked through the archway toward the house. Why did Sarmiento know him? He wore no sword. Of course, young Hernandes. Coming here?

"Your father would seek help from Enrique, Pero—could he speak. Go to the King or the Prince, he would say. Prince and King are interchangeable, though one is at the throat of the other. But your father cannot speak, despite your bullying, therefore I must speak for him and I say not to bother with the hangers-on and commoners. At times you act as if you were common, not noble, and yet you have been advisor to the King, member of the Royal Council, Chief Butler. What has become of you, Pero? Even your mistress is a cipher. Hundreds of ladies of culture, wit, and beauty would sleep with you in a minute—ladies you could be seen with. Yet you choose a whore. Why? What do you see in this Manuela? She is young and beautiful, admittedly, but she has no manners—speaks her mind whenever she wishes. Does she wash? Are you sure she does not infect you? One cannot be too careful, you know."

"I am more than careful. But if I seem strange, Mother, blame the times. If I dally with those you consider toads, then the times demand I dally with toads. You advised me to do so, after all—why should it amaze you? And if I talk to the dead, it is because these days the dead know more than you and I and we should study their example. As for why I implore the blind to see and the deaf to speak, I do that because there are miracles to come of which we know nothing. I am strange, but no fool. The course I have plotted is full of pits and assorted dangers and I will use every power I command to avoid the pits and overcome the dangers."

He stared out the window and spoke to himself. "Navarre is a chance not a certainty, but less demanding than Enrique. Enrique is a last resort which may become a necessity."

Hernandes entered the house.

"Forgive me, Mother, but a young man has come to see me."

"Here? You have an appointment?"

"No."

"Then how do you know?"

"I know."

A servant knocked and opened the hall door. "A señor Rafael Fernán Hernandes, Your Excellency."

"Wait several minutes, then show him in."

"Why would a *marrano* come here?" his mother asked.

"For the same reason the others come here. He wants something."

"He should not see your father."

"My father is a painted statue of an old man. A good reproduction. Almost lifelike. Goodbye, Mother."

Her mouth opened, then closed, and she stalked out through a side door.

A knock, and the servant announced, "Señor Rafael Fernán Hernandes," and closed the door behind Fernán who bowed to Sarmiento.

"Well, young Hernandes, have you come to play at swords or deliver my rug or both? I see you have no sword or dagger, so it must be the rug."

"I know nothing of rugs, Excellency, and I wear no weapon out of respect for your office. I am here to seek your assistance. My aunt, María Hernandes, has been denounced and imprisoned for Judaizing. Excellency, she is innocent of these charges. I assure you, the arrest is an error."

"These Judaizing matters are ecclesiastical, Hernandes. A smart lad like you should know that. The tribunal is under the jurisdiction of the Church. I could not possibly interfere with their work since my role is political and administrative. Where is your father? I assume he is still head of household?"

"My father is indisposed, Excellency. He conveys his regrets. My uncle, Cesario, recovers from the wounds of battle and my other uncle, Antonio Hernandes, husband of María, has departed Toledo at your request. I am the only male member of my house who can plead for your assistance." Fernán stepped forward. "Will you speak to the members of the tribunal, señor? My family and I fear for the life of my aunt. We would be deeply indebted to you."

"You are at this moment deeply in debt to this administration, Hernandes, for your brilliant swordsmanship. I can do nothing for you, nor can anyone. The Church has sole jurisdiction."

"Excellency, I have been to the prison. They will not let me speak to María or bring her food—a privilege granted to the worst of offenders."

"She is a prisoner of the Church and not allowed guests or presents."

"She will starve."

"She will eat prison food, Hernandes. That is all she can expect. Your aunt must be a secret Jew or else she would not have been denounced and arrested."

"My aunt is a lady, señor, of quality and breeding."

"She is a Jew."

"Forgive me, señor, but she is baptised—she is a Christian lady."

"I know the story, Hernandes. She converted when she married your uncle. Very little in Toledo escapes my attention."

"Then you will help her?"

"I said I could not and will not. Now I have been more than patient with you and I bid you farewell."

Fernán hesitated, stared at Sarmiento, opened the door, and then turned back. "Why do you kill us, don Pero? Why do you hate us?"

"Hate? Hate?" Sarmiento pulled his ear and sat on a chair. "Your term is at odds with the facts, Hernandes." He smiled and shook his head. "You are in the way—do you not see that? *Marranos* are a people out of place—a mistake in history. And so you will be removed from history—a gradual process but inevitable. The commoners hate you, but theirs is a misplaced emotion. They hate because you threaten them, your role threatens them. You frighten them. You take their money, you displace them from work, you marry the highborn, you become councilors and advisors to the princes of the land, you move upward in society. They cannot do that. Therefore, they hate you—out of ignorance, jealousy, and fear."

He crossed his left leg over his right. "And the Church responds to their need. The Church reinforces their hatred and assures them that you are evil. That is why you succeed, they say. Not because you are more skilled or clever or industrious—though you may be—but because you are children of Jews, children of the Devil. You employ spells and magic and you threaten the Church." Sarmiento shrugged. "Not all churchmen believe that—the Pope does not, much effect that has. In Castile, we believe that. In Toledo, we do. We believe you are not sincere in your Christianity, Hernandes, that you mock us and mock our Lord, Jesus Christ, and that will not do. You are a people caught between testaments—between testaments, *marrano*. So the forces of Church and commoner have joined together and you happen to be in the center of that combined force and will be crushed. Not hate, Hernandes, destiny."

Why lecture this youth? What possible benefit could be derived from the education of a Hernandes, a *marrano*, who wished him dead? Despite himself, though, Sarmiento continued. "And who is to be crushed first, do you think? Why those who trespass against a neighbor, or insult a servant, or are too comely or clever or rich. No plan, Hernandes, none at all. Luck. Luck rules. Who likes you and who does not."

"Excellency," Fernán said, "arrest me and free my aunt. María is a fine human being and, though young, has had much sorrow."

"Hernandes, you annoy me and I do not care to be annoyed. I have told you repeatedly that these matters are not within my purview. Your aunt is accused as a Judaizer and must be judged. Say no more or join your aunt. That I can do. Now get out."

Fernán nodded curtly to Sarmiento, and bowed to the old man.

"I said get out. He cannot see or hear you and, if he could, he would spit in your face."

Fernán shifted his eyes toward Sarmiento where they stayed a moment, then he left the room. Sarmiento walked to the window as Fernán hurried out of the building and across the courtyard toward the archway.

"What do you think, Father? Was I too harsh or should I have him arrested?"

He looked toward his father. Nothing.

"Too harsh? With all due respect, Father, I think not. However, if he is arrested he will never be able to play at swords with me and that would be a shame."

At the archway, Fernán stopped and stared back at the house. His face was forbidding and Sarmiento, surprised by the intensity of the expression, understood how eight men had been killed. He turned away, then looked again. Hernandes was gone. The archway and courtyard were empty—no carts rolled across the open space, no horses pulled their loads, no one strode by in the brilliant sunshine.

He hesitated and then bent over his father. "Father, should I solicit the support of the Prince, do you think? Navarre may never be forthcoming. You need not move, Father, just close your eyes if you favor Navarre."

The eyelids of the old man never wavered.

"You do not support Navarre? And Enrique? Close your eyes if you support soliciting assistance from the Prince. No? I know you close your eyes when you sleep, so you must disapprove soliciting support from both men. Is that it? Then what should I do, Father? What should I do?"

A sound. A sound which seemed to come from the gut of the old man.

"What did you say, Father?" he shouted. "Did you say something? What was that you said?"

29

The Alcázar of Toledo, two weeks later

Jerónimo was horrified by the appearance of his young master. Fernán lay against the wall of the cell with twenty or more other men in various degrees of decrepitude. Some had broken limbs and dislocated shoulders from the strappado, others bore the marks of whips and shackles, all were covered with dirt and open sores. But the physical breakdown paled when compared to their greater mental and moral debasement. These humans had been reduced to animal existence and that reduction was apparent in eyes that could scarcely look out from beneath their brows, like dogs that have been whipped and whipped again.

Fernán was not at that level. His reduction in state was one of exhaustion and hunger—a stage painfully familiar to Jerónimo. His eyes, though bloodshot, retained their inner strength and intelligence. He had lost weight and his beard had grown, causing him to appear closer in age to Jerónimo. Like the others in the cell, Fernán wore nothing but a cloth around his loins and was huddled in a fetal position, his legs drawn beneath him, his arms wrapped around his upper body, his head hunched down between his shoulders to conserve inner warmth. His body was wasted, the muscles and bones sharply defined. But his will appeared intact—that was clear from his eyes. Jerónimo blessed God for that mercy.

Each prisoner wore a shackle around one ankle fastened by a chain to another chain that led from one end of the cell to the other, linking the prisoners in brotherly degradation. They sat propped against the wall or lay on the filthy straw that covered the floor. Manacles on each wrist were joined by another chain that allowed some independent movement of their arms.

Several buckets were placed in the corners of the cell for the relief of bowels and bladder, though that nicety had been abandoned by many prisoners who had soiled themselves and sat in their own filth. The men and buckets exuded a stench as heavy as a thick fog.

The manacles and stench revived memories to Jerónimo of the galley in which he had served. He had become inured to the smell when enslaved, but this stink unnerved him. Not having had the luxury of a glass, Jerónimo had no idea how he had appeared as a prisoner in the galley and for that he was thankful. How could someone be brought so low in days?

Disguised as a Dominican in a cowl that shadowed his face, Jerónimo made certain no guard was at the cell door, and whispered, "Fernán." The youth raised his head slowly and looked toward the source of his name. His mouth formed *Jerónimo*, but no sound emerged and the steward worried that the voice had been damaged. Fernán pointed to his throat, mimed drinking, and shook his head, and Jerónimo realized that Fernán was so parched it was hopeless for him to try to speak.

Jerónimo stood between Fernán and the cell door and retrieved a flask from beneath his gown. "Slowly, Fernán, else you will throw up and lose the purpose of the liquid. Observe the same slow pace when you eat the bread and meat I have brought."

Fernán drank, smiled weakly, and drank some more. He opened the parcel of food Jerónimo had given him, bit off a small piece of bread, and ate a bite of chicken. Jerónimo let him eat while he watched the door. To be safe, he knelt on the repulsive straw and pretended to pray. He had told the soldier at the prison entrance that he was here to give last rites to a prisoner and reluctantly, the soldier, a corporal, had instructed a guard to take Jerónimo to the cell.

The passage from the world God had made to this Hell of Satan had been well-guarded and, though Jerónimo carried a short sword and dagger beneath his robe, an attempt to escape with Fernán would have been disastrous. Also his swarthy skin and normal height, so distinct from that of Fernán, made a transfer of identities hopeless. He must puzzle out how to rescue his young master—and quickly.

Having finished the drink and eaten some food, Fernán returned the flask to Jerónimo. "I will save the bread and meat beneath the straw. Lovely place, no?"

Jerónimo removed a blanket that had been wound around his body. "I am delighted to rid myself of this encumbrance, Fernán. You cannot know how hot it is. Where will you put it?"

Fernán moved straw away from the wall, lay the blanket down and covered it. "That will do."

"Excellent." Jerónimo said. Then he touched Fernán. "Have they tortured you, young master?"

"Four times they dropped me—the *strappado*. But, thank God, I am strong because of your training and light from not having eaten. I absorbed the weight of my body in my arms. I could have flipped over and relieved stress on my shoulders, but the executioner would have known I could stand the strain and arranged for something worse. After the fourth drop, he said he would try again—when I lost strength."

Jerónimo scrutinized the other prisoners. "Can they hear us?"

"These poor souls neither hear nor speak. Some have been here for months. Although I cannot imagine how one could last that long. Their speech is gone—and not from dry throat. Their minds have cracked."

"How did they arrest you?"

"I had left the house on my way to prison, to inquire whether I could see María, when two guardsmen seized me. I got to prison but not as intended and never had a chance to tell my mother or father—or you. How are my parents?"

"Worried, as you might imagine, but confident you will be released. Did the inquisitors say who accused you and what your offense was?"

"No, they have told me nothing. Who could have denounced me, Jerónimo?"

"I will find out. Whoever it is, his civic duty will be rewarded."

"Jerónimo, will they break me?"

"No, my friend. Have I told you how the pirates tortured me when I tried to escape? No? They tied my hands and feet together and dragged me behind the ship. Most of the time I was underwater, and when I did come up, I inhaled more sea than air. Then I was chained to my oar again."

"How did you come to be a galley slave? You are from Córdova."

"No, Fernán. I was born in Morocco, a Berber village near Melilla on the shores of the Mediterranean. I was Muslim and converted later. Like your father, my father was a merchant. When I was your age, a pirate ship attacked our small town and killed many people, including my family. They needed young men to pull the oars of their galleys and I was unlucky. I had no choice—slavery or death—not unlike the choice your great-grandfather was given—Christianity or death."

"I am Catholic, Jerónimo. Am I a slave?"

"Are you tortured because you are accused of disregarding the dogma of the Catholic Church?"

Fernán stared at the straw-covered floor. "Complete your story."

"The pirates captured many ships but were defeated by a Spanish galleon. I was brought to Cadiz and sold to your father. He saw something other than slavery in my eyes and freed me. As I was saved by God and freed by your father, so God will preserve you and I will set you free. You believe what I say, Fernán?"

"I have always believed you, Jerónimo, since I was a child. Nothing would cause me to doubt you now."

"God save you, Fernán. May He grant you peace and long life. I must leave now. Believe in your strength and you will live. I will return when I am able."

Jerónimo stood and Fernán said, "What of María? What is the news?"

He looked at Fernán. "You must be silent when I tell you or both of us will die. Will you be silent, my friend?"

"Tell me."

Jerónimo closed his eyes a moment. "María is dead—burned for heresy. I watched as she went to the fire. She was not in her right mind. She sang Ladino songs amid the taunts of the crowd, and when her songs stopped, I knew she was gone. María was a beautiful creature, Fernán, full of song."

Fernán quaked with the silent cries he was forbidden to voice and Jerónimo placed a hand on his friend. Despite the cold, Fernán was damp with perspiration. Jerónimo knew the young master had loved María—he had watched his eyes when María appeared and would never tell Fernán the truth of her death, not song but hideous screams as flames crawled up her legs. After her death he had inquired among her jailers, slipped *maravedís* into furtive hands, and learned that María had told her jailers she was with child, that she had missed her monthly time. She could not be put to death, she claimed, for an unborn child is an innocent soul. They had laughed at the mad lady.

Jerónimo blessed his friend in silence and rattled the bars on the door. The guard examined the cowled monk, opened the door, and indicated the direction to the light with a nod of his head.

30

The encampment of Juan II

When the rebels learned that King Juan was no longer besieging Pimentel but had brought his army east to join with Alvaro de Luna and attack Toledo, Sarmiento sent Lope de Galvez, Fernando de Ávila, Juan Alonso, and Felipe Ruano northeast to meet with the King in Fuensalida, five leagues from Toledo. They bore a Petition whose language had been crafted by Marcos García.

Received at field headquarters, they were ushered to a capacious tent filled with officers, aides, and guards. The King was seated on a small ornate throne positioned on a low dais at the rear of the tent, bracketed by Alvaro de Luna the Constable, and Alfonso Carrillo, Archbishop of Toledo. Galvez bowed to the King and nodded to the Archbishop, his superior, who stared at his Vicar. Luna prompted Galvez to explain to His Majesty what business brought them to Fuensalida.

"Your Majesty, we have brought with us a Petition from Pero Sarmiento, Governor of the City of Toledo, on behalf of the people of Toledo."

"And what does this…what did this person call the document, don Alvaro?"

"Your Majesty, the document is called a Petition."

"Petition, yes, we thought that was the term this person used. What is your name, señor?"

"Pero Lope de Galvez, Your Majesty."

"Do we know you?"

"No, Your Majesty. I am Vicar of the Cathedral Church of Toledo during the absence of Archbishop Carrillo."

"And something more than that, are you not?"

"A priest, Your Majesty, that is all."

"Not what we have heard," the King snickered. "Is that not so, Archbishop?"

Carrillo turned to the King. "Your Majesty, it is."

"Well then, we know who we are and now we know who you are. So speak, Vicar, what have you to say to us?"

"Your Majesty, the Governor of Toledo, Pero Sarmiento, has authorized me to request the following before I deliver the Petition."

"Dear, dear. Will this discourse of yours be lengthy, Vicar?"

"No, Your Majesty." Galvez coughed and cleared his throat. "Your Majesty, the people of Toledo wish you to know that they hold you in the highest esteem and invite you to visit their city. However, they request that if you wish to enter the city of Toledo, Your Majesty should come with a reduced force and without Alvaro de Luna and his army."

The King stared and stroked his beard. There were mutterings from Alvaro and from the other attendants.

"Be quiet, all of you," King Juan said, "we very much wish to hear the conclusion of this madness. You have more to say, Vicar?"

"Yes, Your Majesty."

"We thought you might have more wind in your sails. All right, come out with it."

"There are two other requisites for your entrance into Toledo, Sire. That the command of the Alcázar be guaranteed to His Excellency Pero Sarmiento, and that Pero Sarmiento never be held accountable for any actions taken by himself or by others under his command during the rebellion of the people of Toledo."

The King stood abruptly. "Don Alvaro, you will continue to listen to this…this idiocy." The attendants bowed and the King left the tent, followed by all but those few near Alvaro de Luna.

"We will continue this conversation in less regal surroundings," Luna said. "Follow me," and he led the four from Toledo into a small tent that contained a table and stools. "This will do nicely," he said, and sat on one side of the table flanked by two associates, one of whom was a scribe. "Be seated, señores, and proceed with your presentation."

Galvez was perspiring. From the ride, he thought. He began speaking, but his throat was dry and he asked for a drink. A flagon of ale was brought and a mug poured. Galvez drank but his throat did not improve. However, he began again and managed to complete his reading while coughing and drinking after each sentence.

"Let me summarize your statements," Luna said. "When my summary is complete, you will inform me whether my interpretation is correct. If it is not, you will correct my interpretation."

Luna pushed his chair back and walked around the table. "In addition to the statements made previously to the King, the document you call a Petition mentions a series of alleged injustices suffered by the populace and administration of Toledo under the rule of King Juan II. I will not repeat the supposed injustices. The Petition then demands that Cortes be called and that once assembled, the representatives are to be directed to remedy these assumed injustices. As I understand, the injustices mentioned can only be relieved by the elimination of all New Christians, as well as myself, from the administration of King Juan II. The Petition further states that if these conditions are not met, the people and administration of Toledo will deny King Juan his authority as their lawful sovereign and transfer their fealty to Prince Enrique, the son of King Juan. Is that correct?"

"That is essentially what is contained within the Petition, don Alvaro."

"Then, Lope de Galvez, our meeting is concluded. I will convey your demands to the King and my aide will show you to the lodgings we have provided for your party. You will find provisions there for supper. I will see you at dawn. May I have the Petition?"

Luna accepted the Petition from Galvez and left the tent. His aide then led the four to another tent in which were modest beds and a table and stools with food and drink. Galvez and the others talked far into the night and afterward slept poorly, although the accommodations were reasonable for a field encampment. Before dawn they awoke and consumed what remained of their supper. At first light, an aide to Luna directed them to the small tent where they had met with the Constable and, shortly afterward, Luna arrived.

"Señores," he said, "to be direct, your Petition irritated His Majesty and you are requested to leave this place. Your horses have been watered and fed."

Luna turned to leave and Galvez jumped to his feet.

"Don Alvaro, we do not wish to offend His Majesty. However, the King must realize that this Petition is supported not only by those who rebelled against the previous administration of Toledo, but by a considerable majority of the nobles and councilors of the city as well. We do not threaten, señor, but caution His Majesty that the city of Toledo is united in its agreement with the principles of this Petition. Toledo will not yield to threats against its regime. I am instructed to inform you that we are prepared for a long siege, are well armed, and resolved to pursue our goals as outlined in the Petition."

Luna stared at Galvez, then left the tent.

31

That same morning

Their watch near its end, three soldiers stood sentry duty in a field outside the encampment of King Juan. They yawned in sequence and slapped their breasts, attempting to stimulate circulation in their numbed arms and hands while they observed the morning sun struggle to pierce a quartet of rose-rimmed clouds on the horizon.

"May be that we will move today," said one, as he retrieved his pike and adjusted the leather breastplate that weighed heavily on his shoulders.

"All that may move today, Miguel, is your bowels, if you have put anything in them. Toledo is five leagues away and will stay there while we sleep on the ground here forever."

"Forever, Pedro?" the youngest of the trio asked. "We will never taste the food and women of Toledo?"

"Food and women—listen to the *niño*. The only woman Tomás has tasted is his Mamá and he is too old now for her milk—though I would give a good tug if it were offered me."

"You are a coarse one, Pedro. My mother is a good woman. I wish I had stayed where I was born and not been dragged around Castile by King Juan."

Miguel, grizzled and worn, said, "Many pretty women live in Toledo."

"You have been there, Miguel?"

"Many times. I was born near there. We raised sheep in the mountains south of the city, a land of oak and roses. I visited fairs in town and attended my first Mass in the Cathedral. Toledo is a castle, *amigo*. I would hate to attack her. The lady has withstood many assaults over the centuries."

"What is she like, Miguel?" Tomás asked.

"Ah well, how to describe a beautiful woman. She sits on a high mesa, circled by stone walls and strong gates and, on three sides, the noble Río Tajo flows wide and swift. Inside the walls live a few Jews and Moors, some *conversos* and the rest Castilians. Once through the gates, and it is no simple matter to gain entrance through her strong portals, the narrow streets wind round and round like the wiles of a woman, and you may lose yourself and never find your way out. But once inside, you will not want to leave."

"And many beautiful women?"

"Tomás, put beautiful women from your head. You will never see the women of Toledo, nor will the King—not with those walls."

The sounds of horses and conversation were carried to them on the morning breeze.

"Halt and be recognized," Pedro said, as he advanced with lowered pike.

"Pedro, these *caballeros* come from the King, not to him. Let them pass."

"Pass, señores."

Galvez nodded to the sentry and the four continued on their way, riding two abreast—Galvez with Ávila, Alonso with Ruano, their hoods concealing their faces.

"What did we gain, Pero?" Ávila asked.

"Knowledge, Fernando. We know the King and Luna are proud and unyielding. But we demonstrated that we are well entrenched and not likely to surrender to verbal assault."

"The assault will not be verbal, Pero. You saw the number of the forces of the King. How does King Juan know we will not surrender?"

"You heard me say we were well-prepared for a siege and are well-armed."

"And are we well-prepared and well-armed?"

"I am a priest, Fernando, not a soldier, and I must accept the word of those who know of soldierly affairs. I spoke the words I was instructed to speak. How much is bravado I am not prepared to say."

They rode on accompanied by an early swarm of flies. The sun had surmounted the clouds and Galvez grew warm. He threw back his hood and surveyed the countryside—flat, boring land covered with row upon row of olive trees and grape vines. Groggy, resisting sleep, he braced himself against the lulling motion of the horse, swatted at the flies, and recalled the words of the King and Carrillo.

While the King had not recognized the Galvez name, he did recognize the function the Vicar served, and Carrillo was certainly familiar with the role Galvez had in sentencing *conversos*, to the stake—that was apparent from his temper. Galvez was less at ease with Carrillo than with the King, whom he might never meet again. Carrillo, though, would return to Toledo after the siege, however it ended, and then Galvez would face the consequence of his actions. The Archbishop must have found the meeting disagreeable, for he never questioned Galvez as to why he had disobeyed explicit orders and sentenced *conversos* to burn. That omission relieved Galvez somewhat, but he was unsure of Carrillo. He knew the power the Archbishop wielded and the breadth of his immense ambition, and that caused him to be anxious for his own future.

"What will King Juan do, Pero?" asked Ávila.

"Lay siege to Toledo."

"And then?"

"Then we shall see how much of Sarmiento is bravado and how much truth, and we shall act accordingly—or be acted upon."

32

Atop the Gate of Visagra

From the north entrance to the city, Sarmiento observed the encampment of the King—a sea of tents, flags, and small figures who rushed about amid the rising coils of cooking-fire smoke. Galvez had reported delivery of the Petition to the King on his return to Toledo on the sixth of May. On the eighth, the first scouts sited the camp and, during the following days, the encampment expanded and was capped by the arrival of King Juan and the mass of his forces on the tenth. The following day, royal troops established positions at the gates, along the Río Tajo, and around the remainder of the city wall. Toledo was under siege.

García, Galvez, and Ávila joined Sarmiento on the wall. The days had been warm and bright, the nights clear and cool under a brilliant half-moon. After an abortive attack against the Gate of Visagra by longbowmen resulted in the loss of two rebel soldiers, those standing guard on the wall began to wear light chain mail and helmets—not that chain mail could resist a well-placed arrow. The raid on Visagra was followed by a challenge to the Gate of Cambrón, the other portal directly accessible from land. While annoying to Sarmiento, these pinpricks were minor tests of will—the real contest lay ahead.

"You told Luna we were well-prepared to withstand a siege," Sarmiento said to Galvez, "and he said what?"

"Nothing, don Pero. He left the tent without a word."

"And no response from the King?" Galvez shrugged. "Brazen bastards."

Sarmiento drew his sword, stared at the tents, and pointed his sword at the enemy. "Well, we have a surprise prepared for this King and his lap dog that will startle them out of their presumptive dreams of triumph."

"What surprise might that be, don Pero?" García asked.

"Later. How are our provisions?"

"Sufficient to withstand a long siege—longer than the King would like."

"When you say long, how long do you mean?"

"Months."

"How many?"

"A year."

"Without strain?"

"There may be strain in some quarters, don Pero, but not where we reside. The *marrano* borough, for example, will thin down."

"Your friend will certainly thin down, García. He was a subject for the *strappado* today."

"What friend would that be?"

"Young Hernandes, master swordsman."

"I have no friend of that name."

"Forgive me, García. I thought you admired his swordsmanship." Sarmiento returned his rapier to its scabbard and walked along the rampart. "The jailers tell me he withstood the *strappado* well but had nothing to say. They will continue until he gives them what they require."

García followed a pace behind the Governor. "Why is he being held?"

"He was seen leaving the house of Melamed, the Jew doctor, walking in the street with the pretty granddaughter of the house. A neighbor denounced him to the Church, he was arrested, and will be prosecuted for heresy. Torture will uncover the truth, as you well know. Rather a shame."

"How so?"

"I had looked forward to a match with the youth—to test his way with the sword."

"Then why denounce him?"

"Denounce him? I assumed you had denounced him."

"Why should I? Who gives a damn about him? To the devil with Hernandes!" García gestured excitedly toward the encampment. "There is our problem, not some youth. What do we do with the King?"

"Wait and resist, of course. Strange. Who could have tattled on my sword fellow? Well, well." Sarmiento stared out over the rampart. "García, how long will your commoners persevere in defense?"

"Who can say? One month, two, more perhaps. Though not likely more than two months. When the shoe pinches they will go barefoot."

García stood close to Sarmiento and whispered. "Now that we are far enough from the others that no one will hear, will you tell me what it is you would not tell me in front of Galvez and Ávila?"

"In a moment, García."

"Don Pero, why keep me in suspense? Have you heard from Navarre?"

"No. Navarre awaits assurance from his brother, Alfonso, illustrious King of Aragón and Naples, that he will join him when Navarre invades Castile. And who can tell when that will occur, if ever."

"Do we need Navarre?"

Sarmiento leaned against the parapet. At the near edge of the camp, troops drilled with pikes and halberds in mock combat. Far off, the clash of armor signaled knights jousting, sharpening their skills. In open combat the King would devastate amateur rebels. How his commoners would act after a month of waiting, he could not know, but he assumed a precipitous loss of morale after weeks of siege and the occasional attack and, after the first or second concerted assault by Luna, a breach of the walls, then carnage as soldiers and knights on horse entered the city.

Why, for the love of God, had he not anticipated such an outcome before they began this rebellion? Or had he been so overcome with hatred and ambition that he was led to this pass by the Devil? Was it the Devil? If so, let the Devil help him now. Did they need Navarre? They surely needed a champion of some sort. He had a handful of men able to fight on horse, but the other abilities of the commoners were few. They would not hold. They were not trained to fight.

"I have discounted Navarre," Sarmiento said.

"I thought my question had been forgotten. Then what alternatives do we have?"

"One—our Prince, don Enrique. He wants the head of Alvaro de Luna and so do we." Sarmiento turned his back to the camp and looked out over the city. "I have dangled a plum before him. We shall see if he likes fruit. The worm in the plum is Pacheco, favorite advisor to Enrique."

"What are you saying, don Pero? What plum did you dangle before the Prince?"

"I approached the Prince, García, and he has become receptive to a small offer I made."

"You contacted the Prince—how?"

"By messenger."

"What messenger?"

"Myself. Whom else would I trust with such a delicate message? Take no offense, García. You remember when I was ill and in seclusion. I was far from ill. Rather, I was with a troop of horse from the Alcázar, and I met with the Prince and offered him a present."

"Forgive me, but you confuse me, señor. What present?"

"Partial rule of Toledo. Though his father is seated on our doorstep with a sharp sword in his hand and the Prince may not care to have his *cojones* excised."

"You offered him Toledo? And what did he say?"

"What could he say? An offer that allows him to tweak two noses at the same time—one belonging to his father and the other to Luna—while he expands his national reputation and position among the nobility?" Sarmiento grimaced. "However, don Enrique said nothing, then asked me to return the next day. Wily Pacheco whispered in his ear. The man is a worm."

"You mentioned nothing to me of this offer."

"There was no time, señor. The King was at Fuensalida, Navarre was stalling. I saw disaster everywhere."

"What is this talk of provisions and strain and perseverance? Do you pull my beard?"

"Of course not. But nothing is certain until it happens, García. We may yet have to fight and, I assure you, a fight would be bloody. Do you see?" Sarmiento pointed to the camp. "The King struts about with his knights."

"Don Pero, you have led me a merry chase and I am exhausted from your story. What then? What then, señor?"

"Then? When I saw Enrique the next day, he told me he would send a courier to his father and request that King Juan allow him to enter Toledo."

"The Prince alone?"

"No, García. Be sensible. The Prince and his army."

"And the King said...?"

"No."

"Of course he would say no. How in the name of our Lord, Jesus Christ, could the Prince expect his father to allow him into Toledo with a force of men when that same father, no friend to his son, besieges the city?"

"Because Enrique assured his father that, if allowed to enter Toledo, he would return the city to the control of the Crown."

"Woolgathering."

"Agreed, and the King rebuffed him."

"Then we are no better off than before."

"Not quite."

"Don Pero, I surely will be ill, I promise you. Do not prolong this torture."

"Patience, García, patience. We are almost home. Since I returned, I have had a message from our Prince. Apparently, the Prince adores plums and, as we speak, advances toward Toledo with an army that dwarfs that of the King. As you know, he has considerable resources of his own and many nobles have joined his cause." Sarmiento paused in his narration and sighed. "Now, that is what the Prince wrote in his message to me and that is what I believe to be the case. However, whether the Prince does in fact advance on Toledo with a vast force of men and, if he does, what may happen when he arrives, I cannot predict."

"I will faint, don Pero. This exercise in yes and no, this give and take and back and forth has taken my breath and caused me to develop a pain in the head."

Sarmiento, watching the enemy camp, cried out abruptly, "García, mark that party of horse! Mark them! They ride to warn the King that the Prince is advancing. That is their mission. I swear to you, in the name of God Almighty, they have no other reason for such haste. See! The soldiers scurry about like birds before a storm. They will break camp and retreat. I know the sight. I know it in my bones!"

Sarmiento climbed onto the parapet and shouted in full voice. "Pull in your head, tortoise, crawl into your shell! Run, turtle, as fast as your short legs allow! The Prince advances with his nobles and army and ten thousand horse! You are outmanned, Alvaro de Luna! You are undone! Fly! Fly!"

33

In the bowels of the Alcázar

In his grief, Fernán curled within the straw like a dying worm. His eyes were dry. Tears are for minor sorrows, he thought. This pain will kill me and God alone knows that death will be welcome. Had the Lord disapproved of their love and punished them? María had come to him each night for a week, and for a week he had luxuriated in her welcoming body as she taught him to love. His doubts had vanished. He accepted their mission, and each night they lay together his knowledge and love of love multiplied as he prayed for their success. Dear, sweet Jesus, could such pleasure in love be sin? By the end of the week he knew her body better than his own. He had mapped her flesh, each square vivid in his mind, each curve, each orifice elaborated in detail—his fingers and tongue explaining to his eyes, informing his brain of taste, of form, of texture, his nostrils filled with her scent. And as she taught him, he reveled in the new, knowing that this instruction was a speck, a razor edge of the possible, a pinhole view of a universe—a universe now dead.

Each night he asked whether she had conceived and she said, "Silly, I am barren as a cuckoo."

"But cuckoos are not barren," he said, "simply devious."

She laughed, but quietly, so as not to be heard upstairs or down. He had thought she laughed with sorrow, but was uncertain.

And then she was gone, taken by the Guard. Was she in Heaven as she deserved or had love damned her? How, though, could she be damned for wanting a child, for wanting life, a continuation of life? For was that not the will of God? Then how could a just God damn her? And if God damned her, God was not just, not a true God. Fernán questioned and was no longer sure.

He considered himself deserving of damnation for accepting the exile of Antonio and bedding María. *Almighty God, who am I that I can kill men and fornicate with a married woman and live?* Though, in his confused heart, the nights with María were no sin, for he had taken pity on her and planted his seed within her so that God would grow the child she desired. Or had the Devil deceived him? Had lust won his soul and was he truly damned? *Bear me to my grave, oh Lord, that if this love be sin, the memory of its pleasure will be burned from my soul.*

Naomi had sent him away and was married. His prayers had been of no use since Naomi, as a Jew, was outside prayer. And, though Naomi had been untrue to their love, hers was a minor perfidy compared to his betrayal with María. *Oh, Blessed God, have I betrayed You as well?* And he beat his breast with his fists and swayed in his desperation, moaning aloud, so that the guard looked through the bars of the door and shrugged at his antics.

After a long while, Fernán burrowed into the straw, threw the filth over his cold body, and slept from exhaustion.

A rough shove woke him. "Is it time?" he croaked. The shackle was unlocked from his ankle and he was led from the cell up the stairs to the *strappado* chamber. The manacles on his wrists were removed and he was prodded up the ladder to where the executioner waited.

"Shall we try again, señor?"

The head of the executioner was half-covered by a black hood with holes for the eyes. Fernán could see nothing of the face except the mouth, a fleshy void filled with dark teeth, and a jaw like an anvil covered with thick black stubble. *Here is Hell and this the Devil—a fitting end to this life and prologue to the next.*

"Water," he pleaded hoarsely.

The executioner stared at him. "Ale is what I drink, señor, and that you are not allowed. Yet God will look more kindly on me for it." And he handed Fernán the mug. "Here, poor soul, drink."

Fernán grasped the mug and drank. Then he coughed and said, "I thank you for your kindness, executioner, and ask for your blessing—that you may make this my end and that God reward you for it in the next life."

"Though I be damned for it, I shall do my best, señor. But you be a strong one and I guarantee nothing but pain, of that there will be a sufficiency. I do apologize for the inconvenience, but put your hands behind you so that they may be tied. You know the practice."

The man tied his wrists together and tied the rope from the ceiling around the cord that bound his wrists. Fernán could feel his hands begin to numb and wished the rope circled his neck so that his soul would be wrenched into oblivion when the rope tightened. He would not resist, but allow the fall to break his shoulders. And though he might not die from the drop, the pain would persist until they killed him.

He was led to the edge of the platform. Thought stopped. The executioner seized him by the arms and held him over the edge. A moment and he dropped. A second, the rope snapped tight and his arms twisted up behind him. Blessed, blessed pain! But his shoulders held. They would not break. He could not will them to break. His body was independent of his resolve. The muscles in arms and back and chest had tensed and bore his hanging body. Pain, yes, but not sufficient.

"Take him down," a voice said from below.

Two guards lowered Fernán to the ground, fastened manacles on his wrists, and dragged him up the stairs to an empty room. The manacles removed, they washed him with a coarse rag dipped in a bucket of water and gave him sandals and a garment to cover his nakedness, then left him and locked the door. Weak from the *strappado*, confused by the sudden attention, he dressed in the makeshift garment and looked about.

Save for two stools and a table, the room and stone floor were bare. Light squeezed through a small window in one wall, and from that window Fernán could make out the Cathedral spire at the center of the city, the giant finger of God blessing land and sky.

He slumped into a chair, closed his eyes, and dozed.

> *Floating through the window, Toledo spread beneath him. He could see his house and the Melamed house. Mamá and Papá were below him and he waved. They spoke. He could not hear their words and then they were gone. Naomi was seated on the bench in the courtyard with a young man. She looked at him. He saw her face and then the youth kissed her and she waved.*

The sound of a door being unlocked woke him. He staggered to his feet, uneasy in the ill-fitting gown. A figure entered the room haloed by the light behind him, a sword in each hand. Was this the dream or was this the angel of death?

"So, Hernandes, enjoy the *strappado*?" The voice was distant, like the deadened roar of sound in a shell. "I assume you disliked your exercise," the figure said, laying the swords on the table, his voice obscure, indistinct, "therefore I offer you an alternative."

Fernán could say nothing. His sight was blurred. His head cleared slowly. He was in a room with a man and two swords. "A moment," he mumbled. His vision slowly sharpened and he saw that the man was Sarmiento.

"Speak up, Hernandes, I cannot hear you. Do you wish to know the details of my gracious offer?"

"I know your offer," Fernán said, his speech muted but distinct. "You want to play at swords."

"Brilliant. I offer you an opportunity to display your talent, of which I have heard too much. But not play, Hernandes, fight. Fight me and the *strappado* stops. I do not guarantee acquittal and release, but there may be a chance. Well?"

Fernán was sick, his stomach knotted, his body a mass of pain. Here was the creature responsible for the death of María now come between him and torture. Was this a new form of torture, or did Sarmiento fancy himself a swordsman and must satisfy an overblown vanity? He saw distinctly now. Nausea became part of his hatred and a fire rose from his bowels and flooded his brain. His head pained above his eyes and he squinted to reduce the light.

Sarmiento had refused to help María and she had been burned. He would seize the sword and kill this man if that was the will of God or, if God chose, he would die. But death would find him either way. Sarmiento had taunted him—to kill or maim the Governor was sure death. Torture was no path to release. Its intent was to loosen tongues and, once confessed, to burn. Better to die by the cut of a sword or an ax than to burn. But to be out of this life, to be in the hands of the Lord—oh, sweet Jesus, bless me with death. He feared nothing, for despite all, God was beneficent and would surely be merciful to his servant.

"I await your reply," Sarmiento said.

"I will fight, though what satisfaction that will bring you, I do not know. If I kill you, I will be killed. If you kill me it means nothing, for I have no wish to live."

"Winning is not my objective, *marrano*. Your life is meaningless. You are a question and I must have an answer."

"I am no question. I am a man for a short time. I have no answer for you, except that you hate me for myself." Sarmiento wavered in and out of focus. "Why do you wallow in hate, Sarmiento, like a pig in mud? Do you not fear God?"

"My God despises you and your people. He glories in my hatred."

"Then you blaspheme, Sarmiento. You are cursed and deserve to die."

"Not at your hand, *marrano*. Take a weapon. They are equal, fashioned by the armorer, Rodríguez, a month before his death."

Sarmiento stripped the swords out of their scabbards. Fernán chose blindly. The plain hilt of the sword he chose lay in his hand like the hand of an old friend—hard, covered with leather, long enough to be grasped with both hands. The weapon was not quite a long sword, shy of four feet and more flexible, more like his rapier. Nor was the blade as wide as the long sword that had slaughtered the commoners, the sword that Jerónimo had taught him to use. How often had he and Jerónimo faced one another across such swords. He would miss his friend, his intelligence and warmth. So much to miss. Having barely cracked the shell of life, yet he had suffered—and had no time to say farewell, except in a dream. His shoulders had been almost torn by the drop and he wanted sleep—but sleep would come.

Thought fled as he faced his captor. Years of training had molded him and he extended his sword in mid guard and locked his eyes on Sarmiento.

A moment of hesitation, then a thrust by Sarmiento. Fernán parried with the flat of his blade, disengaged, and stepped back, assuming a low guard, sword held with both hands to the right of his knees, pointed at the eyes. Though he held the sword with both hands, he had been scarcely able to parry the thrust and had no strength to respond with his own attack. He wished to die but not before he had killed Sarmiento, though that outcome was unlikely.

"Why have me washed and newly dressed if you would kill me?" he asked, breathing fast. Then he half-thrust at Sarmiento, forcing him to retreat.

"Because you stink, *marrano*. Selfishness, pure selfishness!" Sarmiento shouted, and swung his blade edge down toward Fernán, toward his shoulder where Fernán met it with the flat of his sword. And with swords locked, Fernán pushed close to Sarmiento.

"You too will reek when they imprison you, Sarmiento."

With all the power he could summon, he shoved the blade to the left and circled to his right, away from the other blade. Weeks of confinement and lack of food had punished him and he lost focus a moment—the room twisted and then righted.

"That day will never come, *marrano*." Sarmiento growled, and was at him again with a slashing attack at his side.

Fernán backed off and let the blade slide by, then cut at Sarmiento, at the leg, a low diagonal slash from the left. Too slow. Sarmiento parried, skipped away, and responded with a full cut from high left. But the stroke fell short and the blade whistled in front of Fernán and struck the floor, sending sparks.

"Your people are dead, *marrano*. Time to join them."

"Come close, Sarmiento, or is it that I stink too much?"

Though the sword weighed less than four pounds, wielding it required more effort than Fernán thought he could manage. He circled to his right, slowly, taking his time, breaking the rhythm of the fight, giving himself a breath.

"Who is dead, Sarmiento?"

Sarmiento held his sword high. "Their names mean nothing. Now, *marrano*, you are dead." A quick feint from the right, then, in one move, Sarmiento released his left hand from the hilt and extended his right arm in a thrust straight at the belt-line.

Fernán lurched and sidestepped, parrying to the side and then closed on Sarmiento, the hilt of his sword below the chin line.

"You are a woman with a sword, *marrano*."

Fernán tensed, straightened his legs, and thrust the sword pommel up under the chin of Sarmiento. The head snapped back and Sarmiento staggered and screamed, "Bastard!" raised his sword, and slashed down at Fernán. Desperate, Fernán held his sword above him, point down to ward off the blow, and butted Sarmiento in the midsection with his head and the pommel of his sword.

They lay on the floor. Sarmiento struggling for breath, his sword fallen beside him. Fernán face down, dizzy from the blow, clutched his sword and stumbled to his knees. Sarmiento reached for his sword.

"Set your blade against my breast," Fernán said between gasps. "I will place mine against yours. We will find death together."

"Stupid fool," Sarmiento said, his breath labored. "Death comes soon enough." He dragged himself to the door and knocked. "Put down your sword," he said to Fernán. Two guards entered. "Take him to his cell. You want to die, *marrano*? Die. You will not see me again."

"In Hell, Sarmiento, in the flames of Hell. There will I see you."

34

Ten days later

Sarmiento woke. His body felt abused—his arms and legs ached. Sleep, when it came, had been troubled. Half-asleep he had dreamt of fighting Hernandes again—repeating his attacks, Hernandes responding, then attack and counter, interminably, back and forth, living again the dragging weight of the sword, the fatigue.

Hernandes had been quick, well-trained, audacious. Exhausted, he seemed to gain strength as the fight progressed. How he had used his body—butting like an animal! Sarmiento touched his aching chin where the pommel of the sword had struck and his chest where Hernandes had butted him. The *marrano* was young and youth surely compensated for the deprivations of prison. Ten days since they had fought and Hernandes was putrefying in his cell. So ends youth. What did a man of his age and experience have to prove? That he was a better fighter than a callow boy? That required no test. Though he did need practice—his timing was poor. He would remember that butt.

The three-quarter-moon was high, the unfamiliar bedchamber flooded with light. He remembered that he now slept in the Alcázar, thus avoiding conversation with his wife and mother and isolating himself from the progressive decay of the skeleton that had been his father. As for the children, they cared little for him and he found them difficult. Just as well. Let them play with their mother—keep her out of foreign beds.

A sharp pain pierced his leg when he sat up and he lay back and waited for it to subside. These pains had seized him after the fight that, he admitted, had drained his strength—he was no longer accustomed to such exertion.

A foolish exercise. Dangerous. One slip and the *marrano* would have killed him. He must have pulled a muscle in his groin—tenderness there.

Last night he would have bedded Manuela, but had been apathetic toward her for the first time since the rebellion. Tonight he would see her—or perhaps not. What if the bitch cheated, saw others behind his back? Better to know than to be informed by a supposed friend. He would have a man track her. How could he spend three nights of four in her bed and know so little about the woman?

Admittedly, he knew little of anyone. A wife as dense as pudding. A mother like a cloud, her image shifting from moment to moment. His father dead in all senses. García, hidden behind a wall of words. The only people on whose actions he could depend were the King, Luna, Pacheco, and the other villains. He knew them—self-centered, uncompromising, each dedicated to his own advancement—as he was. And now must he fight them with support from Enrique, the prince of caprice? And at such a price? He should have offered Enrique less. His anxious offer exhibited desperation and he was not desperate, not in the least. He was Governor of Toledo and respected. What would happen when the Prince arrived? Then, dear God, he would be reduced to the state of a vassal. Something must be done.

A cautious knock. Sarmiento slid his dagger from its scabbard, struggled to his feet, and winced with pain. "Come in."

A courier stepped into the room and faltered, eyes on the dagger, and blurted out, "Your Excellency, the army is gone from its encampment. Don Marcos García has asked if you would meet him at the Gate of Visagra in half an hour."

"Tell don Marcos that I will meet him in an hour. And send in the orderly."

35

That same morning at the Alcázar

Cloaked in the hooded robes of a Dominican, Jerónimo stepped down from the open wagon, normally used to carry rugs and other merchandise to market, and led hooded Paulo up the steps of the Alcázar and through its entrance. He greeted the sentries at either side and glanced back. José, the driver of the wagon, had been told to wait. Everything depended on a quick exit, and Jerónimo prayed that the simple man would be there when needed.

Paulo had been chosen, with the approval of Lorenzo, because he was strong and faithful, although ignorant and vain. Jerónimo had warned Paulo away from the servant women, saying he would be whipped if he strayed in that direction.

Paulo had laughed. "Worth the whipping, Steward," he said. "This job is dangerous, no? Getting the young master from prison?

He assured Paulo there was nothing to fear. "Follow my example. Do as I say, but say nothing. Your cowl is sufficient disguise and license. You will be well rewarded when we return."

"To rescue young Fernán from the pit of Hell is reward enough. Trust my silence and my strength."

Brave words, Jerónimo thought, as they descended from the enormous atrium of the Alcázar down spiral stairs to the dungeons. With each step the air grew heavier with damp, and the stench that rose from the cells more potent. At the bottom of the stairs stood a guardsman armed with pike and sword. Another sat at a wooden table, papers stacked in neat piles before him. Jerónimo recognized neither.

"May God grant you peace, Captain. I am Fray Jerónimo and this is Fray Paulo. Forgive the early hour, but we Brothers wake well before dawn to do the business of the Lord."

"I am a corporal, Fray Jerónimo, not a captain. State your business here this morning."

"With the blessing of God, we have authorization for the release of one of your prisoners."

"Papers."

Jerónimo removed a scroll from an inner pocket and handed it to the corporal. "You will see, señor corporal, that the release is signed by Prince Enrique. His seal and signature appear at the bottom of the scroll."

"Why do you think this signature would release a prisoner, Fray Jerónimo? Pero Sarmiento is Governor, not the Prince. The revolutionary administration supervises all prisoners here and only their authorization is valid. You need a signature from the Governor." And he returned to his paperwork.

Jerónimo leaned over the table. "Señor corporal, shut off here in the bowels of this fortress, you may not be aware of what has happened in the world above. But know this—within a matter of days the Prince will be lord of Toledo and the affairs of the city will pass into his hands."

The corporal looked up. "While we may be under the ground, Fray Jerónimo, we are as privy to rumors as those who parade about under the sun. And what you have told me is rumor."

"Forgive my disagreement with your opinion, señor corporal, but what I have told you is not rumor, but truth. Even now the King has retreated and the Prince marches on Toledo." Jerónimo leaned further forward and whispered, "Ask your guard to walk down the corridor so that we may talk in confidence."

"So that you and Fray Paulo may kill me and free the prisoner?"

Jerónimo turned and said, "Fray Paulo, wait for me at the top of the stairs." Paulo nodded and climbed the stairs. "You see, I am a friar and harbor no dark motives, Señor corporal. Rather, our *patrón*, the Prince, wishes to reward you for your foresight and cooperation."

The corporal pushed back from the table, glanced at the guard, and asked in a voice as soft as air, "How do you know the King has gone and the Prince advances?"

"Because with these two eyes I have seen the empty meadow where the King had been encamped, and my brother confidante in the entourage of the Prince assures me that Enrique will be here within days."

"And if by chance I happen to trust you, Fray Jerónimo, what difference will that make? You have no authorized signature."

"Send the guard on an extended errand, señor corporal, if you please."

The corporal looked at Jerónimo, lay his dagger on the table near his hand, and said to the guard, "Felipe, survey each cell. Be sure the guards are alert."

The guard saluted and retreated down the corridor.

"He will return in ten minutes. Who are you?"

"Señor corporal, I am that which you see I am. However, I have pledged to save the life of a young man imprisoned here who is dear to the Prince and who was wrongly arrested for heresy. Your cooperation will be rewarded with advancement and gold when Enrique arrives."

"What proof do you have of this affection of the Prince for my prisoner?"

Jerónimo took a small bag from beneath his robe. "This token is guarantee of his affection."

"And what is in that bag?"

"Examine the contents, if you please. You will find exactly one thousand maravedís."

The corporal opened the bag, reached inside, extracted a few gold coins, and hefted the bag. "One thousand?"

"Exactly. And if we succeed, señor corporal, when the Prince arrives, you will receive that same amount again, be granted a commission as sergeant, and removed from this place of death to a more congenial assignment."

"Why should I trust you, Fray Jerónimo? You may have set a trap for me."

"Señor corporal, I have never seen you before. I do not know your name. How can I have set a trap? And to what purpose? As for trust, you will know I am a trustworthy friar when the Prince arrives, not before. But at the least you will have one thousand *maravedís* in your pocket."

The corporal stared down the empty corridor. "Who is the prisoner?"

"Fernán Hernandes."

The corporal smiled and Jerónimo asked, "You know him?"

"I do. Pero Sarmiento had him removed from a *strappado* session ten days ago. The guards who took him from the torture chamber told me Hernandes and Sarmiento fought with swords."

"Was he hurt?"

"No." The corporal snickered. "But His Excellency has limped ever since." He looked hard at Jerónimo for several minutes and then shrugged. "Have you a plan, Fray Jerónimo?" And Jerónimo described how they would release Fernán.

The guard returned and reported that the cells were well guarded. The corporal signified his approval and told the guard to take Hernandes to the *strappado* chamber.

"He is not conscious, Corporal," The guard said. "The man cannot walk."

"Sancho will help you carry him. Let him die up there. Let it be their responsibility, not ours."

"The cell will be unguarded while we are gone, Corporal."

"But locked, Felipe. Sufficient for the time being. Get on with it."

The guard walked down the corridor and the corporal said, "If Hernandes is dead, I keep the money."

Jerónimo nodded. "Will they be long?" His pulse had quickened when he heard the guard describe the state of health of his friend.

"A minute. They will take him up the stairs."

Jerónimo heard them approach—a noise of dragging feet and cursing guards. When they appeared, he saw Fernán suspended between their shoulders, head bobbing, body drawn, bones stretching his skin.

"Oh, blessed God," Jerónimo said. "Can he not be carried?"

"Carry the bastard," the corporal said. "He cannot weigh more than a sparrow."

"The man is filthy, Corporal."

"Wash after. Carry him under his arms and knees. Now! Upstairs to the *strappado*!"

The guards hesitated at the bottom of the stairs. Fernán hung between them and Jerónimo examined his young friend. His skin was dark from dirt and covered with sores. His matted head lolled to one side, His eyes were closed, his mouth half open. Jerónimo placed a finger on his neck—a pulse, though weak.

"What do they want with this one up there?" a guard said.

"Not mine to ask," the corporal said. "Orders are orders. Up you go."

They climbed the stairs, complaining with each step. The corporal and Jerónimo followed. At the top, the guards paused to take a breath and Jerónimo walked over to Paulo who stood aside, his mouth agape.

"Say nothing, Paulo, but come with me."

"Does he live?"

"Barely. Come. I will explain."

The incongruous company set off down a narrow corridor and reached a door set into the stone wall. The corporal opened the door and they entered. The chamber was free of prisoners or executioners.

"Lay him down. There. Easy. Good," the corporal said.

Jerónimo felt for a pulse. "Oh, my dear God." His voice trembled. "No pulse, no blood in his body. The poor boy is dead."

Paulo crossed himself and cried out, "Merciful God! He has had no Last Rites. No confession or absolution."

Jerónimo knelt beside Fernán. "Dear Lord," he said, "I have no oil with which to anoint the body of this poor soul, no incense or holy water, but I will do without and pray that his spirit will be received in Heaven." And he crossed himself and spoke to Fernán. "May the Lord in His love and mercy help you with the grace of the Holy Spirit. May the Lord free you from sin and save you and raise you up." He looked around him and said, "That is the best I can do, oh Lord."

The corporal shrugged and said to the guards. "Down to the cells. I will be there in a minute."

The guards left. Fernán lay on the ground.

"Quick then!" the corporal said.

Jerónimo unwound a sheet of white cloth from beneath his cloak and they shrouded Fernán, covering his head. His feet protruded from beneath the winding-sheet, but Jerónimo decided they could do nothing to cover them. Then Paulo heaved Fernán up off the ground and carried him in his arms to the door. The corporal opened the door and they walked together to the main entrance of the Alcázar.

"This man died in the cells," the corporal said to the sentries. "The friars administered Last Rites. They are to be passed."

"God protect us, what an unholy smell," one said.

"The poor body cannot help its odor," Jerónimo said. "He must be cleansed and made ready for burial. We are sorry for the odor."

"Need help, Friar?" the other sentry asked.

"Bless you, my son, but we can manage. We have a wagon below."

"God go with you," the sentry said.

They hurried down the steps of the building, Paulo carrying Fernán in the white shroud. Jerónimo breathed more easily when he saw the wagon.

"Gently, Fray Paulo," he said as Paulo laid Fernán in the bay.

"What is your name?" Jerónimo asked the corporal.

"You do not know my name and never will. You will hear from me through the Hernandes family when the Prince arrives." And he ran up the stairs and into the Alcázar.

Jerónimo climbed into the bay beside Fernán. "José," he said, "go quickly. I will tell you where."

The sun began to light the morning sky. Paulo sat next to José and the wagon started. Jerónimo peered over the side and held his breath, for there was Sarmiento mounting a horse at the foot of the stairs. For the second time their eyes met. This time, however, Jerónimo wore the cowl.

36

The Gate of Visagra

Dawn waited for Sarmiento. The sun topped the hills as he and his troop of horse rode up to the Gate of Visagra. The García escort was gathered below the gate and the captain saluted.

"Your Excellency, don Marcos is on the rampart above."

Sarmiento climbed the stairs and stepped out onto the wall.

"A most wonderful morning, don Pero." García said. "If you please, señor, examine the field before us and tell me what you see."

Sarmiento scanned the meadow where the forces of the King had been encamped. The signs of sudden withdrawal were accented by the ascending sun which cast long shadows of the remnants of campfires, piles of gathered wood, and trampled turf—the usual disorder of an army in retreat, the debris of a life Sarmiento had once shared.

"The King has gone, I pray, forever."

"Our patrol reported that Juan marched north toward Valladolid last night," García said. "I am surprised he did not stay and fight. Why scamper away like a cur with his tail between his legs?"

"Three possible reasons, perhaps four. To begin with, Juan is afraid of the Prince—justifiably. He knows the strength the Prince has mustered, the imperfection of his own force, and can add and subtract if not multiply. Then again, a fight with Enrique in the west might tempt Juan of Navarre and his Aragonese friends to attack from the east. Also, Enrique is his son, and fathers prefer not to war with their heirs.

"Finally, this maneuver may be a trick. Are we sure Luna has not led

Enrique into a trap, taking advantage of our imminent rendezvous with the Prince, and will circle back? That would be typical of the fox."

"Our patrol has orders to follow the King. We will be watchful."

"Good. Enrique will be here soon." Sarmiento turned his back on the empty field and hobbled toward the exit. "We should return to the Alcázar, García, and think this through."

"Are you well, don Pero? You appear to limp."

"A muscle, García. I pulled a muscle. Nothing to be concerned about."

They rode off side by side in the van of their troops. The sun cleared the horizon and they walked their horses in the morning light, conversing as they rode.

"What do you know of Enrique, García?"

"What knowledge I have is hearsay. He is reputed to be tall, blond like his father, and with a broken nose pushed flat against his face."

"A fair description. The nose was broken in a childhood accident. A curious appearance. Some wag thought him cousin to a lion—in countenance only, of course. Enrique is far from forbidding, though his comportment is complex. He has amassed considerable power, primarily by blackmailing his father—forming alliances with those who hate King Juan, then relinquishing his new friends for a price. Sweet lad."

"Surprising that Luna has not chastised him."

"Difficult. His vassals comprise a force of over ten thousand mounted knights and almost forty thousand infantry."

"How many on this campaign?"

"Since nobility do little other than fornicate and fight—it is all sport to them—I am sure they will join in the fun. I would say most are with him, eager to down Luna and break a few heads."

"And will the Prince fight?"

"Surprisingly, yes. He has been well-tutored in the manly and martial arts. Bore himself well alongside his father against the Princes of Aragón, the last time he and King Juan were unified."

"Decisive?"

Sarmiento smiled. "You are inquisitive, don Marcos." García shrugged. "Although he can be ruthless, Enrique is not decisive. So you and I should understand that an agreement with our Prince is subject to review by Juan Pacheco. And that fact, García, colors our project and gives us reason to pause before we congratulate ourselves on escaping the snare laid by the King."

He was surprised this conversation with García had gone so well. What had changed? Tension had marked their interchanges in the past. Today, however, García seemed compatible, easy to talk to. There was an element of respect in his demeanor that had escaped Sarmiento before. Perhaps lifting the siege had demonstrated his leadership and, if that were the case, all well and good, but he would keep an eye on the lawyer.

Suddenly, his horse shied and reared. Sarmiento fought the animal and brought the stallion under control with some difficulty. The effort was painful and the nagging ache in his leg returned. "Damned beast shies at nothing and everything," he said, tugging at the reins, driving the bit deep into the tender mouth.

Over breakfast in the Alcázar, Sarmiento and García discussed the original terms of their agreement with Enrique and decided that they had been too liberal and that their concessions must be abridged. The Prince must be restricted in his access to Toledo and the King excluded from the city entirely, although without appearing to deny His Majesty entry. Furthermore, Sarmiento required control of the Alcázar and the chief judgeship.

"Send word to the Prince that we will arrive at his camp by the end of the week," Sarmiento said, "when we will discuss arrangements and welcome him to Toledo."

"Travel to the Prince? That will cause us to appear weak, don Pero. Let his agents come here."

"No, this encounter must be face to face. These are delicate issues easily misinterpreted. We will go to him."

"I protest, señor. We might easily be detained and subject to his whims. And, from what I understand of his whims, our position could be perilous."

"García, I have met the Prince and you have not. We must negotiate with him directly. Therefore, if you would send someone to find his camp and convey our message, I would be most gratified. Another slice of ham?"

37

The encampment of Prince Enrique near Talavera de la Reina

The week following the retreat, a patrol from the Prince intercepted the messengers García had dispatched and led them to Enrique. Their message delivered, they returned to Toledo under a cold, drenching rain.

During administrative review with his aides that morning, Sarmiento noted that Fernán Hernandes had died. The death was one of a series of entries in the documents he scanned, the name buried within those of a dozen or more prisoners who had died of torture, burning, or neglect. Rain had fallen steadily from the dark sky for the past two days and, at that moment, beat hard at the window. Sarmiento stared through the glass. What did it mean that the *marrano* was dead? We all die eventually—though Hernandes had been young. Sarmiento was surprised by the jolt the name Hernandes had caused him. He recalled one move young Hernandes had executed during their swordplay—a feint and slash that took him off guard and almost cost him a leg. An image teased his memory—a cart or wagon at the staircase of the Alcázar, a friar seated in the bay beside a long white bundle. Had he seen protruding feet? The monk had stared at him. Had the shroud contained the *marrano*? Not possible. Too fortuitous.

Thursday morning, the sun shone for the first time in four days, a happy augury according to García. Later that morning, Sarmiento, García, and Galvez, escorted by a troop of horse, departed Toledo. All that week Sarmiento had been troubled by his leg, which made it difficult for him to sit or stand for any period of time. He blamed the weather and was pleased that God had at last sent the sun to bless them with its presence and to dry the mud on the road they must travel. But the pain continued, aggravated by the jolting ride.

They arrived toward evening at the encampment near Talavera de la Reina, west of Toledo, and were guided by the personal guard of the Prince to an elaborate Moorish tent within a city of tents occupied by nobles and vassals accompanying Enrique. The tent was illuminated by numerous oil-burning lamps and filled with the exotic fragrance of incense.

The Prince sat toward the rear of the tent, cross-legged amidst a jumble of ornamental rugs and elaborate, plump cushions. He was dressed in Moorish attire—turban, brocaded jerkin, burnoose, shoes with upturned toes—his costume decorated with gold and silver thread in intricate geometric patterns. The nobles surrounding him were dressed in similar fashion and sat either cross-legged or reclining in the Roman mode.

The visitors bowed. "*Salaam aleikem*," the Prince said, "welcome to my home, don Pero and señores. I am sure you must be exhausted from your journey. My aide will see you and your companions to your tents where you may refresh yourselves. We will talk after dinner." And he turned to a handsome young man reclining beside him and resumed their conversation.

From the restrained sound level within the tent and the temperate behavior of the cushioned nobility, Sarmiento realized that festivities were not yet at their height. As they left the tent, García worried aloud that in such surroundings their trip might be a waste, and Galvez expressed extreme shock at the dissolute behavior he had observed. Sarmiento calmed their misgivings while sharing their concern, realizing that their eyes and ears would be subjected to additional surprises as the evening progressed. They retired to separate quarters—Sarmiento to a tent befitting his rank and García and Galvez to a smaller tent they would share. Their servants and escort were led to less commodious billets.

Sarmiento ordered his servant to wake him in an hour, removed his outer garments, lay down on the simple bed, and closed his eyes. The pain had been intense, but he felt his muscles relax and the misery ease. An hour later the servant entered with a basin of hot water, placed it on a table, and retrieved personal articles from a small leather chest they had brought from Toledo. Then he laid out fresh clothing and awakened his master. His servant helped Sarmiento wash and dress and, within an hour, he was summoned to dinner.

Meats and vegetables grilled on open fires were being carried into the Moorish tent by servants dressed in appropriate costume. Sarmiento questioned one cook as to the menu and was told that there was an assortment of lamb, pheasant, and venison, and a variety of vegetables, fruits, and other delicacies. When he asked about boar or piglet, the cook confounded Sarmiento. Moors do not eat pork, he said, and the Prince refuses to have pig at the table. The devotion of the Prince to authenticity both amused and annoyed Sarmiento and he wondered whether Enrique would apply the same reverence for play-acting to their negotiations. Not having soldiered since the Battle of Olmedo, Sarmiento considered the amenities, provisions, and fantasies he now experienced not what he remembered or expected of an army in the field, and he felt some anxiety about his negotiations with this impractical lord.

The tent interior had been redesigned for dinner with cushions arranged in a large square outside an inner square of low tables. The lanterns had been dimmed and many nobles, including the Prince, were seated and dining. There seemed to be no order to the seating and no one to direct him where to sit, and Sarmiento lowered himself gingerly onto an available cushion. Guests to left and right ignored him, continuing their conversation and consumption of the generous portions of food before them.

No sooner had he seated himself than servants arrived with food and drink, knelt within the ring before him, placed several platters on his table, and asked which of the dishes he desired. He had assumed they spoke only Arabic, of which he had a smattering, but their Spanish was excellent. He chose the food at random and was dealt a lavish plate. No utensils, other than knives, had been provided, and he observed the others using their fingers and wiping them on whatever was at hand—table coverings, handkerchiefs, or costumes.

His rest had eased the pain somewhat but, locked cross-legged on the cushion, Sarmiento knew it would be impossible for him to rise when dinner was over. He resigned himself to further discomfort, examined the plate before him, and began to eat. The food, though simple, was superb. When a servant later appeared and asked if His Excellency had finished, he nodded and his plate was removed.

His glass of wine had been filled repeatedly and, while drinking, Sarmiento was astonished when two other servants appeared with a dissimilar group of serving platters. The process of selection was repeated, a new plate was heaped with food, and his wineglass replaced and filled with a different wine. When the third set of servers, platters, and wine appeared, he stated dramatically that he had eaten enough and wanted no more. Nevertheless, he received another brimming plate and glass. Before long his plate was removed and a dark hot liquid was served in a small cup. The color was black, the taste bitter, the texture grainy. He was unimpressed.

Sarmiento glanced from side to side. The nobles beside him had been in constant conversation since he arrived, their mouths employed in perpetual chewing and talking. Did they eat like this daily? Their acceptance of the feast—the quantity, variety, and masterful preparation—was so matter-of-fact that he imagined they must feel well deserved of their portion. To be sure, they were nobles of the first rank—barons and dukes, owners of fine estates of immense value, and masters of beautiful wives and mistresses. But no one spoke to him. Did they not realize who sat next to them, ate the same food as they, and drank glass after glass of the same wine? Did they not know he was Governor of Toledo, the ancient capital of Castile, a man who had thumbed his nose at the King and Alvaro de Luna—that same Luna who frightened Castile to death? And that he, Pero Sarmiento, had stared Luna and the King in the face and had not blinked while they had? Who must one be to fly so high? Did God apportion His Grace to these men alone while others must grovel for scraps? Sword in hand, he, Sarmiento, could cut them down to size. Then they would acknowledge him.

A servant placed before him a dish of sweets and a glass of liqueur that lay within its bowl like the mercury he had once seen in the rooms of an alchemist. Heavy, portentous, it shone with an inner light, a mystical presence. He raised the glass to his lips, sipped the liqueur, and caught his breath, for the taste and fragrance were beyond his experience and required that he savor the liquid as one would a sacred potion prepared for angels.

He heard music and imagined he had been transported to another plane, for these were sounds such as he had never heard. He knew Moorish music and the music of Jews and, of course, Spanish music, but nothing of this order. The music of stringed instruments, drums, and flute originated with a troupe of players seated in a corner of the tent. They must have been there for some time, yet he had not heard the strains of their instruments. Where could he have been not to have heard such sweet harmonies? They spoke to him of magic.

And then a silken, lustrous apparition appeared at the tent opening, entered the inner ring of tables, stepped to the center as if on pillows, and bowed deeply and gracefully to the Prince, who tossed a handful of gold coins into the ring. His example was followed by the others, so that the carpeted floor glittered with golden reflections.

The music was stilled during the entrance of the young woman, but now it began again with cadences and gliding tones evocative of past times and distant lands. The maiden stood in the center of the tent and sang with such a plaintive lilt to her rich and varied voice that he felt moved beyond himself. His eyes teared with her songs and, though he understood not a word she sang, the refrains wrung emotions from him he had never experienced. While singing, she began to move hands and arms and hips in such a sensual manner that he imagined her limbs ruled by the sea. She was ethereal, and he was drawn to this phantasm as if by some illusory force beyond his power to subdue. So shaken was he that he felt he would cry out in wonder.

The songs ended, the singer bowed again to the Prince, and the tent filled with cries of *Olé* and the clink of coins that were thrown into the ring. Sarmiento felt bereaved, as if at a great loss. The young woman left the tent as she had entered and the musicians gathered the gold coins. He sat transfixed while self-hate grew within him for his weakness—that he had allowed himself to be so enthralled by the songs of a young Moorish woman.

38

Later that evening

Having abandoned all thought of serious discussion that night, Sarmiento was nonplused when toward midnight Pacheco approached him and suggested that they meet outside. As he feared, he was wedded to the cushion and rose with extreme discomfort. He had no relief from the misery in his leg that now throbbed urgently as if in payment for the perfection he had just witnessed.

Outside the tent, Pacheco stood with his face in shadow in the warm dark of the calm night. A sliver of moon had risen in the east.

"We will move to another tent and talk," Pacheco said. "This fête will continue till morning, and there are matters that require resolution from your side as well as ours."

"The Prince will be with us?"

"Yes—the Prince, Girón, and myself. What we cannot resolve tonight we will settle tomorrow or the next day. Your dinner was enjoyable?"

"Extraordinary. Your everyday fare?"

"Certainly not. We would be elephants. The Prince celebrates the withdrawal of his father from Toledo, as do we all. And the music?"

"More than delightful—exquisite. She unmanned me. Who is the woman?"

"A young person of special talents. Would you care to have her?"

"What do you mean?"

"Tonight. In your bed."

"Most tempting, I assure you, but I suffer these pains which appear to originate in my back. The damsel would be disappointed, and such a one should suffer no discontent."

"You were smitten, I see. A pity. The woman is talented in many arts—she might have eased your pain. However. We will meet soon then, don Pero. My aide will come for you."

Sarmiento collected García and Galvez and, uniformly distressed by their consumption of food and drink, they lingered in the night air, content to observe the stars and moon and comment on the singer.

The aide arrived and escorted them to a tent nearby, not half so large but as luxurious as the first, which contained a large oak table on which were carafes of liqueurs and platters of oily cakes. Sarmiento was pleased to see chairs. The Prince sat at the head of the table and a scribe, a Dominican friar, sat at the other end. The Toledans bowed to the Prince and were seated opposite Pacheco and Girón.

"Before we begin," Enrique said, "this meeting and all subsequent meetings will be informal. You will not bow or address me as Your Highness or defer to me in any way. You may address me as 'don Enrique' or 'señor.' We are equal before God and will conduct our affairs as equals. In the world at large there may be a necessity for protocol but not in this tent. Is that understood?"

The Prince glanced at Sarmiento. "Of course, don Enrique."

"Very well, then. I realize the hour is late and we have enjoyed a sumptuous meal, therefore our meeting will be of short duration and will continue tomorrow after noon. Since you requested this meeting, don Pero, begin, if you please."

Sarmiento first expressed their gratitude that the Prince had granted their request for a meeting and again for the elegant meal and entertainment. He trusted that when the Prince arrived in Toledo, his reception would be of similar quality, although he could not hope to equal its abundance or splendor.

Then he cleared his throat. "Don Enrique, these are our requests. When you have assumed the role of *patrón* of Toledo, we request continued command of the gates of the city and of the Alcázar. We also request that the King be permitted access to Toledo only when in your company."

"Don Pero," Pacheco said, "the provision with regard to the King is acceptable and nicely couched. But, señor, how can we be assured access to the city if you control the gates? With control of the gates, a Toledan administration—not yours, of course, but some future administration—might close the gates of the city and deny the Prince access. That is unacceptable."

Sarmiento and García had discussed the gates during their journey and decided that they would request command of the gates as a ploy, then pull back, rather than have Pacheco demand control, which they feared he might claim.

"What then would be justifiable, don Juan?" Sarmiento asked.

"Half the gates," Pacheco said.

Sarmiento and García whispered together as they had planned. "Agreed, señores," Sarmiento said, "that is, if you allow us to control San Martín and allow me to retain my positions as Commander of the Alcázar and Chief Judge of Appeals."

"That is satisfactory, don Pero. We understand your requirement for posts of authority. For our part, we request the gates of Visagra and Alcántara."

Sarmiento had hoped he could retain Visagra to the north or Alcántara to the east, but realized that the Prince desired control of a contiguous area. Again he conferred with García while Galvez took notes.

"Understandable, don Juan. You will command Visagra and Alcántara, and we San Martín and Cambrón. Good."

"Señores," Enrique said. "We have made a good beginning and the hour is late. Let us adjourn now and meet tomorrow after noon. The day has been enjoyable but long and my bones cry out for rest. Until tomorrow."

They parted and Sarmiento found his tent. A light shone from inside and he thought his servant considerate to light his way. He raised the tent flap, and sensed that he was not alone. The tent was relatively dark and his hand went to his dagger, but he had worn no dagger in the company of the Prince.

"Fear not, Excellency, I will be a balm to your suffering."

He could not place the voice, but he knew it was a woman and deduced that she was the singer.

"Who sent you?"

"Your dear friend, don Juan Pacheco. I will calm your pain and bring you pleasure."

"Where are you?"

"Warming your bed, Excellency. Come to me. Let me relieve your pain."

"I thought you were a Moor."

"No, Excellency, though I lived a long time among the Moors and learned their language and songs. I am from Sevilla. Come, señor, one must not live with pain."

39

The Inn of La Fonda de los Reyes

Jerónimo watched as Fernán slept. The room was modest—two windows facing east, a bed in which Fernán lay, and four chairs, three of which were occupied by Lorenzo, Celestina, and Abrahán Melamed. Jerónimo hovered over the bed, as if on guard, as he had been for the past five days and nights since he and Paulo had brought Fernán to the inn.

Last night had gone well for Fernán. His body temperature had lowered and his sleep more tranquil than the first four nights and days, during which he had thrashed and cried out, often flailing his arms as if in combat. His eyes were not yet open and the prognosis don Abrahán rendered was restrained.

The doctor sat in conversation with Lorenzo while Celestina dozed in her chair. She had attended Fernán part of the night while Jerónimo rested—placing cool, damp cloths on his brow, counting his pulse, checking the warmth of his body. Had there been a dramatic change, Jerónimo would have fetched the doctor, though Melamed had said there was little he could do that was not being done by the poor body itself, and they must wait and pray.

Jerónimo heard Fernán breathe in the half-dark and recalled their escape from the Alcázar in the open wagon—jogging down the empty cobbled streets to this inn, chosen because the innkeeper, though Castilian, was a friend of Jerónimo and no friend of Sarmiento. After drawing up to the back of the inn, the steward lowered Fernán from the wagon and Paulo carried him up a set of stairs to a second-floor gallery and into one of the two rooms that Jerónimo had secured.

Paulo had lowered Fernán onto the bed and, after several additional cautions for secrecy from Jerónimo, crept out the door. Jerónimo listened for steps descending the outside stairs and the wagon rolling away. He then turned to the trio standing in the shadows. "Your son is here, don Lorenzo, doña Celestina," he said. "Alive, but just barely. He needs your immediate attention, don Abrahán."

Melamed rushed over to the bed, and Jerónimo and he unwound the cloth to reveal the filthy, emaciated, sore-pocked body. Celestina gasped and Lorenzo cried out, "Dear God!" Melamed searched for a pulse and nodded vigorously when he found it. He felt the body and found nothing broken, although he said that Fernán had fever and they must move quickly to provide him liquid nourishment and treat the sores and remove lice and other insects that might inhabit his body.

"I will wash Fernán while you see to his nourishment," Celestina said.

"Are you able to do that?" Melamed asked.

"Don Abrahán, I will do anything for my son."

Lorenzo took Jerónimo by the arm. "Wherever did you obtain that princely document?"

"A forgery, señor. A good copy that seems authentic."

"Your resources confound me. What miracle will you perform next?"

"Whatever miracle is required by your family, señor."

"Then let your next miracle be this, Jerónimo," Celestina said. "I need hot water and cloths. First, if you please, remove that foolish Dominican costume. I brought soap from the house—in that small bag. The other bag contains a pot of soup. Do not confuse soup with soap. Have the landlord heat the soup and bring it to the doctor. And Jerónimo, come here to me."

He went to her and she looked into his face. Though there was the length of an arm between them, when her mist-laden eyes met his—the most direct contact he had ever had with his mistress—the effect was that of an embrace.

"God bless you, dear friend," she said. "Our gratitude has no limit. Now quickly, do what I ask."

Jerónimo noticed Melamed watching, wearing a sad smile, and he went to work.

That was four days ago and the Fernán who slept in the bed that fifth morning looked nothing like the wraith Jerónimo had rescued. His body had been washed with hot water and fragrant Venetian soap, the insects removed, and the sores treated with ointment. His hair had been washed and cut and lay flat against the pillow. Celestina had trimmed his beard and nails, but Melamed forestalled her from razing the beard, saying it might be wise to hide him in the *judería*, and a beard would alter his appearance and ease his acceptance in the Jewish community.

That remark loosed a series of other questions as to his future now that the authorities thought Fernán dead. An inquiry by Lorenzo at the Alcázar had confirmed that Fernán was officially deceased, the body removed by friars. A false funeral was hastily arranged and, despite the critical condition of the supposed corpse and the superstition that attended the pretense, the black-garbed family walked behind a black wagon to the cemetery outside the gate of Cambrón, where the name 'Fernán Hernandes' was buried with stones in the coffin.

Lorenzo and Melamed had decided that, if Fernán survived, he would recuperate at the Melamed home, far from prying eyes. And when fully recovered, God willing, he would return home as a visiting cousin from another city. The beard and clothes would disguise his actual identity and his familial relationship would account for similarities.

Melamed stood by the bedside and counted his pulse. "The blood beats strong and at a good rate," he said. "Better than yesterday, much better." The sun had risen above the rooftops and the morning light streamed onto the bed. "His color is good." Melamed felt his brow. "And the heat of his body is, thank God, as it should be. Fernán is on the mend, blessed be the name of the Lord. Now we must wait for him to awaken from his long sleep so that we may measure the damage deprivation and punishment have caused. But, Celestina and Lorenzo and you, dear Jerónimo, for the first time I have cause for hope. May God have answered our prayers and returned Fernán to his loved ones."

He went to Lorenzo and shook his hand. "I leave you now, cousin. Watch him with care. This day may produce a good omen."

Melamed then kissed the hand of Celestina, shook hands with Jerónimo, and left by the back stairs. Don Abrahán had protested, but Lorenzo insisted that his carriage be placed at the disposal of his cousin, and Melamed climbed into the waiting carriage and was driven off.

Jerónimo sat by the bed and studied his young friend. Strands of gray wandered through his hair and beard, altering his appearance considerably. He had aged. Was it the gray in his hair, or the beard, or had the experience transformed him? There were lines in his face that had not been there— around the eyes, on the forehead, beside his sunken cheeks. The soft outlines of youth had given way to the harder angles of a more mature age. Not yet eighteen, he appeared older by a dozen years. Truly, Fernán had died and a new soul occupied his body. Oh, merciful God, Jerónimo thought, why have You taken youth from this boy? What purpose shall have been served by this transformation?

40

The encampment near Talavera

He awoke late, alone, the tent fabric glowing with sunlight. For a moment Sarmiento thought the pain was gone, but it struck when he attempted to sit and he lay back and cursed. Finally able to stand, he opened the tent flap and found his servant seated on the ground outside. Sarmiento told the youth to fetch warm water and he washed himself, donned fresh clothes, and sought out García and Galvez.

The two were breaking their fast, and he sat with them in the sun and nibbled on bread and cold venison washed down with ale. After the enormous meal the night before, he was surprised he had any appetite. The pain, which had never disappeared, depressed him. He had slept badly after the singer left his tent, and anticipated the end of negotiations with the Prince and their immediate return to Toledo.

The singer—he had never discovered her name—had departed before dawn after several bouts of lovemaking, if it could be called that. He had been repelled by her heavy, incense-laden odor that troubled his overburdened stomach. Her body had been wrapped in a gauze-like cloth during the performance but, unclothed, he found her flabby, the breasts small and flat, her thighs large and without definition. And her speaking voice was low and coarse, so different from the singing that had enchanted him. Exhausted from the ride, the food, and negotiation with the Prince, he let the singer assume control of the exercise and minister to him. But the experience was dull and disappointing. He awakened with a metallic taste in his mouth, wishing that she had never come to his tent and that he could recall the songs in all their purity. But the music had been spoiled.

"Do we know their requests, don Pero?" Galvez asked.

"No. But we must discuss the disposition of the *marranos* and extract a pardon from the Prince for any of our actions that he may deem illicit."

"What actions?" García asked.

"Appropriation, banishment, torture, execution."

"But those actions are condoned by the Church and employed throughout history by the Holy Father and the Church when dealing with heretics," Galvez said.

"Agreed," Sarmiento said. "Let us wait. Good morning, don Juan."

Pacheco had rounded a tent and come upon them.

"Good day to you, don Pero, and you, don Marcos and Canon Lope. The day is bright and welcome. I sought you earlier this morning to discover whether you would care to join in a hunt, but found you asleep. You missed an excellent ride and gallant bowmanship. But, on to business. The Prince has dined and wishes to conclude our arrangements. There are plans to be made. Shall we join him?"

They met in the same tent as on the previous night except that the noonday sun continued to bathe the tent fabric and interior with a glow that appeared to light a fire in the golden hair of the Prince. Though the tent was open to the air, the sun created heat as well as light and Sarmiento became uncomfortable.

After salutations, Pacheco opened the discussion. "Don Enrique has several requests, señores. We will take them in order. First, the Prince requests that those involved in the Toledo rebellion, including don Pero Sarmiento, don Marcos García, and others of their party, agree not to negotiate with any political party other than the party of the Prince, except with his explicit permission. That excludes negotiations with King Juan, Alvaro de Luna, Juan of Navarre, or any such persons. Furthermore, all such negotiations, should they arise, lie solely within the province of Prince Enrique. Any contrary action by a party to this agreement will be considered an act of treason and dealt with summarily."

Sarmiento gazed at the tent ceiling. He expected to find the sun eclipsed and the ceiling dark. But though the cloth still glowed, a light had been extinguished in the negotiations. He felt the eyes of García hard on him and turned to his confederate and nodded. The return nod was hardly perceptible. Their nighttime requests had been childish dreams, whereas this sunlit demand was a sharp sword on their lowered necks. He had nodded to indicate that a line had been crossed. They were now vassals of the Prince, subject to his will. The nod from García signified that he understood—they had exchanged the chains of the King for the chains of the Prince. But they had no choice.

"Agreed," Sarmiento said, and glanced at Pacheco with a tight smile. Pacheco smiled broadly.

Sarmiento drank a deep draft of ale. "Don Enrique, during the course of this rebellion we have had to resort to extreme measures on occasion to punish treason, to root out heresy, to maintain order. We request that none of those active in the rebellion, comprising those here present and others, be held accountable for any action he may have taken to ensure the success of the rebellion against tyranny—these actions include arrest, torture, banishment, execution or other hardships."

Pacheco rose and whispered to the Prince.

Sarmiento moistened his lips and inhaled another draft of ale. "In addition, the administration has appropriated goods and possessions from some citizens of Toledo as punishment for their actions enumerated before—as is customary under such conditions. We request that all goods so appropriated be retained by the administration."

Pacheco continued to whisper.

"Also," Sarmiento said, "persons removed from posts in the government for similar reasons are to be considered permanently removed and cannot resume prior positions. And those banished from Toledo can never return."

After several more minutes of discussion, Pacheco resumed his seat. "Those requests," he said, "are acceptable to the Prince. However…"

"Don Juan," the Prince interjected, "forgive my interruption, but I will continue at this point, for these are my true convictions and I wish to express them personally."

Pacheco appeared stunned, but recovered and said, "We are most anxious to hear your thoughts, don Enrique."

Enrique paused. "During the course of the rebellion against tyranny, as you call it so poetically, don Pero, you and your people proceeded against many members of the New Christian community—and only against New Christians. You accused them first of treason, that is, complicity with don Alvaro de Luna and against your rebellion, and later of heresy—both major crimes against state and church respectively, if true. You arrested many members of this community, some quite prominent, subjected them to brutal torture, burned many at the stake, and confiscated their goods and properties."

"Only those who confessed to treason and those who would not confess to heresy, don Enrique."

"Yes, yes. Fray Angélico, are you writing down every word of this conversation?"

"I am, don Enrique, every word."

"Good. Thank you. Now then, don Pero, your decision to oppress this limb of our citizenry was based on what facts?"

"That *conversos* were devoted to the tyranny of Alvaro de Luna and therefore treasonous in their belief," Sarmiento said. "And their allegiance to Christ and love for His church was flawed and heretical."

"And all New Christians were guilty of such behavior?"

"Most, señor."

"On what basis did you come to this conclusion, don Pero? Did you investigate? Did you take testimony from reliable witnesses? Did you speak with the Archbishop and others in the Church? Or did you assume yourselves to be correct and proceed over the objections of others—others superior to yourselves?" He raised his hand. "Do not bother to answer. I know what you will say and this is what I say.

"I have been called weak, effete, unmanly." He waved his hand at their move to protest. "I know, I know. That may or may not be so. One fact, however, is irrefutable. One day, God, in the course of His own time, will make me King and, when I am King, I will not abide the persecution of one segment of my citizenry by another more powerful segment. That way lies civil unrest and conflict and we have been too much down that path.

"New Christians are as Christian as Old Christians. They have the same rights in Castile as all Christians whether they descend from Jews, Muslims, Visigoths, Romans, or Greeks. Whatever their origin, they are now Christian. There are many great men among those who have joined our faith in recent times. If they were removed from us it would tear the fabric of Castile so severely that it might not be reparable, and that would destroy us. I will oppose such action with all my strength.

"You, Pero Lope de Galvez, were expressly forbidden by your Archbishop to condemn so-called heretics to the stake. Yet you did so. And don Pero, your administration burned them. No more. There will be no persecution of New Christians in Toledo so long as I am lord and *patrón* of that city.

"I have granted you protection from past crimes. Understand this, however. That protection does not extend beyond this day. On your return to Toledo, señores, you will release all prisoners held by you under charges of treason and heresy. And if you believe that I cannot know what you do, you believe wrongly. If you disobey my commands, I will exact retribution, remove myself as your *patrón*, and abandon you and your rebellion to the justice of Alvaro de Luna."

The Prince stood at his seat. "Fray Angélico will write a fair copy of our agreement and you will sign if you wish me to be your lord. Don Juan Pacheco will see to it. May you have a pleasant journey home."

Enrique left the tent and Pacheco, Girón, and Fray Angélico followed. Sarmiento, García, and Galvez sat hot and silent in their chairs.

41

A small house in Toledo, two days later

Manuela occupied the second floor of a pleasant house on the side of the city opposite from the Alcázar. The first floor was unoccupied and its doors and windows were bolted, deliberately, and would remain so. Sarmiento had chosen the location to be as far as possible from the residence where his mother, wife, and squalling brats lived, and he was thankful for his foresight—particularly tonight. His personal aide trudged up the outside staircase and, after several minutes, returned to say that the way was clear. He had inspected the rooms and found only Manuela and her two servants.

"How does she appear, Carlos?"

"Lovely, don Pero. Expectant."

"I hope not in a delicate way." The aide coughed. "A small jest, Carlos. Tomorrow morning at eight sharp." Sarmiento gazed at the second-floor balcony and then stepped down gingerly from his horse and handed the reins to Carlos. His leg plagued him. "The others in place?"

"Yes, Excellency. They will be relieved at two."

"Thank you. Good night, Carlos."

The ride from the encampment had been difficult and long. Dispirited, anxious, each of them preoccupied with his own black thoughts, they had departed immediately after the Prince and his aides vacated the tent and they had signed the agreement. Yesterday and today, Sarmiento had remained in bed, resting his back or leg, resisting whatever devil it was that caused his pain, struggling to accommodate to the demands of the Prince one moment, scheming how to squirm out of them the next. At last the pain eased and he sent word to Manuela that he would see her at dinner. Perhaps her ministrations would work a miracle and eliminate the discomfort entirely. Nothing else had been successful and he detested being hobbled by pain like an old man.

Lamps on the railing were lit, though the night was not yet dark. Candlelight glowed in the windows. He mounted the steps slowly, not wishing to encourage whatever devil lurked in his back.

Manuela waited in the open door, radiant and smiling, dressed in a long, silvery gown that traced the contours of her body. "Ah, Pero, you have been gone too long," she said, and wrapped her slim, bare arms around him.

"Gentle, my lovely, a devil plagues my back, and the accursed journey has aggravated whatever condition the demon has wrought."

"No, no, Pero. Oh, I am so sorry for my pet. You did not tell me. When did this begin?"

He told her his tale of woe amid clucks and touchings and pouts and kisses and was immediately relieved. He chided himself for having neglected Manuela and, moreover, of being suspicious of this paragon of women, this angel of delight. How delicate her skin, how clear her eyes, how full her bosom. What good fortune he enjoyed in his choice of women.

They dined on a secluded balcony that overlooked an inner courtyard. He wished she lived on the first floor, he said, the entrance would be more accessible.

"But that is exactly the reason why I am here, is it not, my love?" she said. "We want as difficult an access as possible, is that not so?"

He agreed. The sole entrance was the flight of steps he had climbed. His men were stationed around the house—a valid precaution. A spy, a bold *converso*, a relative of the Hernandes youth, any one of them might know of his mistress and attempt to slit his throat while he lay with her. The potential danger enhanced the passion her presence ignited. Ah, the perfume of her skin—he could barely control himself.

She asked about the Prince. He distanced himself from erotic thoughts and told her what had transpired at the city of tents, omitting his dalliance with the singer.

"And so," he said, "we are under the majestic thumb of Prince Enrique."

Was that not the expression García had used referring to Galvez? But then we are all under the thumb of some superior being, are we not? The clergy under García, García under the commoners, and now the lot of them under Enrique.

"This agreement with the Prince has cost us control of Toledo."

"You said he agreed to your demands."

"He did, damn him, but added others of his own. He will not tolerate abuse of *marranos* and that may lose us the commoners, whose only interest in rebellion was to rid Toledo of the accursed *marranos*. I begin to despise them as much as García does. Troublesome lot."

"What will you do, Perito?"

He started and peered at her. He wished this beautiful creature would not use the diminutive. Perito, Perito. So reminiscent of his mother. "I will think of something, my dear. It will come."

The food was delicious, the creation of a Florentine chef Manuela had hired after the rebellion. However, Sarmiento was distracted and ate without pleasure. He put down his knife and moved the plate away. "I am afraid appetite is a victim to worry, Uelita dear. If you please, excuse me to Cook."

"Of course. Cook will understand. Let us enter and relax and talk."

He followed her sinuous body. How does she move like that? Her hips seemed independent of the rest of her. He surveyed the room. Manuela had redecorated the interior in Moorish fashion since he had been here, and he had an unpleasant churning sensation as he recalled the effeminate interior of the princely tent and the now distasteful Moorish songs. Distributed about her sitting room were large, silken cushions in rich colors, and low dark tables decorated with the intricate geometries Moors favored. The walls were covered with silks, and an exquisite deep-piled rug covered the entire floor—donated by Hernandes while seeking the release of his sister-in-law and son. The oil lamps cast a warm, refined glow and delicate incense hovered in the cool evening air.

Manuela reclined on a group of cushions and invited him to lie with her. He sat on the cushions and rested his head in her lap, acutely aware of the junction of her thighs beneath the thin folds of the dress. She offered him a cake, but he refused and she nibbled on the delicacy and discarded it.

"You see," he said, wrenching away from the silken perfume that had begun to suffocate his mental faculties, "at present Enrique and the King are at odds and that works in our favor. However, one day Enrique will awaken and his perspective will have changed. He may have a dispute with the nobility, for example, and need the resources or protection his father can afford him. Then where will we stand? The King will say—return Toledo to me and I will support you. And without warning, Toledo and all within it will be in the royal pocket and we.... Ah well, that may never happen."

"Would Enrique do that?"

"Enrique will do whatever he and Pacheco deem expedient, whatever fits the moment. The story I outlined is not smoke."

"What would such an occurrence mean?"

He sensed a subtle underlay to her question. She wondered, he thought, what the scenario implied for Manuela. Cautious girl. "My love, Alvaro de Luna, Constable to the King, the man who, in fact, rules Castile, is a dear friend of *marranos*. There are many well-placed *marranos* in the administration and the clergy, as you may already know. Those devils would not hesitate a moment to bring me to court. And there I would be, defending my actions, accused by *marranos*, questioned by *marrano* lawyers, in a court presided over by *marrano* judges. A damned nightmare."

"And when does Prince Enrique arrive in Toledo?" she asked.

"In a week or two. Why?"

"What can you do before he comes, dear Pero?"

"Do? Enrique forbids taking any action against *marranos*."

"He means arrest, my sweet—torture, burning. What I ask is, what action can you take to prevent *marranos* from bringing you to court, from testifying against you, from resuming their positions as lawyers and judges?"

Sarmiento raised himself on his elbow and gazed at her. Though she was slightly less than twenty years of age, he had sometimes requested her opinion and been amazed at the layers of deliberation behind her beautiful forehead.

"You intrigue me, Uelita. What should I do?"

"Pass a law. You have accused *conversos* of deceitful Christianity. How can they hold office if they are not true Christians? Jews are prohibited from government and heretics most certainly should be. How can *conversos* bear witness against you or anyone? Jews are prohibited from bearing witness against a Christian. Jews are not true citizens and neither should *conversos* be considered true citizens, as they are baptised Jews."

"Where do you discover such ideas?"

"I hear you speak. I listen to others. My servants bring me gossip from the markets. And my mother taught me to question everything."

"When did she die?"

"Four years ago, bless her soul. Before we met."

"And your father?"

"I never knew him. Typical—the city is full of bastards. Mamá said he was noble. Perhaps. Nowadays, nobility is a commodity."

Sarmiento got to his feet. The pain had gone. He drew Manuela up from the cushions. "With a mind like yours, you should be governor, my sweet, and I should be your mistress."

"My clothes would look grotesque on you, Pero. They would bulge in the wrong places."

"By God," he said, laughing, "you should have been a man."

"Then we would not be here. We cannot make over what God has commanded, Pero, and I approve of the commandments of the Lord. I much prefer my sex. It provides more potential than manhood."

"More potential than manhood? Whatever can you mean? Women have no rights. You may own an estate, but with great difficulty, and you are forbidden in a court of law. You are chattel of men—objects of our pleasure and procreation—nothing more."

"And if women ceased to exist, Pero, what would men do? Some women, not all, have learned to use the assets they command. Those assets which, however men may deny their power, cause men to protect women, to worship women, to serve women. And the comprehension of that power makes women—not all, there are those of my sex who are blind or stupid—that mastery makes women able to rule men."

"And do you rule me?"

"No, my pet," she said laughing. "You are much too wise to be ruled."

He felt discomfited, somehow deceived. The turn in conversation annoyed him. "Where is that wonderful liqueur you hoard?"

"I hoard nothing, Pero dear. My house is yours and open to your needs—all your needs."

Manuela called her servant who brought a carafe of liqueur and glasses. Then she poured the dense liquid into the glasses and gave one to him.

"To your beauty and wisdom," he said. They sipped the liqueur and he lowered the shoulder of her gown, kissed the pouting nipple of her exposed breast, and licked the liqueur from the nipple. "We shall continue the question of your sex more enjoyably in bed."

"Delightful," she said. "You see, you do have good ideas—occasionally."

He cupped her breast, took the nipple between his thumb and forefinger, and squeezed.

Manuela winced. "Stop, Pero!" she said. "You hurt me. Why did you do that?"

"Do not be too wise, my dear. Remember, I am Governor."

42

La Fonda de los Reyes

The oil lamp on the table cast trembling shadows. Jerónimo watched Fernán who sat in the chair by the bed hugging a blanket to him, eyes wide, expression vacant. His head turned slowly from side to side as he looked at windows, door, chairs, bed, and the four seated against the wall.

"What does he think, don Abrahán?"

"God alone knows, doña Celestina. We can only wait and care for him. In time, his body will surely heal. But Fernán must walk and use the other parts of a body that has been wasted by confinement and starvation. As he does, he will gain weight and his bodily functions will return to normal." He sighed deeply. "However, we may assume that, because of the injuries and deprivation which brought his body to the attention of the Angel of Death, he is almost a child again and has lost memory and speech. Therefore, words are as important to his recovery as food." Fernán turned his eyes toward Melamed. "You see, he hears me and wonders what I say."

The light from the windows had dimmed, turning blue as the sky, dark as the nascent night. Celestina smiled at her son.

"He smiled, Lorenzo, when I smiled."

"Poor soul. How brave."

Fernán rubbed his arms against his body.

"Are you cold, dear heart?" she asked. "See how his mouth moves as if he would speak. Talk to me, Fernán." And she touched his face.

Fernán raised his hand to where she had touched him. She took his hand in hers.

"Your hand is cold, Fernán. Are you cold, my dear?"

"We must go now, Celestina," Lorenzo said.

"Yes, it will be night soon," don Abrahán said. "We must leave so that the last light can guide our steps and we will arrive in a dark that conceals us from prying eyes."

"How can we do that?"

"If I may suggest, don Lorenzo," Jerónimo said, "let us see if Fernán can walk. If he can manage a few steps that would help immensely. I will carry him down the stairs and wherever he is unable to manage."

"I wonder if he can stand?" don Abrahán asked, and gently pulled the right leg of his patient and then the left from under the chair. "Help me with this, Jerónimo. Hold Fernán under his arms and lift him from the chair, as you helped him from the bed before."

Jerónimo stood before Fernán who looked at him with the expression of an adoring child. "He knows me," Jerónimo said. "I will help you stand, young master. Rest your weight on me."

He held Fernán under the arms, raised him from the chair, and gradually transferred the weight of the youth to his legs until Jerónimo barely supported his body. At one point, Fernán began to collapse and Jerónimo held him until he felt the muscles stiffen.

"Splendid, Fernán," Lorenzo said.

"You are standing, my love," Celestina said, and Fernán smiled.

"Now we will walk," don Abrahán said. He bent down and moved the left leg, while Jerónimo held Fernán. Then he moved the right leg and repeated the process. "Walk, Fernán." And Fernán shuffled his left foot and then the right.

"God bless him, his body remembers," Lorenzo said.

"He falls," Jerónimo said, and they moved the chair and lowered Fernán into it. And he sat, his arms hugging his body.

"His muscles are weak and his blood poor," don Abrahán said. "These things will come with time."

"He is so thin," Celestina said.

"We must get him to the Melamed house," Lorenzo said. "Can you carry him, Jerónimo?"

"I can, don Lorenzo. Fernán has lost much weight."

"Will someone recognize our carriage?"

"We must hazard the chance, señor. But there is no moon as yet and, when it does appear, it will be a sliver." Jerónimo looked at Fernán. He wore a caftan and hat similar to the costumes don Abrahán and Jerónimo wore. "The young master will laugh when he sees himself—pray God that will be soon. What should we call him?"

"David," don Abrahán said. "Call him David ben Yeuda Melamed, since he is my cousin."

"After his great-grandfather," Lorenzo said.

"Yes. God bless his soul. Now let us go."

Jerónimo knelt. "Fernán, we will take you to the Melamed house where you will see Mosé and Naomi and will recover your strength." Had there been a flicker in his eyes at the mention of Naomi? Well and good. "Can you walk, Fernán?"

"No," Fernán said.

"God bless him, he spoke! He understood and he spoke," don Abrahán said.

"I will carry you, Fernán," Jerónimo said. "When we arrive at the house, you will be called David, so that you may appear to be a Jew and will be protected from harm."

"Is that necessary, Jerónimo?" Lorenzo asked.

"Perhaps, señor, perhaps not. As don Abrahán has said, words are important. We must assume he can grasp what we say so that, in time, he will understand."

"That is correct, Lorenzo," don Abrahán said.

Jerónimo crouched and placed his arms under the body of his friend. "Now, I will lift you, Fernán. Do you trust me?"

"Yes."

Lorenzo opened the door. Jerónimo raised Fernán in a single, smooth motion and held him in his arms. "We can go now." One careful step at a time, he walked down the stairs, resting every four steps.

"If you please, don Lorenzo, step into the carriage. I will place Fernán on the floor of the cab and you will steady him while I get in. Then I will lift him to the seat."

The door to the carriage was opened, Fernán was transferred, and Jerónimo placed him between Lorenzo and himself. Celestina and Melamed seated themselves and they drove off.

Night descended as they traveled through the city. The streets had emptied with the arrival of darkness and the evening star shone bright in the west. The ride to the Melamed house was short. They waited outside the gate while the doctor fetched Mosé to carry Fernán into the house.

In a moment, Mosé came to the carriage door with a lantern. "What have we here? Can that be Jerónimo? Dear friend, have you at last been blessed with supreme intelligence and converted to Judaism, or are you masquerading for a costume ball?"

"Neither, Mosé. You have met don Lorenzo and doña Celestina Hernandes?"

"No, but I am honored, señor and señora. And who might be that queer-looking fellow next to you, Jerónimo, dressed in cap and caftan. God save my eyes, can that be a bearded Fernán?"

"Your eyes are keen, Mosé, but we must call him David now, so that those with eyes as keen as yours will take him for a Jew."

"David? The people of Abraham have become fruitful and multiplied, blessed be the name of the Lord. We shall call him David and welcome him to our home."

"Use your mouth less and your body more, Mosé," Melamed said and took the lantern.

"Yes, don Abrahán. The trumpet has sounded, Jerónimo, I am summoned. Lower David to the floor, if you please. I will bear our friend to his new domicile. And be assured, señor and señora," he said as he cradled Fernán in his arms, "your son is in the most gentle of hands. Dear God, he is a feather—such a little man. Good night all." And Mosé, carrying Fernán, walked through the gate with don Abrahán leading the way, all the while shaking his head.

Jerónimo descended from the carriage and Lorenzo said, "We will go home now, Jerónimo, so as not to attract attention to the carriage. We leave Fernán in your good hands. Tell us when it is propitious for us to visit and how we may do so without endangering our son. We will talk when we see you again. Good night."

They rode off and Jerónimo hurried through the gate and into the house where he found Fernán, Naomi, and Mosé gathered in the study, now converted into a bedchamber. Jerónimo realized that he should use the name David in his mind as well as vocally, or his tongue might slip at the wrong time. Yet, he resisted the logic—the name Fernán was too precious to him.

Mosé lowered Fernán onto the bed and he lay there, eyes closed, exhausted. Naomi stood at the foot of the bed. "He looks so much older, Jerónimo. He has gray hairs. I scarcely know him."

"He does not know himself, señorita. He was much abused. The beard ages him as well. But the bloom will return to his cheeks before long and his eyes will sparkle. You can help him return from the dead and give him the life that was taken from him."

"Blessed God, tell me how I should do that?"

"Speak to him. Remind him of himself and his life. Say anything. He must hear words and feel the presence of those who love him."

"Who will care for him tonight?"

"Mosé will attend him until he can walk and care for himself. And, of course, you and the doctor will be with him during the day."

"Will you be here?"

"Here and there. Most days, here. I will work with him and help to restore him to health."

"Fernán is fortunate to have you as a friend."

"You mean, David. Thank you, señorita. I am fortunate to know such a fine young man. Now I must find the doctor."

"He is in the kitchen," she said and turned to Fernán.

Don Abrahán was seated at the table with a glass of wine and a slice of bread.

"Take some nourishment, Jerónimo," he said. "I know you have had no food since morning and you will need your strength. All of us will." He poured wine for Jerónimo and cut him a thick slice of bread. "Not much to eat, but I know nothing in this house. We shall have to ask Naomi—she keeps the larder." He bit off a piece of bread and chewed with great concentration.

They heard Naomi speaking to Fernán and don Abrahán nodded. "How is she?"

"Frightened, señor. She will adjust."

"I told Fernán that *conversos* would encounter trouble this time, but trouble such as this I never anticipated. I should have known to keep my peace." He looked toward the study and sighed. "She is betrothed, you know."

"No," Jerónimo said, "I did not know. Does Fernán?"

The doctor shook his head and poured more wine for himself and Jerónimo. "I doubt she told him," he said. "Theirs was an impossible match—the Church, everything—though it was clear that their love would have been a miracle. Foolish old man that I am, yet I remember how it can be."

His eyes were far away and then he looked at his hands. "Naomi has no dowry. We have little money. Not that I complain—not for me, so little time remains. But, Naomi…." He shrugged and sipped some wine. "Her intended, Rubén, is a decent man, a farmer from a village south of here. He owns his farm, has people who work for him, manages well enough for these times. Most of the nearby villagers are Jews—farmers, artisans, laborers. Not unusual in the villages—the remnants of those driven from the towns. What else can our people do? They have denied us every line of work—except the few wealthy whose money they covet. We should not own land—the law forbids—yet, we own land. Well. More wine?"

Melamed filled their glasses. "Rubén has cousins here and knows Toledo. We are all cousins here." He laughed. "God bless them, I hope and pray the marriage turns out well. Such a gamble, marriage. A second for him and already he has three children, one a babe. He says he loves her. I hope that is so—with no dowry. And I am old and soon will die. Do not shake your head, my friend. I will, and soon. I have seen enough—too much."

He shook his head. "An old story, no? Older than the *Torah*. Poor, beautiful girl, prosperous man, not exactly ugly, not yet old. Ah." He lay his hand on the arm of Jerónimo. "You see, my friend, she must not be alone in the world. God has given us a pitiless world to inhabit—to plow the field and tame the wild beast."

Tears sprang to his eyes and he wagged his head from side to side. "Oh, that poor boy, such things they did to him. Who could have denounced him? And for what? For a walk in the street with Naomi?" His voice was a hoarse whisper and his grip on Jerónimo fierce. "Say nothing to her, Jerónimo. You have heard nothing. The thought would kill her."

"How do you know that he was denounced, don Abrahán?"

"Toledo is small—this street, smaller still. A rumor, just a rumor." He shook his hand back and forth and then looked toward the study and quickly wiped his eyes. "What do I see? What, indeed, do I see?"

Jerónimo turned and saw Mosé on one side, Naomi on the other, and Fernán supported between them. Fernán took one small step and then another.

"Fernán is walking," Naomi said. "Are you not, Fernán?"

"David," Mosé said, and laughed.

Behind Fernán, the open window framed a bright sliver of moon.

43

The meeting room of the Alcázar of Toledo

"If we deny *marranos* the right to be lawyers and judges," García said, "and Enrique reverses our law, as he can, what then?"

"You omitted the right to bear witness," Sarmiento said.

"As you wish—bear witness and whatever else you may devise. And if we do those things and the Prince accuses us of bad faith?"

"That is a risk we must take."

"The risk is unacceptable, don Pero. How can we risk alienating the Prince? He will accuse us of treason. Then all we have, including our lives, will be lost."

The four sat around the table—García, Galvez, Ávila, and Sarmiento. A breeze blew through the windows, ruffled the papers on the table, and blew several onto the floor. Galvez picked them up and laid a small bronze bust on the stack.

Sarmiento glanced at the statuette—a likeness of King Juan, a gift, a token of affection from the King for the support given him during the Battle of Olmedo. He smirked, drew his dagger, and began to clean his nails, eliciting an expected shudder from García. "In four days, García, the Prince enters Toledo and becomes our *patrón* and lord. Either we act now or in four days we may have to accept whatever retribution *marranos* care to heap upon us, endorsed by Enrique."

"How can we be accused of crimes when there are no crimes?" García asked. "How can they accuse us of transgressions when we are already pardoned by the Prince for any transgressions?"

"In theory they cannot," Sarmiento said. "However, as you above all others know, we rule with the approval of the people, and their approval has been purchased with suppression of *marranos*. Remove suppression and you remove approval. Unless we declare *marranos* unfit to be Castilians, deny their right to be citizens and sever them from Christian society, we will never be safe from their accusations—and we will lose the support of the commoners.

"*Marranos*, don Marcos, are a people conceived by the Devil. Their existence threatens our survival. But think what might happen if the Prince embraced the King. Who would be our judge then? Who but Alvaro de Luna. And if that occurred, how much do you estimate these assurances we have received from Enrique would be worth? We would be better off dead men."

"We would fight them in court," Galvez said.

"Of course—you in ecclesiastic court and we in civil court. For the love of God," Sarmiento sighed, "will we also fight commoners who accuse us of toadying to *marranos* in defiance of their interests?"

Sarmiento thrust his chair away from the table and stared at García who chewed his lip. "This idea, García, is not perfect. To be sure, we must find the perfect response, a permanent response, one that rids us forever of *marranos* and their intrusion into our affairs. But to do so requires time. And to gain time, we need a defense from the attack *marranos* will launch against us. They are not ignorant or stupid. They know we want them dead, and they will fight for their lives. But what better way is there to isolate them from society than to deny them participation in politics? They poison our community. Therefore, remove them—if not physically, then religiously, socially, politically."

Galvez and Ávila sat stone-faced. García glanced at them and fidgeted in his seat. "I do not like it."

"Would you like it better, García, to have *marranos* as our accusers, prosecutors, and judges? Would it be more suitable to your disposition were *marranos* returned to positions of power and influence? Would it enhance your well-being to have the populace berate you for a coward—a coward without the courage to stand against these Jews so as to preserve our society from contamination?"

García thrust himself to his feet—his face livid, his body trembling. When he spoke, his voice was low, his chin quivered, and he clenched and unclenched his fists.

"Never," he said, "never have I been accused of cowardice. I am a Castilian of noble stock. No one, be it the King or his son, and never you, Sarmiento, will call me a coward and live. You have bested me at swords, trod on my name, and hurled veiled insults in my face. I have shrugged off these attacks and wiped off your spittle because you are who you are and we needed you to complete this rebellion. But the rebellion is complete and we need you no more. Before these two gentlemen, you will apologize to me for your assault on my name. You will remove this stain from me and my family, or you and your family will never again lie safe in your beds."

Sarmiento realized that he had overstepped the limits of privilege. What had García meant that he, Sarmiento, was no longer needed? García was mistaken. Pero Sarmiento was needed even more. Without him there would have been no rebellion and, without him now, the rebellion will fail and Luna will win. But Sarmiento also needed García. If García were to die, the people would be a body without a head. As García said—they were chained together like prisoners. How, though, could he retreat without seeming craven, or even worse, foolish? He must apologize, but as a gentleman. If he were seen to be unmanly then, indeed, he would be superfluous.

"Don Marcos," he said, "once more in the heat of argument my tongue has betrayed my intentions. A grave infirmity. Words, those instruments of reason, can become weapons that turn against us and inflict harm on those we love and respect. If I have offended you in the past, señor, that offense was delivered by words intended as jest—not to harm but to express joy in our fraternity—as jocularity, as good fellowship. If I offend you now—and I see that I have—know that the offense was expressed by words run amok and not by my true heart. Know don Marcos that without you our cause would have no cause for survival. I beg you, señor, forgive one whose words have been traitor to his soul and have inflicted profound harm where none was intended."

García squinted and nodded. "I thank you for your most gracious apology, don Pero. In turn, I apologize for taking offense. This time of ours is filled with pressures that exhaust us and raise conflict when our cause would be served better by sober judgment. As for our current situation, your assessment is sound. Indeed, we must do something. Our alliance with Enrique is regrettable, but the dilemma provoked by King Juan seemed hopeless. Let us probe this concept of yours and give it an edge of steel."

"Excellent, don Marcos," Sarmiento said. "Give me your hand, señor." And he and García shook hands. "Now to work."

He had parried that thrust. Once they executed these laws and consolidated their relationship with Enrique, there would be time to secure his guard and attack.

44

The Melamed house, three weeks later

Fernán sat beneath the olive tree in the courtyard, shaded from the intense heat of the afternoon. He had played at swords with Jerónimo earlier that day and remembered everything he had been taught. His legs tired less easily and, though his reflexes were not keen, he had held his own.

Don Abrahán had been called away to a village half a day distant. He was dejected, for he wished to be with his granddaughter since this was her sixteenth birthday. But the invalid he would visit was an old friend and gravely ill and he would celebrate with Naomi when he returned the following morning. Tonight, Mosé and Jerónimo would cook and Fernán, Aharón, and a friend of the family, Rubén Halevi, would attend and honor the day of her birth.

"One young woman for all of us men?" Mosé had said. "What sort of party can that be?"

Few young women lived in the *judería*. Fernán, though, was indifferent to other women. He saw no one but Naomi and behaved as if their love had not been cut short by her arranged marriage or obstructed by their religious difference. His trysts with María had become fantasies, and his near death an illusory nightmare. He acted as if newly born, scrubbed clean—unpleasant memories buried in a forgotten closet.

He experienced lapses. Incidents he recalled, he would forget. When he was practicing with Jerónimo, he performed a feint and slash that Jerónimo had taught him and remembered employing a similar move during his duel with Sarmiento. A few minutes later, when asked to repeat the combination, he remembered nothing of the duel or its occurrence. The loss bothered him.

Then, suddenly, all would be clear in his mind, as if he were in a wood shaded by trees and passed into a glade where the sun warmed his face.

The sun today was hot but he relished its heat. He would bathe before dinner. He could do that for himself. Earlier in his convalescence, he had to be bathed. Naomi would fetch hot water in large pots from the fire and fill the tub. Then he would undress and Mosé would help him into the tub on the floor of his room. He would soap himself and enjoy the scent and bubbles. When he was done, Mosé would pour several pails of fresh water over his body as he stood naked in the tub, and he would take a clean cloth and pat himself dry. He felt fresh then—the clouds in his mind washed away.

Naomi would lay out clean clothes on his bed. When he put them on, he imagined her hands touching the cloth that touched his body. Their evening in the courtyard had fled from his mind but, occasionally, an image would rise out of the fog—Naomi in the dark, his arms about her, his head in her warm lap. And then the picture would retreat again and he would wonder if it had been fantasy or memory.

He could not think of María. If her face appeared, the pain caused him to shudder and his eyes would cloud and he would cry out, "No!" Had it been real? His mind screamed that he had fantasized their week together. She was not dead, could not have been burned. He would not think it. Later, perhaps, when he was strong. He admitted his weakness but could do nothing. He must become strong. Don Abrahán had said he would become strong and could play at swords with Jerónimo. Later he would bathe.

"David."

Strange to be called a name not his own. Naomi wondering where he was. "In the courtyard," he said.

The door opened and she looked out. "There you are. Are you not warm?"

"I enjoy the heat. The prison was so cold I thought I would never be warm."

"That will be a memory soon, Fernán, a bad memory."

He looked straight ahead. Somehow, looking at her was painful.

"I watched you with Jerónimo this morning. You are very good. Does swordplay frighten you?"

"No. I have always played at swords and Jerónimo has taught me well."

"But can you be hurt?"

"Not if I concentrate and make no mistakes. And I do concentrate and rarely make a mistake."

"You are amusing."

He smiled and looked at her. "You make me happy when you laugh, Naomi. But I know why you find me amusing—because I am sure of my swordplay and you believe I should be more humble. Perhaps I should. Come sit with me."

"I have work to do."

"A minute?" She smiled and sat next to him and, after a moment or two, he said, "Did we once sit together on this bench in the dark?"

She looked away. "Yes. A long time ago. Months."

"And did we kiss and hold one another and did I touch you?" She was quiet and he said, "I have this picture in my mind, Naomi. I need to know if it was dreamt or wished or real. Was it real?"

"It was real, Fernán. But we decided that we should not do that again because of our differences."

"And we have not, have we?"

"No. We have not."

"Thank you," he said. "I was not sure. Images sometimes confuse me."

She stood and said, "I am sorry, Fernán, I have work to do. Will you bathe this afternoon?"

"Yes. I had planned to."

"I will help you."

She went inside and he stared at the gate and remembered how it had appeared that night from the street side. He wished he had broken it down. A hot breeze came up and the branches of the trees swayed. Fernán placed his hand on the bench beside him. Was it warm from her body or had the sun warmed it? He rose slowly, walked to the gate, and peered through the barred window. No one in the street. He had seen his mother and father two days ago. Or was it yesterday? Their carriage had pulled up, they had walked through the gate, and stayed but a short while. His mother had kissed him and his father held him in his arms. When he was well he would go home and sleep in his own bed and see his sister and cousins. He walked into the house and lay on the bed.

He closed his eyes and let his mind spin. There were differences between them. Naomi was a Jew and he a Catholic. Was that the difference she meant? Was the difference so great that he could never hold her—never? Perhaps Jerónimo should have let him die. Would she have grieved? The sun warmed him when he was outside in its light, but in the house he was cold.

He slept for an hour and awakened to find Naomi watching him.

"You cried out in your sleep," she said.

"I remember nothing. Don Abrahán said it would take time—until my mind is whole. I may never be a whole person again." He lay with his arm over his eyes. "I wonder if I would mind that? There is so much I want to forget and try to forget. Although trying to forget is the same as remembering.

But all of that is in the hands of God. If God wills me to remember, I will remember and be whole. Now I would like to bathe."

She heated water in a large kettle and, when it was hot, he carried it into the room and poured it into the tub. He did that twice more and then he undressed, took soap and a clean cloth, and stepped into the tub.

Naomi was at the door. "Do you need help?" she said.

"No. I can wash myself. And when I finish I will pour water over my body. I have become very good at that."

"I know. You are very good. I will lay out your fresh clothes."

He finished his bath, dried himself, and donned the clean clothes Naomi had touched. Then he emptied the water out of the tub and sat on his bed. Something in him had been washed away with the dirty water and he sat on his bed and looked through the window at the sky for a long time seeking to remember what it was.

Jerónimo was first to arrive, then Mosé. They sat in his room that had been the study and talked.

"Mosé," Jerónimo said, "introduce me as a friend of David, rather than his tutor or servant. Not because of my sensitivity but because of his safety."

"I understand and will tell Aharón. None of us know Rubén and people do talk a great deal. Not I, perhaps, but others."

"You talk more than anyone, Mosé," Fernán said.

"That is not true, David. I may be stouter than anyone but I am not verbose. Am I, Jerónimo?"

They laughed and Fernán asked, "Why do you laugh?"

"Because one is happy on a birthday. Is that not so, Jerónimo?"

"Yes. A birthday is a happy occasion. When is your birthday, David?"

He would question why he was called David and would always be given the same answer—for his safety.

"Why do you call me David, Jerónimo, when you know I am Fernán?"

"Because we want nothing to befall you. If someone knew you were Fernán, he might harm you, but will not so long as you are David."

Why would someone harm him? He had hurt no one. Then he recalled the battle and the long sword and the men in armor with swords and pikes and the cutting and slashing. Yes, he had hurt men, many of them.

"Who is the someone that would harm me?" he asked.

"We do not know. That is why we take precautions."

"That can be confusing, Jerónimo, but I understand. You may call me David."

The day stretched into evening and clung to the edge of night like a child refusing to accept sleep. Jerónimo had brought newly-baked breads, several flagons of wine, fresh-caught trout, and pastries from the Hernandes house.

"Your mother and father sent me with love for you and blessings for Naomi," he said. "They will see you soon."

Mosé cooked a chicken and Jerónimo grilled the trout on the open fire and Aharón contributed apples and vegetables. A new person, Rubén, walked into the house bearing a marzipan cake.

Then Naomi entered the kitchen where they had gathered and Fernán stared because she was wearing the new white dress he had watched her sew. He had observed her cut the material and sit for hours with needle and thread. Now, wearing the completed garment, Naomi was a revelation.

"You are an angel," he said, "with dark hair." And they laughed and Mosé shouted, "*Olé!*" Mosé and Aharón kissed Naomi on her cheek, Rubén bowed and kissed her brow, and Jerónimo kissed her hand and whispered the blessings of the Hernandes household into her ear, while Fernán smiled from across the room at the vision in the white dress.

They blessed the wine and raised their glasses in tribute to Naomi. They blessed the bread and each tore off a chunk and drank some wine. And they blessed the occasion and drank more wine.

"My only sorrow is that Grandpapá is not here," Naomi said.

"He will be here tomorrow, Naomi. You must be happy on your birthday," Fernán said.

They cut the trout and the chicken into pieces and devoured each piece with bread and wine and fruit and at last they sat before a table cluttered with the shreds of their feast and drank the last of the wine with marzipan, exclaiming at its flavor and texture.

"The Greek gods and the great and mighty," Mosé said, "must feast like this each day of their lives. What do you say, Fernán?" A great gaseous bellow was expelled from his mouth and he excused himself and staggered outside.

"So much for decorum," Aharón said.

"Whom did he call Fernán?" Rubén asked.

Jerónimo looked at Rubén and shrugged and said that there was no one of that name in the room and that Rubén must have misheard. And Rubén protested that he heard clearly and had Mosé referred to Fernán Hernandes? Fernán was busy with the last of his marzipan, but when he heard his name, he asked what Rubén had said.

"Nothing of interest to you, David," Naomi said. "You seem to enjoy marzipan."

"I do. Thank you for the marzipan, Rubén. It seems such a long time since I had marzipan."

"And who exactly are you?" Rubén asked, and his eyes narrowed.

With his slit eyes, Rubén looked not unlike a snake to Fernán, and he expected that a snake tongue would soon shoot out of his mouth to taste the air. He saw the face of the guard at his cell door who stuck out his tongue like a snake, and Fernán shivered and opened his mouth to speak, but Naomi spoke first.

"Why do you ask, Rubén? I introduced you. This is David Melamed, my cousin," she said. "He hurt his head and is here recuperating with us. You must remember."

Amused by the imposture, Fernán realized Naomi was protecting him. But why was this fellow Rubén not to be trusted? Naomi was being too cautious. Then he recalled the face of the executioner—the blackened teeth, black eyes, and black mask. "We have met before, Rubén."

Mosé burst through the door into the kitchen and apologized for his behavior. "I have so many problems," he said, "but the worst is my stomach. Forgive me, Naomi, this is vulgar talk and I plead for your forgiveness."

"You are forgiven, Mosé."

"Ah, the light yet shines, I am blessed with forgiveness. Blessed are the corpulent for they are filled with joy in the presence of food. Hah!"

"Enough, Mosé," Aharón said.

"Your problem, brother apprentice, derives from a lack of appreciation of the better things in life, principally food and drink, of which we have partaken plenteously this joyous evening and for which I pay a pressing price. Catch the alliteration, Jerónimo my friend. I am not without education nor wit, which may at times appear dim."

"You said the name Fernán before, Mosé," Rubén said. "Whom did you mean?"

Mosé leaned on his chair, inclined his head toward Rubén, and smiled with his mouth closed. "You are mistaken, Rubén. In my present condition I slur words, as you may have noticed. But I recall most of what I have said during the days of my life, and cannot recall that name being spoken in this house for some time…"

"The name was not slurred. Did you refer to Fernán Hernandes?"

"… because the person you mention, Fernán Hernandes, whom I knew briefly some months ago, was brutally murdered in the Alcázar and, sadly, graces our land no more."

"Too much wine, Mosé," Jerónimo said.

"Too true, too true. Nevertheless, Naomi should have a birthday every day," Mosé said. "Come along, Aharón, I am no longer accountable for my actions. Good night, sweet lovely lady of sixteen years and gentlemen. Break the plates. They will never witness a happier occasion or more perfect meal and should be sacrificed to the gods—Greek, I should think...."

Aharón took Mosé by the arm, said a quiet good night, and guided his outspoken brother through the door, his voice trailing off into the night.

Fernán smiled at Naomi. Her shy smile warmed him.

"Bless you, Naomi. May the good Lord bless you on your birthday," Rubén said, and stared at Fernán. "Mosé spoke the name Fernán."

Why did the face of Sarmiento impose itself on that of Rubén? There was hatred in his eyes. Had he wronged the man? He could not remember.

Jerónimo stepped between Rubén and Fernán and said in a voice that Fernán knew preceded violence, "You heard wrong." He turned to Naomi, his voice now honey, and said, "Good night, sweet Naomi. Blessings on your birthday. I wish you the best of this and all other worlds. I will help David to his room and then be gone."

Fernán said good night to Naomi and Rubén and then he and Jerónimo left the kitchen.

"Why was Rubén angry with me?" Fernán asked. "Or am I wrong?"

Jerónimo shrugged and opened the door to the study and Fernán sat on the bed. For the first time, his head seemed clear of fog and his mind held fast to a thought. He could peer into the past without slipping into mist.

"I feel better, Jerónimo," he said, "much, much better."

45

That night

After Naomi cleaned the kitchen, she climbed the stairs to her room and fell into a deep sleep. She awakened suddenly after midnight and lay in bed, eyes open, aware of night sounds—a cat wailing, footsteps in the street, the house groaning with age.

She wondered what had awakened her, then remembered Mosé at dinner—such a precious fool—and Rubén, so serious, so insistent when Mosé misspoke and used the name Fernán. Why insist? Was he jealous of the memory of Fernán? True, she had cooled toward him when she met Fernán and he might retain some resentment. Rubén had seen her with Fernán the Sunday morning after Fernán had come to their house with that horrible cut on his throat, and Rubén had ordered her not to walk with other men. Foolishness. But then Grandpapá had overwhelmed her objections and convinced her that she would be wise to marry Halevi. She had resisted, but Grandpapá had frightened her. She had no dowry, he said, and what man would marry her? Not Fernán. He was Catholic. And if she did not marry, how would she live? So, precipitously, without careful thought, without speaking to Fernán whom she knew she loved, she cut her ties to him and said farewell. And then he had been arrested and…oh, dear Fernán.

She must tell him—that was why sleep had abandoned her.

He had stood in the tub like a young prince, lean from prison, innocent eyes on her, indifferent to his nakedness. How pitiful he had been when Jerónimo first brought him—so weak, confused, not at all the firm body she remembered when she held him in the dark courtyard. She had cared for him these past weeks and seen him naked many times, and her love for him had grown—for his body, yes, and his fair face, but also for his beautiful mind, however much that mind needed rest and repair. She had become brazen, drawn to his door whenever she knew he would be bare. He was not whole, he said. Nevertheless, whole or not, she loved him and now must hurt him.

The cathedral bells chimed two and the bed squeaked horribly as she sat up but, despite the noise, she slid from under the covers and walked barefoot down the stairs, a creak at every step. But no one would awaken. The house was empty except for herself and Fernán. Mosé had not slept there for well over a week—not since Fernán had shown he could care for himself. She shivered and, knowing her shivers were not from cold, she turned at the bottom of the stairs and opened his door. Dear God, she thought, how I love this Fernán. How can I tell him?

The moon was now in the west and, in its fragile light, she saw him asleep, his face in shadow, his body a ball. She sat on the foot of his bed and he made a sound and turned on his back, legs outstretched. The substance of his body was outlined beneath the cover and she smiled, for in the dim light she saw that a dream had roused his sex and she wanted to fondle where the cover tented.

"Fernán," she said quietly.

He uttered a smothered cry and his head swung sharply from side to side. She touched his leg and his eyes opened and then closed.

"Is it time?" he said.

"No, Fernán." The dream was of prison. "I must speak to you."

He raised a bare arm and rubbed his eyes with his fingers. Then he leaned on his left arm. "Naomi, is it you? Is something wrong?"

"No, Fernán, Nothing is wrong."

"What hour is it?"

"Two."

"Why have you awakened me?" He peered at her in the semi-dark. "Are you in your nightdress?"

"Yes. I was asleep and I woke. I must speak to you."

"Now?" he yawned. "Must it be now?"

"I cannot speak to you in the daytime when everyone is here."

"What is so important that will not wait till morning?"

"Fernán—I must leave in two days."

"Two days? Two days are days away." He smiled. "All right then, you will leave. Where are you going?"

"You fail to understand."

"What is there to understand, Naomi? You awaken me in the dead of night and say you must leave. What is there to understand? You will return and I will miss you dearly, especially after having seen you in your nightdress. But I will see you when you return. When do you return?"

"Never."

"Never? Now you do confuse me. My head may be woolly, but it has cleared considerably and is nothing as dense as it was. What do you mean, never?"

His beard had grown thick since he had come to them and his hair fell in curls below his ears. She wanted to stroke his face and touch him—the impulse was overwhelming.

"Come hold me," she said, "and I will tell you."

"I warn you, I wear no nightclothes."

"I have seen you many times without clothes."

"When have you seen me?" he said, and pushed himself toward her.

"In your bath."

"Have you? I was unaware." He took her in his arms. "You are warm. I love your body against me."

"Oh, Fernán." She lay her head against his chest and said, "In two days Grandpapá will take me to a village near here and I will be married. Once I am married I can never see you again."

He held her away from him and turned her face up to his. "What do you mean, marry? Whom will you marry?"

"Rubén Halevi. The man you met at dinner last night."

"That man, you will marry? Is that the man with whom don Abrahán contracted your marriage?"

"Yes, Fernán."

"Did I know you were betrothed? Had I put it out of my mind?"

She sighed and reached for him, needing to be held, wanting not to hear what she must say, but he held her distant from him.

"And you love him?" he said.

"When you and I first met," she said, "I was not yet betrothed to Rubén, though he wanted to marry me. Then I met you and I was confused. I could not tell you about him, and then, when I realized that you and I loved each other…"

"Do you love him?"

"… I had to break with you when Grandpapá signed a contract with Rubén. Then the rebellion and the battle and you were imprisoned and came to us."

"Do you love him, Naomi?"

"I am a woman, Fernán. I must have a home."

"Do you love him?"

"No, Fernán, no, I do not love him. But to be a Jewish woman alone in this world is impossible. A Catholic woman can retreat to a convent if she is desperate. But a Jewish woman? A life alone is not a life."

"Come, sweet, come here," he said, and she returned to his arms. "When I was whole, Naomi, before prison, I asked you to marry me. Soon I will be well and my mind will be whole again—I know that now—and then you and I will marry."

"Fernán, I will not become Catholic. I am a Jew. I will always be. I cannot convert as others have done." She put her arms around his waist and pulled herself close to him. "I have no blame for those who converted, Fernán—your grandfather or his father. I blame no one. Life as a Jew is difficult and they were threatened with death. What I would do with a sword at my throat I cannot know. Convert, perhaps, and say prayers in secret. But no sword is at my throat and I need not choose. I am a Jew."

"I know who you are, Naomi," and he kissed her hair. "When I first saw you—when you gave me soup, do you remember?—I loved you. I remember that and I remember how you looked at me. I remember everything now."

"You are not listening, Fernán. I cannot convert, dear soul. Hear me, Fernán." She took his hand and held it to her lips. "Oh, dear God. When I looked into your eyes I loved you and I look into your eyes now and I love you. But I must live, Fernán. May it be years, may it be written in the Book of Life that it be so, but one day Grandpapá will die, as all men must, and I will be alone. And I am afraid to be alone, Fernán, truly I am."

She feared that he would never hear, that no matter how she explained he would counter that his love for her and hers for him would answer all questions. Why did she know that this was false and he did not? He was bright and yet so stubborn. In his mind, all walls could be scaled, all force turned aside. He had suffered and should know better, while she was a girl who had been nurtured in relative safety and yet she knew.

He stroked her face. "When I was in chains, though we had parted, thoughts of you gave me strength. When Jerónimo told me María had been burned, God knows I wanted to die from grief—for I loved María dearly. But when I was near death from starvation and torture, it was your face I saw, and I knew that in the next life I would see you and that sustained me."

"Listen to me, Fernán. Ask me to choose between my love for you and who I am, a Jewish woman, and I must choose who I am. Else, my love, I will be nothing and no love will comfort me."

"I will comfort you."

"Fernán, Fernán, how will you comfort me from the loss of myself? You cannot be a Jew, my sweet, no matter what costume you adopt. And if you did by some strange circumstance manage to convert, the Church would seek you out and have you burned as a heretic and then you would be in Heaven and I in Hell and guilty forever, because your death would be my doing and our love your undoing."

A week from now she would marry Rubén in his small farming village, and would care for him and his three children and nine months later deliver herself of his baby. So it would be for the rest of her life. Fridays she would clean the house and take her Sabbath bath scented with herbs and chamomile. And Rubén would bathe and they would dress in clean clothes and light the Sabbath lamps. Then they would eat the Sabbath meal on a clean white tablecloth and lie together. Now Fernán sat before her and she thought she would go mad. What had God chosen for her life?

She drew herself erect and faced him. "Fernán," she said, "I place myself in the hands of God. What He has planned for me was written when the world was new and what we do now will not change His plan, will not change who we are or what we do tomorrow or the day after or forever. You have always been my love and I will always be yours. Hold me and let us love one another."

They kissed and he said, "There are sins of mine I must explain."

"There are no sins of yours worth the explanation, my love."

She lay her body on his and closed his mouth with hers and said, "You are my husband and I am your wife and our love is sanctified before God."

"You are my wife and I am your husband and God watches and blesses our love."

His hands played with her body and fondled her hills and valleys and she rose above him and swept her nightdress above her head and he sat and she straddled his legs and he kissed her breasts and she ran her fingers down his chest and into the thicket between his thighs, and she said, "I have longed to hold you and play with you and now you are here with me and we shall find our delight with one another."

And their hands and mouths explored each other and she gloried in his touch and the knowledge in his lovemaking and sought to mirror his motions with her own. "How can you know so much?" she asked. "How can you know where the pleasure is so great it cannot be contained?" And she lay back and he knelt between her thighs and his kisses covered her.

"Now you must hurt me, my love," she said.

"The hurt will be brief but gentle, since I must enter that portal from whence all life comes." And she led him to her and he thrust himself between her lips and she cried out but then received him and moved as he moved and rose with him to the crest of their bliss.

They lay together still linked, repeating the ebb and flow of their coupling, and fondled and kissed and spoke words of love. And he said, "Now you are my wife and I am your husband and you will stay with me forever and we will find a way to satisfy the commandments of the world."

"Fernán," she said, and hesitated, "I have given my word. The word of Grandpapá has bonded me to another man. I must complete my destiny."

"What did you say?" He disjoined himself and sat above her, his eyes wild. Then he laughed. "Oh, dear, sweet Naomi, for one horrible moment I thought you were lost to me and now I realize how droll you are."

She eased off the bed and stood on the bare floor. "Not droll but torn. Marriage between us is not possible."

"What was this talk of husband and wife?" he cried. "Did you play with me and have your pleasure and now you will throw me away as you would a whore?"

"No, Fernán. In my heart and with all my life I love you. In my heart and mind you are my husband. But we can never be man and wife within the laws of this world. Did you not understand?"

"How could I understand such a mad idea? To want me for a moment and then discard me? Who can I be that you would do such a thing—a broken soul not fit to have a life? Who is this Halevi that he should have what is mine? I will kill him and then there will be truth in the world, not the farce you have played with me."

"Oh dear God. Fernán!" she said, and knelt on the floor. "Forgive a misguided woman who loves you with all her soul. Kill me, if you must kill. Rubén is a pawn, I am the thief, the deceiver. I have longed for you with such longing that I would die from the loss of you. And now I realize how stupid and selfish I am. I am not worthy of your love. I am not worthy. Oh, Lord God, why have You led me to this?" And she groped her way to the door and fled up the stairs.

She shut the door of her room and fell to her knees. "Almighty God, take this life from me for I cannot bear the pain. I must die, surely. Make it swift, Lord. This misery is more than I can bear." And tears erupted from her eyes and sobs shook her body.

For two hours she knelt and beat her breast and temples and rocked back and forth and moaned and then, exhausted from grief, she lay on the cold floor. At last she staggered to her feet and stole down the stairs, not knowing what she would do or say. The door was open, the bed disheveled as she had left it and, at its center, a bloody stain. And though she searched the house and called his name, Fernán did not answer.

46

Daybreak

The house had cooled during the night, but Jerónimo knew the heat of day would leach the pleasant chill from its walls, thick as they were, and by evening the rooms, having baked in the sun, would be intolerable. So went the weather in Toledo—bitter cold winter, blistering hot summer. Afternoon would pass—dinner at two, siesta, then languid employment, the cool of evening, and supper at ten. Morning was the time for work. He ate bread, downed a mug of ale, and made ready for his morning activity—unpleasant but necessary. The Cathedral bells had pealed four. He should arrive at the house where Halevi boarded no later than five.

So bent was he on his plans that he scarcely heard the tapping at the window. Dawn had barely signaled the new day. He expected no one and could not make out the figure. He loosed his dagger and opened the door a crack.

"Jerónimo, it is I, Fernán."

"Fernán?" He threw the door open and Fernán stepped into the room in clothes Jerónimo had brought him for the time when he would return. "Why are you here, young master? Is something wrong?"

"I have come home," he said.

"That I see. Did don Abrahán release you?"

"No. He is away, as you know."

"Sit with me and have some bread and ale, and then you will go to your room and rest—I can see you are tired. I have an errand to run, but when I return we will inform your parents and prepare for the arrival of your cousin."

"What cousin?"

"Why, yourself—señor Rafael Rivera, cousin to this family. There must be a genuine arrival to suppress suspicion—among the servants in particular." Jerónimo cut Fernán a slice of bread and poured ale into a mug. "I will not inquire of you now, my friend. We will talk when I return." Jerónimo watched Fernán chew the bread and swallow the ale and he grasped what had occurred. The presence of Halevi at the party the previous night had been caution enough.

"I am very tired, Jerónimo, and will go to my room now."

Jerónimo walked with Fernán, scouting the way so as to avoid servants who might be early at their daily chores. When they arrived at his room, Fernán removed boots and doublet, lay on the bed, and fell asleep. Jerónimo covered his young master and closed the door—as it had been closed since the funeral marking his purported death. Then he left the house.

The cousins of Halevi lived in a two-story modest structure in the *judería* not far from the Melamed house. Jerónimo waited across the street. He almost missed the farmer, for the front door of the house opened, Halevi looked first one way and then the other, and rushed up the alley opposite. Jerónimo took a parallel street and, as he reached the corner, saw Halevi scurry up Juan de Dios toward the church of San Tomé. Jerónimo closed on him and grasped his wrist as Halevi was about to open the church door.

"How unexpected but pleasant to meet you, Halevi? I see you are going to church. Must you confess your sins?"

"I am a Jew," Halevi said, and attempted to release his wrist without success. "I do not confess sins. My sins concern only me and my God."

"Then there is no need to go to San Tomé? Come, we will have bread and ale, break our fast, and talk about this and that."

"Who are you? Why were you at dinner last night?" Halevi asked. "You are no Jew."

"No, nor was I dressed as a Jew. But then you are no Catholic and yet were off to church."

"I had business this morning."

"Business in San Tomé? Strange for a Jew, Halevi, to have business in a church. Come with me, or I will rest this blade in your heart?"

"You threaten me?"

"Indeed, and know this—I have killed many men and I would think nothing of taking your life. Though I would rather you came with me and answered my questions truthfully and then went on your way. However, if you decline my invitation, your life is over. What do you think?"

Jerónimo retained his fierce grip on Halevi and led him to a small room in the poorest section of Toledo. The room was less than shabby, containing two crude stools, a table, and a thin, filthy mattress. A small window abutted the ceiling and provided a pittance of murky light. The grimy walls and stools and table exhibited the distress accumulated by years of abuse.

"This is my palace," Jerónimo said, as he tied Halevi to a stool. "Delightful, yes? The stool, by the way, is fixed to the floor and cannot be moved. And if you scream or shout no one will hear. The tenants of this habitat are poor and perpetually drunk, and screaming and shouting are their normal modes of communication. Now, tell me what you were going to confess at San Tomé? I admit I am intrigued."

Halevi clamped his mouth shut and Jerónimo left the room without a word.

Fernán awoke later in the day and was surprised to find himself in his own room. He cried out with relief before he remembered that Naomi was to be married and lost to him. Why had he not stayed and fought for her? Was he weak, a coward? He had sat on the bed after she left him, his body and mind aroused by their impulsive passion and then deadened by the news of her impending marriage. His stomach had pained him as if from poison and he felt pain throughout his body, a pain unlike any he had known. A constant throb tore at his insides and he went into the courtyard and vomited. Then he washed his face, dressed in the clothes Jerónimo had brought him, and walked home through the dark streets, deserted save for a few scurrying tradesmen. He knew Jerónimo would be seeing to arrangements for the day, and he had knocked on the kitchen door and, in a daze, had been fed and guided to his room.

He had slept long and lay on his bed questioning what life meant with Naomi dead to him. A knock on the door and the voices of his mother and father shocked him out of his despair. He realized that it must be past noon and he dressed in black and opened the door to their welcome. His mother kissed his face and held him in her arms and, despite himself, he cried and explained that his tears were of joy. They asked after his health and he explained that he was well and with don Abrahán away, had decided to return home. His father questioned whether he was wise to leave without permission from the doctor, and he said that his memory had returned and his body seemed fit and he longed to see his family and to be in his own home. Gradually, he regained his composure and they talked about his introduction into the household as Rafael Rivera.

Jerónimo was waiting outside the door. The others of the family were at dinner and they walked together into the great hall and introduced Rafael to his sister and uncle and aunt and his young cousins, and explained that Rafael had come to stay with them. He was a distant cousin but, as they could see, from the same stock as their own Fernán, and they should befriend him and make him welcome to their household.

Miguel, the youngest of the children, asked where Fernán had gone, and Cesario smiled at his son and said that Fernán had gone on a long trip.

"I do not like this Rafael," the child said. "Fernán should come back."

"Some day he will come back," Fernán said.

Across the room, next to the dead fireplace, sat Antonio, an apparition materialized from exile, and Fernán, startled to see his uncle, whispered to Jerónimo, "When did Antonio return?"

Jerónimo told him that his uncle and other exiled *conversos* had planned to shield their return to Toledo obscured by the shadow of Enrique and had linked up with the army of the Prince and followed his parade into the city.

"The commoners, though," Jerónimo said, "greeted them with rocks and cudgels while the idiot soldiers stood by and joked. I knew Antonio was due and I waited for him. He was in good spirits and both of us were armed and capable of not a little harm. We worked our way through the mob, leaving a few cuts and bruises behind us."

"But Antonio departed Toledo on horseback accompanied by his servant."

"True enough, Fernán, but the servant deserted late one night while Antonio slept. The bastard took the horse and mule and the goods the animals carried, as well as the bulk of the money. With no horse, no change of clothing, and only the funds on his person, Antonio was unable to travel or purchase goods for resale."

"Where was he?"

"They had gone as far as the town of Madrid. He knew cousins of yours who lived there and sought help from them. They provided him with shelter and, since Antonio is clever with his hands, they put him to work fashioning pots and pans until such a time as he could recover his treasure and practice his own vocation."

"And he sent no word to my father?"

"No. Antonio posted a letter with a traveler who was on his way to Toledo, and don Lorenzo dispatched me to Madrid at once with clothing and money. But oh, young master, that was hard." His eyes were cast down. "When Antonio saw me, he asked how María was bearing the separation. Blessed Christ, he took me by both arms and looked into my eyes and, Fernán, I had not the courage to tell him the truth. God forgive me, I said María was well but missed her husband."

"What you said was acceptable, Jerónimo. You protected him. Has he learned the truth?"

"Not entirely. When he saw your father, Lorenzo embraced him and told him—gently, mind you—that María had been arrested and died in prison two months before, accused of heresy. Brave Antonio broke. Think what he would have felt if your father had dared tell him she was burned. It was a terrible moment, Fernán. At first he blanched and then went purple, tore his clothing, heaped ashes on his head, and vowed revenge.

"Then, in his rage and torment, he shouted at your father that don Lorenzo had denounced María. That he had never approved of María and that he and your mother and Cesario wanted her out of the house."

"How could Antonio believe my father would denounce María? He loved María, although he was severe with her from time to time."

"We were alone with Antonio, Fernán, and nothing don Lorenzo or I said could shake his conviction. He screamed such oaths and uttered such cries. Blessed God, I hope never again to witness such anguish. He was never talkative, your uncle, as you know, but he has been mute since he returned to this house and, when not in his room, sits by the fireplace and moans."

Fernán hesitated, then stared at his father. Lorenzo looked up and smiled at Fernán..

"No, Fernán," Jerónimo said. "Don Lorenzo is innocent. Your aunt was denounced by Paulo."

"Paulo? Our servant, Paulo? Why would he denounce her? He helped free me from prison. He was loyal to our family."

"He was a rabid beast. He hungered for women and fastened on María. One can understand the attraction—she was a beautiful woman. But he hounded her and she laughed at him and he became furious. María was proud, as you know, but pretty Paulo was arrogant and vengeful."

"How did you learn this?"

"He told me."

"Where is Paulo?"

"In the Río Tajo. His throat was cut and he lost his balance."

"Jerónimo."

"I warned him that she was the wife of his master and not to be approached. He replied that she was a Jew, not quite so good as a whore." Jerónimo was stolid, his face a rock, his lips barely moved. "Paulo may have suffered, Fernán, but not a hundredth as much as María."

A cooling breeze had failed to develop and the heat was oppressive. Fernán wiped his brow. He stared at his uncle whose grief and frenzy had transformed him into an animal—an isolated, brooding, ugly creature. The handsome man Fernán knew had been destroyed and the grief Fernán felt at his loss of Naomi was now magnified by guilt over María and Antonio.

47

In the morning

When Jerónimo returned to Halevi, he found the farmer slumped on the stool, his caftan stained. The smell of urine filled the room.

"Mother of God," Jerónimo said, "did I ignore your need for relief? I do apologize. Other than that, I hope you had a pleasant day. I brought some food to eat and drink—for myself, of course. If you are hungry or thirsty, confess your sins to me as you would to a priest. Oh, forgive me, I realize you are not familiar with the ritual. Very simple—tell me what you would have told the priest. If you refuse, I will leave and return tomorrow. Yes? No? Good day."

He turned to go and heard choking sounds behind him. "Is that you, Halevi? If you wish to speak, nod your head and I will give you something to clear your throat. Good man." Jerónimo removed a jar of ale from a bag he had brought with him and fed it to Halevi, who gulped it down. "Now, what was it you wanted to say?"

Halevi coughed and said between gasps, "I would tell the priest that Fernán Hernandes was at the Melamed house."

"As you first denounced Fernán and had him arrested?"

"Yes."

"Why?"

"I want Naomi for my wife. Hernandes would steal her from me."

"Fool."

"You will kill me, I know, but give me ale before you do, if you please?"

"I will release your bonds, Halevi. Remember, though, no one in Castile is as fast with a knife as Jerónimo." He cut the bonds and gave Halevi the jar. "Here is a leg of chicken and a slice of bread. Eat." He watched Halevi down more ale and bite off a healthy chunk of bread. "You are a foolish man, Halevi. Don Abrahán had shaken hands on the marriage and Naomi had agreed. Why, I know not, but she had. Fernán is Catholic and Naomi would not convert, so you had nothing to fear."

"There is always something to fear. Hernandes is a *converso*, not a Catholic—a traitor to his people."

"So you say. You have children?"

"Three. Two girls, one boy. The birth of the boy killed my wife. I cannot work a farm and attend to my children. They need a mother. When you kill me, they will have no mother or father and they will die. The rules of life are harsh. Better that Hernandes should have died than my little ones."

Jerónimo walked to the door, leaned against it, and watched Halevi eat. "This is what will happen, Halevi. I should kill you. As you say, the rules of life are harsh, and you should die for the pain you caused Fernán, pain from which he may never recover. However, by the grace of God he did not die. You will go free, Rubén, but your business in Toledo is done. You will leave this city and you will never come back. But, before you go you will write a note. Can you write?"

"I write Ladino."

"Good. You will write a note to don Abrahán and you will say that relations between Naomi and Fernán were suspicious, that the woman had no dowry, and therefore you revoke your agreement. Then you will return to your farm and take your goods and you will go beyond the Pyrenees and beyond Languedoc and never return. If you do, I will know and I will cut your throat."

"Then do so now. Cut my throat and the throats of my children as well. For if I leave my farm, I will die on the journey over the Pyrenees and my children will die with me. I will write the note and revoke my agreement, though I shall suffer for it, but I cannot leave my farm. My farm is our life. So kill me."

Jerónimo considered the farmer as he drank his ale and said, "Write the note. I know Ladino and Hebrew script. Here is paper and quill and ink."

Halevi wrote the note with great deliberation and signed it with his full name. Then he gave it to Jerónimo who read, paused once, nodded, and said, "You write a good hand, Halevi. Would that your judgment was half as good." He folded the note and slipped it into his purse. "Now eat your food and we will go to the gate of Cambrón and you will leave Toledo. And when you leave Toledo, it will be the last time you will see this city or, if you return, you will see me as well."

"I have possessions with my cousin."

"You have nothing but the life in your body, the clothes you wear, and the few *maravedís* in your purse. That and your loss of Naomi is your penance for treachery—a small penance at that."

"I will take the food with me. The walk to my farm is long."

"The food is yours. Here are clothes. I had them with me for another purpose, but this will do. Change. The smell of you is too much to bear. And Halevi," he said, "from time to time you will hear from me. You will work for me—not in Toledo, but in the countryside and small towns. Light work. Quiet work. Understand?"

"You will pay me for this quiet work?"

"Your pay will be adequate for the job."

"You know my farm?"

"I have been there."

Halevi smiled. "Then I have no objection."

"Good. I will wait outside the door and see you through the gate."

After a moment, Halevi emerged, his clothes changed, and they walked together through the waking streets of Toledo to the Gate of Cambrón. They said nothing to one another as Halevi hurried through the gate. He stopped on the other side, nodded to Jerónimo, and then continued on his way, his pace the steady stride of a farmer. Jerónimo watched as the figure grew small, then he trod back through the streets of the *judería* to the Melamed house and pulled the bell cord. A few minutes and Mosé opened the sliding panel and peered out, eyes puffy with sleep.

"What? Can it be? There is a God in Heaven, as if I ever doubted. But now I know he watches over us and pities mankind. Jerónimo…"

"The same."

"… come in, come in, dear man. Oh," he shook his head, his face a mask of sorrow, "what has become of Fernán? I arrived yesterday, just before the doctor returned from his journey—which, by the way, was not a success, the patient is now with God—and I found that Fernán was gone. Where has he gone? Naomi is inconsolable, poor girl, and the doctor is concerned for his health."

"He is at home, Mosé, and well. Resting. Assure the doctor, if you please, that he is most welcome at the Hernandes house at any time. I bring thanks from my master, his cousin, and this package that you will give to the doctor. Unfortunately, early as it is, I have many chores this morning and must be on my way."

"Oh, you cause me grief, my friend. But you will return another time?"

"Of course. Wait. There is something else." He reached into his purse and retrieved the note. "This note was given to me by Rubén Halevi this morning. I do not know how he found me, but he did, and asked me to present this message to the doctor. I said I would, that I was going this way and would deliver it for him. I found it strange that he would ask me, since Halevi boarded with his cousin a few doors down the street. But that is what he asked and that is what I have done. I am sure he had his reasons. And now I must say good day to you."

With a befuddled expression on his face, Mosé took the sealed note, said good day to Jerónimo, and walked slowly toward the house. Jerónimo waited outside the gate until he heard a commotion from within and then strode quickly across the street and up the alley.

48

La Fonda de los Reyes, later that day

The public room was a nest of sooty tables, chairs, and bodies—some seated, others standing—the air thick with roisterous talk and laughter and the mingled smells of ale, roast meat, wood smoke, and sweat. The hour was one, the city at dinner. Sarmiento and García huddled in a dark corner, wearing clothing that blended with the apparel of the folk around them, as they eavesdropped on snippets of conversation.

A stocky man walked by, a laborer from his garments, and shouted above the clamor, "How long was he here, the Prince?"

"Fifteen days," his friend said. "Fifteen lovely days. And where were you?"

"North with the brother. Missed the rumpus."

The two moved off and three shopkeepers Sarmiento knew by sight wandered by looking for a table. One bellowed, "Never saw such a procession as the day he arrived. First a band of trumpeters dressed in livery—gold, red, white—blowing and blowing…"

"I was there, Francesco, I saw them," another shouted. "And after them that crew of jugglers and acrobats and clowns, and the knights in battle dress…"

"… chain mail, helmets, long swords, lances with red pennants. Such expense. Five hundred knights if one. Handsome animals—the horses, not the knights—never saw the like, never will again…"

"… and the Prince behind the knights. A sight to see. That big white horse, bigger than any, covered with a red and gold blanket."

"On the horse?"

"Where but on the horse, Francesco? On the Prince? Ha! But the armor—a vision to behold. Shone like the sun. The Prince sat that mighty animal—no helmet—you could see his gold hair and blue eyes. Long damned sword by his side. Big man."

"What is he like, do you think?"

"The Prince? I like him, but rough. Broken nose. Ferocious appearance…"

"… and behind him those two—what is their names, his aides?"

"Pacheco and his brother…"

"… and the nobles, one more splendid than the next—the finery, the armor, the weapons. The people howled. Never heard your own shouts. And more knights behind the nobles…"

"… twice the number as in front. Stretched on forever. Pikemen and bowmen behind.…"

The voices of the shopkeepers were drowned in the howls of a pair of young scamps Sarmiento took for pickpockets. He felt for his purse.

"See the city of tents outside the gates?"

"I did. Most knights and pikemen stayed there. Some slept in town wherever they could steal a bed—in streets, whorehouses, inns, anywhere."

"But the tent city with the jousts and games every day—I liked that."

"Profitable business for us—eh, *amigo*?"

Sarmiento leaned over and barked, "Enough of this, García! Where do we meet?"

"Up the stairs. Follow me."

They felt their way to the end of the dingy public room clutching their pocketbooks, mounted the gloomy stairs, and found the door to the chamber García had reserved. The two canons, Galvez and Alonso, and Ávila, captain of the Gate of Alcántara, had arrived earlier and were seated at a round table drinking ale and talking animatedly. They rose to greet Sarmiento and García who shook hands all around, sat on opposite sides of the table, and poured themselves ale from a large pitcher. A knock on the door and the innkeeper, stout and rosy, brought in a platter of roast piglet and bread and another pitcher of ale.

Sarmiento was frustrated by these meetings with the canons and lawyers, always held at odd times in odd places. The whole process was so simple when he alone made decisions in his tidy office in the Alcázar. These interminable exchanges where little was discussed and less decided numbed his mind with futility and wore his patience to a brittle edge which might crack or cut at any time. What might be precipitated by his boredom? Another fracas with García, further threats to his family and well-being? A tiresome business. When would it end?

"Forgive me, don Marcos," Sarmiento said, "my mind was elsewhere. You said...?"

"That I found it unusual there was but one conversation in the public room below and that concerned the Prince."

"Unusual but understandable. Not every day does Toledo bend its knee to a future sovereign and welcome him as lord, friend, and patrón—and that before a battalion of guard in armor in the atrium of the Alcázar."

"Forgive me, don Pero," Galvez said, "as you know I was called away to an ecclesiastic function and could not attend the ceremony. Did the Prince convey any matters of importance?"

Sarmiento squirmed in his chair. Damned uncomfortable seat. "Very little beyond the necessary protocol. The Prince was welcomed as protector and lord, he inspected the guard, ate dinner, and was shown to his rooms which had been decorated to his taste by artisans he had sent to the city some days before. In short, nothing of importance."

"Why bring so many horse to the city, don Pero? And the pikemen and fools?" Juan Alonso asked.

Not the most brilliant head on Alonso. "To impress the city with his magnificence, señor. To alarm the spies of Alvaro de Luna and intimidate you and me. Are you not intimidated?"

Juan Alonso laughed nervously. "An impressive performance, I do admit."

"What you must realize," Sarmiento said, "is that this parade of the Prince and his retinue is a paragraph in a manuscript the Prince and King Juan composed between them. To them, we are a covey of scribblers who write idiotic commentaries in the margins of the text that they, the royals, write. Our words interest us, the commentators, but are rubbish to them. The vital statements—who lives and who dies, who rules and who is ruled—these pleasantries are in the text. We commentators must content ourselves with marginalia—verbal sleight of hand, not authentic magic." Sarmiento fidgeted in his chair. "Enough annotation. Why are we here today and why here?"

"Two reasons, don Pero and señores," García said. "The first is to understand our posture vis-à-vis the Prince. The second, to counter a move our spies inform us the *marranos* will soon make. We meet here because a gathering in the Alcázar might be noted and reported to interested parties. I thought it best to meet in a secluded location. I trust this was not inconvenient."

A murmur of voices was overridden by Sarmiento. "Inconvenient but necessary, don Marcos. Let us proceed."

"To begin," García said, "let us give thanks to Prince Enrique. He has eliminated the threat of war with King Juan and forgiven our supposed crimes. The citizens give thanks for the former and we for the latter."

Alonso giggled and was cautioned by Galvez.

"According to the agreement," he added, "the gates of Alcántara and Visagra have been transferred to the Prince. Our sources inform us that these gates are now reinforced with weaponry, such as guns, powder, and crossbows, and provisioned to withstand a short siege."

"And our gates, don Marcos?" Sarmiento asked. "Have our gates been reinforced as well?"

"Our gates are well-stocked," Ávila said.

"Yet the Prince or Pacheco or some one of their commanders saw fit to improve the condition of the gates they acquired from us. Does that not raise a flag?"

"Raise a flag, don Pero?"

"Sound a trumpet, ring a bell, man!" Sarmiento shifted in his seat. "For the love of God, our gates were found wanting by experienced soldiers. We should follow their example and improve our defenses."

"An excellent suggestion, don Pero," Ávila said. "I shall look to it first thing."

"Now," García said and cleared his throat, "as to policies concerning *marranos*. As you know, the Prince has decreed that all practices aspiring to root out heresy and treason in the *marrano* community should cease."

"García," Sarmiento said, "who in this room is not aware of the events of the past days?"

García reddened. "With all due respect, don Pero, there may be one or two in this room devoid of the benefits bestowed by a prodigious memory such as yours. A review of the major points, however, will occupy little of our precious time and may be beneficial in the long run. May I continue?"

Sarmiento nodded and adjusted himself in his chair.

"So long as the Prince is our *patrón*," García said, "no arrests, trials, executions, or expulsions of *marranos* will be permitted. Those who were imprisoned and awaiting trial or execution have been released. On June fifth, to counter the constraints on our campaign against the *marranos*, we issued the Judgment and Statute, the *Sentencia-Estatuto*..."

"Don Marcos," Juan Alonso said, and glanced sidewise at Sarmiento, "would you repeat the provisions of the *Sentencia-Estatuto*, if you please? I fear my ecclesiastic education did not prepare me for these legislative matters."

García glanced at Sarmiento who shrugged. "Very simple," García said. "The Judgment states that the Jewish problem can never be resolved by conversion of Jews to Christianity—a tacit removal of the distinction between *marranos* and Jews. Therefore, the Statute orders that all *marranos* be deprived of their right to hold office of any kind and to provide testimony in court, and that these restrictions apply to them and their descendants."

Juan Alonso smiled at Sarmiento and said, "Thank you."

"However," García continued, "we did not know the reaction of the Prince to the *Sentencia-Estatuto*—whether he would approve or disapprove. If he disapproved, then he might accuse us of flouting our agreement with him and proceed against us. The Judgment is not the problem. The Prince might disagree with our opinion, but it is an opinion, although a weighty one. The Statute, however, is a decree and another question entirely.

"Since the issuance of the *Sentencia-Estatuto*—and it is three weeks since we did so—the Prince has been here and gone amidst absolute silence from his court. The Prince and Pacheco have said nothing positive or negative. What may we infer from their silence? That they agree with us? That they disagree but do not care to contest the matter? We do not know. We know only that the Prince is silent and that is enough for the moment. The *Sentencia-Estatuto* is enacted, it is law, and *marranos* are cut off from the judicial system and severely reduced in status."

A general murmur of approval from all except Sarmiento, who separated himself from his uncomfortable chair and walked to the window.

"One item more flows from the *Sentencia-Estatuto*," García said. "We are informed that the *marranos* will send a delegation to Nicholas V, our Holy Father in Rome, to contest the *Sentencia-Estatuto* and our general behavior toward *marranos* since the rebellion. What is more, they have enlisted the aid of several prominent Old Christians and clerics to assist in the prosecution of their case."

"Who will represent them?" Sarmiento asked and turned from the window.

"A list of the mighty, don Pero."

"Who are the mighty?"

"Alonso de Cartagena, Bishop of Burgos. The Bishop has written letters to King Juan, espousing the *marrano* cause…"

"Only letters?" Sarmiento asked. García nodded. "Go on."

"The *marranos* have requested that Juan de Tourquemada intervene with the Pope."

"A *marrano* bastard as is Cartagena."

"Don Pero," Galvez said, "forgive me but these are prominent men. Cartagena is the son of Pablo de Santa María, and Juan de Tourquemada is Cardinal of Saint Sixtus and was theologian to the Curia."

"Both are tainted with Jewish blood. Tourquemada was born to a *marrano* mother. And Pablo de Santa María, father to Cartagena, was born Solomon ha-Levi. Undoubtedly, Cartagena was circumcised like his father before him."

"Respectfully, don Pero—and you are aware of my stance with regard to *marranos*—that church notables were Jews does not diminish their status or influence. The Church has welcomed many converts from Judaism to the fold and raised some to positions of importance."

"I know my history, Galvez. Is there more, don Marcos?" Sarmiento asked.

"García Álvarez de Toledo, formerly the Abbot of Santa María de Atocha, has written a refutation of the Statute and has gone to Rome to denounce us and ask that we be declared anathema."

"Another *converso*. No more?"

"One. King Juan has sent emissaries to Pope Nicholas who have urged him to issue a bull that condemns us."

"Expected." Sarmiento ran his fingers over the smooth, cool window glass. "Your sources are reliable, don Marcos?"

"Impeccable."

"Well then, whom do we send to Rome?"

49

The Hernandes house, two weeks later

"The first part of the *Sentencia-Estatuto*," Lorenzo said, "the passage they call the Judgment, appears harmless, but the words condemn us to perdition, Cesario. If we believe the Judgment, the lives of our forefathers and their conversions to Christianity were meaningless. We are alone in a forest of hatred, led to believe that we are a mistake, a people who should never have been, a people with no past or future. Worse, we are lost to God and can turn nowhere. We know too little of Judaism after so many generations and now are denied God through Christianity."

"Do not lose hope, Lorenzo. This is a secular matter," Cesario said. "These rebels cannot erase us. They cannot deny our existence within the Church. They are not empowered to excommunicate nor have we done anything to justify such an action."

"But the Statute robs us of our rights as citizens," Lorenzo said. "With no right to bear witness, how can we pursue our claims in court? Anyone can rob us and we are powerless to pursue them. We can be murdered with impunity. The Statute isolates and degrades us."

"Only if we allow ourselves to be degraded, Lorenzo. I had supposed the Prince would protect our cause, but nothing has changed with his coming. How ironic. The Prince of Peace advances triumphantly into Toledo and sanctions the destruction of a vital segment of its community. Marches in, allows us to be condemned to purgatory, and marches out like a toy soldier. Lorenzo, it is clear that we must be our own salvation."

Supper had been over for some time. The women and children had gone to bed and Lorenzo and Cesario, the wine and fruit untouched, sat at the table turning over this new assault. Fernán and Jerónimo stood near the door to the great hall. Three weeks had passed since his flight from Naomi and Fernán had not returned to the Melamed house nor heard from don Abrahán.

"She will be married by now," Fernán said.

"If the marriage was carried out as planned."

"We would have heard if there had been a change, would we not?"

"We should have, Fernán. Yes." Jerónimo grasped Fernán by the arm. "Turn your mind to other thoughts, young master. Soon a delegation will go to Rome to contest the *Sentencia-Estatuto*. You should be part of that mission. Rome, Florence, and other Italian cities burst with new life. You can learn much and contribute mightily to our cause."

"I am not qualified to argue in court or talk to the Pope, Jerónimo. I am no lawyer. I know nothing of judgments and statutes. My mind has only now become whole again, as whole as it ever will be. No, I am not fit. I have lost Naomi, María is dead, Antonio crushed, and now, what little that was left of our lives has been destroyed by this *Sentencia*-Estatuto. What can Rome teach me that I have not learned in Toledo?"

"The truth of life, dear friend," Jerónimo said. "Blows come hard but pain is not all there is to life. Years lie before you, Fernán. Rome is a beacon."

Across the room, seated beside the dead fireplace, Antonio jumped to his feet and shouted a nameless cry, then crumpled to the floor and sobbed.

"Will he speak again, Cesario?" Lorenzo asked.

"If God wills it. Our brother has suffered a terrible loss. We must support him until his wounds heal and he can once again embrace life."

Cesario walked over to his nephew. His right arm, almost severed in the battle with the commoners, had never regained its function and hung useless at his side.

"Are you well, Fernán?"

Fernán nodded and Cesario asked why he continued to dress in black.

"I mourn María and Antonio who are lost to us." *And Naomi who is lost to me.*

"We were discussing the delegation to Rome, Don Cesario," Jerónimo said. "Has anything been decided?"

"The council will send delegates to Pope Nicholas. We leave in a few days." Cesario considered a moment. "Fernán, had you thought of coming with us to Rome? You have experienced more than we have and I know you can express our position forcibly. Lorenzo will support you, and the council can hardly deny someone who has suffered at the hands of the rebels. Think about it seriously. They will understand your imposture as Rafael."

"Thank you, Uncle, I will," Fernán said.

But would the beacon of Rome offer guidance or warning? By leaving, could he shed the loss of Naomi and recover from the death of María? Prison had transformed him, traced permanent lines on his face and brow, and whitened his hair. Prison had infected his brain—he smelled the stench even now and his prison dreams continued to haunt him. No, Rome would solve nothing.

50

The Melamed house, two days later

The day blazing, the sun a furnace, Fernán stood outside the gate wearing a loose white shirt drenched with perspiration, black breeches, stockings, and low boots, and carried a dagger in a leather scabbard at his waist. He was healthy once again and his heart thumped with anticipation.

His attire was the same as he would wear the following day when he and Cesario accompanied the others of the delegation to join García Álvarez de Toledo, the abbot who had been in Rome for several weeks petitioning Pope Nicholas V. There were four delegates from Toledo—Cesario, Fernán, and two other members of the community, Herrera the lawyer and Husillo the banker.

Jerónimo had persuaded Lorenzo to release him from his duties as steward so that he might accompany the delegates, supervise the servants who escorted them, and attend Fernán and Cesario. The delegates had leased a wagon to carry their possessions and provisions and would tether four additional horses to the rear of the wagon, allowing riders a periodic change of mount. Gentlemen and servants would ride in two columns—gentlemen leading the wagon and servants following—swords in scabbards and braces of loaded pistols at the ready to ward off highwaymen.

They would follow Río Tajo eastward, veer toward Cuenca and, after entering Aragón, proceed southeasterly through Requeña and on to Valencia where they would secure passage to Rome. Horses and wagons would be stabled in that city until they returned. From Toledo to Valencia was about seventy leagues and they estimated that, without serious problems, they would reach their goal in less than ten days. The sea voyage was more of a mystery, since they were ignorant of the craft available to sail the Balearic, Mediterranean, and Tyrrhenian seas to a port near Rome.

Cesario had urged Lorenzo to send Fernán with the delegation, and Lorenzo interrogated Fernán as if he were a stranger, asking him what he would accomplish if he did go.

"I am no longer the son who runs errands, Papá. That son died in a prison cell. Cesario suggested that I knew more about the brutality of this regime than most and, though it has taken me some time, I have come to agree. I am more than qualified and my motives are not commercial. I want revenge against the beasts, Papá, and one way or another I will have it."

Lorenzo regarded his son and nodded. "Agreed, Fernán," he said, "you have my permission. Go to Rome."

"Thank you, Papá, though what I really need is to borrow some money."

"And what do you offer as collateral?" Lorenzo said with a smile.

"My life. I know your question was in jest, but my response is in earnest. I pledge my life to repay every *maravedí*."

"Now you jest, Fernán. How could I send my son to Rome with empty pockets? As for repayment, we will discuss that when you return." Then he tilted his head and scrutinized his son. "What is this I hear about the Melamed granddaughter?"

"What do you hear, Papá? And from what source?"

"The source is of little importance. What is important is that my son is courting a Jew. Was one Jew in the family not enough?"

"Lorenzo," Cesario said, "what can you be saying? You married a Jew."

"Her family converted when she was a baby. Celestina was raised Catholic."

"But we are all descended from Jews," Cesario said. "Why are we hated if not for that? Must we then hate those from whence we come?"

"Do not berate me, Cesario. I hate no one, certainly not my cousins. But why must my son burden himself with a Jewish wife? Would you want your Miguel to marry a Jew when he is of age, be wary of informers behind every bush, and father children who are neither this nor that?"

"Papá, your argument lacks logic and basis. To the best of my knowledge, Naomi is married. And while that does not change my affection for her, it certainly alters any plans I may have had for marriage, were it practical."

"Then go to Rome, my son. But remember that the purpose of this delegation is to legitimize our claim to equality as Catholics. We must eliminate the abuse and persecution heaped on us because of our descent from Jews."

Fernán waited outside the Melamed gate, dreading and, at the same time, longing to know whether Naomi was married. He prayed that by some miracle her marriage had been aborted and he might leave Castile with hope. Though he loved her, he knew that their path to marriage would have been uncertain and might have proved impassable, but youth and blind faith drove him to believe that God wanted him and Naomi to be man and wife, and so he rang the bell.

No response, no sound from within. Oh, dear God, he thought, do not reject me, though I did leave abruptly and said nothing to Naomi, nor did I wait for don Abrahán to return. He rang again and listened. No footsteps. He sighed and turned to leave.

"Would you come this far and depart without a word?"

The quizzical face of don Abrahán was at the gate window. The gate opened and the doctor smiled. "Well, Fernán, you look healthier than when I saw you last. The food at home must be good."

"The food at home is almost as good as in your house, don Abrahán," Fernán said, "but the company lacks a certain charm."

"Thank you for your kind words, cousin. Now do come in out of the heat before we both suffer sunstroke. Though it is difficult to avoid a July sun no matter where one hides."

The study was dark and relatively cool and they sat quietly for a moment and enjoyed the respite. The room had been reconverted from the bedroom where he and Naomi had made love, and Fernán became lost in remembrance until Melamed asked if he would like something to eat or drink.

"A drink, don Abrahán, and I will fetch it for both of us."

"There is ale somewhere in the kitchen. Naomi never tells me where she puts anything. God forbid I should not be able to smell it out."

Fernán stopped midway to the kitchen and said, "Naomi is here?"

"No, Fernán. Naomi is not here."

"Then she is married and I did not wish her well or buy a present for her wedding."

"The present would have been wasted though good thoughts are always welcome."

"What do you say, don Abrahán?" he said, as his heart danced.

"I said that Naomi is not married, but is away from home."

"But why keep me in suspense, señor? You are not a cruel man. Forgive me, but I have suffered weeks of torment not knowing whether Naomi married Halevi."

"For whatever good will come of it, Fernán, Naomi remains single. She lives in this house when she is not elsewhere and—the good Lord forgive her and grant me greater wisdom and patience than I currently possess—she is your dear friend, as am I. Beyond that statement I will not go for the most obvious of reasons. Now, if you please, find the ale before we faint from heat exhaustion."

Oblivious to the heat and all else, though his curiosity boiled and was about to overflow, Fernán surmised that don Abrahán would have told him why Naomi did not marry if he had so wanted. So he asked no more questions but searched the kitchen, found a pitcher of ale, and returned to the doctor with the pitcher and two mugs, without spilling the ale or vaulting into the sky or embracing don Abrahán.

"You are pleased by my news, Fernán?"

"Indeed, señor, I am. With all my heart."

"Why?"

"But you know the reason, don Abrahán. I love Naomi."

"Are you Catholic?"

"Of course."

"Then the situation has not changed—there is a double wall between you. And Naomi will undoubtedly live her life as a single woman since no Jewish man will have her now that she has been refused by Halevi."

"How could he or any man refuse her?"

"Might you tell me, Fernán? Halevi wrote—he did not have the stomach to face me—but wrote that relations between you and Naomi were suspicious, that she had no dowry, and therefore he was revoking our contract. Now he knew she had no dowry before he signed the *ketubbah* and that leaves her relations with you. What did he mean?"

Halevi could not have known of their one night of love. Had he seen them together or was it because Fernán had slept in the Melamed house?

"Did he mean my recuperating here, señor? Was he that jealous?"

"I cannot know, Fernán. Might there be something more?"

"What has Naomi said?"

"Nothing. You both say nothing and yet—yet there is something. Well then, songbirds will sing in May." Melamed finished his ale and Fernán poured more and Melamed said, "Thank you," and shrugged and said, "Ah, well. So, you are a member of this delegation to the Pope."

"How did you know?"

"My spies."

"Don Abrahán, do your spies tell you why the Pope should listen to us? Why the Pope should support our petition? If they do, please tell me."

Melamed drank his ale and nodded his head. "Yes, cousin, by all means. For that I need no spies." He drank again from his mug and sat back in the chair. "Remember, Fernán, that the Pope is more a political than a religious leader. He needs order in the Church and control of its affairs and, for that, order in the world is required, God willing. World order supports ecclesiastic order—the opposite may be true as well. An upstart canon or layman in a wayward parish, as in our case in the city of Toledo, represents a problem for the Pope. Such a priest or lay Catholic might be a heretic or a violator of papal authority or a proponent of political disorder, and the Pope must stamp out these anarchic violations without hesitation.

"Thus, you see, political climate influences his decisions almost more than clerical. For, despite the considerable influence of the Church and its protestations of heavenly superiority to earthly princes—a debatable point, of course—kings live in a political world and the authority of a pope can be limited by the strength of a king. A strong king can disobey a pope with impunity, deflect arrows of excommunication and such, and require a pope to work within a framework designed by the king. On the other hand, a weak king, like our Juan, provides an opportunity for a pope to manipulate affairs of state. And, of course, much depends on the will and wisdom of a particular pope.

"Castile is in a perpetual state of flux, Fernán. Prince Enrique and King Juan are at odds, and Navarre and Aragón and even the Moors play politics with Enrique, in the hope of a share in the spoils. The Pope must be careful to agree with the winner, for to support the loser would be a blow to papal politics.

"Your cause depends on King Juan retaining power—at least for the moment. He must win or you will lose. The argument in your favor, principally, is that this Pope hates anarchy. That is your gauge. Do you know of Nicholas V?"

"No, señor. Though I look forward to meeting him."

"I am sure you do, my boy. A new wind blows in Italy, particularly in Florence, but also in Rome and other Italian cities—though not yet here in Castile. This Pope is sensitive to new winds and the newest goes by the name of *humanitas*. The thrust of *humanitas* is to encourage the most sublime of human capacities. Strangely, Nicholas surrounds himself with thinkers who embrace these thoughts—some quite controversial. Surprising in Rome, the center of Catholicism, to harbor such rebels against the tyranny of dogma. You will find him and his court remarkable and, I think, he will find you equally of interest. Who will be with you?"

"Several members of the *converso* council, including Alfonso de Herrera the lawyer, and my uncle Cesario. We will join Fray García Álvarez de Toledo, already in Rome."

"Álvarez. You speak of the Abbot of Santa María de Atocha in Madrid?"

"Yes, don Abrahán, the same."

"He is a *converso*." Melamed smiled. "How many of our children have assumed the robes of the Church." He sighed. "And you are fluent in Latin and Italian?"

"Yes, señor. Although my father has warned me to conceal that knowledge. He believes that if I keep silent, the Italians may divulge a confidence without realizing that I understand."

"Perhaps. Your mind is clear?"

"In fact, much better."

"And you have recovered your strength?"

"Most of it. My swordsmanship is as it was, and I am not easily winded."

"Good. The streets of Italian cities can be dangerous, especially after dark. Carry your sword at all times. So then, Fernán," Melamed said and rose from his chair, "I will say goodbye to you and pray that God brings you to the shores of Italy and home again without harm and with your mission successful."

"Thank you, don Abrahán. You will tell Naomi that I am sorry I missed her and will see her when I return?"

"I suggest, Fernán, that you forget my granddaughter. There are so many obstacles and Naomi recognizes that now she must find a new life for herself that does not include you. I am sorry, my boy, but those words are hers not mine—although I do share her opinion. Forget Naomi. Your life is just beginning."

"Don Abrahán, I respect your advice and her words. But I will return to Toledo and I will seek out Naomi. For my life begins and ends with her."

Part III

TESTIMONY

"He [Nicholas V] did not know what avarice was: indeed, if he retained anything of his own, it was simply because no one had asked him for it."

The Vespasiano Memoirs:
Lives of Illustrious Men of the XVth Century
Vespasiano da Bisticci (1421-1498)
English Translation 1926

51

A month later, mid-August, 1449

My dear Papá—

Safe in *Roma* in good health, tired but buoyant. This letter will be delivered to the captain of the caravela on which we sailed from Valencia and he will post it on his return to Aragón. With the help of God, these words should reach you within a month.

La María Nueva, on which we sailed, is a small merchantman and bears three triangular lateen sails. The foremast is set just forward of amidships, the mizzenmast mounted at the stern of the poop deck at the tail of the craft, and the mainmast halfway between the two. The mainsail is half the area of the foresail and twice that of the mizzensail—a mathematical approach to sail design. It is a jolly ship and accommodated the seven of us nicely.

The voyage was relatively uneventful but for a near scrape with a pirate vessel near Marseilles. Many ships were tied up in Marseilles harbor, but we were too far out to make port since the pirate bore down hard. The captain put up all sail, changed course, and the pirate gave chase. But our ship was light and more maneuverable and, with a good westerly blow behind us, we ran before the wind all night, outran his galleon and, when day broke, the buccaneer was nowhere to be seen. God was with us.

We arrived yesterday morning at *Fiumicino* at the mouth of the Tiber river—or as the river is called here, *Fiume Tevere*—the weather hotter than a summer day in Toledo. Fray García Álvarez de Toledo had arranged rooms for our delegation in a *pensione* near the Vatican on the west bank of the Tiber, a sinuous river of some width which runs through the city of Rome and empties into the Tyrrhenian sea, the *Mare Tirreno*. Unfortunately, the river is silted badly at its delta on the *Tyrrhenian* and is somewhat shallow upriver, so that the ship could not possibly navigate upstream. Instead, we enlisted the aid of a smaller vessel, no more than a barge or large punt with one small sail. The boat, for it is too small to be called a ship, is propelled by a three-man crew who push against the river bottom with long poles, or employ mules on the bank to pull hawsers secured to the boat. Both methods provide primary forms of locomotion and are used separately or at the same time. The sail appears to be ornamental at best.

This large punt was moored above the delta and we wagoned ourselves and our luggage upriver to the mooring and then were ferried to Rome some five leagues to the northeast, a journey that began at sunrise and ended when the sun set. Once in Rome, we were fortunate in that we found our *pensione, il Gallo d'Oro* or The Golden Rooster, quickly and there procured a pair of small wagons with which to transport ourselves and our belongings from punt to inn.

By nine o'clock last night, settled within our rooms, we were anxious for a Roman repast despite the heat. Supper was strange but wonderful—my first encounter with Italian *pasta*. Then back to our rooms and a comfortable bed.

The *pensione* lies within the old quarter known as *il Trastevere*, a contraction for 'across the Tiber,' one assumes, from the heart of Rome. For from the fourth floor of the pensione where I room, one can see the ruined monuments of Rome laid out as they were in the time of the Caesars—the *Teatro Marcello* near the Tiber, further on the magnificent *Colliseo* where gladiators fought, and in the near distance, the Pantheon. How I look forward to exploring wondrous Rome!

My first impression of the streets of the city was of constant motion. Rome is not nearly so large as it was in the time of the Empire, but much larger than Toledo. The streets are busy night and day with people walking, running, on horseback, or in carriages. Everywhere there are merchants hawking wares from small stands laden with merchandise and foodstuffs, while others bear their wares on their shoulders employing diverse contraptions they have devised. A caution, though. We have been warned that our quarter is home to pickpockets and other thieves, so we wear our weapons and conceal our wealth.

Tomorrow morning we meet with Fray García Álvarez to discuss strategy. There is much to learn and little time. I will endeavor to write as frequently as opportunity allows. However, I must now conclude this note so that it may be delivered to the captain.

May God protect you and my dear mother and sister.

Your devoted son, Fernán

Rome, 15 August, 1449

52

Early the next morning at The Golden Rooster

They met in a private parlor of the *pensione* and sat at a dark wooden table on high-backed chairs with cushioned seats and backs upholstered in patterned brocade. The room was simple, save for a Persian carpet on the floor and several modest paintings and one tapestry that decorated the white walls.

Fray Abbot García Álvarez de Toledo arrived just after the delegates had assembled and was ushered into the parlor by the steward of the *pensione*. A man of medium height, the abbot was generously proportioned, his head accented by a rough growth of black hair surrounding the tonsure. His tonsure and beard, shaved that morning, were tinted blue, attesting to the density of his facial hair. However, the most striking aspect of his rough-hewn features was a blade-like nose with flared, hairy nostrils that lent him the appearance of someone in continual pursuit of suspicious odors. Within this tough cover dwelt a pair of sparkling, but soft gray eyes.

Fray García declared in a profound basso, "Good morning and a Roman welcome to all! I trust you had a pleasant journey." And then, after being introduced to those present, he did not wait for handshakes or pleasantries, but continued, "...being as I am the town crier of the City of Rome, I will bring you up to date with a review of current events," and laughed so boisterously that Fernán thought the walls would shake and awaken the other guests of the *pensione*.

"To date then," García said, after recovering from his brief fit of merriment, "Pope Nicholas has received me and listened to my opinion regarding the deplorable events in Toledo. His reaction was unimpressive. Second, the Pope has received an appeal from King Juan to take action against the Toledan rebels whose acts, the King maintains, constitute sedition—an opinion I share. The King requested that Pope Nicholas denounce the rebels and declare them anathema. The statement may be a reaction to letters from Alfonso de Cartagena, a person of vast persuasive powers who has supplicated the King on behalf of the Castilian *converso* community.

"However, despite the letter from King Juan and my entreaties, Nicholas is silent. Do not expect sudden decisions from this Pope. He is an attentive man, though cautious and not accustomed to precipitous moves. To be sure. Ha!" And he loosed another explosive laugh.

The laughter ceased and Herrera asked, "Why does he wait?"

Fray García, settled at the head of the table, smiled broadly. "We are not alone, my dear colleagues. Rome is honored with the presence of a delegation from the rebels."

"Who represents the rebels?" Cesario asked.

"Before I answer…in fact, before I can manage to speak again, is there something to drink? I dress too warmly for Rome, a city that provides an ample supply of native warmth. This wool cloak is much too heavy—I should have known." Fernán placed before the abbot a pitcher of ale and a mug from the sideboard. "Thank you, dear Rafael," the abbot said, as he filled the mug and drank. "Ah, much better. Now, you ask who represents the rebels. A small delegation headed by my namesake, García de Villalpondo, who arrived in Rome several days after I did, bearing many boxes of putative evidence which they claim form the substance of their investigation into *converso* activity."

Fernán remembered the words that Jerónimo had told him issued from the lips of Marcos García. "… they are Christians in name and hidden Jews in practice, and that is a grave deceit we call heresy. For these Jews in Christian garments are heretics and must be punished."

"They claim this evidence justifies their crimes," the Abbot said.

"Is this Villalpondo the same person of that name who was Deputy Chief Judge of Appeals in Toledo?" Herrera asked.

"The same. Ironically, he was an appointee of Alvaro de Luna and a member of the Council of King Juan. A jurist of some qualification and now a strong advocate for the rebels, he is purported to be a person of principle and spirit."

"A spirit owned by Sarmiento," Fernán said.

"Sadly, young man, sadly."

"I know the man and he is capable, though I would not vouch for his principles," Herrera said. "Has the Pope granted them an audience?"

"No, he has not. Cardinal Juan de Tourquemada, a confidant of the Pope, has convinced His Holiness that to grant them an audience would lend an aura of validity to an otherwise questionable enterprise. However, Villalpondo has availed himself of other avenues."

"What avenues?"

"Why, my friend, the Curia. These people are not without resources within the College of Cardinals." He glanced around the table. "But take heart, brave souls, the Pope is disposed to support our cause but remains uncertain about the future of King Juan—the current situation in Castile being so highly combustible. However, we will continue to enlist members of the Curia on our side, when and if we can, and we must not forget our interview with the Pope on the twenty-first of August at ten in the morning. I suggest we meet beforehand to decide who will speak and what will be said."

53

The Vatican Palace

Armed mercenaries in colorful uniforms stood to either side of the main entrance and, as the Castilians approached, one of several priests assigned to the entrance requested their identity and business. Fray García Álvarez responded that they had an audience with the Pope. The priest inspected a leather-bound book and made a notation. Then he escorted the visitors through the ornate halls of the Palace, past pairs of scurrying priests in long black robes and whispering brothers in brown or white cowls busy with documents, to an open loggia above one of the inner courtyards of the Vatican where the Pope received visitors.

Ceilings in the loggia, as well as in the halls through which they had been led, were decorated with a series of large, square, bas-relief floral panels supported by tall square pillars eighteen feet high and at least two feet on a side. The pillars were encased in variegated marble or covered with framed panels of floral bas-relief sculpture. Fernán found the decoration oppressive, though beautifully wrought.

The Pope sat to one side of the balcony on a gilded, high-backed chair, facing the courtyard. The seat and back of the chair were upholstered in fringed scarlet velvet fastened with rows of silver studs. When they entered, Pope Nicholas was conversing with two priests—one tall and angular, the other short and round. Both wore long black robes with silver trim and were tonsured severely. The fringes of hair that remained on their heads looked to Fernán curiously like the velvet fringe that trimmed the chair. The priest who escorted them to the chamber spoke to the tall priest, who spoke to the Pope, and the visitors were directed to approach His Holiness.

Although seated, the Pope was an imposing figure—large, blocky, in a white overdress with a short scarlet cape on his shoulders and a dome-like matching cap, both garments trimmed in ermine. The cap covered his head, framed his face, and concealed his hair, much of his ears, and the nape of his neck. Nicholas V was fifty-two years old, Fernán knew, but his facial lines, the eyes weary from relentless reading, and the set jaw attested to a man under considerable stress—one who bore his age poorly. Fernán stood against a pillar and sought to remember every word, so that he could describe the meeting to his father.

Fray Álvarez bowed to the Pope and said, "Good morning, Your Holiness," then kissed the papal ring and knelt on a velvet cushion placed before the gilt chair.

"*Buenos días*, Fray Álvarez," the Pope said. "How are you this beautiful morning?"

"Well, Your Holiness, but saddened by the weight of the troubles that plague my homeland."

"Be assured, my son, that your problems are never far from our thoughts. We shall delay no longer than necessary before we rule on this matter."

"I thank you, Your Holiness, for your consideration." Fray Álvarez took a handkerchief from his sleeve and wiped his forehead. "Your Holiness, my purpose in asking for an audience this morning, despite your stressful calendar, was to introduce you to several gentlemen from the city of Toledo in Castile. They are New Christians of the *converso* community and can provide you with more detailed information regarding the persecution of their people in Toledo and the cruelty which has spilled into the streets of other cities in Castile."

Álvarez then interjected his "principal argument and that of many others in the royal and ecclesiastic administrations, that crimes committed by the rebel administration of Pero Sarmiento and Marcos García against *conversos* are crimes against faithful Christians and against the core beliefs of Christianity itself." He waited for a response, but none came and he introduced Fernando Husillo. Fernán hoped that the reply of the Pope to Husillo would be more constructive than that to Álvarez.

Husillo bowed, kissed the ring, and knelt. He thanked the Pope for receiving them this busy morning, and said that his family was converted to the true faith at the end of the last century. He owned a small banking establishment in Toledo founded by his father and was one of those who advocated neutrality and patience when the troubles began. However, after the first few months of oppression, he was convinced that neutrality was a disastrous policy. "The rebels persuaded me by their actions that they wanted the death of every *converso*—man, woman, and child." There was no choice between opposition and neutrality because "Pero Sarmiento removed all choice. And although I live, many died." He implored the Pope to examine their cause, "a cause which has as its origin our wish to be part of the true faith and to worship our God and Jesus Christ, His Son, in peace."

The Pope blessed Husillo and told him that he would weigh his words carefully. As Álvarez had predicted, the response was unimpressive and Fernán worried that their audience would be a failure.

Alfonso de Herrera stepped forward. A slim, fair man, Herrara had some difficulty kneeling on the pillow and the tall priest helped him to his knees. He introduced himself as a lawyer who had defended several members of the community against the "oppressive rule of Pero Sarmiento."

He told of his defense of don Diego Enríquez from the false charges of treason, and the insistence of Sarmiento that, despite his advanced years, Enríquez be tortured, though he knew it would kill him, for under torture his innocence would be proved. "A cruel argument, designed to kill within the law, Your Holiness. When I pleaded leniency for don Diego, Sarmiento smiled and said that I opposed the times, that the times determine what is good or evil, that what appeared good to one era might be anathema to the next." Herrera cited this as an example of the hatred and cynicism exhibited by the rebels, "emotions which mock our law." He said that he could not alter the law with the times nor substitute the law of the street for the law of the court. "But how can we live with a law created by those who hate us?" The Pope alone could answer that question, he said, and right the wrong.

Pope Nicholas nodded his head slowly and said that as a lawyer, Herrera knew the world and "though it is the world of God, there is much that God allows within this world beyond our understanding—much that we can only begin to understand through prayer and belief in His divine wisdom." He said that he listened to Herrera with humility, sympathy, and respect and prayed for the wisdom to act "as God would wish me to act."

Cesario helped Herrera to his feet with his left hand and then bowed, kissed the ring, and knelt. He introduced himself as a man of intemperate spirit, "quick to anger but quick to forgive," a portrayal with which Fernán agreed. Cesario went on, "When I saw that the purpose of the rebel crusade was to reduce our community to ash and ourselves to dust, no matter what we said or did, my gall rose." He rushed into the fight, was struck on the arm, and lost the use of his limb. Reconciled to the loss of his arm, for those were the fortunes of battle, he was not reconciled to the loss of family and friends to the "whims of tyranny."

True, he said, our people were forced into Christianity in earlier times but, once Christian, have embraced the faith. "My sister-in-law…." His eyes teared and he said, "Forgive me, Your Holiness, my temperament masters me."

After a moment he continued. "My brother said that no matter how saintly one might be, or perhaps because one is a saint, a New Christian would be tortured and die horribly. The rebels," he said, "led by Sarmiento, a supposed noble, hate *conversos* because 'God has blessed us and caused us to prosper.' Can prosperity be a sin?" Then he said that Sarmiento killed to seize possessions. "Before God, Your Holiness, my tongue does not lie. We are slaughtered for gold. Is there to be no peace for us, those who no longer remember Judaism or want to be part of that religion? We are Christians, as Christian as those who hate us. What can we do? Must we be martyred to prove our devotion?"

The Pope blessed Cesario for his honesty and candor. "Those are qualities for which one need not be ashamed, my son. Nor should you regret a temperament which gives birth to honesty." The Pope then said that one must live, not be martyred, and that venality would be punished and good rewarded.

Fernán had listened with care. He was disheartened that the Pope had equivocated, said nothing in their defense, told Husillo that he would weigh his words, informed Herrera that he would pray for the wisdom to act as God wished him to act, and praised Cesario for his character, saying that evil would be punished. Fernán knew that patience would never punish the evil he had experienced. Perhaps he expected more than was possible. As Melamed had said, the Pope was a master of compromise, as are all politicians. What would the Pope say to him? More facile words, more compromise?

He would speak in Latin. Only Jerónimo and Cesario knew his true identity and Fernán wished to retain the subterfuge. And though Husillo and Herrera were amazed at his resemblance to the late Fernán, he was obviously 'much older.' After he bowed to the Pope, knelt, kissed the ring, and looked into the face of the man who was the Vicar of Christ on earth, he felt he would rather enter into battle than speak, but this moment was the reason he had traveled to Rome and he composed himself, knowing that he must speak his heart and that, like the Pope, his only power was in his words.

"Your Holiness, with your permission, I will speak in Latin so that I may express my thoughts in a more perfect tongue."

"I hear your fluency, my son. Therefore, proceed."

"I beg forgiveness, Your Holiness. I am young and what I will say is not tempered by the wisdom I hope to gain with age. Therefore, I pray that you will forgive my missteps and hear instead the true words of my heart."

Fernán noticed that the priests nearby, who had been conversing quietly, were now silent and attentive.

"Your Holiness," he said, "we have been driven by desperation to seek your assistance to our cause. First, we were accused of treason by the rebels because of our affection for the works of Alvaro de Luna, whom they despise. When those accusations proved insufficient, we were arrested for heresy because the rebels claimed, falsely, that we practice Jewish traditions and laws. Prince Enrique then interceded on our behalf and forbade such persecution and, in their insatiable desire for our possessions and blood, Pero Sarmiento and the rebels passed the *Sentencia-Estatuto*, the Judgment and Statute.

"The other day my father, Lorenzo Hernandes, describing the effect of this law, said that the Judgment, which claims that Jews can never become Christian, seemed harmless since it is an opinion and not a law, but that the words condemn *conversos* to perdition. He said that if we were to obey the Judgment, the lives of our forefathers and their conversion to Christianity would be meaningless. We would be a mistake, a people who should never have been, a people with neither past nor future. A people lost to God, knowing nothing of Judaism and denied God through Christianity.

"The second part of this edict, the Statute, deprives New Christians of their right to hold office or to provide testimony in court. And these restrictions apply not only to current generations but to our descendants.

"Your Holiness, this Statute deprives us of the benefit of law—of all law. We are reduced to the status of slaves, of animals, of dirt. Your Holiness, this *Sentencia-Estatuto* is the work of the Devil. Only the Devil could have conceived of so evil a pronouncement. To deprive a people of the blessing of God and the blessing of law is to condemn them to a living death, a life without hope. The *Sentencia-Estatuto* is not a law, it is a sentence of eternal death."

Fernán looked into the eyes of the Pope. "Your Holiness," he said, "we appeal to you, the Vicar of Christ on earth, to have mercy on us as a people, and extend to us the mercy Jesus Christ extends to all his followers."

Pope Nicholas breathed deeply and nodded.

"My son," he said, "you wear black. Do you mourn?"

"I do, Your Holiness. I mourn for an aunt who was accused falsely of heresy and burned because she sang a Ladino song. María had been reared as a Jew before she married my uncle, and I mourn for that uncle who was driven mad by her death. I mourn for my godfather, an old man accused of treason for unknown reasons, subjected to torture and killed, and for his wife who died of grief. I mourn for the hundreds of New Christians who have been falsely accused, tortured, and burned, and for the New Christians of Toledo who defended themselves from false accusation and were attacked and killed or maimed in defense of their homes. I mourn as well for the Old Christians of Toledo who attacked our community and were themselves killed in a false cause. And I mourn for the Toledan Church that has been sullied by its complicity in these attacks and killings. That is why I wear black, Your Holiness."

"You have not told me your name, my son."

"Your Holiness, I am called Rafael Rivera. I am, however, Rafael Fernán Hernandes de Toledo, the fourth generation of my family reared in the Catholic faith. I was arrested for heresy and reported to be dead from torture and deprivation in my cell in the Alcázar. However, I was stolen from the prison, more dead than alive, and revived. I pray you will preserve the secrecy of my continued existence. If the fact that I live were to reach the ears of Pero Sarmiento or Marcos García or their operatives, my life would be forfeit. I am still young, Your Holiness, and I hope to live."

"To the best of our ability, my son," the Pope said, "this office will ensure that your life is preserved." Nicholas studied Fernán for a moment and then said, "You have more to say than this brief audience will permit, Rafael Rivera. This evening there will be an informal salon here at the Vatican Palace. We would be pleased if you would attend. Bring your associates with you."

"Thank you, Your Holiness. We would be greatly honored."

"It is we who would be honored." Nicholas closed his eyes and then opened them. "The matter we discuss is multi-faceted, Rafael. The attitude of the Church toward Jews and foreign gentiles is one of openness and welcome, yet there are recognized problems with the implementation of that policy. Some part of this dilemma in Castile may be traced to the delicate and confused nature of the political situation within your country and between Castile and its neighbors. But the confusion is not limited to Castile. We will not pursue this matter further this morning. However, be assured that we view the events in Castile and Toledo with grave concern. We look forward to a more informal conversation this evening. Father Tomasso will provide you with details."

The tall priest nodded to the visitors and led them from the chamber.

54

The Golden Rooster

The sight of a despondent Jerónimo peering over the iron courtyard fence greeted Fernán when he and the others returned to the *pensione*, and he urged his sad friend to join them for dinner. Herrera called for the steward of the *pensione* to bring beer, and the six Castilians sat across from one another at a trestle table in the courtyard, anticipating dinner, drinking beer, and mulling over the audience with the Pope.

The lance-like, leathery leaves of the tall olive trees shaded the courtyard and filtered the hot afternoon sun. The patterned sunlight threading through the leaves and the terra cotta tiles beneath his feet returned Fernán to the Melamed courtyard and Naomi—her oval face, dark-rimmed eyes, and delicate mouth. His throat was parched and he downed the beer in one swallow, but his thirst seemed unquenchable. Memory of the faces of Naomi and Jerónimo that occupied twin halves of his mind distracted him from the lively conversation that began to swirl about him. Eventually, the voices broke through the barriers of melancholy and longing and he heard Husillo say that he had been pleased with the audience that morning.

"The Pope understood my argument. He had great sympathy for our decision to fight."

Herrera disagreed. "The Pope was a block of red and white stone," he said, "unmoved and unmoving. What does he mean, 'as God would wish us to act'? Does he expect an angel to deliver a message from God?"

Fray García objected. "The Vicar of Christ carries the weight of the world, don Alfonso. We cannot know his mind any more than we can know the mind of God."

"With great respect for your person, Father, that manner of talk is prattle and not worthy of a man of your intelligence. The Pope is a man with the concerns of a man, elected by other men to do a job. Though I admit his responsibilities are large, they are no larger than that of a king—though the papal bureaucracy would have us believe them monumental and deserving of reverence, an opinion with which I disagree."

The steward brought several loaves of bread and a large carafe of white wine. Fray García said Grace and they helped themselves.

"Señores, we are drifting," Cesario said. "Rafael, what did you say to His Holiness—and why did you speak Latin?"

Fernán put aside his concern for Jerónimo and his desire for Naomi and repeated the essence of his conversation with the Pope, avoiding references to the question of his identity. "I spoke Latin because Latin is a more serious language than ours, although I treasure Spanish."

The steward brought a large bowl of *tagliatelle* seasoned with mushrooms and peas.

"Was anything accomplished this morning?" Cesario asked.

Herrera questioned their success. "You ask do I respect Nicholas? I know he must make concessions and compromises and that there are factors beyond our struggle with the rebels but, señores, the Pope abandoned us to wander in the wilderness."

Fray García raised his head from the dish of pasta to say that his business here was done and that he would leave Rome in the morning to attend to problems at home. He had learned of a barque with berths to spare that would leave on ebb tide the following night and he planned to sail with it. Cesario expressed surprise, but Herrera agreed with the decision and said that he and his servant would join the Abbot since it would be a long time before the Pope weighed all the imponderables, tested the wind, and decided whether or not to support their cause. His family and legal practice required his presence in Toledo. Husillo admitted that the trip had been arduous and costly, and that he too would return to Castile with the others.

The steward brought brown trout on trenchers and they sprinkled lemon juice on the fish and ate in silence.

"Will you come to the salon this evening, señores?" Fernán asked.

"Not I, Rafael," Herrera said. "We should make an early start tomorrow and I must gather my goods together."

Husillo and Fray García agreed, and the Abbot asked Cesario to make their excuses to the Pope and explain their absence. "But you must wear your best clothes to the salon," Husillo said, and Fernán, in an antic mood, replied he would wear white hose with black stripes, a bright red doublet, and a yellow hat. No one laughed.

The steward brought melon and they cut the fruit and speared the pieces with their knives. As they ate, juice ran down the sides of their mouths and they exclaimed at its sweetness and became reconciled to parting. Before adjourning for siesta, Cesario and Fernán wished the others a safe journey and reunion in Toledo. They parted company and Fernán went to his room.

Waking an hour later, Fernán returned to the empty courtyard, sat under the olive trees with pen and paper, and began writing a letter to his father. Jerónimo emerged from the *pensione* and joined him, his face somber.

"Are you well, dear friend? Your complexion has changed."

"I am well, Fernán, but seem never able to sleep during the day and less than half the night."

"Are your dreams troubled?"

"I dream, but my dreams are spirits that disappear when I wake."

"My sleep overflows with evil dreams," Fernán said. "I have come to dread sleep and yet am always tired." He had dreamt of Naomi, the same dream of flying and farewell that came to him while he had dozed in the Alcázar before the fight with Sarmiento.

"You are newly released from pain, Fernán. That will change."

"Perhaps." Fernán signed his name and sealed the letter. "Why do you think the Pope invited us to his salon?"

"The Pope dreams, just as you and I do. I imagine that among other perplexities this controversy in Castile plagues his nights. He may want to understand more than was provided this morning and perhaps that a less formal setting will be more conducive to its procurement. He is a man of wide interests and formidable powers, despite his belittling by don Alfonso."

"So don Abrahán had said. Is Nicholas more concerned with secular or ecclesiastic matters, do you think?"

"Nicholas is a scholar of the new *humanitas* and surrounds himself with others of that persuasion. Since *humanitas* implies an emphasis on the individual, on the development of human capabilities and the balance of thought and action, he must lean toward the secular." Jerónimo grasped the railing of the iron fence and shook it. "I feel imprisoned here, Fernán. Isolated. That may be what you see in my face. I should never have come to Rome."

"Join us this evening at the salon."

"No, young master, I would be out of place."

"Then return home with the others, Jerónimo. This wait may be long and you can help in Toledo more than here. Once in Castile, your color will brighten."

"I promised your father I would be at your side."

"Do you see my right arm? It could take you on and best you."

Jerónimo smiled and Fernán said, "Yes, I know better, but I am fully recovered and Cesario and I will care for each other. Go home, Jerónimo. Take this letter to my father and another I will give you for Naomi, and tell my mother that my heart is with her."

"And Cesario?"

"I will convince Cesario. Have no fear. We love you."

"I am torn, Fernán—Toledo is unstable but your need is here."

"Cesario and I will be well and safe, Jerónimo. Return tomorrow with the others. There, my friend, you see, like good *umanisti* we have balanced thought with action."

55

Evening at the Vatican Palace

The conveyance was more wagon than carriage, with benches that faced one another in the bay and a multi-colored cloth suspended above as dubious protection from the elements. A single ancient horse pulled the vehicle, guided by an ancient man with wizened features and bent back who drove the nag the quarter league from the *pensione* to the Vatican Palace while appearing to sleep all the way.

The Pope held the salon in a small chamber of the Palace. On arriving, Fernán and Cesario found the Pope surrounded by a dozen dignitaries—men forty and fifty years of age, most in ecclesiastic costume, all drinking wine. They bowed to the Pope, kissed his ring, and were introduced to the cardinals, monsignors, and secular members of the salon.

When Nicholas introduced him, Fernán started at the sound of his true name. The Pope reassured him that the gentlemen seated with him were members of his select circle and were to be trusted.

"These signori, Fernán, know everything that transpires in the Vatican. Some are papal executives, others are employed on projects for us. All are discrete. You may trust them with your life."

"I thank you for your reassurance, Your Holiness," Fernán said, though he experienced qualms at the disclosure.

Cesario expressed the regrets of Álvarez and the other Castilians and the Pope nodded distractedly.

"Please sit, signori," he said. "You understand Italian, signor Hernandes?"

"Not as well as my talented nephew," Cesario said, "but I understand most of what I hear and I speak your beautiful language, though haltingly."

"Good. Then we will speak Italian." The Pope drank from a glass of water. "You must wonder, Fernán, why I asked you to attend our soirée."

"I am delighted to be here for whatever reason, Your Holiness. But your invitation was a source of some concern."

"Then let us say that your experience may influence our decisions regarding Castile. I would like these signori to hear what you have told us and to have them ask whatever questions they feel are pertinent to our inquiry. Are you amenable to this procedure?"

"Your Holiness, that is why I am in Rome."

"Very good. By the way, Fernán, I neglected to ask how old you are."

"Seventeen, Your Holiness."

"But you appear at least ten years older, my son. Your face is lined and your hair and beard are flecked with gray."

"My youth was stripped from me by the torture and deprivation I suffered when I was confined. That is not a complaint, Your Holiness. The others in my cell suffered far more than I—and I escaped—not by my own means but through the efforts of family and friends."

"Why were you imprisoned?" asked one of the cardinals, a gaunt man with twin lines between eyes enlarged by round, metal-rimmed spectacles.

"For heresy, Your Eminence—a false heresy which, I understand, may have consisted in its entirety of a walk with my cousin, a young Jewish woman. I cannot understand nor know what the substance of the accusation was—I was never told—but the prison experience left me near death and aged me as you see."

"Signor Hernandes," a gentleman said, "I am Leon Battista Alberti, sometime *umanista*, sometime writer, sometime architectural adviser to His Holiness. May I ask how long you were imprisoned?"

Battista was a handsome man of imposing presence whose name was familiar to Fernán. Jerónimo had inquired about the people surrounding the Pope and Alberti was mentioned as gifted and influential. A remarkable man of forty-five with accomplishments in many fields and a member of one of the prominent merchant-banker families of Florence, Alberti was a poet, philosopher, author, architect, grammarian, and mathematician—as well as a man of outstanding physical valor. Fernán was immediately drawn to him.

"I was imprisoned from April ninth to May twenty-fifth of this year, signor Alberti. It required over a month for me to recover my senses. I have not yet returned to my full strength."

"What you suffered must be difficult for you to describe," Alberti said, "but did anything of substance occur which might relate to the current problems of New Christians in Castile?"

"I do not believe what happened to me was very different from that which other New Christian prisoners suffered," Fernán said, "but I will describe my experiences as best I can." And he spoke of the conditions in his cell, the torture, and the duel with Sarmiento.

"Pero Sarmiento forced you to fight a duel?"

"A strange, abortive duel, signor. I had been starved for about three weeks and had suffered the latest of a series of drops of the *strappado*. I was not at my best." And he recounted the details of the bout with Sarmiento. "Sarmiento appeared to be obsessed with my supposed prowess with a sword. He declared that I was a question that must be answered."

"And you hit him with the pommel of the sword and butted him?"

"Yes, signor. I was exhausted and desperate. At the time I cared little for the niceties of swordplay and was so depressed that I did not much care whether I lived or died, but I wanted to die taking Sarmiento with me."

"Incredible."

"Signor Alberti," Cesario said. "If I may. My nephew is modest. He is a master swordsman. During our pitched battle with the rebels, Fernán saw me wounded, took my long sword, and rushed into battle without armor. He slew eight men, maimed an equal number, and turned the tide of the conflict."

"I am not proud of that episode, signor," Fernán said. "My passion overwhelmed my sense."

"Signor Hernandes," Alberti said, "the gentlemen of Florence, my birthplace, pride themselves on their physical as much as on their cultural achievements. I would consider it an honor to play at swords with you, to learn from you."

"My uncle does me a disservice, signor Alberti, though not out of ill will. He is a brave man and a dear friend. I would be honored to show you the little I know if, in return, you would explain *humanitas* to me and describe how and where I may educate myself as to its virtues."

"With great pleasure, signor."

"Fernán," the Pope said, "beware Leon Battista Alberti. He is a fine swordsman and an excellent athlete."

"A better athlete than thinker."

The man who spoke, Lorenzo Valla, Jerónimo had characterized as the gadfly of Rome. Accused of discomfiting the orthodox, Valla attacked sacred tradition he found disagreeable without regard for his own welfare.

"Ignore Valla," Alberti retorted. "Valla criticizes everyone. He studies the teachings of Epicurus among other nonsense."

"Do you know Epicurus?" Valla asked Fernán.

"Signor, I do not."

"Then you must learn. Come to me after you have taught Alberti the wisdom of the sword."

"Signor Valla, I know your reputation and would be most honored."

"Careful," Alberti said, "Valla will corrupt you. He makes enemies as others make friends, though he is undoubtedly something of a genius."

"Ah, Alberti," Valla said, "why only something of a genius? Have I displeased you? How could that be?"

"You have never displeased me, Valla," Alberti said, laughing. "Especially not in the occasional discourse that you provide out of kindness to us ignorant beings."

"My kindness," Valla said, "is that of the asp which relieved Cleopatra of pain and life. If I am permitted to live and converse, one must be wary of my sting. I understand, signor Alberti, that in your role as architect you are considering the reconstruction of the tattered Basilica of St. Peter."

"Secrets are impossible in the Vatican. Yes, we are considering reconstruction since the basilica shows its age more each day. First, however, we must find the funds and then the designer."

The Pope interrupted, saying that they were rebuilding the north and west walls of the Vatican Palace, which had been constructed by Nicholas III, and were in dire need of repair. Also he would enlarge the Vatican Apostolic Library. "I have my eye on an extraordinary collection of books and manuscripts we should acquire, but it would require Heavenly intervention to secure adequate funds to release the volumes. I am afraid the good Lord has more important things on His mind."

Fernán was astounded by the manner in which the Pope spoke of God. Then Nicholas turned and Fernán saw that mirth had fled from his eyes.

"Fernán," Nicholas said, "I have given one reason why I asked you to join our salon this evening, but there was another. I can understand the others of your group being members of the delegation—the merchant, the banker, the lawyer—but your participation surprised me. I would like you to explain your presence. Do you mind?"

Fernán was unprepared for this new question. Why was he in Rome? A brother to the question his father had implied—what could he, a youth of seventeen years, accomplish? He had told Lorenzo that he was more than qualified to testify to the Pope, that he knew more than most of the brutality of the regime from his personal experience, and that he wanted revenge against the rebels. He had no fear of Nicholas—the Pope was a man such as himself, with dreams and fears like his own. But he hesitated and then spoke without conscious deliberation, the words streaming from his mouth.

"Your Holiness, my father asked me a similar question before I left and I answered him, but differently than I will answer you. I told my father that I was no longer the son who ran errands. That son, I said, had died in a prison cell. My father understood and sanctioned this trip to Rome.

"With humility and circumspection, Your Holiness, I say to you that I am an artifact of persecution. Before the rebellion, I was a boy like other boys, distinct only in a talent for swordsmanship and foot races and an aptitude for languages. After the rebellion, after killing, after imprisonment, after the loss of loved ones, I have become the person you see before you—indelibly stamped with hatred for my persecutors. I have been subjected to their brutality, deformed by their destruction of those I loved, and blunted by anticipation of a future made desolate by their venom against my kind.

"With all respect, Your Holiness, I was created by the indifference of the Church to the excesses of its radical clerics and, through them, to the excesses of the tempestuous rabble. The resulting massacres brought my family and me into being through forced conversion. Now the excess has reemerged and, if allowed to continue, will destroy us—those New Christians it created.

"That is why I am here—as a living question—whether or not my community and I have a right to live as members of the Church, or whether we must now vanish because of a new indifference or hatred.

"Why would the Church want us removed? Do we embarrass the Church? Do we remind the Church of its origin—the same origin as our own? An origin as a people who wandered in the desert with belief in a single God and who were then scattered to the winds?

"I am a challenge, Your Holiness, a challenge to the Church, sent here because I was tortured, abused, left to die and then, in a sense, reborn with this white hair as a mark, a sign from God, a reminder of the blessing of life. Your Holiness, if we New Christians are to remain children of a Church that was created and created us out of that wandering tribe of Jews, we must not now be turned away. For if we are turned away and destroyed, that would contradict the laws of God, the teachings of the Church, and the lessons of our Lord Jesus.

"I speak too much, Your Holiness, but I speak from my heart. I appeal to your greater wisdom to heal this insult to the body of the Church before the wound to our branch festers and the limb is cut off."

Fernán had risen as he spoke. Now he sat and waited for a response, but when it came it was not what he expected.

"Thank you, my son. We will consider your remarks and include them in our deliberations. We wish you a pleasant evening."

And so they were dismissed. Fernán and Cesario nodded to the assembled dignitaries and, as they walked toward the door, Fernán sensed someone behind him.

"Fernán," Alberti said, "may I call you that? Very good. Do not forget to visit me—you and your uncle. The best time would be eleven in the morning. We will play at swords and then dine. Monday would be excellent. Agreed? Good. Valla lives not far from my residence and I shall invite him to dine with us. I look forward to our meeting." And he gave Fernán a card on which his name and address were written in elegant script. Then Alberti nodded to uncle and nephew and returned to the salon.

56

Palazzo Alberti

Alberti resided in a small but elegant *palazzo* in *Roma Medievale*, the Old Rome, not far from the Pantheon and a short walk across the Tiber from the *Pensione il Gallo d'Oro* in *Trastevere*. Cesario was in an ill mood and declined to accompany Fernán. He had criticized the responses of his nephew to the Pope but received no apology.

"How dare you challenge His Holiness?" Cesario had said. "Who are you to confront a pope in the Vatican before those distinguished men? Where do you find these insane ideas?"

"Perhaps I found them in prison, Uncle, having been imprisoned and tortured for no reason."

"You were accused of heresy and that is the procedure."

"You approve of what they did, Cesario? Approve burning María? Approve killing de Ribas and Enríquez?"

"Close your mouth, nephew! Watch how you talk to me. I am your uncle, not a friend at whom you shout."

"I did not shout."

"The volume of your voice makes little difference. Your words were shout words and you were disrespectful."

"Cesario, I spoke the truth. I told the Pope nothing he does not know. I reminded him that we are Catholic because of the massacres, that we are of the Church, and that the Church is responsible for its own.."

"You said more, and you are no one to reprimand a pope."

"I did not reprimand the Pope. His Holiness asked why I was part of the delegation and I told him."

They argued for hours—in the carriage, in the *pensione*, in their rooms, at supper that night, the following day—so that Cesario developed a peeve that became a pout and then a mood and said he would not go to the *Palazzo Alberti* on Monday. Fernán shrugged, but would not appease his uncle.

Buckling on sword and dagger, he walked over *il Ponte Fabricio* spanning the Tiber and then north toward the Pantheon and the *Palazzo Alberti*. His brain was seething. How could he concentrate on swordplay or the sights of Rome when he had spoken so bluntly to the Pope? For the dear love of God, the Pope! Alberti would turn him away. He will be arrested for his words. What he said will have been interpreted as heresy and this time he will surely burn. Why did he say what he said? What else might he have said that would not cause him to burn?

Fernán raised the knocker and let it fall. Once more he knocked. The door opened and a manservant in livery ushered him into a sitting room and said that the master would join him momentarily. The room was sizable, the furnishings elegant, the paintings on the wall religious. Fernán was distraught by his quarrel with Cesario. He loved his uncle, but his reply to the Pope… sweet Jesus, his words to the Pope, and he could not retract them. He would apologize. He would apologize, recant, confess his error, and then would not be burned.

Alberti arrived, dressed in comfortable clothes. He appeared to be the same affable man Fernán had met last Thursday. There was no change in his attitude. Fernán had been welcomed into the *palazzo*, no reference to his remarks had been made, and he was not bound in chains. Nothing adverse had occurred. He would wait and be watchful and, at the first sign of trouble, he would gather Cesario and their possessions and leave Rome. Once on the water they would be safe.

They entered a large chamber whose furniture had been placed against the walls, which left space in the center for swordplay. Fernán surmised that the room was used as a ballroom or could be converted to an additional parlor or dining room for an important affair. The floor was stone and polished, though not slick.

"We will play in this chamber, Fernán," Alberti said in a pleasant voice. Was it pretense? "May I see your sword?" Fernán gave it to him. Alas, the first sign—now he would be detained. Alberti held the sword, balanced it, waved it about, and nodded his head approvingly. "Spanish swords tend to be longer than the Italian, but then you are tall and it suits you. However, would you mind if we used my swords today?"

Fernán agreed and Alberti fetched two swords from a chest of drawers. Apparently, the room had been used for swordplay before. He chose a sword and tested its balance and heft. Lighter and shorter than his own, the weapon had a blunt point and a dull blade—a rapier for play. He had not used such a harmless instrument in years, not since Jerónimo had insisted on deadly weapons. "How can you know your behavior in a real fight?" Jerónimo had asked. The steward had been gone for just two days and already Fernán felt empty, devoid of friends.

"If you please, Fernán, show me how you butted Sarmiento," Alberti said.

"I was half dead, signor Alberti, but I will try to recall the moves."

"Use my Christian name, if you please, Fernán—Leon."

Was Alberti playing cat and mouse? Would he lead him on and then close the trap? "As you wish, Leon." A curious man, this Leon Battista Alberti—a man of redoubtable reputation and impressive skill who treated Fernán Hernandes as if he were an equal. Was he wrong about the arrest? Perhaps this eminent man was a friend, though more than twice his age.

"You must remember, Leon,"—Leon, by God!—"we used two-handed swords, though they were fully a hand or more shorter than a true long sword."

His father would be amazed that Alberti had become his friend—if he truly was a friend and not a pretender—and that he, Fernán, had taught the great Alberti swordsmanship. *Fantástico!*

"Sarmiento held his sword high, like this, then feinted to the right and thrust straight at my belt line. He released his left hand and passed with his right foot, you see, to achieve greater depth. A difficult move to make and even more difficult to avoid. But, signor, God was with me and I turned sidewise, like a *matador* with a bull, and backed right while parrying, sword point down. Thus, I engaged his sword with the flat of mine, the pommel just beneath his chin. Then I stepped in tight with two quick steps, thrust the pommel up under his chin, and snapped his head back. He did not care for the pommel, I can tell you."

"Ha! Neither would I."

"Nor I, signor. He was disturbed, for he roared at me. But he retained his focus and swung his sword in a great arc that cut straight down toward the top of my head—like this, you see. I had no choice. I could not move fast enough to the side or back and the sword whistled at great speed toward me. So I ducked under the flat of my sword, with the point somewhat down to direct his blade away, and rushed him. Head and pommel drove into his stomach, just below his ribs—a delicate spot. Knocked him flat and out of breath. I fell too, though I held my sword and he lost his. Had I wanted, I could have killed him."

"Why did you not kill him?"

"Why not, indeed? You see, I had begun the fight depressed, drained—I wanted to die. I knew his guards would kill me if I killed him and, for one reason or another, I found that I wanted to live, though I knew the chance was slight. So I let him live. I had no altruistic motive, my self-interest was pure." And the hope to escape death and see Naomi once more.

"Wonderful," Alberti said. "You have inspired me, although these swords are puny compared with a long sword. So. I am not close to your class, but let us play."

They engaged one another for a while, and then Fernán stopped the play and explained where Alberti might have improved his position. They continued, Fernán stopping the action periodically, as would Jerónimo, to demonstrate technique and strategy. He would relate this to Jerónimo, sure that his friend would laugh.

A half hour passed quickly. Fernán had not yet begun to feel fatigue, while Alberti breathed heavily. "That is enough for me, Fernán. Most entertaining and instructive, but sufficient for an old man. And soon Valla will join us for dinner. I will show you to a chamber where you may make yourself comfortable. Valla should be here within the hour."

The room contained a large bed, a bowl of hot water on a dresser, soap and towels, and several comfortable chairs. Fernán removed his clothes, relieved himself, and washed his body. A fresh overshirt had been laid out on the bed and he dressed, put on the shirt and belted it, surprised that it fit. Then he sat in a chair, mulled over his fears and obvious reprieve, and waited for Alberti or a servant to call him to dinner.

A half hour later, the manservant appeared and led him to the dining chamber, a modest but refined room containing a large table with fixed legs, chairs, and a sideboard for serving. Valla was there, talking to Alberti, and they broke off their conversation when they saw Fernán.

"So," Valla said, "I see you have left my friend Alberti in one piece. That is surely preferable to two or three pieces which might not agree with one another."

"You may or may not become accustomed to Valla and his attempts at humor, Fernán," Alberti said. "However, you will not be criticized severely if you do not. Rather you should find yourself in the company of the majority of Italians."

"I find both of you, signori, to be excellent company. And I thank you for your hospitality to a stranger of little worldly experience, knowledge, or worth."

"On the contrary, Fernán, Valla and I discussed your comments to His Holiness yesterday. We were impressed with your command of our vernacular but, more than that, with your words which were marked by a candor and sincerity rare within our circle and the world at large—virtues to be valued above all else."

"To be truthful, signor," Fernán said, "I feared that I would be put in chains and made to sample your papal prison."

"Have no cause for alarm, my dear boy," Valla said, "His Holiness was impressed with your statement, and even more so with yourself. Though a positive outcome of your appeal is far from assured."

"Shall we dine and continue our discussion?" Alberti said.

He sat at the head of the table while Fernán and Valla sat opposite one another. The manservant appeared and placed bowls of a cold black bean soup before them.

"I hope you enjoy our cuisine, Fernán. Much of it is from my Tuscan homeland."

"Then it will be delicious, for Tuscan cuisine is prized by all Castile."

"Fortunate that you come from Castile, then, Hernandes," Valla said, "and not from Rome, where we appreciate more robust food."

Fernán noticed that the soup Valla ate disappeared at a greater rate than that of either Alberti or himself.

"So then, I will call you Fernán, since Alberti uses the familiar and you are younger than we are. You may call me Lorenzo."

"My father has the same name."

"A fortunate choice. Tell me, Fernán, you have studied rhetoric?"

"Very little, Signor Valla."

"Lorenzo, if you please. Really? Very little? Then you must have an aptitude."

Jerónimo had told him that Valla had taught rhetoric at the University of Pavia but was forced out because of his attack on the barbarous Latin of a legal colleague.

"You speak Latin, I understand," Valla said in Latin.

"I spoke Latin to His Holiness," Fernán said in the same tongue, "because I wished to be precise in what I said. Latin fills that need for me."

"Yes, I hear it in your speech. Interesting syntax, excellent pronunciation. Personally, I prefer the vulgate," he said, and switched to Tuscan dialect. "The people speak a more vibrant tongue than did the ancients, though all wisdom can be found within the Latin corpus. Have you read Petrarch?"

"Signor Lorenzo, I am embarrassed to say I have not."

The next course had arrived, a narrow pasta enriched by a delicate tomato sauce and a crisp white wine. Fernán watched the practiced way Alberti had with the pasta and followed his example.

"You must read Petrarch, and you should stay in Rome and study rhetoric with me. Also you must read the classics—all of them. And you must learn Greek. Then you will begin to appreciate *humanitas* and become one of us."

"Your offer is most kind, signor Lorenzo. Do not think I am ignorant of its worth, but I must return to Castile, my family, and our struggle. Perhaps I will return to Rome some day—but not now, I have a duty to perform."

"A pity."

"You know, Fernán," Alberti said, "Valla is papal secretary to His Holiness. Until last year, however, he was employed by Alfonso of Aragón and Naples and resided in the latter city. For how long were you there, Valla?"

"Thirteen contentious years as royal secretary, historian, and general nuisance."

"Did you know that Valla had discounted the Donation of Constantine while he was with Alfonso?"

"Forgive my total ignorance of the classics, Leon, I am not familiar with the Donation."

"A grave deficiency," Valla said. "The *Donatio Constantini*, a document purportedly written by the emperor Constantine, granted the then Pope and his successors spiritual supremacy over all bishops in matters of faith and worship and—this is the critical phrase—temporal dominion over Rome and the entire Western Empire. You can see where that might be of some minor importance to papal authority and where Alfonso, who was at war with the Papal States at the time, would want the papal claim to Italy overturned.

"In any event, I determined that the Latin of the document was coarse at best and could not possibly have been written in the time of Constantine. In short, the Donation was a damned fake. Alfonso was delighted."

"But now you are papal secretary."

"Thus with the passing season do green leaves turn gold."

They consumed the next course—beefsteak and spinach, Tuscan style—with a red wine from the Chianti region.

"Fernán, Valla has retained contact with the court of Alfonso," Alberti said, "and Alfonso, always ready to seize an opportunity, is prepared to pounce on Juan of Castile, your King..."

"If he receives encouragement from the Castilian nobility," Valla interjected.

"... and the nobility are ready to pounce if Alfonso invades. However, neither Alfonso nor the nobles will move without the other. Correct, Valla?"

"Exactly. We thought you should know that, Fernán," Valla said. "You see, His Holiness, Pope Nicholas, wants no part of civil war in Castile, although he does support your King in principle. But he does not wish to provoke Alfonso, his neighbor in Naples, into any further action against the Papal States. Therefore, Nicholas must be cautious."

Valla, then, with contacts in the court of Alfonso, must have informed the Pope that Alfonso planned an invasion of Castile, and warned him of the dire consequences to King Juan. And so His Holiness bided his time, watched the drama unfold, and waited to applaud the winner.

"Thank you, signor Lorenzo," Fernán said. "Then we too must be cautious."

57

Afternoon on the streets of Rome

After dinner, Valla excused himself—papal duties called—and Fernán and Alberti continued their conversation. Alberti took Fernán into his extensive library, explained its organization, and invited him to use the facility for as long as he was in Rome. He suggested they meet at ten each morning, engage in an hour of swordplay, and afterward discuss *humanitas*. Fernán agreed eagerly. Some days, Alberti said, he would be required to supervise construction projects at the Vatican—Fernán could accompany him if he wished—but most days his mornings were his own.

Fernán left while the sun was high. The way toward the Tiber and the pensione led him past the Pantheon and he recalled Alberti remarking that the diameter of the ancient dome was exactly equal to the height of the walls, accounting for its remarkable visual coherence. He felt blessed by his acquaintance with this polymath, this versatile and accomplished humanist who, in a simple conversation, could reveal such knowledge and explore its significance.

The sun was strong and he was glad to be in Rome, but wearing a hat with a wide brim, a peasant hat he had purchased on the street. Although unsure of the deliberations at the Vatican, his spirits soared for the first time since the rebellion. He admired the well-dressed gentlemen and ladies taking the afternoon air. The dark eyes of the women glanced his way and he nodded and touched the brim of his hat. How splendid to be alive. Thank You, dear Lord, for Your gift of life. His step sprung, he felt his heart beat, and he saw Rome for the first time as a place in which one could live. Perhaps Naomi and he would dwell in Rome for a time and he would study and she...would she be welcome in this most Catholic of cities? There were Jews here, he knew. But he would allow nothing to spoil their life together. Oh, Naomi, how he missed her!

Walking toward the Tiber he found himself in the Jewish ghetto on *Via Portico d'Ottavia*, not far from the Roman Forum and near a bronze-roofed synagogue on the riverfront. His drifting walk led him to *il Ponte Fabricio* and he crossed the Tiber and the island of *Tiberina* in its center and proceeded toward the *pensione* in *Trastevere*. Caught up in musing, he failed to notice the three toughs until he walked down a side street that led to the *pensione* and heard footsteps behind him. He stopped to adjust his hat and pretend to admire the timeworn facades of the buildings. The sounds stopped. He loosened his dagger and rapier, resumed walking, and the sounds recurred. Turning down another narrow, twisting street, the footsteps followed. He quickened his step and the sounds quickened.

Fernán raced down the street, sprinted up a narrow alley on his left, turned a corner at the blind end, and faced a wall. The only way out was the way he had come. He drew his sword and dagger and peered around the corner—the toughs had entered the alley and were stealing up the narrow passage toward him, single file with drawn swords.

"I am Rafael," he shouted, "angel of the spirits of men, here to heal the earth which the fallen angels have defiled and to slay the demon Asmodeus." And a battle cry rose from his lungs and he lowered his sword toward the assassins and charged. The one in front, seeing Fernán bolting toward him, tried to turn, but the others behind him were too close and he spun back toward Fernán, sword extended. While running, Fernán lowered his sword, moved it right, then left, then up again, and the sword of the assassin followed his lead and Fernán, at full tilt, caught the sword on his own, raised it, and sank his dagger from below into the heart of the would-be assassin. The force of his charge drove the dead man back onto the sword of the tough behind him and Fernán slashed the upper arm of the tough over the falling shoulder of the first. Both dead and wounded assailants tumbled to the ground. And the last, seeing the Devil at work, sped out of the alley and down the street.

Fernán put the point of his sword to the throat of the second assailant. "Who hired you to kill me?" he said. "The name or you are a dead man—but slowly, a piece at a time."

The man said nothing. His eyes bulged from his head.

"Then we begin. First the ears, then the nose, the eyes, and so forth. Stay silent and lose an ear."

"Villalpondo!" the man cried.

Fernán checked that neither the dead man nor the wounded had pistols and walked out of the alley, taking care to keep an eye on the live assassin and on the street for other possible assailants. He put up his dagger and, holding his sword in its scabbard, ran back the way he had come to the *pensione*. The day was spoiled but his heart was full.

Cesario was waiting outside the pensione, staring up the road.

"What happened to your shirt, Fernán? I worried about you. My God, the blood. You were in a fight."

"A small fracas, Cesario. Three assassins followed me. One is dead, another has a useless sword arm, and the third fled. Villalpondo sent them. From now on, when in Rome I will ride a horse, and God will ride with me."

58

A month later at the pensione

Fernán sat in the courtyard, writing. Cesario had arranged for their departure—hired a punt to ferry them down the Tiber and verified their passage on a ship to Valencia. They had settled accounts with the steward of the pensione and most of their belongings were packed. He could scarcely believe they had been in Rome for over five weeks and that during that time he had petitioned the Pope and enjoyed a burgeoning filial relationship with Alberti. He would send this letter with a sailor shipping out today for Barcelona and hope that it reached his father in Toledo. He read what he had written.

> My dear Papá—
>
> With your permission I will continue this narrative beginning immediately after returning from my first visit to the *palazzo* of Leon Battista Alberti and the subsequent *fracasso* which resulted in the death of one assailant and the injury of another. This missive is late because much has happened between then and now. But I write because the news is glorious—God is with us—the Pope has ruled, and we have won our suit.
>
> However, let me put that aside for a moment and present this good news in context—though you may be aware of the events of the last few days from other sources, due to the long delay between the writing of this letter and its reading. In point of fact, this letter will, I pray, precede our persons by a very few days, as Cesario and I take ship for Valencia on Friday and I hope to see you and my dear mother and sister less than a month after that.

To the narrative.

As you must have surmised, Cesario and I are again dear friends. I promised him after the attack that I would make my way about Rome on horse, and I have—a congenial but spirited mare named Laura, after the fair lady who was the unrequited love of the great Petrarch. No matter where we go—and we go everywhere—Laura and I are never bothered.

The period after the attack was filled with delightful visits to Alberti and several valuable conversations with Valla, of whom I have spoken at some length. Such a curious man—a combination of curmudgeon, wit, and scholar. Alberti told me that Valla has three children by his mistress in Rome but no intention of marrying the woman. Roman culture is indeed different from ours—or am I naive? One would think that within the Papal States especially, adherence to conjugal law would be strict, but that is not the case. In Italy, love in all forms is a disease without cure, and I sympathize with the afflicted.

Cesario will, I am sure, fill you in on his own exploits since, during this period, I most often went my own way—to the Alberti library and the Vatican—though I joined Cesario from time to time exploring Rome. Several times I followed in the footsteps of Alberti during his supervision of construction—more of that when I return—and visited Valla, whose quarters are more modest than those of Alberti.

I learned from Valla that Alfonso of Aragón and Naples had ordered an invasion of Castile—remember I mentioned the potential for invasion from that quarter—but surprisingly, the Aragonese Cortes turned its back on their king and refused to sanction war with Castile, having just concluded peace with our homeland. Kingly prerogative has its limits—at least in Aragón.

Juan of Navarre argued with *Cortes*, Valla said, but to no avail. The Aragonese parliament would not have war and Alfonso and Navarre were thwarted in their design. How different we Castilians are from the Aragonese, and yet we are fellow Iberians and joined by culture.

To continue—although much of this may, as I said, be familiar to you from other sources. With Castilian invasion thwarted by the Aragonese *Cortes*, Juan of Navarre and Prince Enrique were forced to reexamine their own aggressive plans. Navarre, according to Valla, invited the Prince to unite with him in a plan to eliminate Alvaro de Luna, whom he and Enrique both despise. Prince Enrique took up this cause as his own and called a meeting of Castilian nobles and others opposed to Alvaro. But, Papá, not one soul joined the Prince—not Navarre nor the Castilian nobles—and the plan was dashed.

Therefore, King Juan and Alvaro are reprieved and we win. For Pope Nicholas, reassured that the rebellion of Prince Enrique and the Castilian nobles was as illusory as the Aragonese invasion, no longer feared an attack from Naples and decided for us.

Once bent on that course of action, the Pope signed three bulls against the rebels in which he blasted them and others who opposed us. The details of these pronouncements may reach you sooner than this letter but nevertheless I will continue this outline. The bulls attribute three types of crimes to Sarmiento and his cohorts. The crime of *lèse majesté*—an affront to the dignity of the King—an attempt to overthrow the laws of Toledo, and various other crimes against the inhabitants of Toledo. However, sadly and inexplicably, the Pope does not mention the deaths by burning of our beloved friends. Does His Holiness suggest that our people are now with God, and, therefore, we are not bereaved, that we mourn them less? Or is he circumspect and sees threatening shadows everywhere? As you may see, I have formed an opinion of this Pope that is not altogether favorable.

However, Nicholas has imposed a sentence of excommunication on Sarmiento and his familiars. He has denied them the right to give testimony, removed all their properties, lands, honors, dignities and offices, ecclesiastic and secular, and made them subject to other sentences normally passed against such perpetrators. I have a copy of the bulls before me, as you soon will. The Pope also issued a call to all nobles, councils, and towns to proceed by force against Sarmiento and his aides and hold them until due satisfaction is taken by the King for their offenses. Also, all officers of the Church are directed to publish the crimes of Sarmiento and his aides and the punishments required by the Pope.

Papá, we shall have to wait to see how effective these pronouncements are. I have learned several things in Rome, one being that the Pope is powerful but not all-powerful. Though he is the Vicar of Christ, his words are words like other words and the power of words depends on the interpretation placed on them and the belief of the reader in their truth and spiritual strength. Belief is everything.

The King and Alvaro trust the Pope. They have an interest in doing so. The Prince may not. Since we live in thrall to the Prince at present, we have yet to see how effective the words of the Pope will be for our welfare.

And so I come to the end of this narrative. Friday, God willing, the wind shall fill our sails and we shall be blown eastward to Iberia and home. I trust that the good Lord has kept you and Mamá and Beatriz and the others of our family strong and in good health. I hope to see all of you and hold you in my arms before the wintry winds of November blow past the turrets of Toledo.

Your devoted son, Fernán

Rome, 24 September, 1449

Fernán read the letter through once again and made a few corrections. Then he wrote a fair copy in lemon juice, taking care to use the liquid sparingly. After allowing it to dry, he wrote a short, inconsequential note in black ink on the back of the page, placed the letter within a sheet of oiled paper on which he had written his family name and address, and folded and sealed the cover sheet. When Lorenzo received the letter, he would hold it over a warm fire and the transparent, dried lemon juice would turn brown and legible.

Lorenzo had often used this technique and its variations to convey secret instructions to his mercantile contacts, and Fernán had been instructed to employ it whenever the content of one of his letters was the least provocative or controversial. He would provide the sailor more than sufficient payment to care for and post the letter in Barcelona.

With departure imminent and their cause in Rome won, his thoughts turned to Toledo. What might he find when he returned? Toledo was so distant and no word of home, other than that provided by Valla, had reached him. But now he anticipated seeing Naomi and thoughts of her welled up within him. He counted the hours until they would depart.

Part IV

JUDGMENT

"Having forgotten the fear of God...and the loyalty that he owed me...as his King and natural lord, [Sarmiento] rose and rebelled together with some of my disloyal individuals of the common people of [Toledo]... conspiring with them, and making with them a conspiracy... against me and disobey me, and take over the said city and rise with her against me..."

Cronica de Juan II de Castilla
Alvar García de Santa María (1370-1460)
Quoted in *The Origins of the Inquisition*
B. Netanyahu, Random House 1995

59

One month later, October of 1449, the Alcázar of Toledo

The wind strengthened and blew through chinks in the stone walls of the fortress, the afternoon gray, rain presaged by dark clouds in the west. Sarmiento watched the clouds slowly obliterate the blue sky and damp the light of the sun.

"Have you read them?"

García nodded. "Yes. Unpleasant."

"Villalpondo was a bad choice. You should have chosen a cleric not a lawyer. The man selected inept assassins and was altogether a failure. What now?"

"I think you must read the bulls, don Pero, and evaluate their effect. A first reading did not encourage me, but your opinion might differ from mine."

"It might. You have another copy?"

"I do." García put a sheaf of papers on the table.

"Select the statements you find bothersome while I read."

"Many statements are bothersome, don Pero. The first bull aims at our hearts."

"How poetic. I will read, then listen."

García resumed his seat and Sarmiento read the bulls. The test was near and García would surely fail.

"So, García, where do we start?"

García eliminated the third bull as trivial, and began with the first, which described crimes against the King. Then there were crimes against Toledo, its laws and nobility, and finally, crimes against the people.

"This first bull weighs most heavily against you, don Pero. As you see, the Pope singles out *marranos* as those grievously wronged, saying you fabricated charges of heresy against them so as to arrest and rob them."

"*We*, García, not I alone. But go on."

"The bull reads that you 'laid violent hands on clerics…' what can that mean?…and committed other offenses which posed a danger to the faith and the kingdom."

"Papal rubbish." He raised his head from the page he was perusing and stared at García. "Why do you insist on saying *you*, when it is *we* who did what *we* did. *I* did what was necessary to promote and defend *your* rebellion. We prosecuted *marranos* for treason and punished their heresy. *We* did these things, not *I*."

García stared at the ceiling. "The Pope denies their heresy."

Sarmiento noted the shift of subject. "The heresy of *marranos*? Certainly he does. The Pope knows nothing. He was not here. He accepts hearsay from *marranos* and it becomes truth. But see, García, he says nothing about burning *marranos*. Nothing. Why is that, do you think? He complains of everything except burning and on that His Holiness is mute. Then he proceeds to condemn us, excommunicate us, demand we be punished on pain of ecclesiastical censure, and all the while says not a word about the stake."

He tilted his head and smiled at García. Sarmiento sat on the edge of his table, leaned toward García, and spoke in almost a whisper.

"Do you know why Nicholas says nothing about burning, García? I will tell you." He looked at the window and wet his lips. "His Holiness is afraid. He fears the people. He fears that if he supports *marranos*, he will alienate the people from the Church and then…. Well, one cannot tell what might happen if the people of Castile, all of whom hate *marranos*, defy the Pope."

Sarmiento walked to a window on the other side of the room. "Might the people be drawn to some heretic sect, some apostate creed? Might Nicholas be toppled? Might he—can one think it—be assassinated? Our Pope is not that popular, and yet he surrounds himself with these free-thinkers, these intellectuals, these Italian *umanisti* who tolerate radical ideas—placing individual worth above duty to Church and God. Oh, yes, Pope Nicholas fears the people and through them fears us and hopes to defeat us with words. Words. Ha! Nicholas has nothing to his name but words. The man is weak, García. The people are with us, we have their strength. More than the people, we have the nobility on our side."

From the window he could see the whole of Toledo now cloaked in melancholy shadows of heavy rain. "Rest assured, García, the people and nobles approve the *Sentencia-Estatuto*. They want *marranos* humbled and destroyed. And with the people and the nobles behind us, we are stronger than our Holy Father in Rome."

"You think so, don Pero?"

"Think so? García, we are lions in this contest. The Pope is a wee lamb. Why does he not mention your good friend Pero Lope de Galvez in his precious bulls? Is it because your friend Galvez, for all his faults, is of the Church and untouchable? Or is it because he speaks for the common people of Toledo? If Nicholas is so determined to punish the guilty for crimes against the clergy, why would he not punish Galvez who ousted the Archdeacon of Toledo for no reason other than that the Archdeacon failed to honor his oath to me—to me, a layman. And Nicholas accepts that dismissal, says nothing more, and does not condemn Galvez for burning *marranos*. Although the Deacon had no such authority, as you well know, and so knows the Pope.

"These precious bulls, García, say more by silence than by words. Their silence whispers that Nicholas is afraid and that his fear is our strength."

"But what will happen, don Pero?"

"What do your spies report? Where is our dear friend, the Prince?"

"On the road to Requeña. He was with el conde de Haro and el marqués de Santillana until now. Haro would never agree, never come to terms, and they have broken off," García said.

"Broken off?"

"The alliance. The Prince has abandoned his plans—they will not attack Alvaro de Luna."

"So there you are," Sarmiento tapped on the glass now shrouded by rain. "Luna is safe—damn his eyes. Enrique has resigned the field and hunts small game in Requeña. Wonderful. Invasion and revolution are dead, García. What happens next is a matter of negotiation between the Prince and his royal father."

"Will they reach an agreement?"

"There may be some difficulty, but they will agree. The Prince has run out of opportunity. He holds a single card—our Toledo."

"And are we vulnerable?" García said.

Sarmiento stared at García a moment and then turned to the window. The rain obscured his view. He felt numb, somewhat faint. Though he shook his head, the numbness persisted.

"Are you well, don Pero?"

"What? Yes, of course, García—a late night. Our business for today is complete. I will see you tomorrow. Good evening."

As Sarmiento hurried from the room, he noticed García shaking his head in disbelief, but the Governor continued on his way.

60

The Port of Valencia

After an uneventful passage from Rome, Fernán and Cesario arrived in Valencia on the Feast Day of the archangel Rafael, the 24th of October, the name day of Rafael Fernán Hernandes. Fernán was welcomed to the stable where they had boarded their mounts by an energetic nuzzling from Margarita—reminding him pleasantly that he was in Iberia and less than a week from Toledo and Naomi.

Cesario and he secured lodgings near the stable and, together, celebrated his eighteenth birthday with a hearty dinner of roast boar and wine. Early the next day, after a sleep free of the pitch and roll to which they had become accustomed at sea, they saddled their horses, rode the thirteen leagues to Requeña with two pack animals trailing, and stopped at an inn for the night. The next morning after early Mass, they departed ancient Requeña, the bells of El Salvador and Santa María ringing farewell behind them, and began their descent onto the Utile plain holding Río Magre on their left, following the course of the river. From there they would ride toward Cuenca and home.

The day was bright with a sharp touch of autumn and, though Fernán was leagues from Toledo, his heart sang and he laughed aloud.

Cesario smiled and asked, "What is it you find amusing so early in the morning, Nephew?"

"Nothing amusing, dear Uncle, I am filled with joy at the prospect of home."

They had not traveled far from Requeña and were still high above the plain when they saw a caravan of wagons and horsemen below them. The riders appeared to be a mix of gentry, knights, and servants as would be found in the train of any nobleman of stature. Cesario expressed concern that if they encountered the troop they would be treated badly, but Fernán could not imagine that the retinue of a nobleman would behave improperly to strangers. His uncle chided him for his naiveté, and reminded him that they were in Iberia and that *conversos* in this land were subject to the temperament, good and bad, of Old Christians.

Fernán shrugged off the reproof. "I have faith in my God who protects his children, and in my sword which has never failed me."

"Have you forgotten prison so soon?"

"Never. Never can I forget prison, Uncle. I live with prison in my heart every day of my life. But this day is so pleasant that I know no harm will befall us."

Since the double file of men and wagons lay directly in their path and was traveling in their direction, they had no choice but to keep to the road that was, in truth, a wide path beside the river worn to dirt and stone by the passage of men on horse and foot over hundreds of years. And so, within a few hours, they had drawn close to the rear of the column.

Exchanging greetings with several knights who constituted the rear guard of the caravan, they discovered that the entourage belonged to Prince Enrique. The Prince and his retinue were returning to Toledo after a hunt in the wild country near Requeña, having achieved some success with boar and deer, as well as bustard, partridge, and small game taken by falcon. Fernán, less restrained than Cesario, asked whether they might ride with the company, since Toledo was their destination as well. The knights welcomed them but, to ensure propriety, dispatched one of their number to secure permission from Juan Pacheco. The knight soon returned with a welcome from Pacheco and an invitation to take midday dinner with the Prince.

The remainder of the morning passed quickly in conversation, the knights charmed by Fernán and his tales of Rome. Sometime after noon, the caravan encamped off the road in a grassy meadow surrounded by tall oaks, rock roses, and other fragrant plants. The servants of the Prince set fires to prepare the meal and erected a series of trestle tables and benches on which to feed the company that numbered almost a hundred.

Fernán and Cesario tied their horses to graze and were introduced to Pacheco who asked their names and family. Fernán presented himself as Rafael Rivera and Cesario as his uncle, both from *Hernandes y Familia*, merchants of Toledo. They asked after the city, having had no word from home for over two months, and Pacheco told them that all was relatively quiet.

"Were you in Toledo during the rebellion, señores?" he asked.

"I was, señor," Cesario said. "My nephew joined us after the Prince took charge. I remember it well for I had two good arms before the rebellion."

"You were wounded in battle, señor?"

"Defending our home."

"And were in Rome petitioning the Pope. With what objective?"

"To overthrow the *Sentencia-Estatuto*, don Juan. You are familiar with its provisions?"

"I am. A bold, perhaps too bold, maneuver."

"Just so," Cesario said. "As you may know, the good judgment of His Holiness has prevailed and he has signed bulls excommunicating Sarmiento and the others and excoriating them for their attacks on New Christians—in fact, repudiating the *Sentencia-Estatuto*. You have copies of the bulls?"

"Though we have been in the woods, literally, for a good while, we have the bulls, señor, and have read them. Prince Enrique found them entertaining. By the way, when you meet the Prince, señores, do not bow or call him Your Highness as you might feel required to do but, if you please, address him as 'don Enrique' or 'señor' as you would any nobleman or gentleman of rank. The Prince abhors formality and welcomes good fellowship."

Fernán was surprised but pleased that the Prince would shun formalities of title. Cesario thanked Pacheco for his advice and, at that moment, Enrique emerged from his tent and joined them. Expressing his pleasure at meeting two gentlemen recently returned from the Vatican, he asked after the health of His Holiness.

"The Pope," Cesario said, "is well and busy with many projects, don Enrique. My nephew, Rafael, spent much time in the Vatican with the esteemed humanist and architect, Leon Battista Alberti, and the papal secretary, Lorenzo Valla, formerly royal secretary to His Highness, King Alfonso. And so Rafael is better versed in the affairs of the Vatican than I."

"How fascinating," Enrique said to Fernán. "Of course, I have heard of Alberti and Valla, distinguished men both, but have not met them. We must talk at length." Pacheco whispered to the Prince, who said, "Our dinner is ready, señores. Sit opposite me, señor Rivera, and we will discuss your journey to Italy."

Fernán had heard stories about the Prince—that he was ill-kempt and neglected his bath—but his appearance was much less disconcerting than the reports. As tall and well proportioned as Fernán, he had pleasant features, particularly his light eyes. Dressed casually for traveling, the Prince was impeccably groomed and would have passed unnoticed among the other gentlemen at the table but for his flattened nose. Perhaps he, like other men, wished to make a good appearance before strangers.

Once seated, the Prince asked Fernán for details about the Pope, what Fernán and the others had told him, and what the Pope replied. He had not met His Holiness, but said he planned a trip to Rome when the political climate cleared.

Pacheco, meanwhile, asked pragmatic questions of Cesario—where they had stayed, what the weather in Rome was like, where they had eaten, what means of transportation were available—so many specific questions that it appeared he would soon be on his way to the Eternal City. Later, Fernán discovered that Pacheco gathered trivia—bits and pieces of fact and speculation that he filed away in his capacious memory—fodder for an active intelligence busy on disparate subjects yet jealous of the knowledge of others. Pacheco sat hunched on the bench, his spherical head thrust forward, his eyes screened behind narrowed eyelids, his mouth another slit into which food was stuffed and seemingly swallowed whole.

"But what transpired with the three men who followed you?" the Prince asked.

Fernán had described the meeting with Alberti and Valla and his pleasant walk back toward the *pensione*. In doing so, he had mentioned the three assailants. The Prince was on the edge of his seat, eyes wide with anticipation, as were others within earshot of the story. Fernán told them about the charge and the killing.

"You took them on, all three?"

"Don Enrique, forgive me. I may have implied that I stood and battled three men at once. That was not the case. The alley I chose was narrow, deliberately, as you would choose to defend a narrow mountain pass through which one soldier at a time could traverse. The attackers assumed surprise was on their side but, in reality, it was on mine. For when I charged and shouted, the walls of the alley reverberated with sound and deafened them, prevented talk between them, and muddled their thoughts. My sword was longer than that of the first assassin, and I rushed him, my rapier aimed at his eyes. The man could not back up or move to the side and those behind were blocked from assisting him. My charge was designed to frighten—and he was frightened. He had no choice and no chance."

"A good lesson and an excellent strategy, señor Rivera—guard your flanks, narrow your focus, and attack. Excellent. But now you return to Toledo?"

"To report to the others of our community."

"And what will you report, señor?"

"Pardon, don Enrique, one additional question if I may. I understand that you have read the bulls. By the time we return, their content will have been broadcast throughout Castile. Do you believe the bulls will be effective? Will you follow through with the directives against Sarmiento and the others?"

"You counter one question with two, señor. That is not polite. However, I will reply." The Prince drank some white wine while Pacheco whispered in his ear, and then Enrique shook his head. "Don Juan Pacheco has requested that he be allowed to state our position." Pacheco seemed to close his eyes completely and retreat within himself, and the Prince continued. "Normally don Juan would do so. Today, however, I prefer to speak for myself. My answers may not be complete, since we must be silent on many issues. However, it may be prudent to reveal something of our position, something you may carry back to your community which, indeed, has suffered an injustice."

Enrique hesitated a moment, pulled on his ear, and then continued. "Pero Sarmiento, Marcos García, and the other rebels of the administration of Toledo will be removed. Among their other faults, the *Sentencia* was a grave mistake, and far beyond their authority. What may happen after they are removed depends on factors outside the purview of this conversation." The Prince smiled. "I am sure you understand, señor. I know how dearly you may wish for retribution, however we must deal with political reality. Is that not so, don Juan?"

"Politics is an art, señor Rivera," Pacheco said. "Now, if you please, answer the question don Enrique posed. What will you report?"

Pacheco annoyed Fernán. He had put the question to one side, not knowing how much to reveal to so powerful a man and, still unsure, he delayed again.

"Once more, forgive me, don Enrique and don Juan. An additional question and then, I assure you, I will respond. The bulls call for excommunication of Sarmiento and his followers, and also for their imprisonment and eventual delivery to the King—for his satisfaction. Will Sarmiento and his followers be imprisoned?"

"Señor Rivera," Pacheco said, "your question is out of order and will not be answered. Your response to the Prince, if you please."

Fernán knew he would extract nothing more from the Prince or Pacheco and said, "As you wish, señores. The Pope calls for actions that others may choose not to accept. We pray the Prince will follow those papal instructions and act forcefully against Sarmiento and the others. However, the future actions of Prince Enrique cannot be dictated by the Pope or by any man. His agenda is his own. His responsibilities are his own. Therefore, we must continue our fight, independently of don Enrique. We note that the Pope did not denounce the burning of our fellow New Christians by the rebels— the most grievous of crimes. Apparently, His Holiness, like the Prince, is faced with weighty political, as well as spiritual and ethical, considerations. Therefore, we must follow our own dictates to secure our future. We must depend on no one but ourselves.

"That will be the substance of my argument, don Enrique. My uncle, Cesario, and others will differ from me in many ways."

"Yours is a realistic position, señor Rivera," Enrique said, "though not optimistic."

Two knights approached Pacheco and spoke quietly. Pacheco looked at Fernán who tensed under his glance.

"Señor Rivera," Pacheco said, "one of our knights has challenged you to a contest with sword and dagger. He is aware of your exploits and would appreciate the opportunity to test your skill. Are you willing?"

Cesario whispered to Fernán, "You spoke too much, Fernán. Do not accept. If you win, we will die."

"You will be provided a helmet and chain mail," Pacheco said. "No one will be hurt, I assure you. I shall judge the match."

Fernán turned to the Prince. "Don Enrique, is it your wish that I engage one of your knights?"

"The choice is yours, señor," Enrique said. "But no harm will follow from that choice, either way."

61

The duel

The knight was taller than Fernán. His head sat flush on his shoulders without benefit of a neck, and his thighs and legs were stoutly muscled. The clothing he wore was rich, that which could be seen beneath the coat of mail that reached from his shoulders to below his groin. In the crook of his left arm he carried a helmet with nose guard and in the right a rapier, all of which lent him the appearance of a walking coat of arms.

"He is large, Fernán," Cesario said.

"He is a man, Cesario. Rapier and dagger are instruments of wit, not muscle."

"This match conceals an objective other than sport."

"Perhaps. Be brave, Uncle, or you will frighten me," Fernán said with a smile. "This being Sunday, the appearance of this knight would indicate that we are at a *corrida de toros*. However, *picadores* would have trouble finding the neck of this bull."

An aide appeared with a coat of mail and a helmet for Fernán, who donned the mail and inspected his opponent, judging his stance and attitude. Then he placed the helmet on his head and strolled about the grassy area in which the contest would take place, noting defects in the terrain and assessing the reaction of the knight to his survey. His helmet felt warm but tolerable—though its leather smelled of the sweat of those who had worn it, and the helmet guard resting on his nose shadowed a narrow window of his vision.

The match bothered Fernán as much as it did Cesario, but he did not express his misgivings. He placed his faith in God that the Prince would deal with him honestly, since Enrique had forbade mistreatment of *conversos* and, because of that, had won his trust. Pacheco was another question—his reputation was well advertised.

Pacheco asked the two contestants to approach and introduced them to one another. "Rafael Rivera, gentleman of Toledo, your opponent this afternoon will be Miguel de Moya y Oropesa, knight."

Fernán looked into the face of the knight, but the small eyes would not meet his. The jaw worked, the muscles in the cheek bunched beneath the helmet, and the mouth turned down—altogether an unpleasant face. The man appeared to be a minor noble, perhaps the youngest son of a count, possessed of a long history of oppression by his father and older brother and the knowledge that life would be a continual struggle for recognition. What advantage might that bring Fernán?

"Señores, you will engage each other at most five times." Pacheco said. "The first to touch his opponent three times will be declared the winner. You will take care to measure the strength of your thrusts—we want no blood on the grass—a touch will be sufficient. You will salute each other before each assay. I will hold this scarf above my head and you will begin when it is dropped. I will shout 'touch' when there has been a touch, after which there will be no further action. Both of you will then retreat and wait until I say 'proceed.' When I say 'proceed,' you will approach each other, salute, and wait with swords engaged and daggers in low guard until I drop this scarf. A break in any rule of conduct or honor will not be tolerated and will be considered the loss of a 'touch.' All decisions are mine. Questions? Then, if you please, assume your positions in the center of the area."

The company had formed a wall of bodies around a circular area about forty feet in diameter. Fernán walked to one side of the center of the circle and waited. The sun was high—there would be no advantage from shadow or sunlight.

Moya spoke briefly to Pacheco and then joined Fernán. His sour face wore an offensive smirk. Fernán was attentive. He anticipated a break of rules. The knight looked dishonest—a peevish sort with little brain and no humor. This match, he feared, would be a useless exercise, fomented by these knights to amuse themselves or to extract some pleasure from the pain of a stranger—a *converso* at that. Cesario was correct—there would be no limit to this contest. Fernán searched for a strategy but found none. He would play one moment and then the next and pray that God would grant him vision.

Pacheco said, "Proceed." Fernán and Moya walked toward one another, stopped, saluted, extended rapiers until they touched, and waited. Pacheco raised the scarf and hesitated. Suddenly, Moya thrust and Fernán parried, pushed the rapier away, and stepped back.

"What was that?" Pacheco said. "I did not drop this scarf."

"The *marrano* attacked," Moya said, "and I countered."

"Don Juan," Fernán said to Pacheco, "believe what you will, but I did not attack. However, I will not be insulted by any man, noble or beggar." Fernán walked up to Moya and said quietly, "Insult me again, Moya, and I will fight to kill and I *will* kill." Then he stepped back and said in a loud voice, "Don Enrique, continue or end this contest at your pleasure, señor. I have no desire for this match but follow your charge."

The knights surrounding the contest muttered and grumbled. A few sotto voce remarks prompted laughter. "Fight not talk," a knight said. Others echoed the comment.

Enrique, seated in a chair watching the match, said, "Señores, I expect men of honor to remain silent. Señor Rivera, what occurred was an innocent error produced by the tension of the moment and not sufficient to discontinue the match. Proceed, señores, without prejudice."

Fernán caught the eye of the Prince. Enrique nodded imperceptibly and Fernán realized that this match was a test of sorts. Then he faced Moya, walked a few steps toward the man and saluted. Moya executed a perfunctory salute and they engaged rapiers.

Pacheco dropped the scarf and Moya lunged.

Fernán caught the rapier on his dagger and, noting that Moya carried his dagger well out, feinted to the right with his rapier to draw him and then, with a turn of his wrist, touched Moya just above the groin. Moya, startled, bent at the waist reflexively and stepped back as Pacheco cried, "Touch!"

"That was not a true hit, don Juan," Moya complained.

"A hit is a hit, señor. You may expect to be hit anywhere on your body—head, foot, front, back, wherever your opponent finds an opening. Protect yourself. In battle, your opponent will not care how he kills you, he will kill you and you will be dead."

"You will never be so lucky again, *marrano*," Moya said.

"What a pity, Moya, that one so young must die," Fernán said. "I did warn you not to insult me. This pass I will hit you on the nose. Then I will kill you."

"You will die first."

"Show me, knight."

They saluted and engaged rapiers. Pacheco raised the scarf.

The scarf dropped and Fernán and Moya stood with rapiers pointed at the eyes of the other and daggers thrust forward. Fernán moved his left shoulder. Moya flinched. Then Fernán shrugged his right shoulder at Moya while tapping his rapier. Moya stepped back and Fernán realized the knight was inept and tedious as well as offensive. He would win this match quickly and then they would leave.

Fernán moved his rapier to broad guard and stretched his dagger and sword wide while he directed the points of rapier and dagger at the eyes of Moya. Then he circled slowly, his body apparently open to attack. He feinted with both weapons and the knight retreated. Fernán knew this open stance was a dangerous play. The man was an amateur and might attempt something foreign that Fernán could not anticipate.

Fernán had completed a circle around Moya and was planning his next move when Moya rushed. Fernán engaged rapier and dagger with his own weapons and, as the momentum of the knight carried Fernán rearward, he rolled back onto the ground, caught Moya with his bent legs and, straightening his legs, thrust Moya up and over his head. The knight fell heavily on his back. Fernán sprang to his feet, stepped over the body behind him, and touched the nose-guard with his rapier.

"Touch!" Pacheco shouted. There were cries of outrage from the soldiers and knights watching. One called out, "*Olé!*" and was roughed by those near him.

Two friends of Moya helped him to his feet. He had dropped his rapier but held his dagger in his hand, and he shook off his friends and charged Fernán who engaged the dagger with his own, stepped aside, and tripped Moya. The knight went sprawling, face forward, onto the ground.

Cesario walked over to Fernán. "You have made an enemy."

"I made nothing—the enemy was there to begin with. We leave camp after this next touch, Uncle. If you would please get our possessions ready and the horses saddled, I will come directly to you. The pack horses should stay with the caravan—they would be an encumbrance and I sense that the Prince will accommodate us after this fiasco."

"Be on guard, Fernán. This knight is an animal. He has lost honor and pride and, with nothing left to boast of, will be unpredictable."

Fernán reassured him and Cesario walked away as Moya got to his feet. The knight had truly lost his humanity and reminded Fernán of a wounded boar. Fernán glanced at the Prince. Enrique was pensive and whispered to an aide who hurried over and told Fernán that the Prince would speak to him after the match. Fernán saluted.

Pacheco had not moved during the last assay. He now cautioned the contestants to obey the rules. Shouts and hisses of disapproval burst from the crowd. Pacheco shouted, "Proceed!" Fernán faced the knight.

Moya did not salute. His face was hideous, bruised by the fall and by his internal state. "I will kill you, *marrano*," he said.

"You insult me. You threaten my life. What choice do you leave me, Moya? You have learned nothing from life in this world and, therefore, must die."

Pacheco dropped the scarf. Fernán was disgusted with the fight and quickly disengaged his rapier, feinted with both weapons, and touched Moya with his dagger above his heart.

"Touch!" Pacheco shouted. "Señor Rivera has won the match."

Fernán removed the helmet and coat of mail and the aide relieved him of both. As he walked toward the Prince, Enrique jumped to his feet, his hand pointing, his mouth open as if to shout. Fernán felt movement in the ground behind him and swung his sword in a wide arc while turning. He saw Moya rushing at him and his rapier nicked the knight in his shoulder and throat. Fernán stopped the swing of his sword in high guard and Moya dropped his weapons and held his throat. The knight had halted his charge just short of Fernán whose dagger touched him just below his breastbone. Moya cried out in pain and fear.

Fernán was enraged and shouted, "You are scratched, you fool, scratched! God watched that you did not die. Why He should care about an idiot who refuses to accept defeat escapes me. Perhaps God does love fools." Moya was dabbing at trickles of blood that fell from his throat and arm. "You were dead a dozen times and are alive only because I chose not to kill you."

"I will kill you."

"You bore me, Moya. You will have no chance to kill me. Do you not recognize who I am, Moya? I am Death and you cannot kill Death." His rage spilled over and he shouted into the face of the knight, "You sicken me—you idiot with a sword and no brain! You think you own Iberia and can kill or maim whomsoever you wish? My people were here before yours, ignoramus! Before Christ! They tilled the soil of Iberia when Toledo was a Roman outpost, when your people were scrabbling for roots in a Nordic forest!"

Moya spit and hit Fernán full on the cheek.

"Rivera! No!" the Prince shouted.

Fernán slowly wiped his cheek with his sleeve and, abruptly, kicked Moya in the groin with the point of his boot. Moya bent over in pain, held his crotch, and moaned.

"I pray that your balls were crushed," Fernán said, "that you may not father more fools."

"Señor Rivera, enough," the Prince called, and sent two aides to see to Moya. Then he spoke out to the soldiers and knights, "Rafael Rivera and his uncle are not to be molested, either in or outside this camp, now or ever—on pain of death by beheading! Come, señor Rivera, stroll with me." They walked in silence until they were alone. "I suggest that you leave immediately, Rafael."

"That was my plan, don Enrique."

"Good. You see how it might be imprudent for you to stay. I regret our treatment of you. My knights normally mean well and are hospitable, even gracious, but Moya is impetuous and stupid. He is of a noble family and was both coddled and abused as a child. We rich and powerful are not always adept at protecting our legacies." He looked at Fernán. "I would not have taken you for a warrior, señor. You seem more bookish, a scholar."

"I am not a warrior by inclination. Had I been, Moya would be dead."

"True. That may be a fault, Rafael. Your next opponent may have no qualms about sticking a dagger in your belly."

"Thank you for your concern, señor, but I have no regrets when I need to kill. As you see, God has given me strength and skill and some courage. I trust I do not abuse my gifts." He sighed. "Don Enrique, may I request that your servants care for our pack horses? They slow us considerably, and it would be wise to put a good distance between us."

The Prince smiled. "Your pack horses will be cared for and delivered to the Hernandes house. However, I would like you to come to me in Toledo, at the Alcázar, midmorning the day after I enter the city. You are an unusual man, Rafael Rivera, with many fine qualities. We may be of use to one another. We will talk when I see you next. May God protect you on your journey."

They shook hands. Cesario had mounted and brought the horses close. Fernán mounted, saluted the Prince, and he and Cesario rode off.

"West toward Cuenca, Cesario. Then we will head off the road, wait till dark and, if no one follows, continue. The moon will be full and up early."

"I am of no use, Fernán. I cannot fight."

"Do not belittle yourself, Uncle. The warning the Prince declared may be futile—they may disobey. I expect, however, that Moya has had his fill and that the warning has cooled his blood. If they do come, however, we will not wait for an attack. We have two pistols and will choose a good place for an ambush. I will take the crossbow and you the pistols. Your good arm can shoot a loaded pistol."

They rode by the river until dusk, found a site protected by large boulders, and waited for several hours. No one followed, and they mounted and rode off, the full moon lighting their way toward home.

62

Ten days later, several leagues beyond Cuenca

The Prince, and Pacheco and his brother, Girón, ate supper in their tent. They had assembled a large contingent of knights and foot soldiers in the city and welcomed the Bishop of Cuenca, don Lope de Barrientos, to their fold. Pacheco had suggested the inclusion of Barrientos, despite the fact that the Bishop was loyal to the King, since there would be hard negotiation ahead. Don Lope would lend strength and balance to their position.

Pacheco had seemed testy since the episode with Rivera, and Enrique smiled. Was Pacheco annoyed that Rivera had won so handily or fearful of his prerogatives? Or were those attitudes one and the same? And when would Girón utter a word? This brother of Pacheco was perpetually mute. He ate and drank and followed his brother like a favorite spaniel waiting for supper.

"I find it queer," Pacheco said, "that Jerónimo has never mentioned Rivera."

"Why queer?" Enrique asked.

"Surely Jerónimo would know a nephew of his master, since Rivera resides under the same roof as Jerónimo."

"Do you doubt he is a nephew of Lorenzo Hernandes?"

"Not at all, don Enrique. I wonder at Jerónimo and his silence."

"But Jerónimo is silent by nature. He says little except to report what we demand he learn."

"An ideal spy," Pacheco said.

"You trust him?"

"Totally. A trove of valuable information."

"What do you think of Rivera?"

"A good fighter," Pacheco said.

"Is that all?"

"Other than his facility with a sword, don Enrique, I have had no opportunity to observe his additional qualities."

"I would wager Jerónimo was his tutor."

"Most likely," Pacheco said. "I know Jerónimo tutors Arabic and swordplay and knows more about most things than he should."

"We will make good use of Jerónimo during negotiations with my father,"

"Then you will negotiate, señor?"

"As you advised—we have no choice. I will end this business using Toledo and Burgos Castle to buy conclusion. I am tired of this eternal battle. Such wrangling over nonsense. Castile must be unified under a strong monarch and the nobles brought to heel. My father and Alvaro are too old for the task and, without the monarchy, my arm is weak. But I cannot unseat His Majesty without the help of God, for the good Lord controls Death and we must wait until He chooses to orphan me. I have no stomach for patricide."

"Will you approach the King or wait for his tender?"

"I will approach him when we reach Toledo—a few days at most. I love the life of the road, Juan, but a dusty path is no venue from which to negotiate. I must have a stable platform. A military encampment would satisfy, but not this endless march, day after day. Have you made preparations for our entrance into Toledo?"

"We will return as we left, don Enrique, after the agreement with Sarmiento—the same number of troops, the same encampment for foot-soldiers, the same accommodations within the city for higher ranks. I saw no need to change the plan."

"Good. You will send word ahead of our arrival." Enrique pushed his plate away and a servant removed it. "No acrobats."

"They are not in the plan, señor."

"Excellent. You read me well, Juan. But then we know each other such a long time, do we not?" Enrique sipped his wine. "Sarmiento will protest vehemently when he learns my mind. Proud bastard. His flag flies too high. We will haul it down."

"It flew badly to begin with. He has little talent for administration."

The Prince chewed on a segment of sweet orange from Sevilla and spit the pits into his hand. "I have asked Rafael Rivera to see me the morning after we arrive in Toledo."

"Why is that, señor?"

"He intrigues me. Rivera is far from stupid, Juan."

"You know that?"

"I sense it. He will provide another perspective."

"You think a *marrano* attitude would be valuable, señor?"

"In this case, yes. Arrange to have him admitted to the Alcázar when he does arrive, Juan, if you please. And I will want him at the Town Hall."

"What are you thinking, don Enrique?"

"Nothing in particular. Indulging a whim."

"A dangerous whim?"

"Hardly." Enrique took another segment of orange. The juice ran down his hand as he bit the fruit and a servant offered a cloth. The Prince dabbed at his hand and chin. "As you know, Juan, I am always on the prowl for bright lights. Rivera appears to glow. The glow may be the herald of dawn or the dim light of a small fire—one never knows—but men like Rivera are rare. There was magic in his swordplay, an intuitive response to the moment. That back flip, for example. Had you ever seen that before? Remarkable. So deft."

"I wonder," Pacheco said. "Rivera is undoubtedly loyal to Alvaro, like all *marranos*. Be careful, señor, this coincidental linking may not have been coincidental. His tutor may have taught him duplicity as well as swordplay."

"I hear your warning, Juan. I will step carefully, thank you. But I may need a man such as Rafael Rivera as messenger to Alvaro. I can see him in that duty. Luna would feel empathy for him."

"If you believe so."

"I do." The Prince motioned to have his plate removed. "We must conclude a peace with my father since there is no alternative. And we must employ whatever guile is required to secure our goals, even that of dispatching a handsome fellow to carry our letters."

"Agreed. How will you…dismiss Sarmiento?"

"Sarmiento will have been forewarned by the papal bulls. However, he may not think we will follow through. Therefore, I will avoid overt dismissal to begin with but inform the Toledans that Luna must remain what he is, the undeniable ruler of Castile and, therefore, Toledo. And if Luna rules, then the *Sentencia*, with or without the bulls, is trash. Alvaro will insist that New Christians be returned to their position of equality with Old Christians, and that will make the position of the rebels and Sarmiento untenable."

"The Old Christians will fight. So will Sarmiento," Pacheco said.

"If they do, I will crush them. The authority of the Crown must be established, for now and forever. When we are enthroned, we will not tolerate such dissension among our subjects. The bulls support Luna and the *conversos* and provide us with a stage on which to play out this farce—a farce jointly authored by Sarmiento and His Holiness." He popped the last segment of orange into his mouth. "Such a curious pair of playwrights. Unfortunately for Sarmiento, he has written himself out of his own production."

63

Homecoming

The moon had not yet risen and the narrow streets were dark as Fernán and Cesario approached the Hernandes house. Fernán felt the urgency in Margarita. His mount sensed her stable nearby and thrust against the bit, wanting her head. He held her tight and his heart beat faster as he passed each house or shop, minute by minute, each step closing the interval between himself and home.

They rode behind the house to the stables, and the horses neighed, shook their great heads, and reared in high spirits. Cesario left orders for the mounts to be fed, watered, and bedded down on new straw, and for the saddlebags to be brought into the house. Then they rushed up the stairs into the great hall.

"*Papá*," the little ones cried, bounding off the bench and running to Cesario who knelt and gathered them to him with his good arm, kissing each on the brow and then again and again wherever his lips met their young bodies. "*Papá*, are you home?" his oldest daughter asked, tears wetting her cheeks. "Are you home at last?" His wife hurried to Cesario and embraced him, and he held her with his good arm while the children clung to their legs and giggled and cried.

His mother left her place at the table and went to Fernán. Celestina held her son from her and looked at him. Tears formed in her eyes and she kissed him. "How good it is to see you, my son," she said.

"Good evening, Mamá. I have missed you and Papá and the children." And he kissed his sister, Beatriz, and asked her how she was and how were her lessons, and she recited as much as she could in her gentle voice as she walked with him to their father.

"Good evening, Papá," Fernán said.

Lorenzo stood and grasped his son to him and Fernán kissed the bristly cheek. "Fernán, God bless you. How tired you look, son. Come, sit and eat and tell us about your journey, and then you will sleep and tomorrow you will tell us more."

Cesario joined them and he and Lorenzo embraced and Lorenzo said, "You too need a good rest, my brother. Was the journey hard?"

"No more than expected, Lorenzo. We traveled fast from Valencia." He looked away. "I do not see Antonio. How is he?"

"The same, brother. He eats alone—in his room. When he does come down, he sits at the fireplace and stares into a void. I pray he will wake one morning and the nightmare will have ended but, to be truthful, I think his mind has been damaged and the Antonio we see will not change."

His family appeared so small to Fernán. Was it the fact of the journey and his expansion of vision that made it seem so? Or was it the loss of María? Fernán was profoundly aware of her absence. Before this, her presence would have filled the great hall. She would have bounded to Fernán and teased him and kissed him soundly and danced and sang a song to commemorate his return. Her enthusiasm had been childlike, and he would have smiled at her and been filled with love. Now her absence drained the room of warmth—the fire could not compete. The hollow in his chest would remain there forever.

Jerónimo stood at the door. Fernán walked over to him and they shook hands and embraced each other.

"I have so much to tell you, my friend," Fernán said.

"We will have time, young master. The Pope has issued his bulls and they support our position."

"Indeed. However, I do not presume that our personal intervention influenced the outcome. The politics of Aragón and Rome decided the issue. The Pope is king of an extended nation and, like all kings, must protect his regime. The schism between secular and ecclesiastic is enormous, especially when seen so close. Do you agree?"

Jerónimo smiled. "How you have grown, young master. What can I possibly teach you now?"

"Forgive me, I have become a bore."

"Not a bore. New knowledge floats like bubbles on water, Fernán. After a while, the bubbles burst and mingle with the other waters in the pool. That is all it is—new knowledge."

"So good to see you."

"And I you." He held Fernán by the hand. "I am grateful you sent me home to Toledo. There was much to do and, with Cesario and you in Rome and Antonio not recovered, Lorenzo was pleased to see me, I assure you."

The children were led off to bed with kisses for each and Lorenzo called Jerónimo to come and sit with them. "We will drink wine and hear Fernán and Cesario talk of Rome and their voyage."

This was new for Fernán. His father had never asked the steward to sit at the table with the family or the men. Family was precious to Fernán and he was pleased that Jerónimo was finally recognized as part of that family.

Fernán and Cesario ate and talked about the journey and Cesario boasted of Fernán and his performance before the Pope and then his duel with the knight.

"I never taught you such a trick," Jerónimo said. "Over your head? Indeed, it was over your head. You must have been mad as well as lucky. Suppose he had fallen on you, what then?"

"Then I would have stabbed him…

"And I am sure he would have let you stab him and, if you had, you would have been assaulted by the whole troop. No, a trick may be stirring and supposedly courageous, but the overuse of art demonstrates a prior fault in strategy. We shall have to practice more thoroughly than I had planned."

The men talked for hours and then, exhausted and somewhat drunk, wandered off to their wives or empty beds.

Fernán awoke early the next morning with one thought—Naomi. He broke his fast, dashed out of the house, and ran toward the *judería*. The sun was low on the horizon and the air warned of winter. Otherwise, all was as it had been. He no longer dressed in black, but wore mourning in his heart. The wall, the door, and the bell faced him and he shivered with anticipation in the chill air. Would she be at home?

He rang the bell and, after a while, rang it again and was rewarded with footsteps in the courtyard. The panel opened and Mosé peered out.

"By the blessed and eternal God,…," he opened the door and looked up and down the street, and then grasped Fernán in his arms and whispered hoarsely, "… Fernán!" And then he looked up into the sky and said, "Thank you, Oh Lord. You are indeed good to Your children for You have permitted us to look into the face of our dear friend who has been gone these many days into the distant land of Italy. By Abraham, Isaac, and Jacob, you are a blessed sight, Fernán. You are well and…oh, but bless our house with your presence, dear friend. Come in, come in. The doctor is at home and will offer infinite prayers of thanksgiving for your deliverance from the iniquitous Romans."

"Thank you, Mosé, and thank you for your greeting."

"More than you deserve for deserting us for such a dreadfully long time but…come this way, please. The doctor will deny me my life if I detain you longer."

His footsteps sounded hollow when he entered the kitchen—as if the cupboards were empty, the shelves bare, and the room stripped of possessions. The aroma was of stale food. No windows were open. The chairs and stools were in disarray, the house cold.

"Is don Abrahán well?"

"You might say he is and you might not. But he is not happy since Naomi has gone. Nor am I or Aharón, for that matter."

"Where has she gone, Mosé?"

"To speak the truth, and it is my habit to do so, I do not know."

"Where is the doctor?"

"In his study. That is where I left him. His hearing has suffered in recent days. You must speak loudly or he may not hear."

Fernán walked into the study. Don Abrahán was seated at his table, writing.

"Don Abrahán," Fernán said. The doctor continued to write and Fernán spoke more loudly, "Don Abrahán."

"Yes," he said in Ladino, "I am busy, Can you not see that I am busy? Come back later."

"Don Abrahán, it is Fernán, returned from Italy."

The doctor put down his pen and turned slowly. "Ah, Fernán Hernandes, my dear cousin," he said, "whom I welcomed into this house when he was recovering from the wounds of prison and who traveled to Rome to see the Pope. Come into the light, Fernán. You will have to excuse me. During this past month my hearing and sight have degenerated and you must speak loudly and stand in the light. Good. I can see you now and I see that you are my cousin."

Fernán was puzzled by the slow, slurred, and disordered speech, and thought that the same affliction which had affected the doctor in sight and hearing may have affected his language. He prayed that was not so.

"Are you ill, don Abrahán?"

"I have suffered a slight *apoplexia*, Fernán—a stroke. The result is as you see, although the cause is a matter of debate. However, I am not incapacitated and may recover normal function—for a while. Mosé and Aharón have been very helpful. They will be good doctors—as good as doctors can be, given the limited knowledge we have of the human body and soul." He peered at Fernán. "Let me look at you. Sit, sit, Fernán. Good. You seem well, your color is satisfactory, you have filled out since I last saw you. Good. And were you successful? You saw the Pope?"

Fernán described the trip briefly—the interviews with the Pope and the content of the bulls.

"Then you must be pleased, my boy. I hope this new papal prescription will improve your lot. Tell me, how is your family—your father and mother—they are well?"

"Yes, señor. They are well."

"You will convey my best wishes for their health, if you please?"

"I will indeed, don Abrahán." Fernán hesitated. "And Naomi is well?"

The doctor turned his face away but not before Fernán saw the confusion and pain. "I do not know," don Abrahán said. "I assume she is well." When he spoke, his words were halting, separated by silences during which a muscle in his cheek twitched. "We argued, she and I, and when I woke she was gone. I do not know where. I can only pray that God will care for her and lead her back to me before I die."

"If I may ask, don Abrahán, what did you argue about?"

Melamed looked at Fernán. "You, my dear cousin. We talked about you and I asked about Halevi and his rejection of her. Whether there was something I should know that she had not told me." His speech a series of staccato bursts between great breaths. "She said that you and she had become man and wife before God. That had she married Halevi she would have betrayed you and God and could not have lived with her guilt. The note from Halevi, she said, was a blessing and a sign." He took a handkerchief from his sleeve, wiped his eyes and blew his nose. "I called her a bad name and she wept. She said I did not understand. That I was old and no longer felt love for her or for anyone. Our talk worsened, became deplorable, and she went to her room. I could hear her weep. But I was upset and could not find it in my heart to comfort her. In the morning, her room was empty. She left as you left—without a word or a note."

Fernán fell on his knees before the doctor. "Don Abrahán, how can you look at me?"

"Then it is true?"

"Yes, señor. Naomi and I swore before God that we loved each other and were husband and wife and that God sanctioned our love. I beg your forgiveness, señor, not that we acted without your blessing, but that I was not brave enough and concealed the truth from you to protect Naomi and myself. You have been a father to me and I have not been worthy of your love and trust. And now Naomi has gone from both of us. But I swear to you, don Abrahán, as I am a man and as I kneel before you, that you will see Naomi with your living eyes."

"How can you say that, Fernán? She may be with God."

"No, señor, she lives, I know she lives because she must. And I will bring her to you, don Abrahán. I swear it before Almighty God."

The doctor shrugged and Fernán kissed his hand. With some difficulty, don Abrahán put that hand on the head of Fernán and blessed him with an old Hebrew blessing that ended with the words, "may the Lord cause His countenance to shine upon you and give you peace." Then he said that seeing him was a blessing in itself, that he was tired and would rest, and that Fernán should return another time.

Fernán left the house and walked through the city, not seeing people or houses but only the face of Naomi. Later in the dark and cold, he became weary and desolate and walked home. He excused himself from supper—the trip had tired him, he said—and went to his room. The feeble coals of a dying fire offered no warmth and little light and, as he lay in bed, he heard quick footsteps above him and was reminded forcibly of María. The familiar pain returned to his breast, but he realized that what he heard was not the spirit of María but Antonio, wandering about, unable to sleep.

64

The conference room of the Alcázar of Toledo

Drops of rain dribbled down the window. Sarmiento watched the steady fall that had damped the city all day—not sufficient to raise the level of its cisterns but enough to slick the cobbles and make hazardous a casual walk or ride. Across the room, slumped in a chair, Marcos García imbibed his endless stream of wine, while Galvez and Ávila, huddled at one end of the conference table, whispered, and glanced from side to side as if planning an escape from life.

The weather pained Sarmiento. His leg and head were virtual storehouses of discomfort—each ached from the week of ceremonies and fiestas that had followed the return of the Prince. The foolish Toledans saw Enrique as a messiah, a savior who would release them from the supposed tyranny of the rebels and protect them from Luna and the King. But when they learned what the Prince planned for the city, their heads would ache like his own. No fiestas would gladden Toledo.

That morning the Prince had called the rebel leaders and luminaries of the city to a forum in the Town Hall and struck Sarmiento a fatal blow. It is time, Enrique said, to resolve our differences with the King. That resolution would require the people of Toledo to accept Alvaro de Luna as the de facto head of government of Castile and Toledo, and to reject the *Sentencia-Estatuto* as an illegal document, disallowing its arguments, conclusions, and false laws. Furthermore, New Christians were to be considered equal in all ways to Old Christians. Therefore, a new government that would support the law, and which the Prince would assist in forming, must replace a rebel administration that did not.

Sarmiento felt the hurt of each word in his limbs. They reverberated in his head and echoed in the shivers that trembled through his body. García dulled the blows with wine, while Galvez and Ávila, dull to begin with, felt the words of the Prince as elements of another quagmire, another mess to be sidestepped and ignored. Sarmiento envied their lack of wit.

"I warned you, don Pero, of the consequences of the *Sentencia*," García said.

Sarmiento swung from the window and faced García across the room. "Warned *me?*"

"In this very room. I warned you what would happen if Enrique reversed himself on the *Sentencia*. You, however, said we must take the risk."

"On the contrary, don Marcos, I warned *you* of the consequences of a rapprochement between the King and Enrique. I warned you that if we did not restrict *marranos*, cut them out of the life of Castile and the body of Christianity, we would lose the support of the commoners. And do you recall the alternative, García? Do you remember what I said would happen if the Prince entered Toledo and *marranos* were again ensconced in their judicial robes? If they were allowed to proceed against us? If they could bear witness against us?"

"Is the current situation better?" García stepped to the table and faced Sarmiento across its width. "The Prince promised to safeguard our rights and privileges. Now the King and his son walk arm in arm. And why did you not remind the Prince of our agreement?"

"What are you saying, García? Did I not proclaim in a voice as loud as I could raise, without deafening the ears of those around me, the terms of the agreement we signed in the tent before the Prince and Pacheco? Did I not remind the Prince that it was *we* who made him *patrón* of Toledo in exchange for *his* assurances, *his* promises, and *his* signed agreement?"

"He promised to protect us from Luna," Galvez said.

"You were there, Galvez," Sarmiento said, his voice troubled, "when I repeated the terms of the agreement this morning, word for word, were you not? When Enrique ignored me and went on to discuss a new government for Toledo with the dignitaries?"

"I was there. I heard and was sickened," Galvez said.

"But you failed to press the case, don Pero," García said. "You read the terms but never demanded that the Prince hold to his agreement."

"Do you expect a Prince to hold to every agreement he makes? He would not be a Prince if he did. Like a tall tree, he must bend with the wind or break. Do you think I expected him to hold to the letter of his agreement? How foolish do you think I am?" Sarmiento returned to the window and, with his finger, traced the run of a drop of rain down the glass. When he spoke, his voice was contained. "The dignitaries support our position. They reject control of Toledo by Luna. They oppose *marrano* equality. Did you hear Ayala? All nobles support us, except Silva. They want the *Sentencia* to remain in force and, though they may not be fond of us, they are most certainly less fond of *marranos*."

"What did Enrique mean by concessions from the King?" Galvez asked.

"Concessions?" Sarmiento hissed. "Can you see Luna conceding anything? In your ass, you can."

"The Prince promised a pardon from the King," García said.

"How can Enrique promise a pardon from the King? He will be fortunate to get one for himself."

"Señores," Galvez said, "past decisions are beyond recall. Let us avoid recriminations. We must decide what to do. The Pope has ruled and we are accused. I will have accusers to face in ecclesiastic court and, I assure you, that will not be pleasant, but I place my faith in a just God, that He will have seen that our actions were in accord with the precepts of the Church and will hear and accept our pleas for justice. I suggest, señores, that your best hope for pardon is to plead with the King. Explain your motives. You are loyal servants of His Majesty. What you did you did for the King and the good of Castile."

"Are you witless, Galvez?" Sarmiento said. "With Alvaro de Luna in the chamber? You believe Luna will look kindly on us for defying his will? For mounting an army and resisting his entry into the capital of the monarchy?"

"The Prince can be brought around," García said.

"You think so? And how do you propose to convince Prince Enrique and Pacheco that they committed a grave error and must mend their ways?"

"The Prince wavers, don Pero, as you say, he sways to and fro like a…like a weathervane. After he left, I urged the dignitaries not to be influenced by the appeal of theoretical offices in a new regime. Many nodded in agreement." García drew a scroll from within his outer garment. "And I have prepared a response to the bulls. The arguments within this document are irrefutable. Listen. Once you hear them, you will agree and so will the Prince."

The words Sarmiento heard García read were stilted, flattering, and servile. They referred to the Prince as illustrious and powerful and concealed plain language behind a veil of allusion. García reminded the Prince of his promises and written agreements and admonished him for retreating from his word and embracing the *marranos* and his father, the King. Then, berating him again, García warned that no "false bishop," meaning the Pope, could absolve the Prince from his solemn oaths to the city and that, if he did renege, the city would once again take up arms.

Sarmiento was appalled at this childish whimper. Their cause was dead.

"The Prince said he would try to obtain a pardon from the King for the city and its citizens," Ávila said.

"Try, indeed," Sarmiento said. "Where is Enrique now?"

"Returning to Requeña," García said.

"The Prince is tired—tired and bored. The bastard hangs about for a week impressing commoners with his love for them and then fires his bolt. Now he is off to Requeña to hunt deer and play with his favorite falcon while we stew in the pot he has left to boil. And in the meantime, the *Sentencia* is doomed and *marranos* are in power and set equal in stature to Old Christians. And we? Why, our offices will be stripped from us and our bodies thrown into the river. What in the name of God did we fight for? What was this rebellion?"

"We must make peace with the King," García said.

Sarmiento wheeled on him. "What is it you want—to have your head cut off or your body burned? Perhaps Luna will do both for the same price."

He approached García and spoke softly across the table. "García, as you love life, listen to me. Make no move without my assent. You and I have come a long way and this is not the time to wander off on a new path. The path you would choose might prove to be sand and water that will weaken under your weight and swallow you whole."

65

Two weeks later, La Fonda de los Reyes

The four sat at a table in a private room. Dinner finished, they drank wine and waited for don Enrique to establish a new administration, for their lives to end.

"Enrique has made up his mind," García said. "His assurances are not worth the hearing. Were Luna to require our heads, the Prince would deliver them by fast horse. Enrique is not to be trusted, no more than Luna."

"Enrique has his finger in the wind," Galvez said, "make no mistake."

"We are pawns, merely pawns," Ávila agreed.

"We must appeal to the King, don Marcos," Galvez said.

"Sarmiento will never agree."

"Why inform Sarmiento? He is a noble."

"True," Ávila said, "he is not like us. Nobles have their own code. Luna will excuse Sarmiento, fine him a few *maravedís*, and send him off to his estate. Don Marcos and I will lose our heads, not Sarmiento."

"And if the Prince discovers our approach to the King?" García asked. "Do you remember what Pacheco said in the tent? That all negotiations lie in the province of the Prince, and any contrary action will be considered an act of treason and dealt with summarily. You know what summarily means? No trial, no judge, quick time to the block or the stake or worse."

"You remember all those words?" Galvez said.

"I am a lawyer. I live by words."

"Why should Luna listen to us?" Ávila asked. "Why should he not kill us outright?"

"Indeed, why not?" García said.

Then, suddenly, he rose from his seat and stood silent as if posing for an artist. When at last he spoke, his voice was almost a whisper, a ghost of a voice. "If we approach Luna before Enrique does, he may have Toledo with little bloodshed and without submission to any demand the Prince might present, for the Prince will surely require payment for Toledo."

"But how can we deliver Toledo?" Juan Alonso asked.

"We own the Gates of San Martín and Cambrón." García leaned on the table and looked at each of them, his voice now whole and strong. "And if we were to capture Visagra and Alcántara, which Ávila commands, Luna could stream through all four open gates without a struggle. The city would be his."

"We can secure Alcántara," Ávila said. "The facility may be strong but the force is weak and suspects nothing. We can take Alcántara and the Gate of Visagra at night."

"Yes," Galvez said, "it can be done."

"Then are we agreed?" García asked. He examined each face. Ávila nodded, then Alonso, and finally, Galvez. García raised his glass. "To the King!" he pronounced, and they drank.

"Who will negotiate with Luna?" Galvez asked.

"Lope, you should go," García said. "Alvaro knows you. Being a priest, you can come and go freely."

"I will not go alone," Galvez said. "Who will go with me?"

"I will go with you," Alonso said.

"Thank you, brother. Then let us decide what we should say."

66

The Hernandes house

He woke with a start—his hand on his dagger, his wrist held by a firm grip.

"Fernán," Jerónimo whispered, "it is I."

"Jerónimo? Are we attacked?"

"No, young master." Jerónimo released Fernán. "Our world is safe. Forgive me waking you, but this is a matter of serious import."

"What is the hour?"

"Midnight. The house sleeps. Dress for travel, if you please, and we will talk."

Dressed in warm clothes, Fernán lit a taper and followed Jerónimo down the stairs. Seated on a stool in the buttery, he drank warm mead Jerónimo had prepared and ate wheat bread with orange preserves.

"What I tell you," Jerónimo said, "must be guarded from all persons, even from your family, for my life depends on your silence. May I burden you with my story?"

Fernán smiled. "When I was in that stinking cell, Jerónimo, my life was forfeit until you redeemed it. I will guard your secret with the life you saved."

"You are my true friend, Fernán," Jerónimo sighed. "To begin. I have told you some of my past but omitted a few important details.

"Some seven years ago, when the Prince was your age, I was not yet steward but helped your father with the delivery of merchandise. I was younger and stronger than I am now and I made quick work of heavy rugs and other materials that your father sold. One day we delivered a large order of rugs and carpets to a wealthy young man. This man was impressed with my strength—he was curious, he said—and he inquired after my background and interests and was intrigued that I tutored swordplay and languages as well as assisting your father.

"The man was Juan Pacheco, then and now advisor and friend to Prince Enrique. I had told you, Fernán, that my family was killed during a pirate attack. That is essentially true, except that my youngest sister survived—she was an infant and away from our house with a wet nurse during the raid. I learned of her survival some time after I had begun work with your father and I inquired about her and, periodically, sent what little money I had to the family who had assumed responsibility for her well-being.

"The time came for my sister, Fatima, to marry. However, as you know, girls need dowries to marry and neither her adoptive family nor I had the means to finance a marriage. When Juan Pacheco suggested he might have use for my services from time to time, I accepted his offer eagerly. Since then, on occasion, I have worked for Pacheco.

"My special talent, other than those of which you are aware, has been the collection of information by hidden means—that is, the talent of a spy. Some information I have gathered for Pacheco has been of great value. But let me assure you, Fernán, never have my nocturnal pursuits interfered with my loyalty or duties to your house or your family. Your family has been sacred to me. Do you believe me?"

"Indeed, Jerónimo, I do."

"Thank you, Fernán. Your friendship and trust are precious. Now I must describe the business at hand."

Jerónimo told Fernán that he had been assigned to observe the actions of the rebel leaders, and had done so for some time with the aid of informants in sensitive positions. He had learned, not an hour ago, that the rebels planned to negotiate with King Juan. Now he must inform the Prince.

"You require a message to be delivered to the Prince?" Fernán asked.

"I am ashamed to ask, but there is no one I can send whom the Prince will trust, other than you. Pacheco and Girón are with Enrique, and the others of my group are engaged or not trustworthy. Normally, I would do this myself, but I must be here to observe the rebels during this sensitive time."

"I will do anything to defeat Sarmiento. But what will we tell my parents?"

Jerónimo examined Fernán. "You have not mentioned Naomi since you returned."

"I cannot find her." Fernán told Jerónimo of his visit to don Abrahán and his desperation. "I have inquired and searched for her in Toledo and the near villages but without success."

"Then I will tell your parents that don Abrahán is not well and that you search for Naomi so as to calm his fears. You left suddenly tonight because you were informed that she might be in a village nearby and in need of your help, and you instructed me to take that message to your parents. While you are gone, I shall make inquiries of my own to find your Naomi. We shall exchange roles."

"Will you find her? Where does one start? Every turn I take seems wrong. I fear she may have been harmed."

"Have no fear. I will find her, Fernán. But now, if you please, young master, ride to the Prince."

Jerónimo described where Fernán would find Enrique, and they roused and saddled Margarita and bridled the gelding Jerónimo rode. He had named the horse, Almohada, Arabic for *pillow*, because a ride on the gelding was silken. Fernán would alternate horses when one tired. Jerónimo handed him several bags filled with provisions, clothes, pistols and ammunition, and his sword and dagger.

"The weapons are clean and sharp, young master. I pray they will not be required. This letter explains everything to the Prince. Deliver it to don Enrique or Pacheco, but to no one else. This other document identifies you as Rafael Rivera and will allow you to pass through the Gate of Visagra. Go with God."

Fernán nudged Margarita and, leading Almohada, walked the horses through the streets of Toledo to the Gate of Visagra. Once through the gate he headed east toward Cuenca and Requeña at a trot, a pace he knew Margarita could sustain for hours. He would have to test the stamina of Almohada, but he felt secure. The night was clear, the air crisp, and the moon, full the previous night, brightened his way. He would ride a few hours, then groom and water the horses, and sleep before setting out again at dawn.

Two weeks before, he had attended the assembly of the Prince, dignitaries, and rebels at the Town Hall at which Enrique pronounced the death of the *Sentencia*. The words of the Prince caused Sarmiento to blanch, and Fernán noticed García whispering to the Governor, but Sarmiento did not respond. The lawyer seemed to have ballooned since Fernán had last seen him. Sarmiento, however, was gaunt, his mouth turned down in a perpetual sneer.

The Prince requested that Fernán attend him after the meeting and, once the hall emptied, asked if Fernán had ever met Alvaro de Luna or the King. Fernán said that he had not, but refrained from comment, unaware how the conversation might develop. Enrique inquired whether he would carry a message to Luna and Fernán consented. Nothing, however, was asked of him.

His days since had been occupied with the futile search for Naomi and he was dejected and concerned for her safety. He prayed that Jerónimo would turn up some clue as to her whereabouts.

The journey to Requeña passed quickly, segmented into meals, care for the horses, and rest. Fernán saw few people on the road—most were peasants and local merchants. The passersby would doff their hats and bend their heads in greeting—weighing the quality of his mounts, his sword, dagger, and pistols. A man with two handsome horses was at least a *caballero*, certainly a gentleman, perhaps a knight, and deserved and required their respect. Once near Requeña he inquired of the locals whether they had seen the entourage of Prince Enrique and was led to the camp within a few hours.

The knights securing the camp remembered him well and remarked on his bout with Moya. "He is dead, the fool," one said. "Picked a quarrel with a man who was not so considerate as you." Then one of them escorted Fernán to Pacheco.

"So, Rafael Rivera, what brings you to us once more?"

"I bear a message of serious import from Toledo, don Juan, and have been instructed to deliver it to you or to Prince Enrique."

"You have taken up the life of messenger with a vengeance, señor."

"A temporary occupation. I hope to find a more engaging livelihood soon."

"I am sure you will. Of serious import, you say? Then we shall find the Prince together. Meanwhile, my fellow will care for your horses. You must plan to stay with us and hunt."

They walked toward a large tent and Fernán thanked Pacheco. But he knew that the invitation to hunt would be void and the camp broken and on the move before sunset.

67

Toledo

Once informed of the rebel approach to Luna, the Prince raced to Toledo, taking with him a small group of lightly armed knights—the main body of the encampment would follow. Fernán accompanied them and, once within the gates of the city, took leave of the Prince and returned home. The search had failed, he explained to his parents. Naomi was not to be found. His mother consoled him while Lorenzo remained withdrawn.

In the morning, Fernán sought out Jerónimo and found him in the stable watching the horses being groomed. Margarita neighed when she saw him and he stroked her great head, telling her they would not ride that day.

"Thank you, Fernán," Jerónimo said. "I am most grateful. The Prince has expressed his gratitude as well." Then he told the groom to make sure that the coats of the horses were curried, and he and Fernán walked outside.

"What will happen now?" Fernán asked.

"The Prince has ordered an inquiry—who initiated the approach to the King, what was intended, and so on. Of course, the inquiry is a sham. Who would negotiate with the King but the rebels? Sarmiento was not involved, apparently—he is far shrewder than the others."

"How can they know he was not involved?"

"The Prince apprehended and tortured several rebels. I doubt Sarmiento would have been accused in any event, being noble. Enrique will assemble the dignitaries and councilors in the Town Hall and accuse the rebel leaders of treason—he wants them out of the way. The city must be turned over to the King with a clean administration—the rebel leaders eliminated and the city purged. Everything must be in order for Luna."

"Which of the rebels will be accused?"

"García, Ávila, and the two canons—Galvez and Alonso."

"Sarmiento was the fulcrum of the rebellion, Jerónimo. Without him there would have been no rebellion, no persecution, no burning. Noble or not, he must be punished."

"Perhaps, later."

"And Naomi? You have said nothing of her."

Jerónimo shook his head. "I asked about her among those I know in the city, young master. Naomi has not been seen. I am sorry that I have no good news, dear friend, but we shall find her."

68

Late December, the Alcázar

His desk in the Alcázar was bare of papers to be signed or orders to be executed—the conference table, with regimented chair, pen, ink, and paper arrayed before each seat, was the sole occupant of the room other than Sarmiento. No one was expected. His administration was finished. Christmas was near, the year at an end. Well, he was alive and that was more than he could say for the others. He would wriggle out from under, but soon they would be as dead as his father.

After his father died, Sarmiento had made the Alcázar his permanent residence. The funeral, held the week before the Prince returned to Toledo, was attended by few other than García and some rebel leaders. Sarmiento and his mother walked behind the black-draped coffin followed by Clara and the children. Then the interment and a brief funeral meal at the family home at which Sarmiento, stiff in mourning clothes, accepted awkward condolences from those who cared not a damn or hated his father and himself. His mother, dry-eyed, gossiped in a corner with a few friends, and the children ran about while their nurse attempted to control their exuberance. The day finally over, Sarmiento left for the Alcázar and silence.

Troops in the Alcázar knew the regime had been terminated. Sarmiento saw it in the casual salute, the arrogant upturn of a mustache, the occasional disreputable uniform. Discipline had drained from their behavior, their fear of him dissipated.

His adjutant entered the silent room and announced that García was waiting. Sarmiento had not spoken to the lawyer since he had warned him not to move without his assent. Yet the rebels had dispatched Galvez to negotiate with Luna, and the indiscreet canon had been stopped at the Gate of Visagra on his return from the King. Enrique would have their heads. Fools. He had misjudged García, credited him with greater intelligence than the lawyer possessed—an admitted failure. Now he and García would play solo end games—the chain that bound them broken.

"Señor García," the adjutant said, "states that Toledo has become a trap for him and the others and he seeks asylum in the Alcázar. He asks to see you, don Pero. What shall I tell don Marcos?"

"Say that the troops of Prince Enrique will search the Alcázar first, and that I cannot endanger the forces under my command. I wish him good luck. Should he return to the Alcázar, however, I shall have no recourse as an officer of the court but to have him arrested."

"That is all, Excellency?"

"Exactly."

69

Nine days later, the Town Hall

Fernán was roused from worrying about Naomi by a knock on his bedchamber door. A message from Prince Enrique had been received—Rafael Rivera was required.

He found Pacheco in the chair formerly occupied by Sarmiento in the chamber of the Chief Justice of Appeals. "The Prince desires that you take a message to Alvaro de Luna, Rafael," Pacheco said. "The weather could be better, but you will make good time—the roads are in good repair."

The air was leaden both in color and temper, and the breeze, while not strong, was damp and chill. Fernán had ridden in bad weather before and was not concerned.

"You have been to Valladolid?" Pacheco asked.

Fernán said he had not, but the route was direct and he should have no problem. At that moment, the tower bell of the Cathedral Church began to peal without rhyme or rhythm. The chamber of the Chief Justice faced the Plaza Ayuntamiento and they could observe the bell tower directly across the plaza from Town Hall. A crowd had gathered near the tower entrance.

Pacheco wondered at the commotion. A guardsman entered the room to inform them that García and his forces had fortified themselves in the bell tower.

"Imbeciles. How many?"

"Somewhat more than a dozen, don Juan."

"Notify the Prince. Tell him where I am and that señor Rivera is with me." Pacheco frowned. "Why would García want to isolate himself in the tower? He will die either by assault or starvation."

"Perhaps he wishes to call attention to himself," Fernán said. "He may believe that the people will rally and prevent the Prince from punishing him and the others."

"If that is his reasoning, he is mistaken. Above all else, the people are fickle and self-serving."

Accompanied by two knights in light armor, the Prince entered the room, went immediately to the window, and surveyed the situation near the tower.

"How long have those idiots been up there?" he asked.

"We do not know, don Enrique," Pacheco said. "We heard a disturbance and then were informed that García and his friends had fortified themselves in the tower. Rafael believes that they may seek sympathy from the commoners."

"For what purpose?"

"To prevent you from penalizing them, don Enrique," Fernán said.

"Interesting. But then they do not know me, do they, Juan? Does the city have a town crier? If such a person exists, ask him to come immediately."

Rodrigo the town crier, an older man with a sharp tenor voice, appeared within a half hour.

"Your services are required, Rodrigo," the Prince said. "Are you paid by the city?"

"I am indeed paid by the city, Your Highness, or by any person who needs a loud, clear telling of a message to the public. I am paid by the length of time my voice is used and by where and when the service is to be performed. If the announcement is simple and to be delivered in the Plaza for those who may stroll about, that fee will be small. If, however, the message is long and to be announced to all the folk of the city for an extended period, that fee would be large."

"Then," Enrique said, "let me tell you what I want you to say and you will charge the city accordingly. Will you write my message down as I speak?"

"Begging your pardon, Your Highness, but I cannot write words and, if you were to write them down, I could not read them. I will, however, remember your message—sound by sound—and vent it as if your voice were speechifying the sounds themselves."

"One cannot ask for better, can one?" Enrique smiled and enunciated his message in a clear voice while strolling about the room, accenting specific words he wished Rodrigo to emphasize.

"People of Toledo. Today, Thursday, the eighteenth of December of the year 1449, the leaders of the January rebellion, Marcos García de Mora, Pero Galvez, and other members of the rebels, in all fewer than twenty, have barricaded themselves in the bell tower of the Cathedral Church with the intent to deny justice to the people and the city of Toledo and to your *patrón* and lord, Prince Enrique. For these rebels have negotiated with Alvaro de Luna and King Juan for the purpose of delivering possession of Toledo into the hands of Alvaro de Luna by stealth and trickery, and those are acts of treason.

"Therefore, His Highness Prince Enrique requires your assistance to remove these rebels from the bell tower of the Cathedral so that they, who would deal secretly with the enemy, may have their crimes judged. All men who support the city of Toledo and its *patrón*, Prince Enrique, come with your arms to the tower. The Prince will there direct you to remove the traitors from the tower so that they may be arrested, judged, and punished.

"That is the message, Rodrigo. Can you repeat it to me?"

"With the help of God, Your Highness," and he repeated the message word for word.

Fernán was amazed by what he heard. Although he had witnessed Rodrigo work before, he had never heard such a long message repeated with such accuracy, both for its content and tenor.

"Then, Rodrigo," Enrique said, "broadcast this message to the city, if you will, and continue to do so until you are told by my messenger to stop."

"As God is my witness, Your Highness, I will do as you instruct." And Rodrigo left the room, repeating to himself, *sotto voce*, the words of the message.

"Why do you want the commoners involved, don Enrique?"

"This is their city, Rafael. If we are to govern now that Sarmiento and the rebels are removed, we must have the cooperation and approval of the commoners—as did Sarmiento till now. Also, we shall be able to test whether the people are with us or are still enthralled by the idea of rebellion."

"Will they come?"

"We shall soon see."

Within an hour, the mass of people in the Town Hall Plaza had grown substantially. Fernán could see that many of the men had buckled on swords and brought other weapons with them to join in the attack. Enrique, Pacheco, Girón, Fernán, and the knights and guardsmen of the Prince walked out of the Town Hall and marched toward the tower. A path opened before them and the crowd hushed as the Prince approached and entered their ranks. The response to the message spoken by Rodrigo had been considerable. Fully a thousand people, most of them men, stood in the Plaza with swords and other weapons in their hands. As the Prince walked toward the Cathedral, the silence was superseded by shouts of approval and applause, and then a rhythmic chant was taken up by the crowd—"Enrique, Enrique, Enrique"— as the Prince and his entourage mounted the steps of the Cathedral. Enrique raised his arms and the crowd quieted.

"People of this ancient and glorious city of Toledo!" he called, and the people responded with a roar. "The rebellion is over. There is no further requirement for rebellion, for your Prince and *patrón* understands your needs and will install an administration in this city that responds to you, the people." A great shout arose from the crowd and the chant of "Enrique, Enrique" was repeated and then died as the Prince raised his arms again. "But, my people, the rebel leaders of the January rebellion—Marcos García de Mora, Pero Lope de Galvez, and the other rebels who would betray our city to Alvaro de Luna—these traitors have barricaded themselves in the tower of the Cathedral Church with the intent to deny you justice."

"No!" the crowd shouted. "Punish the traitors!"

"Then those of you who would help us bring these traitors to justice form yourselves around the tower. Leave a space of ten paces between yourselves and the tower and beware of arrows shot from above. We will select those who will storm the bastion and bring the traitors down. Move slowly. Do not push or hurt your fellow citizens. There is work here for able-bodied men." And then he shouted, "For Toledo!"

"For Toledo!" they echoed. And gradually, under the direction of knights and guardsmen, a space was emptied around the tower. Pacheco walked along the front line of men, selecting the most warlike of those with weapons, and asked them to step forward.

Fernán inspected the empty windows in the tower. He pictured the defenders cramped within the small space above, listening to the mob outside, knowing that they would be overwhelmed and murdered. Had they thought the people would protect them? If that was so, they knew now they were wrong. The people had deserted them, had flocked to Enrique either in hope of reprieve for crimes committed during the revolt or out of disillusion with the rebels. But that knowledge would offer no solace to the twenty in the tower. Their hearts were frozen with fear and nothing would thaw their hearts or save their souls.

Enrique ordered several knights to lead the attack. The people would form a phalanx behind them.

"I wish to be part of this force, don Enrique," Fernán said.

"You have no armor, Rafael."

"My sword and passion are my armor."

The Prince smiled. "Do not be foolish, my friend. You have more important work."

"I will not disappoint you, don Enrique. May I suggest a stratagem?"

"Your thoughts are always welcome."

"Señor, the windows of the tower are too high for arrows or fire and you do not wish to destroy the structure. Therefore, assault the door. Place a charge at each pin and harness two draft horses to the door. The charges will fire and the horses will loose the door and open the tower. Since the tower steps curve round and can be defended effectively, a suitable charge thrown through the door will create a cloud of white smoke whose purpose is to confuse as well as injure those defending the stairs, and to deny them the sight of those who will enter. That will allow men with sword and buckler to attack, supported from behind and below by crossbow. A charge of powder thrown up the stairs from time to time will disperse its defenders and allow our attackers to advance. In this way the top will be reached and the prisoners secured."

"Where did you study this strategy?" Enrique asked.

"I have practiced with arms for years, señor. May I participate?"

"May God go with you, Rafael! You will supervise the placement and use of the charges." And he called to his armorer, who was responsible for powder and charges and told him to follow the instructions related by Fernán.

Francisco the armorer, an older man with white beard and brilliant blue eyes, was enthused at the prospect of heading the attack, and he and Fernán conferred together, discussing the proper powder and how it should be packed and lit. Then Francisco rushed off to secure his equipment and produce the charges and a guardsmen was sent for horses and harness.

The knights, meanwhile, had assembled the commoners and drilled them in what they should do, while other commoners, who would be held in reserve, shouted curses at those in the tower. Francisco returned, covered the eyes of the horses, and led them away from the tower. He then placed the explosive at the door hinges and led a cloth fuse a safe distance from the door.

"Are you ready?" Enrique asked the knights.

"We are ready!" they shouted. Francisco lit the fuse and it burned across the ground and up to the door. An instant, and then a loud explosion. The door shook but held.

"Apply the harness," the lead knight shouted. The harness was fastened to the loose hinges and the horses strained and pulled and a massive roar went up as the door was dragged away. Francisco lit a fuse on a large charge and handed it to Fernán, who ran up to the door, stood to one side, and threw the charge into the space where the door had been. In a moment another explosion resounded deep and hollow within the cavernous tower. Then crossbowmen loosed bolts through the doorway and knights charged into the void followed by crossbowmen, commoners, Fernán, and the armorer with his charges and a lighted taper.

The interior of the tower was thick with whitish smoke. Fernán could see the man before him but others beyond were dim shadows awash in white. He heard the ring of swords and cries of wounded men and, sword in hand, he ran with Francisco toward the sound, passing crossbowmen loading their weapons. Several bodies, dead or wounded, lay on the bottom stairs, thick smoke smudging the contours of their faces. The stairway was slippery with blood and the air heavy with acrid smoke and the sickening odor of bloody sweat.

Fernán heard fighting above him—the grunts of men heaving swords, the shouts, the clash of metal, the screams of pain. He pushed up beyond the first bodies—a knight with a pike protruding from his breast, a commoner with throat cut, surprised eyes distended, two defenders resting athwart one another, swords clutched in dead hands. More fighting above. He pushed ahead.

And then he was at the battle. Here the smoke had thinned and he saw men straining to reach above to where two or three were fighting with swords. Above them were the defenders and beyond that a crossbow pointed down.

"Crossbowmen!" Fernán shouted down the stairwell. He heard men call and then two with crossbows were behind him and he pointed to their opposites above and said, "Shoot well and quickly." They aimed, shot, and caught one in the throat and another in the shoulder.

"Francisco, prepare a throwing charge," he said. Francisco handed Fernán a charge. "Light it," he said. The charge was lit and Fernán held it a moment and then threw the charge beyond the wounded crossbowmen above. An explosion and several bodies were blown over the balustrade and fell to the stones below. Then, as if a cork had been pulled from a spigot, the men before him surged forward and Fernán followed, avoiding dead and wounded, and was soon at the top defending himself with sword and dagger.

The fight was over quickly and the rebels taken. García, Ávila, Galvez, Alonso, and several more were dragged down the bloody stairs between the bodies of the fallen and thrust into the sunlight before the howling mob. Guardsmen seized Galvez and Alonso and led them to cathedral cells where they would be held for ecclesiastic trial, while García, Ávila, and the other captives were dragged across the plaza through the bedlam of their former supporters to the Town Hall. There they were put in a guarded room until their fate could be determined. The wounded were taken from the tower and their wounds tended. Several died from loss of blood and the dead, bodies and faces covered, were arrayed on the platform near the tower.

A shout from across the plaza. The words were carried as a whirlwind through the crowd from mouth to ear. "García and Ávila escaped! Bribed the guards! Were caught!"

Fernán stood near the Prince and asked, "What will happen, señor?"

"The people will have their pleasure, Rafael. The rebels will die."

"They will be tried first?"

"They will not. This horde will have them drawn and quartered before the hour is out."

"And you will allow it, don Enrique?"

"One cannot stop it. The best one can do is to step aside."

"But no crime deserves such punishment, señor."

"A matter of opinion, Rafael. We shall see."

Fernán watched as García and Ávila were dragged across the plaza. As they passed through the crowd they were beaten with sticks and rope. From another direction, as if by common understanding, came the executioner followed by men carrying his table of death. García and Ávila were hauled up the stairs to the platform before the tower and Fernán heard a sound like the soughing of wind in the trees, like the beating of blood—an ebb and flow that rose and fell and grew until it became an inhuman scream—"Draw and quarter! Draw and quarter!"

Dear God, he thought, these people are no longer human.

He looked at the face of García and saw death. Ávila was curled within himself, sobbing. Fernán walked down the steps and through the crowd. No one noticed—their eyes were on the platform and the table where Ávila was now tied. He crossed the plaza and walked toward home. Then he heard the first shriek and began to run. He ran faster and faster, but could not escape the fearful sound.

70

The house of Manuela

The bed was warm, the night cold. Manuela lay beside him, her head on a pillow, hair spread behind her, eyes closed. Her body was covered with a light blanket, her left arm and half her breast exposed. He moved the blanket, gazed at the puckered nipple for what seemed a long time, and then ran his tongue around the blushing areola.

"What are you doing?" she said, her words dull with sleep.
"I love your breasts," Sarmiento said.
"Is that all of me you love?"
"There is nothing about you I do not love."
"You love me?" Her voice firmer, roused.
"I had not thought of it before," he said.
"Do you?"
"I suppose I must."
"That is nice. You are not sleeping?"
"I awoke. Something woke me and I began to think."
"What did you think?"
"Nothing pleasant."
"Then go to sleep and your dreams will please you."
"They will not."
"Oh, Pero. How sad. Tell me what you think, then it will leave you."
"These thoughts will stay."
"Put your head on my breast and close your eyes."
"If I put my head on your breast I will make love to you."
"Then you will think pleasant thoughts."

He lay his head on her breast and his cheek sank into her yielding flesh. Her breast was warm, almost hot.

"You thought about García and the others," she said.

"Yes. We will never recover—the rebellion is dead. The people have deserted us. I did not imagine Enrique could be that sudden, that severe."

He heard her heart beat and felt the rise and fall of her breasts. His hand wandered to her belly.

"Pacheco moves the Prince like a chess piece," she said.

"Not this time. Enrique was in command. He ordered the attack and approved the deaths by quartering. Surprising. The Prince is more forthright than I had imagined."

"Never mind. He cannot touch you," she said.

"Don Lope de Barrientos, the Bishop of Cuenca, told me to relinquish the Alcázar and the Chief Judgeship. The Prince has decided to rid himself of Pero Sarmiento. The Bishop said Enrique will not waver from that decision—there is no way to turn him from it."

"Barrientos is an old woman," she said.

"A tough, wealthy old woman. The Bishop was a favorite of the King—now he bows to Enrique. All our gates will soon belong to the Prince. Barrientos said it would be my death to confront Enrique and I told him I would be pleased to relinquish the Alcázar and the Chief Judgeship, but I required payment for their surrender—custom demanded an award."

"You said that?"

"It is the custom."

"How can you be so bold, Pero?"

He moved his hand between her thighs and traced a wandering path from sacrum to mons where it rested.

"I am noble," he said. "It is the custom. I also demanded protection and safe passage—for who can know where an assassin may hide with a deadly message from our King. Enrique acquiesced. He granted safe passage for my family and me and assured me that I could accompany him to Segovia. Wait," he whispered, "what do you hear?"

"Something. I thought it was you."

He sat on the edge of the bed, reached for his sword, and unsheathed the blade. There was no moon. He could see nothing but gray forms and black shadows.

"Talk to me as if I were with you," he whispered, and he stepped softly toward the dark doorway and stood there listening. A dog barked far away. Manuela was speaking to him as he had instructed her. No other sound. He stepped through the doorway into the room beyond, his feet on the thick carpet. A chill ran down his back. He could discern the door to the outside stairway and the lighter gray windows. His hand was at his knee, the sword pointed directly before him. He took another step into the room.

An arm circled his neck and a sharp point pricked his chest below his heart. He struggled but the arm on his neck was strong and the point dug into his skin.

"Who are you?" he croaked.

"Your death, Sarmiento," the voice breathed into his ear. "I am Antonio Hernandes, whose wife you killed. You killed my life and now I kill yours. Say farewell to life, Sarmiento."

The point of the dagger bit into his skin and he felt the body behind him push hard against his back. The dagger fell, the arm withdrew, and the body dropped away. A taper was lit. In the light of the candle he saw Hernandes on the floor, a dagger protruding from his back. Manuela stood above the body holding the candle. Her face was calm. She knelt, withdrew the dagger, and wiped the blade on Hernandes. A rivulet of blood flowed from the wound onto the carpet.

Sarmiento had held his breath and now he breathed deeply. Blood trickled from his chest where the dagger had cut his skin.

"I will bind the cut," Manuela said. "Come with me."

He followed her into the bedchamber. She washed off the blood with a cloth dipped into a basin of water and tied a strip of clean white cloth around his chest. Sarmiento donned a robe and sandals, walked into the other room, and stared down at Hernandes. He felt for a pulse, but there was none—the dagger had pierced the heart. The Hernandes carpet was stained with Hernandes blood. He picked up his sword, walked to the outside door and down the steps to find the sentry. There was no sentry. He walked to the rear of the building. The sentry saluted.

"Where are the others?" Sarmiento asked.

"At their posts, don Pero."

"If they were at their posts I would not be here. Find them and your lieutenant and both of you report to me. Immediately!"

"Who was the assassin?" Manuela asked when he returned.

"Antonio Hernandes. His wife was burned for heresy. I exiled him instead of his nephew who subsequently died."

"How did he get into this room?"

"I do not know. Either the sentries are dead or will be."

Manuela had wrapped a gown around her body. She asked if he would like a liqueur to dispel the bad taste and he said he would.

"Where did you learn to use a dagger?" he asked.

"Mamá insisted I learn to defend myself."

She poured two glasses and he suggested they drink to life.

"That is what Jews say, Pero."

"Not everything Jews do is wrong, Uelita."

"What will you do now, Pero?"

"Once I give up my positions of honor and trust? Retire to the countryside and live well. Travel. And for that and other things I require a companion."

"You have your family."

"They travel badly. You are my perfect companion. We should visit Italy, France, England. Paris, they say, has become quite civilized. It was not so when I was last there."

"I would miss Toledo," she said.

"But I will not be here."

"I know, Pero, and that will be a pity."

"You will not come with me? Your face would light the civilized world."

"Thank you, Pero. You flatter me. But I think not. I am a simple girl."

The sentry and lieutenant arrived. The bodies of two sentries were found in an alley near the house, the lieutenant said, and he saluted formally with his sword. "I apologize most profoundly, don Pero, but I must congratulate you. Your dispatch of this assassin was most swift and effective. I am honored to be in your service, Your Excellency."

Manuela took Sarmiento by the arm. "Don Pero," she said, "is the foremost swordsman in Castile."

The lieutenant squared his shoulders and bowed. "The mastery of don Pero for rapier and dagger is well known throughout Castile, señorita Manuela. My salute to His Excellency was from the heart." Then the lieutenant apologized and asked if there was not some way he could make amends for the laxity of his staff.

"Indeed, there is," Sarmiento said. "Have this carcass rolled into the carpet and delivered to the Hernandes house. You know the house? Place the rug in front of the door, so that when Lorenzo Hernandes awakens tomorrow morning and unrolls it he will be greeted by his brother."

"But, Pero," Manuela said, "that will leave me with a bare floor."

"I will buy you a new carpet, my dear, twice as beautiful."

Part V

RETRIBUTION

"[Juan II] issued commands for the suppression of the revolt in Toledo, the pursuit of the fleeing Sarmiento, and revocation of... anti-converso decrees. Pope Nicholas V approved....
Two years later, in 1451, the same pope authorized, at the request of [Juan II], the establishment of an Inquisition ...for the trial of *conversos* suspected of adhering to Judaism."

A History of the Jews in Christian Spain
Yitzhak Baer (1888-1980)
Translated from the Hebrew
The Jewish Publication Society 1961

71

The middle of January, 1450, the Toledo Town Hall

"You ask me about Pero Sarmiento, don Enrique. As you know, I am a New Christian, a son of *conversos*. How then should I reply?

"The policies and actions of Sarmiento and García caused the death of my Aunt María, burned for a heresy she did not commit. Antonio Hernandes, my uncle and husband to María, lost his mind over the death of his wife and was killed by Sarmiento. Many *conversos* were killed and their possessions stripped from them. Many were left homeless and without means because of Sarmiento and his rebellion, used as objects to promote his ambition and greed.

"Now he has come before you to plead his case. He claims we New Christians are linked to the Devil and he warns you against us, saying that we caused him to fail as part of our alleged scheme to defeat the people of Castile and Christianity itself. Where is the proof for these fantastic fictions? Only in the crevasses of his disturbed mind. We *conversos* are Castilian and Christian and would commit suicide were we to pursue such a ridiculous course.

"You ask if Toledo will enjoy greater harmony and peace with Sarmiento gone. I say, yes. The man is the very center of a whirlwind that destroys all in its path. He has no respect for others, whether they be Christian, *converso*, Jew, or Muslim. His is an overreaching ego that tramples on the less fortunate and envies and hates those more prosperous or gifted than himself.

"Don Enrique, you have been persuaded by Juan Pacheco and your aides that risk to your position and life would be lessened with Sarmiento removed from the city. To that I say, amen. Therefore, you have demanded that Sarmiento relinquish the Alcázar and Chief Judgeship and withdraw from

Toledo, and he claims that he is willing to do so as long as he is compensated for his withdrawal, asserting that such reward is a matter of custom. To remove Sarmiento from the sinecures he holds would be a blessing for Toledo, but to compensate him for his removal would be immoral.

"Señor, you have not only granted Sarmiento an estate with considerable properties to compensate him for his supposed loss, but say that he may retain those goods and possessions that were stolen from those poor souls who were falsely accused of heresy and treason, and then tortured, killed, and robbed. Oh, señor, loss can be true only when honesty acquired its value. Stolen goods can never be lost, for they were never truly possessed. Sarmiento was not rich before the rebellion but acquired wealth by stealing the assets of the accused—symbols of the value of life that were snatched from New Christians by this Sarmiento, who knows nothing of the meaning or value of life. To restore them to their rightful owners is the least consideration these persecuted people deserve.

"You have argued, don Enrique, that Sarmiento is noble, that he has a great deal of land and many vassals. Does the quantity of his possessions make a man noble? A peasant can own land but is not noble. Nobility requires qualities of high moral character, such as courage, generosity, and honor. None of these virtues belong to Sarmiento. His courage is that of a hyena, not a lion. As for generosity, he has neither generosity nor honor and deserves nothing a noble person deserves.

"Don Enrique, you have sent word through Bishop Barrientos that Sarmiento must terminate his business in Toledo and leave. He has expressed his willingness to do so, for he has no choice, yet he requests permission to take his family and his stolen possessions and settle in your stronghold, Segovia. He claims that he has no safe haven in Castile outside of Toledo, that the King and his agents will hunt him down and kill him. Surely the King, your father, has more important affairs to concern him than the life of Sarmiento. But had he wished the death of the man, would it not be deserved? Consider, señor—Sarmiento warred against his sovereign King and defied his authority, as Pope Nicholas V has testified and as we have observed.

"He says that he is afraid he will be attacked. Oh, señor, that he would be attacked and stripped of the gains he derived from the rape of the *conversos* of Toledo—his very motive for joining García and the rebels in their ill-conceived revolt. He should be put on trial, convicted of his crimes, and punished.

"These, señor, are my thoughts regarding this vulture."

The Prince listened carefully while Pacheco whispered in his ear, but the arguments Fernán raised did not move him.

72

A forest near Toledo, three weeks later

By force of the bulls of Pope Nicholas V, the Bishop of Sigüenza ordered all Christians to shun Sarmiento, declaring him anathema, and the Prince, feeling the weight of the pontifical office, ordered Sarmiento to leave Toledo immediately and without princely protection.

When he learned of the order, Jerónimo alerted the spy he employed in the Sarmiento household to inform him when the family would move and by what route they would travel. A week later, the young nurse reported that a caravan would leave Toledo through the Gate of Visagra that Sunday, sometime after midnight, heading north to Segovia along the road that followed the Guadarrama river. The woman was concerned for the safety of her charges but was assured they would not be harmed.

During the day and early evening of Sunday, Fernán, Jerónimo, and a company of *converso* friends, comprising some twenty young to middle-aged men with swords, daggers, pistols, and crossbows concealed in their saddlebags, rode into the countryside. They departed Toledo by twos or threes and at different times through the gates of Alcántara and San Martín, their passes counterfeited by an associate of Jerónimo and sanctioned by the forged signature and seal of Enrique.

The company gathered three leagues from Toledo near a small forest that would provide cover for their nighttime actions. A trio of scouts was assigned to watch the Visagra Gate for the Sarmiento caravan. When the wagons passed, one would gallop to warn Fernán while the other two would follow the wagons at a discrete distance. If the caravan departed from its anticipated route, the two who followed were to continue surveillance until they were sure of the actual route, then apprise Fernán and continue pursuit.

At quarter past two in the morning, the scout informed Fernán and Jerónimo that the Sarmiento convoy—two carriages, three wagons, and several men on horseback—had passed through the Visagra Gate. Sarmiento rode ahead of the first carriage and armed servants guarded the other vehicles. They traveled the expected route along the Guadarrama and, at their current pace, would cover the three leagues to the rendezvous within an hour.

Fernán and Jerónimo had scouted the likely routes and selected the best locations for ambush. The men felled two large trees across the road near the river and waited for the convoy—some on horseback, some on foot.

After a time, the creak of leather and chink of bridles announced the caravan and, in the light of a half-moon, now high above the scene, Fernán sighted the first carriage. Sarmiento, riding slightly ahead of the lead carriage, pulled up several yards before the fallen trees, ordered the carriage driver to halt, and called to those behind him to stop and be wary of an ambush. As the caravan halted, the *converso* men, strung along both sides of the road, struck the wagons and subdued the few defenders. The path was too narrow for the wagons to execute a quick turn and the company drew swords and leveled crossbows to enforce the capture. They then seized the vehicles, forced the drivers from their perches, disarmed the mounted servants, and bound them hand and foot.

Fernán, Jerónimo, and three of the company approached the lead carriage with pistols drawn. Fernán called to Sarmiento to dismount and disarm.

"I am Pero Sarmiento, Governor of Toledo," he said. "We travel under the safe-conduct of Prince Enrique."

"We know who you are and we are not in Toledo," Fernán said, "but alone in a wood in the Kingdom of Castile y León. A safe-conduct is worthless here. King Juan rules, and your crimes are to be brought to account."

"What crimes? Who are you?"

"A spirit," Fernán said. He and Jerónimo stepped around the trees in the road and advanced toward Sarmiento. "One who died at your hand and now is risen to avenge his death and the deaths of his friends and loved ones. I am Rafael Fernán Hernandes de Toledo."

Sarmiento stepped back and looked from side to side—men with pistols and swords surrounded him.

"Your name was on the list of the dead."

"An error in judgment. Jerónimo, if you please, remove the sword and dagger of señor Sarmiento, tie his hands behind him, and lead him to the clearing. I will see you presently."

Fernán then inspected the caravan. The first carriage was occupied by the wife of Sarmiento, his mother, and four female servants. The wife stared at Fernán. He ignored her. The mother was asleep, her head propped against the wall, her mouth open, stretched out on one of the two benches that ran along either side of the carriage. The second carriage contained the children, the nurse, and three servants—children and servants sound asleep. The nurse looked down and was silent.

The wagons were loaded with goods of every description. Fernán asked his boyhood friend, Diego, to supervise the removal of all personal Sarmiento family belongings from the wagons, leaving only those that he judged had been seized from *conversos*—strongboxes, paintings, furniture, and carpets. When the men finished off-loading personal materiel, they were to move all confiscated goods from the forward wagon to the two rear wagons and place Sarmiento possessions in the forward wagon. Then Diego and three others were to reverse the two rear wagons containing the confiscated goods and drive to a prearranged site near Fuensalida where they would await Fernán. The first wagon and the two carriages containing the women, children, and servants were to remain as they were and to be protected.

Fernán thanked his friends for their help and embraced them.

"Go with God, Fernán," Diego said. "We do His work tonight."

"As God alone knows, *amigo*," Fernán said. "Until later!" And he left Diego and the others to their labors and walked into the forest.

The light of the half-moon threaded through the branches of the winter-bare trees and cast dark shadows on the floor of the woods. Alone in the dim forest, Fernán knelt on the shaded ground strewn with twigs and dead leaves and silently offered his prayer that God would approve his purpose that night and guide his hand, for he would duel Sarmiento and he had experienced the fury of the man during their encounter in the Alcázar. This would not be swordplay with the dull knight Moya or the three assassins in Rome. Sarmiento was shrewd and venomous.

Then he prayed for the souls of María and Antonio and his godfather Diego Enríquez. He prayed for his parents and sister and family and for his dear friends, don Abrahán and, particularly, for Jerónimo. And he gave thanks to God for redeeming him from prison and prayed that God would look kindly on him, should he survive the night, guide him to Naomi, and bless their union. For he knew the good Lord would approve their love and help them find their way.

Refreshed by prayer, he rose and walked ten feet before he remembered he had forgotten to cross himself. How could he have omitted an act he performed at least once each day? His prayer had ended with an entreaty to God to bless his union with Naomi. Had he crossed himself, knowing

Naomi was a Jew, would that have invalidated his prayer? He was sure that was not the reason he forgot—his mind was preoccupied with the upcoming bout—that was all. Then through the trees he saw the light from the fire in the clearing and he crossed himself and walked toward the flame.

The pear-shaped clearing was lit by the cold half-moon, an hour or so from its zenith, and a hot fire set in the center of the fat end of the pear. A group of men stood at the narrow end—Jerónimo quiet while the others chatted. Sarmiento, hands tied behind his back, watched the dancing flame.

Fernán knew that Jerónimo was disturbed by the prospect of the fight and, though he was well prepared, he felt the hollow in his gut that had preceded every encounter except his mindless charge with the long sword. The hollow would disappear once the bout began, but he wished the fight were over.

He thanked his friends for taking care of their guest and asked one of them to bring the weapons, Fernán then faced Sarmiento. "Several times you have asked that I cross swords with you. The last time was in the Alcázar, when I was half-dead from the *strappado* and fought you with that ungainly long sword. Neither of us won, since we are both alive, although I am sure you have convinced yourself that you, in fact, did win." Sarmiento turned his head in a lazy arc and gazed at Fernán through lidded eyes. "Tonight, we will fight again—this time with rapier and dagger. The night is cold but you will be warm before long—if not dead. In truth, I do not want you dead. I have other plans for you, some already put in motion."

Sarmiento turned away.

The weapons, bound in a cloth, were placed on the ground and displayed. Then the men took their pistols and walked to their positions—one at each quadrant of the pear. Jerónimo would cover the narrow end.

"The clearing is relatively smooth," Fernán said. "I walked it earlier this evening. A stray twig or two may be under foot, but there are no holes or sharp changes in level." Sarmiento glanced at Fernán. "In a moment, your wrists will be untied and you will select your weapons and walk into the clearing where I will join you. You will find that the weapons are equal in quality and well-balanced."

"You realize, Hernandes, that Prince Enrique will kill you if I do not."

"The Prince and I are on excellent terms. He will find it expedient to ignore this episode, should he learn of it. Now we begin. You will don this white overshirt, as I will. In that way we shall see one another more easily, and blood, if there happens to be any, will be apparent. There are no rules, except to remain in the clearing. If you attempt to leave, you will be shot. Untie our guest, if you please, Jerónimo."

Jerónimo cut the bonds. Sarmiento massaged his wrists, then looked at Fernán. "You make a mistake, señor. Ours was a professional encounter."

"The mistake was yours, señor. Our encounter was neither professional nor personal. You never saw me or my people as human. You sought to eliminate us and overstepped the bounds of your power. Select your weapons."

Sarmiento selected a rapier and tested its balance and heft. Choosing the other rapier, he tested it and dropped the first, performing the same steps with the daggers. With both weapons in his hands, he walked into the clearing.

"God be your guide, young master," Jerónimo said.

"God is in my heart, Jerónimo. My mind is as clear as fresh water." Fernán picked up the remaining rapier and dagger and walked toward Sarmiento, who stood in the right quadrant, midway between the fire and the trees where men waited with pistols.

Fernán realized he must not look at the fire for it would blind him—its light far stronger than the moon that hung above them in a sky spotless save for a thin wisp of cloud. How many times had he seen the moon in all its phases? Would he be alive to see it after tonight? Predawn would coat the sky in an hour, first light an hour later, and an hour after that the sun would rise above the low hills. This venture would be completed well before dawn.

He recalled the fight in the Alcázar. He had wanted death to release him from the pain of María and her death as much as from the torment of prison. Tonight, he wanted life, but that desire would not direct his rapier. He would fight, oblivious to death, aware only of the eyes of his opponent and the points and edges of sword and dagger.

His eyes became accustomed to the mixed light and the firelight on the weapons and his heart was steady. He approached Sarmiento who faced him, feet parallel, rapier at his knee, dagger arm stretched straight. The dagger and rapier pointed toward Fernán, directly at his eyes—a traditional opening. Fernán assumed the same stance and studied the eyes and weapons of Sarmiento.

The fire was to his left, the acrid smell of wood-smoke defeating the fecund aroma of earth and foliage. He had not visualized the full effect of the blaze. The rapier and right side of Sarmiento were lit, while his own rapier was in partial shadow. If the opponents exchanged places, the reverse would be true. And were his back to the fire, his body would be in shadow, whereas Sarmiento would be lit and his motions more discernible. But the fire was a trap. He must not place his back against it despite the promised visual advantage.

He walked a few steps. Sarmiento waited. Their rapiers touched and, in one motion, Sarmiento circled the rapier of Fernán, pressed down, lunged, and swiped at Fernán with his dagger. Fernán stepped back—his motions deliberate, reactive. He loosed his sword from the other rapier, feinted with his dagger, and thrust at the midsection of Sarmiento with his rapier. Sarmiento twisted away and countered over the rapier with his own weapon. Fernán caught the rapier on his dagger, carried it left, then slashed with his extended rapier in reverse at the chest of Sarmiento. The tip of the rapier missed the chest but caught Sarmiento on the inner arm.

Sarmiento retreated several steps, though the cut was minimal. His white shirt had been ripped and a red stain blossomed over the wound on his arm. He lowered his weapons, looked from side to side, and caught his breath. Their positions had not changed. Was Sarmiento listless or was this phlegmatic stance a ruse? The man was silent, had said nothing—no boasts, no taunts—unlike their duel in the Alcázar when he had used his mouth as a weapon.

Now Sarmiento walked to his left, away from the fire. Fernán wanted the fire on his left and he matched Sarmiento step for step.

Sarmiento began to walk backward around the fire and now called out while motioning with rapier and dagger for Fernán to follow. "Come, *marrano*. Follow me. Attack. Kill me, if you can. But careful, *marrano*, first blood means little in a fight to the death. And I will not be so generous tonight as I was in the Alcázar."

Fernán followed, watching his footing, watching Sarmiento.

"Come, *marrano*. Be not afraid. Death will be quick. There will be no pain. Touch my rapier. Here, touch it." And he whipped his rapier in the air. "Come. Kill me, *marrano*, Kill me."

They were close to the outside of the clearing when their weapons met. They had walked a quarter way around the fire and Fernán stepped forward with his right foot and rapped sharply on the other rapier, then slashed left in reverse and up toward the face of Sarmiento. Sarmiento avoided the slash and ran back around the fire, laughing.

"You want me close to you, as when you smelled like a sewer rat? Come then, embrace me, *marrano*, embrace death. You are much too far away. I cannot smell you. Do you stink? Has the stench of death left your nostrils? Do you wake at night in your cell, your leg chained, and wait for the *strappado*?"

The wound seemed not to have affected Sarmiento. His dagger arm was strong.

"What have you done with my goods, *marrano*? You think I cannot read your mind? Do you steal as all Jews steal? And my wife and mother and children, do you kill them while I kill you?"

Abruptly, Sarmiento advanced, his rapier descending in reverse. Fernán caught the rapier with his dagger, but his overshirt captured the point of the rapier and Sarmiento withdrew the rapier cutting Fernán along his ribs.

"Now you are cut, *marrano*. The first but not the last. I lied before. Death will be slow and painful. I will slice you into pieces, one cut after the other, and you will die, *marrano*. Slowly. I will skin you as I would skin a fox."

The cut burned, but Fernán pressed forward, slashed with his rapier and stepped toward his right, forcing Sarmiento toward the fire.

"You want my life, *marrano*? You want revenge? Play *torero* and I will play the bull. But remember, *Torero*, a bull has sharp horns. Which horn do I favor? Do you know? Left or right?" And he lay his weapons either side of his lowered head, pawed the ground, and laughed. "Come, *Torero*. Test me. As you thrust your sword I will gore your gut."

Fernán stepped forward and Sarmiento circled to his right. Sarmiento had his back to the fire and the firelight rimmed his shadowed figure. He is the Devil, Fernán thought, now in his Hell. He blinked. His eyes smarted from smoke.

"But why kill me, *Torero*? My work is done. Soon I will be gone. What is it you want, Torero? Do you know? Do you ambush the bull out of frustration? You think the bull fears death, *marrano*?"

Time slowed. He was in a void—the voice of Sarmiento a fading echo. He heard nothing clearly but the extended beat of his heart, sensing each muscle contract to control his arm, his hand, his rapier. His feet in his boots on the grass and dirt responded to each slight variation in compaction and texture. Thought was silenced. He held his weapons with such lightness of touch and fine perception that the pressure of the soft breeze on each plane of steel was a force to be counterbalanced.

Within him a heat like the fire grew stronger and the memory of María, of Diego, of Antonio, of the dead and maimed grew hotter and hotter until he was consumed with their memory and his hatred. And he attacked Sarmiento with both weapons, the eyes of the other contracting slowly and then opening and the motion of each weapon glinting in the firelight now displaced point by point to intercept his own dagger and rapier. Dagger on rapier, rapier on dagger, Sarmiento caught and blocked his weapons, but the strength of the attack forced Sarmiento back one step toward the fire and then two more steps—the heat of the fire a living presence. And Sarmiento, sensing the heat, glanced over his shoulder, and in that instant, in time expanded, beat by heartbeat, heartbeat by footfall, Fernán drove forward against both weapons, twisted his rapier loose, and thrust.

The rapier caught Sarmiento in the flesh and muscle of his inner thigh, and the wicked strength and cut and pain of the thrust threw Sarmiento backward. The weakness and agony of the injured leg caused him to lose balance and, as he fell, he dropped his weapons and collapsed on his back into the fire, crying out in terror as the heat struck his body and flames crawled up his shirt. He scrabbled with his boots and legs against the turf seeking frantic escape from the flames, his hands striving to press and push against blazing logs and branches. But his body was caught in a net of burning brush and he could grasp nothing.

The smell of burning hair and flesh now mingled with the smoke and Fernán hesitated, restrained by the justice of it, and he shouted, "Die, Sarmiento. Die!" Die by fire as María had died, not filled with gracious song, as Jerónimo had lied, but with an agony cruel beyond the scope of human knowing. Suffer a piercing wound as Antonio had suffered, and die in such a duel as he had provoked with Fernán when the pain of the *strappado* still racked a body enfeebled by starvation and prison barbarity. These penalties were so clear and true that Fernán watched instant by instant as flame ate at the body on the fire.

Let him die. Death deserves him. Let the fire wash him clean and carry him to Hell. Then Fernán saw the face of the executioner on the *strappado*—the devil with the black hood and broken, discolored teeth. Dear God, do I now wear the hood? Had he driven Sarmiento into the fire? He had defeated the man with his rapier, but was the thrust that drove Sarmiento into the flame deliberate? God had given him a talent for killing. Had He also give him a talent for torture? And was he condemned to use that talent?

The rebel attack, the long sword, the killing, the question Naomi had raised—how can one be splendid and yet kill—these thoughts now stirred within him. How when he found Naomi, could he explain what had happened tonight? He thanked the Lord she was not here as witness. Or Alberti, the calm, considered humanist who valued reason and humanity above all else—how explain why he had acted as he did, why he had thrust Sarmiento into the fire? Alberti was not there nor was Naomi, but he was and so was his God.

He threw down his weapons, grasped the boots protruding from the fire, and dragged Sarmiento out of the flames. The overshirt and hair and hose were burning, and Fernán ripped the overshirt from the body and smothered the flames on the head and back and thighs and shouted to Jerónimo for water. And Jerónimo ran with the bucket and splashed water on the writhing form on the ground, extinguishing the remaining flames.

Blood flowed freely from the wound in the thigh and Fernán shouted, "Stanch the blood, Jerónimo!"

Jerónimo quickly cut away the clothing where the rapier had entered. "A clean stab, Fernán, but you injured a large blood vessel. Bright red shows we should stem flow from the heart." And he tied a rope around the leg near the groin and tightened. Sarmiento groaned.

After a few minutes, bleeding was reduced to a minor discharge and then halted altogether and Jerónimo released the tourniquet. Bleeding began again and he tightened the rope and continued to tighten and loosen until the oozing blood was minimized. Then he placed a pack of folded cloth on the wound and held the pack against the wound with a length of white cloth tied around the leg.

"First the blood must clot. When bleeding stops, we will change the cloth."

They rolled Sarmiento over on the ground and Jerónimo cut the remnants of the shirt away and examined his back and wiped dirt off the skin with a clean cloth. Sarmiento moaned and was quiet.

"He has fainted," Jerónimo said. "We need fat to cover the burns, young master. Fire has blistered the skin on his back and neck and charred it on his shoulders and buttocks in several places. Scarring will be severe."

"We have no fat, Jerónimo," Fernán said. "Have they brought cooking fat with them, do you think?"

They dispatched Ruy and the other men to ask the wife for fat and cloth, and to refill buckets of water from the river.

"Make him comfortable, Jerónimo," Fernán said. Make him comfortable so that he will know our revenge for María and Antonio. Make him comfortable so that he will experience the death de Ribas and Diego Enríquez suffered.

Sarmiento lay on his side. The bleeding had stopped. Such wounds, Fernán knew, were hell. The blisters and charred skin on his back and arms and the wound would hobble Sarmiento for months or more, unless the thigh mortified and he lost the leg or his life.

"What now, young master?" Jerónimo asked.

"We cannot do as planned. Sarmiento is defeated. We have stripped the stolen property from him. He is wounded decisively, perhaps fatally. Added punishment would prove nothing except that we are monsters. God protect us from that. There is no proof in revenge, only a transitory and demeaning satisfaction."

"Sarmiento deserved to be punished."

"And he has been, Jerónimo. I did not foresee the effect of the fire, yet I drove him into it." Fernán stared at the body of Sarmiento. "He would have killed me. In a way, he did. I died in that cell—I am not the same man."

"Nor is Sarmiento," Jerónimo said. "This is not the man you knew, Fernán. That man has been broken."

"Will our friends consider it a weakness—not pursuing punishment?"

"No, Fernán. Not weakness, but strength. Although the opinion of another means nothing when truth is within yourself."

Ruy and the others returned with a small tub of butter and buckets of water. Jerónimo washed the dirt off Sarmiento, who had awakened. He fainted again, and they treated the burned areas with butter and covered them with clean cloths where the skin had suffered the fire.

"When you finish, Jerónimo, if you please, have Ruy and the others take Sarmiento to his carriage. Make a sling to carry him. First check his wounds and change the dressing. Then ask our people to remove the fallen trees and release the guards and drivers. Warn his wife that her husband fell into a fire and has been burned and will require immediate care. She should travel quickly to Segovia and find a physician. I will take a few minutes to extinguish the fire, then we will join Diego in Fuensalida. Our work here is done."

They changed the dressing, applied more butter to the burns, made a litter of branches and cloth, and carried Sarmiento from the clearing. Fernán separated the logs of the fire and quenched the embers. His side pained when he moved the logs and he raised his shirt and examined where Sarmiento had cut him with his rapier. Bleeding had stopped and the cut seemed clean. He would visit don Abrahán when he returned to ensure himself against corruption. Then he sat against a large oak and watched the burned logs hiss and smoke and, at last, lie still.

The oak he leaned against was hundreds of years old, the bark rough and massive against his back. The fire was dead, the half-moon at its zenith, the clearing cool. Diego was in Fuensalida, waiting.

73

In search of Naomi

The valuables Sarmiento had confiscated were delivered to an empty barn outside Fuensalida, and later that day Fernán and his *converso* friends split into pairs and surveyed their community, requesting each family to list property or sums of money that had been seized by the rebel administration. The lists were then compared with the contents of the barn and families with matching items were invited to claim their goods. A considerable sum, was distributed to those with the greatest need—families who had lost a breadwinner or could demonstrate a valid emergency. Items not claimed nor identified were auctioned and the money distributed among the poor. The process occupied the better part of a week and, by its conclusion, only a few families had not been compensated.

One morning, Fernán and Jerónimo were comparing notes while breaking their fast. Without preamble, Jerónimo said that he had found Naomi.

Fernán leaned across the table and held Jerónimo by the arm. "How long have you known?"

"Since late last night, young master. You were asleep when I returned and I would not wake you—the news would keep till morning."

"How did you find her, Jerónimo?"

"By chance. For over six months I have employed Rubén Halevi to observe certain persons of interest to Juan Pacheco. I would harvest this information periodically and, last night at our first meeting since early November, I asked if he had seen Naomi or knew where she was. Halevi has learned the spy trade well. It provides a nice supplement to his farm income...."

"Jerónimo," Fernán interrupted, "where is Naomi?"

"A moment, Fernán. The story has importance. When Naomi left don Abrahán, she believed Halevi might provide her suitable employment while she gathered her thoughts—puzzled as to how an orphaned Jewish girl without marriage prospects might survive in a hostile world. She walked to his farm—a considerable distance on foot—and found that, while Rubén had married and thereby fulfilled his need, a neighbor of his required a responsible Jewish girl to care for and teach his children. Halevi sent Naomi to the neighbor who offered her employment. She has been there since."

"You might have awakened me, Jerónimo." Fernán walked to the window. Night was slowly yielding to dawn. "I have barely lived through one delay and then the next before I was free to search for Naomi and then, when able to do so, could not find her though I inquired everywhere—within Toledo and as far as Orgaz." Fernán searched the deep-set eyes of his friend. "Do you not find it strange that Naomi would approach Halevi?"

"Why strange, Fernán?"

"Halevi rejected her and cast doubt on her reputation."

"She was in desperate need, young master, and Halevi was the only Jewish person she knew who might help. He did, at one time, say he loved her."

"Naomi would never have lowered herself to ask Halevi. She has her pride. Might there be part of this story that has been concealed from you—or from me?"

"Concealed? By whom?"

Fernán examined the sky above the outbuildings behind the main house—a touch of rose tinted its hue. "You must know, Jerónimo, that I trust you above all men, save my father. As you once said, you would not hurt me except to save my life. However, it occurs to me that you may have done just that."

"What do you mean?"

"Concealed Naomi from me, thinking that you would save my life."

"Why would I do such a thing, Fernán?"

"To restrain me from a grave error of judgment—in your opinion. You may have thought that marriage to a Jew would expose me to great danger—that I would be seized for heresy. Or, that Naomi was not a match for me, that she might impede my growth toward some miraculous future of your imagining." His smile was sad. "I would love you no less if you thought that, dear friend, but I must know."

Jerónimo rose slowly, disturbed, hesitant, and faced Fernán where he stood beside the window, one side of his face cool in the predawn glow, the other warm with candlelight. "Here, Fernán," he said, "take my weapon." And he drew his dagger and held the point against his breast. "Grasp this dagger and thrust it into my heart. I am overcome with shame. I have not defended you as I swore I would, but have deceived you. I have betrayed my honor."

"Put away your dagger." And he took the weapon from Jerónimo and returned it to its scabbard. "Death has no part in this. The hurt is not permanent and your intention was honorable."

"Dear Fernán, you have grown beyond me. I am ashamed. Forgive me, if you can find it in your heart. I have been alone too long with my secrets. My judgment has been affected. I realized, finally, that you would be incomplete without Naomi, that she is your perfect mate. I will tell you how to find her."

"I am grateful. But first, Jerónimo, tell me how Naomi came to be with this neighbor."

Jerónimo said that after Naomi and don Abrahán had words, Mosé found the girl crying. She explained that she must leave the house and asked Mosé to help her find a place to live. Mosé, a person of little worldly experience, turned to Jerónimo, swearing him to secrecy. Jerónimo then approached Halevi and asked about employment for Naomi.

"That is the story, Fernán. I was derelict keeping this from you."

"The subject is closed, Jerónimo. I understand your motive and you know mine. This breach does not affect our love. Now, the name of her employer?"

"His name is Aboav, Yaacov Aboav. I will tell you how to find Halevi and Halevi will direct you to Aboav."

"I pray to God she is still there."

Fernán nibbled on bread while listening to the directions and deciding how to proceed. He would take Margarita for himself, Almohada the pillow for Naomi, and food for the journey. Halevi lived near Orgáz, some seven leagues from Toledo. If he left shortly and the good weather held, he could be at the farm in early afternoon and then, perhaps, see Naomi before sundown. First, he must inform his father and then, don Abrahán—the news might buoy his spirits.

He found Lorenzo in his study, a room off the great hall where his father kept records of the family business. Lorenzo had been desolate since the death of Antonio, blaming himself for neglecting his younger brother. When they were children, Lorenzo, as the elder son, had assumed responsibility for his siblings. His eyes would fill with tears as he told stories to Fernán about their escapades as youngsters—how when his father caught them at some prank, Lorenzo assumed the blame and spared his brother from the inevitable whipping.

When the carpet from Sarmiento was discovered on their doorstep, Lorenzo was called. He knew where the carpet came from and he ordered it spread before him. On seeing his dead brother, Lorenzo fell to his knees, beat his breast, tore his clothing, and wept. Since then he had retreated from discussions of political affairs and devoted his time to mercantile transactions from early morning till late at night. He avoided Mass and was silent at dinner. Often, Fernán would hear him speaking, sometimes to himself, sometimes to Antonio or to his father, laughing at a remembered joke or a bit of mischief from childhood.

Fernán had not told his father about the letter from Rome in which Alberti invited him to join Valla and himself. The offer included an apprenticeship with Alberti, tutoring in the classics from Valla, and a small stipend from both men that would allow Fernán to study rhetoric, law, and architecture. He could further support himself, Alberti suggested, by teaching swordsmanship.

He stood at the open door to the study and watched his father, bent over a sheaf of papers, a waybill of the latest shipment of goods from the East. Lorenzo looked up and smiled at his son, but the half-sad smile, Fernán knew, was instinctive, his mind was elsewhere. Nevertheless, he told his father of the letter from Alberti and of his desire to return to Rome and study with the masters who had honored him with their invitation.

His father listened attentively. "You would be far away, Fernán. I had plans for you to succeed me at *Hernandes y Familia.* Your mother and I grow old, my son. When will we see your countenance?"

Words and phrases from prayers and the Testaments now crept into his language. Lorenzo would sometimes quote psalms at length, surprising Fernán who had never realized that his father was learned in spiritual matters.

Lorenzo shook his head from side to side. "However, these gentlemen must find you exceptional, and that I certainly understand. A young man must follow his heart," he said, sighing, "and the old must step aside. That is what we shall do. Go to Rome, my son. Study with these wise men. Then return to us with knowledge of the world and use that knowledge to better our lives in Castile." He inclined his head and peered at Fernán. "When will you go, Fernán?"

"I had thought early April or May."

"So soon? Does your mother know?"

"I have not spoken to her. I wanted your approval first."

Lorenzo lit a candle and motioned to his son. "Come with me, Fernán. There is something you should know." They walked down the stairs to the giant storeroom under the house. Lorenzo unlocked the door. They entered, locked the door behind them, and walked to a blank wall behind a stack of crates and oddments.

"Hold this candle," Lorenzo said, and he removed a brick from the wall, pulled a lever within the cavity and a section of the wall moved forward revealing a small closet. He reached inside the closet and removed a small book and two velvet bags with Hebrew inscriptions in needlepoint. Other similar packages lay on the shelves of the closet.

"These books and bundles belonged to your great-grandfather who, as you know, converted to Catholicism to save his family during the riots of 1391. When we rebuilt this house, your uncles and I moved them from their former place of concealment to this closet. This is a book of Jewish prayers. I know you speak Hebrew—yes, Fernán, I know about your Hebrew—so you will understand the meaning of these prayers. These two bundles contain phylacteries or *tefillin*, which a Jewish man fastens in a special way to his arm and forehead when he prays in the morning, a prayer shawl or *tallith*, which he wears during prayer, and a skullcap worn at the same time to cover his head, as a sign of respect for God."

He turned to Fernán. "You are surprised, I know, but once a year at the time of the great fast, the most holy day of the Jewish year, *Yom Kippur*, the Day of Atonement, your uncles and I would pray as Jews. At midnight of Yom Kippur, when the servants were asleep, we would come here and pray as our father and his father prayed. We would pray for forgiveness for our sins and, especially, pray to be forgiven for the pretense that we are Catholic. For, in truth, we are neither Jew nor Christian."

"And you have concealed this practice all these years."

"Yes, my son. What choice did we have? Your great-grandfather had a sword at his throat, and his wife was threatened with strangulation. Yet, they were Jews in their hearts, and they did what they could to remain Jews."

"Why did you not tell me this before, Papá?"

"Because your uncles and I became sick with the pretense, the duplicity, and decided to raise you children Catholic. When you reached manhood, we would explain and leave the choice to you. That choice is now yours."

Fernán realized that his life had changed again. He was recognized as an adult and given the choice of remaining Catholic or becoming...what would he become? He had no idea and he said, "Are you alone in this practice, Papá?"

"No, many are like us, and many not, so that one must be careful to maintain a disguise, like one of the disguises Jerónimo assumes—yes, I know of his nighttime employment as well as your Hebrew," he said. "That is why we have married within the community, Fernán, to maintain our heritage and our secrecy."

"But Papá, why then object to a marriage with Naomi?"

"Because Naomi is overtly a Jew and would cast suspicion on you, my son. She is a wonderful child and don Abrahán a dear soul and our cousin, but I would fear for you if you married her. We are deer in a forest of lions, Fernán. You know that better than I. To be safe, we must be invisible."

They returned the religious articles to the closet and closed the wall. Fernán thanked his father, kissed his cheek, and excused himself, saying he must tell his mother about Italy. The revelation had confused him further and he must now work that new intelligence into his life.

He found Celestina in her bedchamber teaching Beatriz needlepoint. He explained to her that his father had granted him permission to return to Italy to study and that he planned to leave later that spring.

"So soon, Fernán. Dear soul, it seems you are never here, and we miss you when you are away. Do we not, Beatriz?"

Beatriz nodded shyly and smiled at Fernán. Though bewildered, he was proud that his father had thought to confide in him and, full of love for his small family, he knelt before Beatriz and hugged her to him. Her brother had never expressed his love so openly, though she knew he loved her as one would love a favorite puppy, and she was so overcome that she began to cry and had to be comforted by her mother. Fernán kissed the top of her head, told his mother he had an errand to run, and left the two emotionally muddled.

The sky and streets were clear and the weather brisk, and he ran to the Melamed house, reveling in the exercise that had been denied him. His rapier wound had healed of itself with no sign of infection and he had not consulted don Abrahán. Now, though, he would lift the spirit of the doctor with his good tidings. Mosé answered the bell at the gate and Fernán experienced a rush of friendship for the round, pleasant fellow, despite the fact that he and Jerónimo had concealed Naomi from him. But the face of the apprentice revealed distress beneath his natural ebullience and he told Fernán that the doctor was not well. He had suffered several additional strokes since Fernán last saw him and was confined to bed.

"Then it is all the more important that I see him, Mosé. Jerónimo has told me about Naomi."

"What has he told you?"

"Everything."

"Do not think ill of me, Fernán. Naomi was most positive about concealing herself and when I asked whether she referred to you as well, she said yes."

"The time to hide is over, Mosé. Don Abrahán must see Naomi. They must be reconciled. I am off this afternoon to bring her home."

"That is welcome news. Let me see if don Abrahán is awake. He sleeps most of the day. The rest does him good."

Mosé returned and motioned to Fernán who entered the study, once again a sick room. The morning light shone through the east windows and illuminated the face of don Abrahán. Fernán was dismayed by the change. The doctor was sallow, his face haggard, the skin deeply wrinkled. Fernán knew he must hurry to bring Naomi or she would never see her Grandpapá.

"Don Abrahán," he said quietly.

The old man opened his eyes. They were rheumy, faded, distant. He saw that don Abrahán was making an intense effort to discern who this man at his bedside might be. And then the struggle eased and he said in a stumbling, weak voice, "Fernán. Such a long time since I saw you. How is your family?"

"Well, don Abrahán. But I have excellent news. I have found Naomi and will bring her to see you tomorrow or the next day."

"Naomi?" he said, and hesitated as if searching his memory. "My granddaughter, Naomi? I have not seen that stray little lamb for so long. How pleasant that will be. Tell her, though, she must not tire me with her running about. I am so weary." And he closed his eyes and fell asleep.

"Stay well, Grandpapá," Fernán said, "stay well."

A wind had risen from the west and the sky was overrun with clouds. He must hurry.

74

Near Sonseca

Jerónimo had the horses groomed and food prepared for the journey and, after a light dinner, Fernán rode out of Toledo on Margarita, leading Almohada. Several hours later, the bitter wind he had experienced in Toledo blew in from the west. Clouds that followed him concealed the sun and heavy flakes of snow began to fall. Fernán donned a warm cloak. If the snow continued he must find shelter for the horses until the weather cleared.

The Halevi farm was a league beyond Sonseca. He had hoped to make the journey in three or four hours at the most, but the snow worsened and the treacherous surface slowed him. The sheltering branches of a dense pine forest furnished temporary refuge, and he brushed snow off the horses, made a fire, and warmed himself. After covering the horses, he fed them, ate some dried meat and fruit, and pushed on. Fernán had memorized the directions to the farm but, although the snow lightened, the snowfall had reduced landmarks to blobs of gray.

The day turned to dusk and he rode for another league or more in intermittent snow before he saw, through the haze, a group of simple adobe and wattle-and-daub structures that fit the farm Jerónimo had described. The family home was a small adobe building with a thatched roof from whose chimney a stream of smoke issued. To one side, a primitive barn, part of which was not yet bound into a structure and covered with clay, revealed twigs and branches intertwined with poles and whitened by snow. On the opposite side of the house rose another crude, thatched-roof construction, perhaps a henhouse. If this was not the Halevi farm then, at the least, the people who lived there might guide him or provide shelter for the night.

Fernán tied his horses to the gatepost of a rude fence, walked to the house, and knocked on the plank door. The door opened instantly and Halevi stood in the doorway, grim-faced, a thick cudgel in his fist. Fernán had not expected a warm welcome, but he stepped back when he saw the club.

"Good evening, Rubén. I am Fernán Hernandes, sometimes called David, sometimes Rafael. We met at the birthday party for Naomi last year when I was recuperating from an injury. You may remember."

"I remember, Hernandes. Why are you here?"

"May I come in, Rubén? Snow is falling down my neck and I will take but a moment of your time. First, if you please, is there some place I might shelter my horses out of the storm?"

Halevi nodded and pointed to the barn. "In there. They will be warm enough and there is hay. Then come inside."

Fernán led the horses into the barn. The back half of the building was open to the weather, but the front provided cover from snow. A series of stalls lined one side of the completed section of the building, home to several cows and two horses who neighed when they saw Margarita. The first stall was empty and Fernán tied the two animals to a post near a pile of hay and removed the saddles. Then he trudged through the snow, which was now ankle deep, and again knocked on the door.

"Come," a voice called.

He opened the door and stepped into a simple whitewashed room. An open hearth in the center of one wall provided heat for the house and a grill for cooking. Shelves along the far wall were filled with jars and other containers of foodstuffs. A hand-hewn table and two benches occupied that end of the room while several handcrafted chairs and a crude bed covered with sheepskins and blankets filled the near half. Halevi sat in one chair while, in another, a young woman fed a toddler.

"Take off your cloak and sit, Hernandes."

Halevi motioned toward the woman. "My wife, Judith, and my daughter, Rahél."

Fernán removed his snow-laden boots and cloak, nodded to the wife, and smiled at the little girl whose large, dark eyes never wavered from his face. Rahél was the Hebrew name María had been called before she converted and Fernán felt tears behind his eyes. "A beautiful child, Rubén. You have other children?"

Halevi nodded. "Two. Asleep. So, Hernandes, why are we honored with your presence this bitter night?"

"I hoped that the weather would have been more pleasant, but don Abrahán is not well and I am searching for Naomi. She must return with me to Toledo."

"He is that bad?"

"I am afraid so. He could leave us at any moment."

Halevi looked at his hands. "Has Jerónimo told you about me?"

"He told me that you work for him from time to time, that he spoke to you about employment for Naomi, and that you directed her to a neighbor."

"That is all?"

"All he told me. Yes."

Halevi nodded and squirmed a bit in his chair. "You will stay with us tonight and tomorrow I will show you where to find Naomi."

"Thank you kindly. I have blankets and will sleep with the horses."

"You will sleep in the bed, Hernandes. The floor is warm from the fire and Judith and I will sleep on the floor. Have you had supper?"

"Many thanks, but I have eaten and my horses are munching your hay."

Halevi then asked about Toledo and Fernán recited the events of the past months without mentioning his own participation. The baby yawned desperately and Judith carried her into the other room through a doorway in the far wall. Then she made a bed for herself and Rubén on the floor near the fire. Fernán was discomfited by their offer of the bed, but he could not refuse. After several minutes of chatter, Halevi damped the fire, removed his boots and jacket, and lay down beside his wife. Within minutes, Fernán heard him snore.

In the morning, they broke their fast with bread and ale and eggs from the hens they kept in the small outbuilding. The day was bright and the sun glinted sharply on the snow. Fernán saddled his horses, mounted Margarita, and once again thanked Halevi. The three dark-haired children hovered around their parents in the doorway, squinting into the light.

"A quarter hour, Hernandes, and you should be there," Halevi said, then looked up at him and cocked his head to one side. "You love Naomi, Hernandes?"

"With all my heart and soul."

"Then may God go with you and Naomi and see you both safely home."

Fernán smiled to the children, nodded to Judith and Rubén, and turned Margarita toward the road.

The farm of Yaacov Aboav could have belonged to Halevi—an adobe house, a wattle-and-daub barn, and another indeterminate, half-finished building. Aboav, a short, sturdy-looking man, was working outside the house and he called to Naomi. She came to the door and she and Fernán stared at each other for several minutes without speaking. At last Fernán roused himself and asked her to walk with him. The sun had melted much of the snow, and he took her hand and they walked away from the house.

He said that don Abrahán was very ill and that they must leave immediately if she was to see her Grandpapá before God took him. Naomi looked into his eyes and the tears came and he held her.

The journey to Toledo seemed long, though they rode at a good pace and were at the Gate of Cambrón just after noon. They led the horses to the Melamed house and tied them to the wall.

"Should I come with you?" he asked.

"Yes, Fernán, if you please."

Mosé and Aharon met them at the door. Their faces hid nothing and Naomi wailed and rushed into the house crying, "Grandpapá!" Fernán followed her to the study and the three men stood by silently while Naomi walked slowly to the bed on which her grandfather lay. She knelt and lay her head on the sheet which covered him and sobbed and keened and tore her skirt.

Mosé told Fernán that he had shaved the hair from the body and cut the nails, as was the custom, so that don Abrahán might be clean before the Divine Countenance. Then the neighborhood women had washed the body in hot water, dressed him in new white linen, and covered his face with a white linen cloth.

Fernán knelt beside Naomi and held her until the desperate wailing ceased and she cried quietly.

"He did not suffer, Naomi. Death was gentle to your Grandpapá."

Naomi looked into his face and pulled him close to her. "Bless you, Fernán. How cruel I am to have left him and doubly cruel to have hidden from you."

"You did nothing wrong, Naomi. He loved you and blamed himself for driving you away. And I would have found you no matter where you had gone."

She then went to Mosé and Aharón and they held her.

"He died early this morning, Naomi—at first light," Mosé said while rocking back and forth. "Your Grandpapá turned his head to the wall and breathed his last—he knew it was time. Fernán," he said, "the funeral is tomorrow in the synagogue of Samuel Levi. The community knows. And Fernán, I informed your father."

Fernán thanked Mosé and said that he must tell his family he had brought Naomi home. He would return soon. Naomi nodded and looked at him, eyes wet with tears. They held one another and Fernán kissed her forehead, shook hands with Mosé and Aharón, and left the house.

75

A funeral and a wedding

The service was simple. The rabbi read the psalm, "Keep me, O God, for I have taken refuge in You," and the body in a wooden coffin was placed on an open wagon and drawn slowly through the streets of Toledo, followed by Naomi, Fernán, Mosé, Aharón, the Hernandes family, the small Jewish community, and a multitude of *conversos*. At the graveside, the rabbi read the psalm, "O you that dwell in the shelter of the Most High," as the coffin was lowered, followed by the *Kaddish* which admits "submission to the judgment of God and acceptance of His justice." Fernán held Naomi by the hand and wore the skullcap his father had given him.

Neighbors and the Hernandes family provided food for the funeral meal, the *cohuerço*, and for three days Naomi observed intense mourning during which she ate only eggs and bread with water while sitting on the floor at a low table. Then another four days of the seven days of *shivah*, during which neighbors and friends attended her.

On the eighth day, Fernán sat with her in the courtyard. She looked tired, drawn from grief and mourning, and he held her hand and smiled. He had sent a note to Yaacov Aboav explaining the death of don Abrahán and expressing regrets that Naomi would not return.

"What will I do then, Fernán? Grandpapá was my rock. We had a little money, but not enough, and that will soon be gone."

He kissed her hand. "You know I love you and at one time you said you loved me."

"I love you now, but a wall between us prevents our love."

"Not if we are brave."

Fernán told her of the letter from Alberti, and that his father had given him permission to pursue the Italian venture.

"But I will be alone and will surely die," she said.

"Not if you come with me." She began to protest and Fernán raised his finger to her lips. "Italy is not Castile, my love. It is more understanding and indulgent than Spain for a man and woman who love one another but cannot marry in a church. In Rome we can live together as man and wife without the blessing or interference of the Church. Valla himself has such an arrangement and has fathered several children with his mistress.

"Come with me to Rome. We swore our love before God and we are man and wife in His eyes. Our children will be Jews since their mother is a Jew, and I will be a man, not Catholic nor Jew but a man whose ancestors were Jews."

"It is not possible."

"Possible and certain. But I have taken you by surprise and I do not expect you to say yes—not now. Think about what I have said. Believe in me as I believe in you, then say yes." He looked away. "One thing more I must tell you." He held her and told her about María. "When I thought that I had lost you and María came to me, I felt pity and love for her. I cannot deny that we made love and that she gave me pleasure. But you were gone from me and María, sweet soul, was desperate. I sympathized with her cause, although I was uncertain."

Naomi was quiet. She looked into his eyes and he could not read her expression.

"You are not the only one who has made love," she said. "Nor are you the only one who was uncertain. I made love with a young man. I came to him in the night and seduced him, though I was promised to another."

"And did you love the young man?"

"With all my heart, and I love him now. He was not well, but we swore our love to one another and then he was gone." She looked into his face. "You tell me not to say yes now because you think a woman has not mind enough to decide quickly. But you are wrong and I defy you. I say yes, yes, yes!" She stood and took his hands. "Take me to Rome, Fernán. Be my husband and let me be your wife as men and women have been husband and wife since before Abraham or before any church or priest or rabbi sanctioned their love.

"I ask but one thing, my love, for the memory of my Grandpapá and my mother and father, may God bless their souls. Let some venerable man—not of necessity a holy man, but someone whom we trust and respect—say a few words to us and to our friends and family gathered around us, and read a psalm and declare us man and wife."

Fernán was silent for a moment, and then he said, "Did God not love man and woman before they knew of Him? Do birds have priests or rabbis? We will be as birds—natural people without class or clan who are blessed because they love."

"Fernán," she said, and knelt before him.

"Never plead, Naomi," and he raised her to her feet and held her. "I will always respect your needs. For love of your grandfather and for the memory of your parents and because I love and honor you, we will do as you say. We will find a place in the open air, safe from hateful eyes, and we will be joined as man and wife before those who love us."

"Oh, Fernán!" She kissed him. "Say nothing more but hold your loving wife."

Naomi told Mosé and Aharón that the house belonged to them, and the apprentices blessed her and kissed her hand. And Fernán and Naomi walked out of the courtyard together to the Hernandes house where Fernán gathered his family and informed them that he and Naomi were married before God and would leave for Italy at the beginning of May.

After their initial shock, his father and mother acknowledged their union and blessed them, and Lorenzo said he would give them a gift that would finance their travel to Rome, furnish a modest place to live, and leave them a little to start their life together. After that, they must make their own way.

There would be no formal wedding, Fernán said, because no one would marry them, neither Jew nor Catholic, but they hoped that some honorable man who loved them would say a few words before their family and bless their union.

"With all my heart I would be that man," Lorenzo said. "I will join you in a bond no one but God can break."

"Bless you, Papá," Fernán said and embraced Lorenzo.

Celestina kissed her son and embraced Naomi. "You are so beautiful, Naomi, so like your mother whom I knew and loved. Your father was handsome and brave, like my son, and a gentle man. We miss them both, may they rest in peace. And may God bless you and grant you a long and peaceful life filled with laughter and the joy of children."

Fernán asked Jerónimo to come with them to Italy, but his friend declined, saying he would welcome them when they returned to Iberia. The Hernandes family had need of him in Toledo, he said, and Lorenzo and Cesario had made him a partner in the firm of *Hernandes y Familia*.

"I have taken the name Hernandes, Fernán. Now we are truly brothers."

Fernán held his friend and wished him well as a member of a family fortunate to have him.

"I have a present for you and Naomi from don Enrique, Fernán. He wishes you Godspeed and suggests that when you return from Rome, no matter when, you must visit him."

Fernán opened the package. A handsome wooden box with the golden crest of the Prince of Asturias on its face lay inside. The box contained two small daggers with handles ornamented with the crest.

"Either dagger will gain you admission to the Prince."

"Thank you, Jerónimo, and convey my love and thanks to the Prince." He looked into the distance and said, "What of Sarmiento?"

"He is in Segovia for the time being, under the care of a physician—a Jewish physician. He lives, but is in continual pain. His back is covered with wounds that have not yet healed and which inhibit his ability to move about. It is rumored he will depart soon for his estate near Navarre. Be on your guard, Fernán, and may God be your guide."

Then Jerónimo held Naomi, and she said, "We will miss you, dear brother, for the strength of your soul and your love for my love."

Their marriage was celebrated on the last day of April. Jerónimo had remembered a low hill on an estate that belonged to the Prince, covered with grass, wild flowers, and an occasional oak. Lorenzo and the others teased him for remembering such a romantic site, asking how often he had used it for liaisons. But Jerónimo protested that it was virginal and perfect for this exceptional day.

The Hernandes family and Mosé and Aharón and the few remaining members of the Melamed clan bundled into wagons with food and drink and rode through the streets of Toledo and through the Gate of Cambrón into the countryside in late afternoon, singing songs of love. People hallooed and waved at the happy riders, the angry colors of race and religion paled by the songs and the bright sunshine.

Grass on the hillside was lush, sprinkled with the reds and purples and yellows of wildflowers, and on the crest of the hill stood a tall oak with spreading limbs that shaded a substantial space beneath its branches. Lorenzo exclaimed that here was the perfect stage for the marriage—the tree formed a canopy, a *chuppah*, he said, under which bride and groom would stand as in a traditional Jewish marriage ceremony. Fernán and Naomi smiled and called it ideal.

After they gathered the children from their romp on the hillside, Lorenzo called everyone to the base of the oak. Naomi and Fernán stood before him surrounded by family and friends. Naomi wore a white gown Celestina had given her, a dress she had worn for her own marriage, altered slightly to fit Naomi who was shorter and slighter than her mother-in-law. On her hair she wore a white linen square decorated with small yellow, red, and blue flowers. Fernán wore a white shirt embroidered with similar details on his cuffs and collar, pale gray breeches, black boots, and a white cap. The sight of the beautiful couple brought tears to the eyes of Lorenzo.

"Dear friends, cousins, and family," he said, "Naomi and Fernán stand before us today to receive our blessing for their union as man and wife. For those interested in such matters—and I cannot imagine who that might be—there will be no wedding contract, no *ketubbah*, nor is there need of one. For when these young people are united, Naomi will be our daughter—as if she were born into our family. And that bond shall live for as long as God in his wisdom allows this sweet angel to dwell on this earth—and may it be a long, long time."

There were amens from those surrounding the couple.

"I am no rabbi, as you know. I am not even a Jew, though I am proud of the lineage of my fathers and know something of the customs of my cousins. But I am here to witness that our son, Fernán, and Naomi, granddaughter of our late beloved cousin, Abrahán Melamed, are united as man and wife. And so I ask you, Fernán, my dear son, to place this ring on the third finger of your bride and say, 'You are consecrated unto me according to the law of Moses and Israel.'"

Fernán placed the ring on her finger and intoned the blessing. Then Lorenzo instructed Naomi to do the same. And she smiled at Fernán and placed a ring on his finger and repeated the blessing.

"Now hold each other by the hand, Fernán and Naomi, and in turn drink from this glass of wine."

They did so and Lorenzo said, "May God bless you, my children. May He grant you happiness and long life. Now, Naomi, take the glass and sprinkle the remaining drops of wine on this hillside that you may be as fruitful as a meadow in spring."

And everyone followed behind Naomi, laughing, as she danced around the hilltop sprinkling the remaining wine—except for the children who, following the example of Mosé, picked wild flowers and strewed them before Naomi.

"Now, Fernán," Lorenzo said, "take the glass and throw it high into the air."

And Fernán threw the glass so high that all one could see were sparkles of light as the glass flew, fell to the ground, struck a rock, and splintered into shards.

"May God grant that you live and are happy," Lorenzo shouted, "until these bits of glass reassemble themselves and hold a full glass of wine!"

They clapped and shouted, and the women cried and the men slapped Fernán on the back and embraced him and Naomi, and the women kissed them and all wished them good luck.

Lorenzo held Naomi to him and said, "Welcome to our family, daughter," and kissed her forehead.

Flagons of wine were opened, and the wedding party drank to the health of the newly married couple and ate berries and grapes and small pastries filled with ground meats and fruits. Mosé gathered the children around him and they sang and danced in a circle until they became dizzy and fell on the grass. Lorenzo took Naomi by the arm and walked around and around in a dancing way and told Fernán that he must wait until the old man had enjoyed his beautiful bride. Fernán laughed. Then a young woman he did not know, a cousin of Naomi from the maternal side, began to sing a Ladino song about a bridegroom robed in gold and silver and a silken bride.

And Fernán held Naomi and they danced on the grass and were entranced by the perfection of the afternoon and their vision of one another.

The day passed into evening, the sun fell behind the hills, and the air cooled. And they climbed into the wagons and returned to Toledo—Lorenzo singing and the children dozing—and drove to the Hernandes house for the wedding supper.-

The following morning, the first of May, Fernán and Naomi, riding Margarita and Almohada and followed by a pair of loaded packhorses and two trusted servants riding guard, passed through the Gate of Alcántara bound for Valencia. As he rode out of the city, Fernán stood in his stirrups and looked back at the gray palisades of Toledo, at tier upon tier of houses and shops, at the spire of the Cathedral which searched the blue sky like the finger of God, and at the ever-present warning of the dark mass of the Alcázar. And he sat his horse and took Naomi by the hand and they walked their mounts together down the road toward Cuenca, Requeña, Valencia, and Rome.

Manufactured by Amazon.ca
Acheson, AB

13337752R00224